Julie Bozza

The
Butterfly Hunter
Trilogy

LIBRAtiger

Published by LIBRAtiger 2018

ISBN: 978-1-925869-07-1

Butterfly Hunter first published by Manifold Press 2012
Of Dreams and Ceremonies first published by Manifold Press 2013
Like Leaves to a Tree first published by LIBRAtiger 2014
The Thousand Smiles of Nicholas Goring first published by Manifold Press 2014
The Butterfly Hunter Trilogy boxed set first published by Manifold Press 2014

Text: © Julie Bozza 2018
Proof-reading and line editing: F.M. Parkinson, W.S. Pugh
Editor: Fiona Pickles of Manifold Press
Print format: © Julie Bozza 2018
Set in Adobe Caslon and Adobe Gothic

Cover design: © Gayna Murphy of Mubu Design | mubudesign.com

Characters and situations described in this book are fictional and not intended to portray real persons or situations whatsoever; any resemblances to living individuals are entirely coincidental.

libra-tiger.com | juliebozza.com

Acknowledgements

With love to my stalwart technical advisor, Mr B.

With thanks to the person whose comment on Goodreads unknowingly inspired the first novel.

With love to Pete Murray for his honest, emotional songwriting and his passionate performances.

And with gratitude in anticipation of the reader's tolerance. I wrote some of these stories conscious that I am an outsider looking in at things some will say don't concern me. I did so with nothing in my heart but a love of and a wish for interdependence between all our peoples – and for that perhaps any infelicities will be forgiven.

Table of Contents

Butterfly Hunter   1

Of Dreams and Ceremonies   165

Like Leaves to a Tree   293

The Thousand Smiles of Nicholas Goring   305

Butterfly Hunter

one

Dave Taylor looked down at the perfect little human creature he held cradled in his hands – delicate skin, warm scent, fragile bones – and asked, "Tell me again why she isn't ours?"

Over at the kitchen bench, Denise snorted, her hands busily assembling their lunch. "You know why, Davey."

"I still haven't found what I'm looking for?" he hazarded.

"See? I knew you'd listen eventually."

"I didn't know that I even *had* to look …" Dave gazed down at this exquisite tiny replica of Denise, and let out a sigh, wondering why she was so sure he wasn't looking for this, exactly this. They had been Denny-and-Davey for so very long, since his very first day at school over twenty years ago, and it bewildered him why they weren't Denny-and-Davey-and-Zoe now. The baby's fine hair glowed golden, as his own and Denise's did; Zoe didn't even have any of her father's dark Italian looks, at least not from what Dave could make out.

"Hey," he murmured a greeting as the baby's eyes fluttered a little and then opened to return his gaze with solemn blue. "Hey there, Zo. I'm Davey." The baby turned to curl trustingly into his chest. "I'm your … Well. I'm your mum's best mate. I think."

"Course you are," Denise put in with brisk scorn for the notion that there could be any doubt about it. There was a brief scowl of frustration from Zoe, and then a yawn which threatened to become a wail. Denise came over and put a plate of sandwiches down on the table before Dave, and then took Zoe, settled in a chair round the corner and rearranged her own clothing so that Zoe could feed. Denise's very matter-of-factness emphasised that Dave was considered as mostly harmless now; not even the ex, but only the friend who had no chance at all of regathering what he'd lost.

"Where's Vittorio?" he asked, reaching for a sandwich, and keeping his eyes politely averted – as if he hadn't known that very breast as intimately as anyone might, not so long ago.

"Work. He got called out; he'll be a while." Denise paused to shift Zoe a little in her arms, as if still trying to find the right hold. The baby wasn't even two weeks old. "What did you want to talk about? You said you had a trip coming up?"

"Yeah. I could be gone for a while. It's all happened very quickly."

"That's good," she replied – then added as if bracing him up, "It's good for business. Tour group, is it?"

"No, just one guy. An English earl, for God's sake! Well, the son of an earl, or something. I've been dealing with the father's butler, and he wasn't real specific. What does that make him? The son, I mean."

"Out of place. Out of time! What's he doing over here?"

Dave groaned. "Chasing down some mythical butterfly. Apparently no one's even sure it ever existed in the first place."

"A quest!" Denise's eyes had lit up, though Dave knew well enough it was at least half in humour. "A knight on a quest! A *genuine* knight!"

"Um, yeah, so –"

"And you're his squire!"

"Oh God, shut up, would you?" he grumbled good-naturedly. "It's just as well that Japanese tour group cancelled for June. He's booked me for three months."

That sobered her up. "You're gonna be out there for *three months*?"

Dave essayed a shrug. "Not the whole time, of course. But the idea is that we get this done, whatever it takes. When I told them I had that week's trip in July with the Americans, he said he'd come along, too, if he was welcome, or he'd wait for me to meet up with him again afterwards. And if we find the damned butterflies early, he's paying me the full fee anyway."

"Huh," was her only response. A thoughtful silence stretched while Zoe finished up on one breast and was switched to the other. Dave stared out the French windows at the backyard until Denise was decently rearranged.

"I just don't know what to expect," Dave said.

"Why? Not cos he's English. Your dad was English!"

"Yeah, I always forget that." Dave smiled a bit wistfully. He still missed his dad. "But that's not it."

"What's the problem, then?"

"I only hope he's up to it. The guy who made the booking – his butler or secretary or whatever – he said –"

"What?"

"Just before he hung up, he said – Well. To treat him kindly. So I'm left thinking God knows *what* to expect."

"He didn't tell you why?"

"Nope. And I even asked; I followed up with an email. He just shrugged me off, all very proper and dignified, as if he hadn't even said it in the first place."

"Huh." Eventually Denise asked, "So where do you start, when you're looking for a butterfly that may or may not even exist?"

"The other side of Cunnamulla. There's supposed to be a waterhole – though it's not on any maps – and that's –"

"A *mythical* waterhole?"

"Pretty much straight out of Dreamtime. Yeah."

"You'll need to talk to Charlie, won't you?" Denise visibly relaxed at the notion. "You talk to Charlie before you head out there, and you take care, do you hear me, Davey? *You take care.*"

"Course I will," he scoffed. "How many years have I been doing this?"

"No, I mean it. You have to come back, see, cos you're gonna be – well, whatever the irreligious version of a godparent is, for Zoe."

An irreligious godparent … ? Dave just laughed. But before he left he pressed a gentle kiss to the top of Zoe's milk-scented golden-haired head, and he silently wished her well. Just in case.

The plane was due in just after seven in the morning. Dave made sure he was there in plenty of time, even though the Englishman would need to go through passport control, collect his luggage, and then get through quarantine. All of which would take an hour, probably – but it would be just Dave's luck if he turned up at eight to find that the earl's son had been processed as a VIP or some such thing, and had been waiting on him ever since.

Dave found a place to lean on the waist-high barriers with the drivers and others carrying signs. His own read GORING. That was the guy's name. Nicholas Goring. Which perhaps made his father Earl Goring, or was it the Earl of Goring … ? When Dave wasn't chatting in an early morning haze to his current companions, he spent the time trying to remember whether he'd had any clue about whether Nicholas was the eldest son or not – and if he was, whether that meant Dave should address him as 'my lord' or as 'sir'.

He'd looked it up on Wikipedia, realised he'd need to email the butler for more information, and then promptly let it all slip his mind.

He was kicking himself, metaphorically at least. He was always more professional than this. Always. And all right, maybe titles didn't matter very much – though he was sure they'd matter more to an Englishman than an Australian – but no one could afford to be this slapdash in the Outback. Why would Goring trust Dave with his life, if he couldn't even get this detail right?

Dave sighed, and watched in a desultory way as the passengers from other flights straggled through. No one looked their best after a 24-hour flight. No one. This pair now, for instance – a father and a young daughter, Dave assumed – appeared beyond tired, irritable, dishevelled, unhappy. That all fell away, however, as they were greeted by an older couple. The man's parents, the girl's grandparents: they had to be. Faces brightened, postures lifted, hugs all round.

It would take a miracle to perform the same transformation on the next pair who came through the gates, though. A married couple, perhaps, whose marriage didn't look like it would survive the rigours of an international flight. Dave and Denny had done that once, of course – headed off on the obligatory backpacking holiday in their late teens. They'd done all right together, despite having laughably little money and even less sense. But then, they'd always been friends first, and a best mate could see you through anything. They'd taken turns seeing each other through.

Dave tried not to sigh again, and then tried not to yawn, as he absently watched the next fellow come through. The luggage came first, on a trolley, and the guy came after it, almost tumbling as he negotiated the doors and got a foot caught against the trolley wheel. Everything teetered as he tried to break free, prevent the door from slamming closed, and head down along the barriers to his right, all at the same time. He almost succeeded in achieving all those things, and probably would have, too, if he hadn't suddenly decided to head to his left instead. He went sprawling on the floor, long limbs everywhere, while the trolley trundled off by itself for a few feet and finally came to an unconvincing kind of halt.

Dave felt for the guy, he really did. Just his luck if he was meeting his lover at the airport or something, and had managed to gawk out entirely. Everyone was either tactfully looking somewhere else, or smiling ruefully at the guy. There wasn't anyone nearby to help him up, because none of them were dumb enough to go past the barrier; security didn't seem to have noticed yet, and for now the blunderer was the only arriving passenger.

And he was still lying there on the floor ... Why on earth was he still down there on the cold hard floor? He hadn't broken something, had he? Dave looked at him – properly – with a frown. Considered each of those gangly limbs, but they seemed to be whole. He wasn't lying at an awkward angle or anything. But his head was tilted back, and he was grinning a bit stupidly ... and he was looking right back at Dave!

Which would have been fine, except that once he realised Dave was looking back, the guy seemed to wink. Or was that blink? But upside down like that, his smile seemed to have a wicked kick to it – and really, if they were in any other situation at all, if this wasn't early morning at an international airport, Dave might have thought the guy was checking him out ...

He turned away with a bit of a grimace, kind of a sneer. Which wasn't like him, not really, and he wasn't prejudiced, he'd swear it, but honestly it was *way* too early for lascivious stares from awkward strangers of the wrong gender. It just was.

A moment later he regretted the rudeness, of course, and his heart thudded once, punishingly. He turned back to see if he'd given offence, and perhaps to offer an apologetic shrug. But security had finally arrived, and were helping the guy up to his feet, dusting him off, making sure he would remain upright for now, retrieving his bags. Listening to him chat, and apparently letting themselves be charmed into considering him harmless.

Dave watched, vaguely glad that everything seemed to be in order. Until they were past the barriers, and the guards ushered the guy out towards the exits, and he declined to go. Instead he turned, and his searching gaze soon landed on Dave again. Dave stood up slowly, warily, as the man approached with the guards trailing behind with matching frowns.

"I believe you're looking for me," the guy said in a cultured English accent.

"What?" Dave replied stupidly.

A long pale hand indicated the sign Dave carried. "I'm Nicholas Goring."

"Oh God."

The corner of his mouth kicked slightly, though the man was no longer smiling. "Just *sir* will do."

They were silent while Dave led his client out to the car park, paid off his ticket, found the car and put the bags in the boot, insisting in a mutter that he didn't need Goring's assistance.

It wasn't until they were heading into the city on Kingsford Smith Drive that Dave finally spoke. "I'll take you to the hotel. I booked it with an early check–in. I'm sure you'll be glad of a shower and change of clothes." When he risked a glance at the man, Dave was disconcerted to find that Goring's smile once again had a wicked kick to it. "Um," said Dave, "*sir* …"

"I always had a thing for chauffeurs," the man confided.

"Huh." Dave frowned, and stared very hard at the road ahead, though he wasn't entirely sure how much he was actually seeing. "Well. What do you do when they don't have a thing for you?"

Goring chuckled, sounding genuinely amused. "Ah, come on. Seize the day!"

"Mate, life's not *that* short."

The chuckle turned into a laugh – and Dave liked that. Still, he was relieved when Goring said, "All right, I'll stop. Don't mind me. I hardly got a wink of sleep on that damned plane."

"You weren't exactly travelling cattle class. Were you?"

"No, but …" Goring looked away, biting at his lower lip. He was a tall, scrawny man, and his lips were the plumpest thing about him. They were a dash of pink on his pale face. They were almost pretty. "Too much on my mind, I suppose."

Dave let a beat go by, and then headed for safer ground. "Common wisdom is to stay awake for as long as you can today, and try not to sleep until tonight. Get into the new time zone as soon as you can."

"Yes, so I've heard."

"And I find that people like to start with a good breakfast, to keep their energy levels up. The hotel – you're at the Hilton – is known for their breakfasts."

"I see."

"It's up to you, but I'll keep you company, if you like. For as much of the day as suits."

"Starting with breakfast … ?"

"If you like," Dave repeated. "And later, if you have people here, I can drop you off wherever. Just tell me what you want to do and then, you know, feel free to change your plans if you can't stay awake any longer or whatever."

Goring was staring at him. "I understand." After a moment, he added, "I don't know why I was expecting laconic rather than loquacious."

Dave glanced at him. "Dunno if I'm your typical Aussie, mate."

Another laugh, though wry this time rather than genuine. Then Goring asked, "Will Mr Taylor be able to join us for breakfast?"

"What?" Dave grimaced as he turned right onto Albert Street. They were almost there. "No, I'm – *I'm* Dave Taylor."

"Oh."

"I guess I didn't – No, I didn't introduce myself. The meeting at the airport didn't, uh –"

"Didn't quite go as planned," Goring smoothly supplied.

"No. My fault. Look, we're here," Dave said. "I'll drop you off, and you can check in while I park."

"No need. I'll stay with you."

Dave glanced at him, and thought that Goring wasn't merely being polite. In any case, he needed to decide right away, as he was already approaching the car park. He nodded, and flipped on the indicator. So be it. Almost nothing this morning had gone as intended, so why not this as well?

They were silent again as Dave collected a ticket, and then quickly chose an empty space on the ground floor – it was still too early to be busy. Once he'd parked, they both got out, and met around the back of the car. Dave looked the man in the eye, and held his hand out. "Good morning, uh, sir. I'm Dave Taylor."

Goring shook his hand with a cool firmness before disengaging. "I'm pleased to meet you, Mr Taylor. Call me Nicholas."

"Dave."

"David," said Nicholas.

Dave grinned, and turned to open the boot, started lifting the three bags out. "All right, but no one calls me that. It's Dave or – well, my friends call me Davey."

"Would you join me for breakfast, David?"

"Sure. Thanks," he added, quite genuinely. "We can talk over your trip.

I've brought maps and such."

"Good. Here, let me –"

But Dave only handed over the cabin–sized bag, and insisted on wheeling the larger cases. "I've got it," he said. He attempted the three syllables as they emerged into sunlight: "Nicholas." He wondered how long it would be before he was allowed to go with Nick or Nicky.

"Thank you." The man's smile was a little gentler by now.

Of course it had all gone horribly wrong so far, and God only knew what that meant for the rest of the trip, but it seemed that at least Dave had been forgiven for his part of the shambles. He nodded, both accepting and returning the thanks. Nicholas seemed to understand. As they walked shoulder to shoulder into the hotel, Dave dared to think the next three months mightn't be a complete disaster.

Barely half an hour later, Nicholas reappeared, bright and fresh and cheerful in the diffuse sunlight of the restaurant. While still standing there towering tall and lean, he offered, "I apologise for the chauffeur thing."

Dave couldn't help but grin. "You're sorry about your thing for chauffeurs?"

"Well, no," was the reply as Nicholas sat down around the corner of the table to Dave's right. "That dates back to my first love. Always a formative experience, wouldn't you say?"

Dave huffed an empathic breath. "Hell, yeah."

"What I'm sorry for is being so outrageous so early in the morning with no provocation on your part whatsoever."

"Don't worry about it. We already started over, didn't we?"

"With our proper introductions," Nicholas agreed.

A waiter appeared, and Dave ordered coffee while Nicholas ordered tea.

Perhaps it was all best forgotten about, but Dave was still curious about the misunderstandings. "You know, I always do this bit. Meeting my clients off the plane, or whatever. To me, that's the professional thing to do. Maybe you're used to butlers and maids and secretaries – and chauffeurs," he added, as he caught Nicholas trying to suppress a wicked smirk – "doing that for you, but here there's just me. The business is mine, and I try to do things properly." Having forgotten the point he was trying to get to, Dave tailed off, "Well, I wouldn't just send a car to collect you."

"Of course not," Nicholas stoutly agreed. "It was my mistake entirely."

For some reason, Dave felt the need to persist. "There are a few people I employ to help me when I have larger tour groups, but for smaller groups – and for you – I'm afraid it's just me."

"That's perfectly fine. Of course."

A silence stretched. Dave frowned, unable to either follow his own thought processes through to their outcome, or track them back to their origin.

"Look," said Nicholas after their tea and coffee had arrived. "I won't flirt. I won't make a nuisance of myself. If that's what you're worried about. What I said this morning was stupid. But if an apology and a promise aren't enough, then –"

"That's enough," Dave insisted. But then he blurted, "The chauffeur. What happened to him?"

Nicholas's head went back in surprise. "Oh. Well. He went on to lead a full and happy life, I suppose. What do you mean, what happened … ?"

"He lost his job, right? Sacked without a reference?"

"Good grief," Nicholas exclaimed with a laugh. "Even I don't characterise my life as a Gothic romance. No, he didn't lose his job. Quite the opposite. He retired last May, and still lives on the estate."

Dave stared at the man.

"He was very kind to me," Nicholas continued. "Very patient. And," he confided from under a lifted brow, "very discreet."

"Oh!" Dave hadn't felt so idiotic for years.

"So, you see … it isn't *always* an unmitigated disaster to be fancied by me."

"No. No, of course …"

"Shall we go raid the buffet for breakfast?" Nicholas smoothly supplied.

Once they were done eating, they ordered more coffee and tea, and Dave reached for his folder of maps and notes. "Can we talk about the trip?"

"Yes, please." Nicholas sat forward with an eager little smile, his hands spread on the table either side of his cup.

"Look," said Dave after a long moment.

Nicholas's face fell. "There's a problem?"

"I just don't want you getting your hopes up, is all. The information you gave me – a lot of it's contradictory, or it doesn't make much sense."

"I know it's only clues. That's why I was hoping we'd have plenty of time to explore. Maybe it will all start falling into place while we're out there."

"That's the thing. And I tried having this conversation with your butler or whatever he was, so I'm hoping he passed all this on. Heading into the Outback – it's not like taking a stroll through the Cotswolds or whatever. If things go wrong, we could die."

"I understand," Nicholas solemnly replied.

"So we really need a better plan than just wandering about at random, hoping the clues will add up. If they even *are* clues."

"I understand, I really do. And I'm prepared for it all coming to naught. I know I might get nothing more from this than a rather peculiar holiday."

Dave grinned despite himself. "You don't seem the type to give up, though."

"No. I'd hope to come back next year, and try again. With you, if you can stand it; with someone else, if you can't."

"All right," said Dave. "I'm glad you said that about having plenty of time. You realise we're not going to be leaving Brisbane right away? There are still things to organise. And if we're heading north, the Wet's really only just ended – the wet season. It ran quite late this year. There's no point in hurrying."

"From what I understand of the geography, I don't think we'll be heading that far north."

"Aren't butterflies generally a tropical creature?"

"Not these ones." Nicholas's fingers skittered against the edge of the table, as if he wanted to drum impatiently but was too polite. "When will we leave, do you think?"

"A few days at least. Maybe a week. We need to plan exactly where we're going, and if we're going to be leaving the established roads, then we need to ask permission of whoever owns the land."

"Is that likely to be a problem?"

"I shouldn't think so; if the owners don't already know me, they'll know people who'll vouch for me. But it's only fair to ask before rather than after, if we can."

"Of course. I understand."

"Then it's a fair drive, just to get to Cunnamulla. So I'll leave one day, and you fly out the next, and I'll ... collect you from the airport. Again."

Nicholas's smile was quirking irrepressibly.

"Or I'll send a driver to fetch you and bring you to the hotel, maybe. If you're lucky."

"No, I'd rather it was you," Nicholas said with a little more warmth than might be expected. "And anyway," he continued with a rather cooler directness, "I'd rather stay with you. I'd rather you drove me. Unless there's some particular reason why not."

"It's a long way, and there's not much to see. You'll get bored."

Nicholas shrugged. "I'd rather experience it. I'd rather ... get a feel for the country."

"You have no idea about the distances involved. I mean, you can drive across England in an afternoon, can't you?"

"All the more reason to, um ... broaden my horizons." The man really had the most infectious grin.

"Well –"

"It's like watching cricket," Nicholas said, overriding any protest that Dave had been about to make. "You're an Australian, you should know about cricket."

Dave made a noise tentatively indicating agreement and conveying an unwillingness to get into an argument over such a contentious issue just now.

"It's like watching a Test match. It might get a bit tedious on occasion, watching the full game. But you get a sense of it unfolding that way. You get a real feel for how the game is playing out. You never get that from watching the highlights."

Dave laughed, and surrendered. "Well, I can't argue with a cricket analogy."

"My best guess," said Nicholas, peering down at the state map and circling a region with a fingertip, "is that we start around here." He had long pale fingers; they were, perhaps, the most elegant thing about him. Dave watched as they traced lightly across the map as if the man could feel the land's contours. "Yes ... and then we head further west, if we don't find anything there." After another long moment passed, Nicholas looked up. "What do you think?"

Dave shook himself out of his silence. "Area the size of Wales," he remarked.

"Yes. I realise it's a needle in a haystack and all that, but I have to *try*. This might be the only thing I –"

When the conclusion wasn't forthcoming, Dave prompted, "The only thing you what?"

Nicholas's gaze remained fixed on the map. "Never mind."

Dave let a moment go by, and then got the conversation back on track. "Okay, take me through the logic of it again. You started with a settler's journal."

"Yes. Clemence Hall. She's not very well known."

"And she mentioned a blue cloud."

Nicholas nodded enthusiastically. "They were travelling south–west from the Wyandra region, taking it slowly. This blue cloud would appear near the horizon each afternoon. She thought it was a mirage, but it stayed in the same location while their expedition continued on south. She wanted to go investigate, but one of the party was quite ill, and they didn't have enough water to take another detour." Nicholas's eyes were afire with the possibilities. "And I thought, what could that blue cloud be, but butterflies rising in the afternoon sunshine?"

"All right," Dave said. "But then didn't she say something about being north of the stone–curlew? If she meant Quilpie, then they weren't travelling south–west from Wyandra. Quilpie's to the north."

"I think she was referring to a Dreamtime site, not a settlers' town."

"Oh. Of course." Dave felt supremely idiotic. Imagine a Pom making that leap before a dinky–di Aussie …

Nicholas spared him a sympathetic look. "I've been obsessing over this for a while, you know."

"So I guess you did your research about possible sacred sites? Your butler or whatever didn't mention anything to do with the Dreamtime."

"I haven't found anything in the Dreamtime stories about the stone–curlew, or not yet anyway … but I did find a story about the Barcoo grunter – Great name, by the way."

"The fish … ?" Dave clarified, having to make yet another leap. "What's

14 | Butterfly Hunter

that got to do with curlews?"

"Yes, the *Scortum barcoo*. And the connection is with the butterflies."

"Right ..." he prompted, feeling rather bewildered.

"The story ended with the Barcoo grunter ancestor returning to his long sleep, sinking deep *deep* down into his waterhole, and pieces of the sky – this is a loose translation, I admit – rose up to lament and flutter in farewell."

"But ..."

"He was farewelling his love," Nicholas supplied, "who lived in the sky."

"Your butterflies were, like, the Barcoo grunter's tears?"

"Yes."

"Have you *seen* a grunter? They're ugly things."

Nicholas sat back with a disapproving sniff. "Even ugly creatures feel love, you know. Even ugly creatures can create beauty."

"Of course. I –" Dave hardly knew what to say. This contradictory Englishman had taken that personally, which meant that he must count himself among the ugly creatures of this world, when it was surely blindingly obvious to anyone with eyes that ... Well. Dave wasn't about to tell some guy he'd just met – or indeed *any* guy – that he was beautiful. Nicholas Goring was strange, perhaps, yet undeniably beautiful with his long face and longer fingers, his deep blue gaze and his wicked smile, and the way he lit up when he talked about his mythical blue butterflies ...

And what was Dave even doing, thinking things like that? About a *bloke*?

"All right," Dave said, his voice unaccountably rough. "So we need to find out about sacred sites for stone–curlews and Barcoo grunters, if we can. I know just who to talk to. I'll call ahead, but if he's home then we're heading for Charleville first. As long as the sites aren't off–limits. There might be secret elements to the story that –"

"You think I don't know that? Of course I'd respect that."

Dave let the matter drop for now. That was the first sign of irritability from a man who'd survived a hellish twenty–four hours on a plane. Dave himself wouldn't have gone half so long without snapping.

"If you're in the mood for a walk," Dave offered, "the city botanic gardens are about ten minutes away, on a bend of the river. They're pretty cool. And they date back to convict days, so they're historical as well."

Nicholas considered him for a moment, and then said rather remotely, "All right."

15

"Stretch your legs. Get some fresh air."

A reluctant smile tweaked the corner of Nicholas's mouth. "Don't humour me."

"Is that what I was doing?" Dave asked with mock innocence. "Well, what d'you say to a stroll around the gardens?"

The smile was small but genuine by now. "I say yes."

Dave watched as Nicholas ambled along, hands snagged in his jeans pockets and long face turned towards the sun, long eyelashes fanning darkly down over his cheekbones. In the strong light, the Englishman appeared beyond pale – almost translucent, like the fine china Dave's grandmother used to treasure. So pale and fine, but with an odd tinge of cool colour, as well. Nicholas looked as if he'd been raised in the shade all his life. God only knew how he'd cope with the harsh realities of Australia.

"You know about protection, right?" Dave asked.

Nicholas tilted his head to quirk a suggestive eyebrow at Dave.

"*Sun* protection," Dave clarified.

"Heavens, can't I soak in a bit of warmth – just for a few minutes?"

"Yeah, but *only* for a few minutes." Dave added, "I'm going to buy you a hat."

Nicholas laughed. "You assume I don't have one? Or that it's inadequate?"

"Well –"

"You think I came out here equipped with my grandfather's old pith helmet, do you?"

"Mate, I am going to buy you a genuine Akubra."

The man's expression turned fondly droll. Or drolly fond. Whichever was worse for Dave's peace of mind. But all Nicholas said was a soft "Thank you."

The two of them wandered on quietly for a while, until they reached the river, and turned to follow along the bank. Well, Dave turned – and then he had to reach back and snag Nicholas by the elbow and turn him before he walked off the path and right into the water, he was so busy gazing up at the trees and the sky.

"Mate, you've got to look where you're going," Dave advised.

Nicholas murmured something appreciative, and continued on with his head metaphorically in the wide blue expanse above.

"Okay," Dave announced, "it's time for The Talk."

"Oh dear!" said Nicholas, though he didn't sound very worried.

"I've let you talk me into a few things today, but you've got to understand that when we're out there, what I say goes. I make the rules, I make the decisions, I get the last word. Every time. Do you understand?"

Nicholas pulled a long face. "Well –"

"No quibbles, no arguments, no second-guessing. This isn't a democracy."

"The whole point of this is to find the butterflies."

"I'll find your butterflies for you, if we possibly can. But that's only ever our second priority, all right? Our first is to return home, safe and whole. Those are my priorities, and those are going to be your priorities, too."

Nicholas immediately brightened. "Oh, if that's all –"

"No, that's not *all*."

"What else, then?"

"I mean, you can't just dismiss it like that. This is serious. There aren't many places left in the world where your survival depends on you alone, but this is one of them. And your survival depends on you and on me."

"I see." Nicholas turned his face up towards the sun again, though he no longer seemed to be basking in it quite so happily. "I understand."

"Do you?" Dave sounded sour and sceptical, he knew he did.

Nicholas laughed. "You bring me to this beautiful place to read me the Riot Act … ? How am I meant to take you seriously?"

"Mr Goring," Dave began with stiff formality, "I really must insist –"

"All right, all right! The only rule is to listen to you, and do as you tell me. I get it."

"And you agree?"

"Yes! For heaven's sake," the man softly grumbled.

Dave sighed. He liked to be liked, he knew that about himself. It could be the hardest part of this job that he sometimes had to insist on being completely unlikeable.

And perhaps Nicholas could already read all of that in him, because without any further prompting he offered, "I *do* take your point, and I agree, and I promise I'll behave myself out there. It would break my heart to lose a chance at the butterflies, but if you decide my heart is to be broken, then so be it."

"I wouldn't do anything without reason," Dave offered in turn.

"I trust you entirely."

They'd both paused in their wanderings, and now they stared at each other. Dave had pushed, that was certain, but he hadn't meant to go this deep.

Nicholas shrugged lightly. "I realise I am trusting you entirely, with my life and with more besides. That doesn't necessarily come easily for me, but I'll do it with a good grace."

And all Dave could do was nod in acknowledgement, and then turn to get them moving again. They paced slowly on, shoulder to shoulder. Soon he observed, "I've known Englishmen before. None of them talked like you do."

"Ah, well. I'm not just English, am I?"

"No?"

"I'm the youngest son of an earl. And gay. Incorrigible. And a quarter French."

"That would do it," Dave agreed. He left a pause, but then sought to get the conversation back on a firmer footing. "Okay. Thank you for agreeing. Now, the trick to returning home, safe and whole, is to make sure nothing goes wrong. Nothing at all."

The man's eyebrows climbed. "Is that likely? I was assuming you'd plan for every contingency."

"I do, and I have backups, redundant supplies, emergency procedures. We should never be further than a half day's drive from the nearest bit of civilisation. We'll never be more than a two hour helicopter ride away."

"So … ?"

"We can cope if one or two things go wrong. It wouldn't be a problem. But trouble is like a row of dominoes. Things happen; that precipitates more things happening; it quickly becomes a horrible mess, and we're in the midst of it, dead or injured. And there aren't many second chances in the Outback, you know. Not many at all."

"Look, I assure you that –"

"Camping in the Cotswolds or what–have–you, five minutes from the nearest pub, doesn't cut it. Not the same thing at all."

"All right!" said Nicholas, rather sharply. *"I get the point."*

"Did I scare you a bit?" asked Dave.

"Well. Maybe a bit."

"Good. Thank you. And I'm done now. Unless I think you need another dose sometime to make you see sense."

"Consider it seen," Nicholas stiffly replied. After a moment, he said, as if forcing out the words, "Well. I suppose you need to know that I am on medication."

"I do need to know that, yes. Do you have sufficient supplies? What is the condition? We should probably consult a doctor before we leave."

"That won't be necessary, I assure you. There won't be any problems. It's not that kind of condition."

And he so obviously didn't want to talk about it – and Dave had already pushed so very hard – that Dave took pity on the man. "All right," he said gently. "That's all right." They still had days to go before they left, after all.

When it became clear that Dave wouldn't insist, Nicholas nodded slightly in gratitude. And they finished their walk in silence.

Denise called that evening, and as usual cut right to the chase. "How's your earl?"

"Not an earl."

"Well, your baby earl, then ... Which makes him an earling!" she declared with a laugh. "How's your earling?"

Dave frowned for a moment over the day's jumbled impressions, and then ventured, "Unexpected."

"Ah," Denise wisely responded, as if this actually meant something to her. "Are you getting along all right?"

"Yes, it's almost as if ... Well, you know how once you've known someone for a while you get past the difficulties, and it's as if you've known them forever already?"

"You get comfortable. Especially when you're on a long trip."

"Yes, and it's just the two of you, and –" He sighed, though it was more in puzzlement than sadness or frustration. "Well, it's kind of like we're there already. Like we just skipped ahead."

"Well, that's good, isn't it? I mean, so you don't drive each other crazy these next three months ... ?"

"Yeah. Yeah, um ..." He tried to think it through, this sense of unease that accompanied the ease. "Unless the difficulties just come later. I guess."

"You'll be right, mate," she said stoutly.

"Will I?"

"You've been doing this for ages, yeah?"

"Yeah. Six years with Dad; nine on my own."

"Well, you've never yet hit a client over the head with a shovel and buried them under a red gum, have you ... ?"

"Actually, no. No, I haven't."

"See? You'll be fine."

two

Five days later Dave drove out of Brisbane in his Land Cruiser, with every space in the back and on the roof rack efficiently crammed with supplies, and Nicholas beside him in the passenger seat. The Englishman sat there quiet and still with his hands resting placid on his long thighs, yet he seemed to *tingle* with anticipation; it was infectious, the very air seemed to sparkle with it. Dave grinned to himself. Despite having done this for most of his life, he was as susceptible to the excitement of a new trip as anyone could be.

And, after all, it wasn't just the trip – it was the new Cruiser that had Dave himself tingling. She was a beauty. He'd just upgraded to the 2011 model in Magnetic Gray with a roo bar, side rails, snorkel, long-range fuel tank, and the rest. This was her first real trip, and to be honest he'd been a little disappointed to know he wouldn't have her to himself for this first stage of the journey. Nicholas remained quiet, though, which allowed Dave the chance to revel in all the joys of his Cruiser. She was solid, of course, but also sleek and smooth, and she handled with just the right responsiveness – easy but not skittish. They were only on regular roads for now, but Dave thrilled to how she held to the planes and curves.

He and Nicholas didn't talk. Not that there was much outside to distract or interest. The Warrego Highway had soon taken them out of the suburbs, and then through apparently endless farmland and towns. Dave had to assume the landscape wasn't very exciting for his English companion, but Nicholas paid careful attention, apparently genuine in his wish to get a feel for the countryside and how it slowly oh-so-slowly changed as they left the coast behind.

They didn't talk. They'd spent that entire first day together talking, then they hadn't seen each other since. Dave had been busy making the last preparations for the trip, and closing up his house. Nicholas, meanwhile, had apparently been happily occupied with the insect collections at the university, the museum, the Department of Primary Industries, and God only knew where else. In fact, they'd been going to meet for dinner on the Tuesday evening, but Nicholas had been so engrossed in his studies that he'd called to cancel at the last minute, having let the afternoon slip by unnoticed.

He'd been keen to meet the following day, but Dave hadn't wanted to cancel his plans to spend a last few hours with Denise, Vittorio and little Zoe – especially as it had been made clear that the invitation was issued on behalf of all three of them. Dave might have worried about not getting to know his client well enough under other circumstances, but it seemed to him that they'd connected on that first day; he was blithely confident that any problems between them would be small, and that they could handle them as they came.

After about an hour and a half, the road started winding through what seemed to be real bush. Nicholas smiled happily, and sank a little in his seat as if luxuriating in it. Dave had to disillusion him.

"Make the most of it," he advised. "There's a scrap of bush as we head through the hills, and then we're into Toowoomba."

"The city."

"Yeah. D'you wanna stop for a cuppa tea, or something?"

Nicholas dragged his gaze away from the countryside for a moment. "I'd never say no to tea, but wouldn't you rather keep going? We're not even a quarter of the way there yet, are we?"

"No, but we're not in any hurry. We might as well make the most of it. Like I said before, I don't think we should try doing it all in one day."

"But you would if you were on your own. Wouldn't you?"

"That's different."

"A cup of tea, then," Nicholas concluded. "If you don't mind stopping."

And they were into suburbia again. Dave drove along sedately, barely a kilometre or two – well, maybe five – over the speed limit. "You're the client," he observed mildly. "You can always say if you want a cuppa."

Nicholas smiled at him, softly – and then he changed the subject. "You were right, we would have been halfway to Wales by now."

"We'd have been *in* Wales."

Nicholas laughed, but couldn't help quibbling. "Driving in Britain is qualitatively different, not just quantitatively."

"Spoken like a true scientist."

"It takes a lot longer to get around. It's much more built–up and crowded, so there's more effort involved. There are far fewer empty stretches of road."

"You've got the motorways."

"That's different. And they create their own problems."

Dave shrugged, and found somewhere to park.

A polite request in his English accent and a winsome smile earned Nicholas a pot of tea delivered with a wink – in response to which Nicholas beamed up at their waitress happily. Suzie stood there with a bit of sass in her posture as she considered the man in turn. "Ah, Davey, you can bring this one back any time you like."

"Developing a thing for Poms, are you?" Dave asked with mock sourness.

"With that smile, who cares what flavour he is?"

"That smile?" Dave echoed blankly, having to think for a moment to work out what was wrong with the sentence. Then he got it. "Those smiles," he corrected her. "The man has a whole repertoire."

"Does he indeed … ?" She sounded intrigued.

But Nicholas's attention had been caught by Dave. As he gazed across the rickety old cafe table, his smile turned wistful – though when he spoke, he addressed Suzie. "I would have thought you'd be encouraging David to return for his sake, not for mine."

"Ah," she grieved, taking a metaphorical step back, and snapping her chewing gum. "That's how it is, is it? Well, mate, Davey here is no use to either of us, I'm afraid. He's strictly a one–woman man."

Dave tried not to splutter in protest. "We broke up *ages* ago! A year or more!"

"What's that got to do with anything?"

"She's –" Dave was having second thoughts, but said it anyway, glancing at Nicholas with a plea for rescue. "Denny's married with a kid already! She's *long* gone."

"Uh huh. Whatever you say."

"I'm gonna be, like, the kid's *godparent*."

Suzie looked at him flatly. "I rest my case." And she belatedly put Dave's mug of coffee down, before turning her back and sauntering off.

Dave's mute plea kept Nicholas quiet. Well, he was obviously gay enough to be curious, but at least he was bloke enough to know that some things just couldn't be discussed. "Um," said Dave, scrambling for a different topic of conversation. Just in case. "Um … Oh. Did you learn anything new about your butterflies? I mean, from all those collections?"

Nicholas's gaze turned intent and his smile fond for a long slow moment. Then he gently chided, "I would have told you, if there was anything that would change our plans."

"I know," Dave responded easily. "Not why I asked."

The smile grew as another moment lengthened. It felt as if Nicholas was happy in their mutual sense of trust. Eventually, Nicholas said, "No. No, if I find them, then there's a chance it will be a new species discovered. There's been very few sightings of the Lycaenidae reported in that area. At least, not of the sort of thing I'm expecting."

"The what?"

"The Family Lycaenidae: the blues. And when I say that area, I mean that entire south–west corner of the state. Though I guess … Well, I am extrapolating rather a lot from very little data. It could all come to nothing, of course."

"Huh." Dave hadn't quite realised the full significance of this quest of discovery. "An entirely new butterfly … You'll be able to give your name to it, then?"

Nicholas was smiling with slow contentment again. "Yes, I will."

"In Latin, like Whatever Goringi. Or Blah–de–blah Nicholasi. Nicholai … ?"

The smile became a laugh. "Something like that."

"Cool."

"And I'll write it up for *The Australian Journal of Entomology*, and I'll say I couldn't have done any of it without Mr David Taylor of Brisbane."

"Fame at last!" Dave laughed. "Thanks, mate."

"Might be good for business."

"Butterfly hunting. Dunno how much call there is for it, to be honest. Most people who brave the Outback are wanting to go crocodile wrestling instead."

"Ah, but if you want to attract the more charmingly eccentric clients …"

Dave couldn't help but grin; Nicholas's wicked brand of happiness was definitely catching. "Well, it's working for me so far," Dave finally agreed.

The Warrego Highway took them north–west from Toowoomba. The countryside around them was still mostly cultivated, but the number of lone houses and small towns slowly decreased. As their journey continued Nicholas eventually relaxed, realising that he wouldn't miss anything new if he let his attention wander for a moment or two. They still didn't talk much, however.

They stopped for lunch in Chinchilla, and then drove on. A while later the highway turned towards the west; they were getting close to the town of Miles.

"I thought we'd stop there overnight," Dave said into the silence. "Stay at the hotel. Not that there's anything much to do in Miles, but we can drive out into the bush, if you like. Get a better feel for it than we can driving past. And there might be precious few trees where we end up. Might as well enjoy them while we can."

"We can stop?" Nicholas asked. "Do you mind?"

"Course not. I mean, of course I don't mind," Dave clarified. "Just say, whenever."

"Oh, but it's *your* rules," was the teasing response. "What you say goes."

Dave chuckled. "We're not quite at the life–and–death part of the trip yet. But thank you," he found himself adding, "for taking me seriously."

"My pleasure," the man replied with light simplicity.

And Dave metaphorically kicked himself for saying far too much.

Dave had booked them into the hotel rather than the motel, as the narrow rooms with painted eucalypt–green wood–panelled walls felt more genuinely Australian to him. The rooms were each sparsely but elegantly furnished with a single iron bed, a wardrobe, a dressing table and a chair; simple white curtains hung by the tall sash windows. It wasn't the Hilton, but Dave thought Nicholas would appreciate this more than the kind of motel room to be found on road trips anywhere.

They checked in and headed upstairs with their overnight bags. Nicholas chuckled when he discovered that they'd been given adjoining rooms – and then he cast a wink over his shoulder at Dave as he slid past his door and into his room.

Barely a minute later, there was a knock at Dave's door. "End of the corridor on your left!" Dave called out.

"What? Oh!" Another chuckle. "No, I just wanted to say it'd be great to head out again. Whenever you're ready."

"Oh." Dave went to open the door, and considered the man. "You're keen."

"I am. But if you need some time out –"

Dave stretched out an arm to grab the keys from the table. "Let's go, then."

They headed off north past the old cemetery and up Pelham Road for a way, until Dave turned off down a track that took them into the living quiet amidst a scatter of gum trees. Not that it was wilderness or anything, but neither was it like anything else they'd experienced that day – or would again, probably, for several days to come. Nicholas was all hushed expectancy, staring around them as Dave drove along at a fair pace.

Once he felt they'd left civilisation as far behind as they could for now, Dave said, "What d'you want to see? What are you looking for?"

"Anything." Nicholas turned to him, his dark blue eyes alight with eagerness. "Honestly. Anything. There's still so much to discover here!"

"Well, it's your first trip …"

"No, I mean – Australia's so *vast*. And there's so few people really studying it. You'd be astonished – Well, maybe you wouldn't be. But the discoveries people make! And the things that have been found and then lost again … And the place is so *old* –" Nicholas stopped with a laugh. "What am I telling you all this for? You'd know it better than me."

"I dunno, not really," Dave admitted. "I mean, I know *bits* of it. Sounds like you've got a bigger perspective. And I'm not – I never went to college or anything. I liked geology in high school though."

"That's all right – you've been living it. Not just reading about it, like me."

"So we both know different things," Dave tried. "Or we're coming at it from different angles."

"We're going to have *so much* to talk about," Nicholas concluded rather happily.

Dave glanced away. "Where d'you want me to stop?"

"Here," said Nicholas, without even looking.

And Dave immediately pulled over, even though it was a completely random place. He parked carefully, just off the track, despite them not having seen any other traffic since they'd left Miles. Nicholas grinned at him for a moment, before slowly turning away, unfastening his seat belt and letting it slide home. Then he opened the passenger door and carefully stepped out.

Dave got out, too, and headed around the back of the Cruiser to retrieve a box. He may or may not have patted the Cruiser's rear in grateful admiration, he wouldn't like to say. Then he continued on round to find that Nicholas had barely taken a step. He'd barely even moved, but seemed to be looking here and there, his eyes darting, as if torn over which direction to take.

"Here," said Dave – and Nicholas turned a grateful gaze upon him, as if glad to have the matter decided for him, at least for now. "Here, I got you this."

Nicholas was as delighted as a kid at Christmas. He reached to carefully take the box in both hands, and beamed happily at Dave. It was perfectly obvious what it was from the branding on the box, never mind that Dave had already announced he'd buy this for him. Nevertheless, Dave was blown away by the power of Nicholas's smile. He watched as, with a kind of awe, Nicholas unfolded the box, unwrapped the tissue paper, took out the Akubra – and marvelled at it for long moments before slipping it on. It fit neatly, and looked just as Dave had imagined.

Nicholas's smile grew so overwhelming that Dave scrambled for refuge in words. He had to clear his throat before he could voice anything meaningful, mind. "It's the classic style. You know? The Cattleman."

"It's like yours," Nicholas observed.

Dave had put on his own old Cattleman as soon as he'd gotten out of the Cruiser. It was part of him, and had been for more years than he could remember. His father had bought it for him ... well, it must have been for his eighteenth.

"It's perfect!" Nicholas was continuing. "How did you know –"

"I emailed your butler, and asked him how big your head was. He said *very*."

Nicholas went pink round the cheekbones. "He did not."

"Nah. He sent me your measurements. Well, you know. For hats, anyway."

"And the colour?"

It was the Bluegrass Green. Dave had been going to get the Sand, like his own, because that was also classic. But then he'd thought about Nicholas's black hair and dark blue eyes. The blue jeans he'd worn on that first day, with the sage green t–shirt, and the black sweater. Nicholas was wearing blue, black and green again today. And Dave had thought about how the darker hat colours – the Black, the Graphite Gray, the Western Navy – would absorb the heat. He'd thought again about the unsettlingly oceanic depths of Nicholas's eyes. And he'd gone for the Bluegrass Green.

"You asked him about the colour, too?" Nicholas persisted.

"What?"

"You asked Simon about the colour … ?"

"Oh." Dave could feel his cheeks heating. "No, I just guessed."

"It's *perfect*." Nicholas had it in his hands again, turning it about, and admiring it. When he went to put it back on again, he grinned at Dave – and made the usual rookie mistake. He pinched the crown at the front between his thumb and second finger, and lifted it one–handed.

"Not like that!" Dave cried, instinctively reaching for Nicholas's narrow wrist to stop him. God, now they were both blushing. Dave took his hand away.

Luckily, Nicholas didn't take offence at any of that. "What did I do wrong?" he asked, apparently keen to know the answer.

"I know that's how they hold it in the movies. And it looks good, doesn't it? I mean, it's like you should be able to hold the crown like that. But you'll put pressure on the creases here, and that's where it'll end up cracking. Maybe not for years, but you don't wanna –"

"No, I don't," Nicholas agreed.

"Um, so, you know, it should last you a long long while …" He trailed off uncertainly.

"So, how should I hold it?"

Dave looked, and snorted as he saw the Akubra's brim now warily balanced on the very tips of Nicholas's long fingers. "Not like that, either! Here, you can grasp it as strong as you like with both hands, at the front and back." He demonstrated with his own hat, taking it off, and then putting it back on again. "Fit the front low on your forehead, then push it down at the back until it's in place … That's it," he added approvingly, surveying the results.

Nicholas was still smiling, gratefully. Even with a wry kind of sweetness. "Thank you," he said, in tones that matched his smile.

"You're welcome," Dave responded, feeling completely at a loss now.

And it seemed that even Nicholas was, too, for he finally turned away, and slowly wandered off, apparently scanning the undergrowth in search of something. Hiding his face, when he could, behind the lowered hat brim.

Dave followed him, watching him, occasionally glimpsing those pretty pink lips, slightly parted now in concentration. How strange it was, Dave pondered, that he'd become so very fixed upon Nicholas's marvellous smiles. How very wrong it was to be thinking so much about another bloke's mouth …

The quiet of the bush was calming. A delicious full silence was augmented by the occasional bell-like chirp of a bird, the bustle of a four-footed creature carrying on with life unconcerned by these two human intruders. Dave sighed contentedly. Flora and fauna weren't his strong suit, beyond the necessary survival knowledge of what he could eat in an emergency and what he couldn't, but he really did love it out here, in the bush, in the Outback. He loved that, mostly, the flora and fauna were willing to coexist with him, if he only paid them their due respect.

Dry bark crunched under Nicholas's footfall, and Dave's attention was back on him again. The Englishman was moving slowly, peering about at the lower shrubs, at the ground, at the sparse grasses – ducking and frowning now and then, weaving to and fro, until – "There! My first Australian butterfly."

"What?"

"Well, my first one in the wild, as it were."

Dave eased closer, astonished. "You're making discoveries already?"

"No. Oh, no … This is just a Cabbage White or one of the Pearl Whites, I should think. I'll have to check the field guide."

"What is?" Dave asked dumbly, looking about for beautiful white wings. "Where?"

"Here." Nicholas crouched, and indicated a grub-like casing. "It's in the pupa stage. One day, not too far distant, it will break apart, and the most glorious butterfly will emerge."

"Oh. Oh, of course." Dave felt like an idiot. He'd done some research, but then he'd also felt that the butterflies were Nicholas's area, and the organisation and safety of their travel were Dave's. Apparently his reading – or, more to the point, his browsing – had gone in one eye and out the other …

Nicholas had straightened up to consider Dave a bit kindly, as if he were to be pitied. "You know nothing about butterflies, do you?"

"They're pretty, I know that much."

"Yes, they are."

"I like the colours," Dave babbled, probably not redeeming himself. "When I was browsing Google images, I liked the blue ones best."

Nicholas was nodding earnestly. "Ours – *our* butterflies – are going to be *gorgeous*. Like bits of the sky come alive." He took a step closer to Dave, his hands in the air between them as if trying to shape adequate words. "But you're only thinking about their last stage of life. They *transform*."

"They do," Dave agreed, looking at the pupa, which might as well be an old bit of stick. "Is that – is that why you're so interested? In butterflies, I mean. Because of how they change so much?"

"Sorry … What?"

"I was just wondering," Dave blundered on: "*Why* butterflies?"

But Nicholas had taken a step back, and his long face sobered. It was as if the sun had gone in.

All right. Time to change tack. "D'you want to walk about a bit more?" Dave asked. "Seeing as we're out here."

A brief nod.

"We'll get the field guide, eh? Is it in the Cruiser?"

"Yes," was the quiet reply.

Dave hardly spoke after that, not wanting to spoil things any further. They went back and fetched Nicholas's satchel which contained his guide, his camera, a notebook and pens. And then Dave followed around as Nicholas ducked and weaved, searching around at random, and he kept track of where they'd left the Cruiser. It didn't take too long – not even half an hour, really – before the peace settled over them again.

three

They were into the acacia scrub the next day, as they headed west for Charleville. The gum trees grew sparser, and the acacia shrubs took over with tussocks of dry grass dotted about, and plenty of bare red–brown dirt between. The land was quickly flattening out. A lot of people hated this semi–arid countryside, and Dave would agree that none of the individual elements were particularly attractive. There was a spartan kind of elemental beauty about the overall effect, though. And he knew that it harboured all kinds of life, some secretive and some not. It was in a landscape such as this, he thought, that Nicholas would find his butterflies.

Nicholas was sitting in the passenger seat looking around with that strangely childlike eagerness of his. It was really quite endearing, but Dave couldn't help teasing. "Don't soak it *all* in at once. Take your time. We'll be seeing a lot of this."

"Yes?"

"We might see nothing *but* acacia scrub, depending on how far afield we go. It'll thin out more as we head west, and it'll be mostly low–level. You're gonna get bored with it pretty quickly."

"Not yet, though," Nicholas said with a grin. "Um ... Can we stop?"

"Sure." Dave glanced in the rear–view mirror, just in case, but there was nothing between them and the horizon in either direction. He pulled the Cruiser over, taking it safely off the road. Kept his gaze tactfully averted. "Loo roll in the glove box, if you need it."

"Oh! No. Thank you, but no."

"Well, then. Let's go see how many grubs you can find."

Nicholas grinned, put on his Akubra, grabbed his satchel, and clambered out of the Cruiser. "It's all useful," he explained with endearing earnestness as Dave trailed around after him. "It's like I said: there's so few people working on this. Any reliable observation is welcome."

"That's great." Dave obligingly held items as necessary, kept an eye out for anything Nicholas might find interesting just in case he didn't notice it himself, and made engaged or impressed noises occasionally as Nicholas nattered away.

At some point after Dave's attention had wandered, Nicholas abruptly sat down in the dirt, and Dave stepped towards him anxiously thinking, *Could this guy be any gawkier?* and, *How the hell am I gonna keep him safe?*

But of course Nicholas was fine. He sat there offering a dazed smile to Dave, and said, "I just looked up."

"Oh yes. The sky."

"It's rather larger than the one we have at home."

Dave put his head back and looked up. There wasn't a cloud to interrupt the enormous arc of pure blue, which if you didn't – scarily – let into your soul, would indeed make anyone feel insignificant. Dave huffed a breath. "You matter to me. If not to the sky."

"It's not that so much. I got dizzy there. Just for a moment."

"Like you'd fall up into it?"

"Yes. And float away."

"I'll keep you grounded. It's all right."

Nicholas looked down at his hands for a moment, as the long pale fingers meshed together. "Is that another reason for the hats? To keep the sky out?"

"No! No, you'll get used to it." Dave chuckled. "Wait until you see it at night." Out here, with few lights around, the stars were beyond awesome. Dave had never yet gotten tired of it.

"Spectacular?"

"You got it. Not tonight while we're in Charleville. Wait till we're camping out."

Nicholas grinned, and lifted a hand, which Dave grasped. "I will," Nicholas murmured as he unfolded from the ground, some of his weight a not unwanted test of Dave's strength, and the rest borne up by those long thighs. Nicholas didn't move away once he was standing again. Not immediately. He stayed there for a moment, right up into Dave's space, and whispered in Dave's ear, "I'll wait for you to show me."

Dave tilted his head in closer, as if about to confide in the other man – but what he said was, "You promised you wouldn't flirt."

"Not *my* fault you're so gorgeous, not to mention promising me spectacular nights."

"Huh." Dave stepped away. So gorgeous, yes, he reflected sourly, when the only person he'd ever wanted to hold such an opinion had proved it untrue just over a year ago. And that was that. It hardly mattered if some eccentric English earling had taken it into his head to feel attracted. Dave

32 | Butterfly Hunter

muttered a few choice swear words under his breath, and kicked disconsolately at the nearest shrub – which sat there, sturdy and unmoved.

"David …" Nicholas sounded infinitely compassionate, all sorrow and grace.

"Leave it be," Dave insisted. Then he said, rather more reasonably, "Take your time. There's no hurry. I'll wait with the Cruiser."

"Of course." And Nicholas crouched to examine something at ground level, his Bluegrass Green Akubra tilting to hide his face.

Dave made as cool an exit as he could.

When Nicholas finally returned to the Cruiser, Dave was deep into *The Nutmeg of Consolation* – and he felt all the better for it. He lifted his head once Nicholas had clambered back into the passenger seat, to find the man smiling at him fondly.

"You're a reader," Nicholas commented. "That actually explains a great deal."

"Not really." Dave shrugged.

"You like the Aubrey–Maturin novels, though? That's wonderful! And what else?"

"There's twenty of them," Dave explained. "Twenty-one if you count the last, but it was only half done when he died. When I finish, I just go back to the start again."

Nicholas laughed, though he sounded more delighted than cruel.

"I've read *The Last of the Mohicans*. And *Moby Dick*. But mostly just these. Denise is the serious reader. She loves George Eliot – who's a woman. And Tchaikovsky."

Nicholas took a breath, and glanced at him askance, before deliberately not saying anything.

"All right, so I've got the name wrong again, don't I?"

"Um … Dostoyevsky?" Nicholas hazarded.

"That's the bloke," Dave equably agreed. He didn't pretend to be educated, after all, but he did love these novels. "I think I'll be reading these all my life."

"I can't think of anything better," said Nicholas.

They reached Charleville late that afternoon, checked into the hotel, and then met half an hour later in the lobby. Despite the fact that they had adjoining rooms again, Dave had been very firm on the location for their rendezvous, and he went down early, while he could still hear Nicholas moving around next door, apparently taking his time unpacking and freshening up.

Once Nicholas joined him, they headed off down the street to the pub that was Charlie's regular. The westering sun bathed them in gold as they walked along side by side.

"Now," said Dave, breaking the silence in his best *this is me setting the rules* voice. "We need to be tactful here. We're not gonna blunder in where we're not wanted, all right?"

"Yes, David," Nicholas replied with a fair crack at a *this is me being the meek and obedient client* voice. The trouble being that it was always undermined – *always*, Dave had learned this already – by a happy little smirk loitering around the man's shapely pink lips.

"Charlie's a mate; we go back for years. We'll say g'day and I'll introduce you, just as soon as it feels right. I mean, just like with anyone. He might already be hanging out with his friends, or something. I mean, his own people. In which case, we don't interrupt unless it's clear we're welcome."

Nicholas nodded, seriously. Apparently now hanging upon every word.

"It's not that Charlie's not completely comfortable in both cultures. But if he's hanging with his Aboriginal friends, then we don't expect him to switch over to our register right away."

"No, of course."

"And once we're talking, then you need to take your cue from me, all right? When you start asking about Dreamtime stuff, then you go easy, and you have a care about whose toes you might be stepping on. If something's secret, then it's secret, and we're not pushing to know who or what or why."

"I understand, David."

"Do you? And can you stick to it? Cos all you can do is explain yourself and ask, right? You can't have any expectations about getting any answers. And even if you sense he's holding back, you've got to let it be his decision."

"Well, you know," Nicholas responded with at last a spark of ire, "I'm not a complete boor."

"I *do* know that," Dave said. "I'm just trying to say – that even more tact is called for than usual."

34 | Butterfly Hunter

Nicholas huffed out a breath. "One day I'm going to look back at this and laugh. An Australian teaching an Englishman about tact!"

They'd reached the pub, so Dave led the way through the door, too caught up in the argument to pay any real attention beyond registering that the place was as crowded as usual. He turned back to Nicholas, and let the noisy buzz of the pub's patrons give him an excuse to raise his voice. "Oh yeah, cos you Poms have learned so much from hundreds of years of good relations with the Aboriginals, haven't you?"

Nicholas had been about to take his Akubra off, in an instinctive politeness, but Dave shook his head in annoyance and, after a glance around, Nicholas must have realised that no man took his hat off in such a place. He pushed it back on, and stood tall. "Don't try to pretend, *mate*," Nicholas crisply replied, "that you're not on the white side of the equation. All this pussyfooting around makes you look like part of the problem, not the solution."

"Respect isn't pussyfooting!"

"I'll respect him enough to just tell him straight out what I need, and then I'll leave it to him to decide what he tells me."

"That's what I was asking you to do!" Dave cried in frustration.

"You were not; you were telling me. And I didn't need to be told."

Dave found himself completely undermined by an unexpected fondness as he contemplated the folded arms, affronted shoulders, and loftily lifted nose of his client. He let out a laugh under his breath. "Nicholas," he started in mollifying tones –

"Nicholas … ? Nicholas Goring!"

It was Charlie, of course. Nicholas had already turned towards the enquiring voice, and now he burst into a happy grin. "Charles!" The two men shook hands enthusiastically, while Dave looked on in bewilderment. "How marvellous!" Nicholas was saying. "I didn't dare hope it was you David was bringing me to meet."

"Who else would it be?" Once Charlie was finally done with Nicholas, he turned to greet Dave, and they shook hands, too.

"Hello, Charlie," Dave said, not too grudgingly. He wasn't going to ask, though. The world was a small place, after all. He already knew that.

"We follow each other on Twitter," Nicholas explained, and he was actually sounding friendly, and rather apologetic.

"Come on," Charlie said, leading the way. "Let's get a table, and some beer."

"I'm sorry, David. I should have said."

"No, I shouldn't have assumed."

"Nicholas here is *all right*," Charlie assured Dave as they all sat. In fact, Charlie dragged Nicholas down to sit very close beside him, Dave noted to his own annoyance and chagrin. "Nicholas has Butterfly Dreaming, you know?"

Nicholas laughed happily. "Oh, now you're just flattering me. David's not going to believe that any more than I do."

"Anyway, you're Australian now, Nicholas. You've got the hat."

The man's cheekbones went a happy pink. "David gave it to me."

"Did he now … ?" Charlie turned a pondering gaze on Dave.

"I'm sure he does the same for all his clients."

"Not that I ever heard of," Charlie replied.

"Oh shut up," Dave grumbled.

"In *fact*," Charlie continued as if he hadn't even heard, "I'd say you were in like Flynn there, Nicholas …"

The man's bashfully pleased pinkness bloomed further.

Before Charlie added with regret, "If only Dave weren't a one–woman man."

"Oh God!" Dave cried. "You all think you know what you're talking about, but you don't. You just don't."

"We don't?" Charlie asked.

"No. That's just –" He made it a rule not to swear around clients, even if they expected him to. "Nonsense. That's just nonsense."

Charlie put his head back and considered Dave for a long long moment … before nudging Nicholas with an elbow. "In like Flynn, mate."

Nicholas guffawed quite happily.

"Fuck's sake," muttered Dave. And he went to get a round of beer.

Despite the pub's incessant cheerful noise, Dave was close enough to hear that Charlie and Nicholas were soon nattering away about Dreamtime sites and blue clouds and stone–curlews. Dave shook his head in self-mocking disbelief. So much for tact! He was sure that Charlie would fill him in if they reached any practical conclusions, so he was happy enough to leave them to it.

While waiting to order, Dave thumbed through to a browser on his phone. He'd joined Twitter a couple of years ago, because Denise had gotten into it, but he'd hardly even looked at it since they'd broken up. He was already connected to Charlie, of course. And as soon as he started scrolling through Charlie's list of followers, he found Nicholas. His profile image was, unsurprisingly, a photo of a beautiful blue butterfly. Dave thumbed the Follow button, and then started browsing the man's tweets. Nothing particularly significant, beyond an excitement over the prospect of this trip. Otherwise it seemed to be chat with a wide variety of friends, interspersed with vaguely philosophical questions relating to a butterfly's life and transformation. *Does the butterfly remember its former larval self?* Dave read. Another one earlier in the timeline: *What does a pupa dream of while becoming fabulous?*

Nicholas my man, Charlie had replied to that one, *you tell me. What did YOU dream of?*

No, I'm still the caterpillar. I'm not fabulous yet.

Are you so sure about that, my friend?

Charles, I'm hardly even dreaming yet…

Dave looked up, and found Nicholas's deep dark blue gaze upon him, and for a moment the world around them went still and quiet. They stared at each other, and Dave knew. He knew, somehow, that something within Nicholas had changed since that exchange of tweets. Something that wouldn't – that couldn't change back. He wondered if…

But then Charlie nudged Nicholas and indicated a location on the map they had spread before them, and Rosie behind the bar asked, "You right, Dave?" and the moment was gone.

Dave frowned, pretending to be considering which beers they had on tap. But it was a no–brainer, and Rosie knew it. "Three Cascades, thanks, mate."

When he got back to the table, Nicholas and Charlie still had their heads bent close together over the map. Charlie sat back, and accepted the beer with a grateful nod. The glass was already beading with condensation. Nicholas accepted his, too, with a happy smile – and then he turned to consider Charlie for a long moment. Took in Charlie's thoughtfulness, and then tactfully lowered his gaze. Waiting, with no expectation. Sipping at his beer.

If Nicholas had looked up at Dave in those moments, Dave suspected that he would have found a very fond expression looking back at him. Perhaps it was as well that he didn't.

Half of Dave's Cascade slid coolly down a welcoming throat.

Eventually Charlie sat up, and said to Nicholas, "Show me again."

"Here," murmured Nicholas, one of his long pale fingers marking a rough circle towards the south–west corner of Queensland. "This sort of area."

Charlie nodded, and glanced at each of them in turn, taking their measure. Then he pressed a finger–pad to a place within the lower half of the circle. "Here. Stay north of here, I reckon. That's just a guess," he added, "from an old fella who hasn't been out that way in a *long* time."

"No, that's great," Dave said, knowing that Charlie had just shared a secret with them, even if only implicitly. "Thank you."

"Thank you," Nicholas echoed, with exactly the right quiet restraint. "I really appreciate it, Charles."

Charlie sat back again, relaxed, and downed half his beer. "We've got to find you your butterflies," he said to Nicholas. "I think … we'll all learn something from them."

"I'll do my best."

"Don't wanna have come all this way for nothing," Charlie continued, his expansive gesture somehow taking in Dave as well as the butterflies.

Nicholas went pink round the cheekbones, and laughed. It was a delightful sound. Which Dave might even have appreciated if he hadn't been so set on muttering complaints under his breath.

And Dave wasn't even halfway done grumbling yet, when Nicholas obligingly offered, "I'll get the next, uh – shout."

Charlie crowed with laughter. "You're even talking Strine now, mate!"

Nicholas grinned, but dipped his head towards Dave to surreptitiously ask, "What exactly do I order?"

"Three Cascades," Dave supplied. "And say thanks, not please."

An uncomplicated pleasure broadened the grin. "Three Cascades, thanks," Nicholas practised.

Dave nodded encouragement, and ignored Charlie's wondering look until Nicholas was safely at the bar, attention fixed on sorting through the colourful Australian dollar notes in his wallet. And then Dave said, "What?"

despite knowing exactly.

"You can't even stay angry at him," Charlie observed.

"Oh God, will you *please* give it a rest."

"Mate, you didn't even set him up for a fall just then."

"Course not. He's a client."

"Ah, come on. Classic chance for a bit of fun, and I know you've done it before. Rosie would have played along, too, and you know it."

"Look," said Dave, determined to take this chance at least. He propped his elbows on the table and leaned in closer to talk in confidence. "How well do you know him? Nicholas, I mean."

"Yeah, who else would you be obsessing over?"

"How well?" Dave insisted.

"Hhhmmm …" Charlie responded in a quibbling manner.

"It's just that his butler or whatever told me to treat him kindly, but wouldn't explain what he meant."

"Maybe he didn't mean anything."

"No, he did."

"Then maybe he just meant that Nicholas is a nice guy. Worth looking after."

It wasn't enough. Dave shook his head.

"And coming out here all alone," Charlie persisted. "He just wanted to make sure that Nicholas could count on you."

"There has to be something more specific. There has to be."

"What are you worried about? He looks fine! Happy as. Nice bit of a glow to him."

Dave nodded reluctantly. "He *has* got more colour to him lately. I reckon it's being out in the sun, despite the hat."

"See? He's fine."

"Dunno …"

"Davey," said Charlie.

"Yeah?"

"You worry too much, mate. You'll be fine. *Both* of you – will be fine."

Well, and Dave could only hope it was true.

Late that night Dave lay awake listening to the quiet rustling of rhythmic movement against bedclothes audible from the next room, and Nicholas's gentle panting breaths. Dave wondered if Nicholas was thinking about him. It already felt inevitable that that was the case. On the other hand, if Dave was going to leap to such conclusions, he should probably just get over himself instead. He wasn't the centre of anyone's universe. Not anymore.

Nicholas finished soon enough with a soft groan, and then quiet fell through the hotel, through the town, through the countryside surrounding them. The hush was vibrant, though. Energised with longing. Somehow Dave got the impression that Nicholas was lying there still awake. Not quite satisfied.

Dave sighed, and turned away. Settled himself for sleep with his back towards the wall he shared with Nicholas. As if even that mattered. He closed his eyes, and with another lonely sigh slipped away into the dark.

four

Dave was at the Cruiser early the next morning with his checklist, making sure they had all they needed. He couldn't think of anything he'd missed, anything they'd need to visit the Charleville shops for – and that in itself worried him. It would almost be a relief to think of something he'd forgotten. Dave sighed, and slid the checklist away with his other paperwork.

Which was when Nicholas appeared from the hotel in a bit of a flurry, with his black shirt buttoned up yet misaligned. He was barefoot, but already had on his Akubra. "Am I running late? I haven't packed yet. Won't take me a minute, though. Good idea of yours, to have a separate overnight bag," Nicholas added, before squinting up at the sky. "But I didn't oversleep, did I?"

Dave chuckled. "Nah, I'm just doing a last check through. Think we'll be fine – but this is your last chance for any shopping for a week."

A cloud passed across that long mutable face. "I should think that I can manage without shopping for a week." The gay man was offended.

"I just meant that if you need any essentials …"

But Nicholas was grinning again, with a mischievous little kick to it. "I know."

Dave just rolled his eyes. "*Anyway,*" he continued, "we've got to have one of Billy's full cooked breakfasts before we go. Won't need to eat again until we're back in civilisation."

"Cool, okay. And then –" Nicholas's smile was quieter now, but pure and true – and Dave really had to quit obsessing over the man's smiles for God's sake! "And then we'll be off for real."

"Yup. Off like a bucket of prawns in the hot sun."

"What?"

"Never mind. Yeah, we'll be out into the beyond." Dave wasn't immune to the excitement of it, even after all these years. But he touched a hand to Nicholas's suitcase where one side of it appeared amidst all their belongings and gear and necessaries – and he frowned. "Um … Got your medication all right?"

"Yes, darling," Nicholas replied in a long–suffering spouse voice.

"Good. Yeah. Bit anal about this sort of thing."

"It's life and death!" Nicholas protested. "Of course you take it seriously."

Dave grinned at him. "All right, all right. Now, go back up and get your shoes. I can't have you wandering around the Outback barefoot any more than you can be bareheaded."

"I *did* remember the Akubra," Nicholas commented with mock innocence.

"I am *not* buying you shoes as well," Dave responded with mock severity. "Go on! And then we can have breakfast, just as soon as you're ready."

"David, I am *always* ready …"

Dave just growled – and Nicholas scarpered with a gurgling giggle.

Nicholas didn't even want to stop for a cup of tea late that morning – their last chance for one that they didn't make themselves – so Dave kept driving, and they shared a bottle of water. Within a couple of hours, they were into the search area – which was massive. While they were still around the edges, at least, Dave had negotiated Nicholas down from stopping every mile to stopping every ten kilometres. They'd pull over, and Nicholas would look around, identify anything butterfly-related that he found, take handwritten notes, photograph it. And then they'd drive on. He didn't discover much, and nothing unexpected, though sometimes the identification would take a while of frowning over the guide.

At one point in the early afternoon, they found a flurry of white butterflies amassed over a particular spot that looked just the same as any other to Dave in the relatively featureless scrub. Nicholas lit up like it was Christmas – God only knew what he'd look like when they found his blues. They pulled over, and by the time Nicholas was done recording all the pertinent details, Dave had set up two folding chairs in the shade of the Cruiser, and brought out cold drinks and the makings of sandwiches for lunch. They sat there together watching the drift and hover of tiny scraps of white against the huge curve of bright blue sky. Nicholas was just *wallowing* in the sight.

But Dave was prompted to raise something that had given him pause. "How do we find a *blue* cloud? I mean, I can *see* this. And I get the cloud idea. But how on earth do we spot them against a blue sky?"

Nicholas was too happy to doubt. "If Clemence Hall could see them, we'll be able to, too."

"Maybe we need it to be overcast, so the blue shows up against the white haze."

But Nicholas shook his head. "Not if they only fly in the direct sunshine. Butterflies have to be warm enough to be able to fly, you see. Otherwise, they remain settled."

"That's why they only fly during the day," Dave said with a sense of realisation.

"Yes." Nicholas looked at him, obviously knowing there was more and waiting for it.

Dave shook his head. "A story I heard once. I'll have to remember it properly before I tell you."

"All right," Nicholas agreed contentedly.

They sat there for a while longer.

Eventually Dave cleared his throat. "Is there more to see?"

Nicholas turned to him with an apologetic look. "Can we wait until they settle again? Any observation –"

"– is useful, yes. No worries," Dave added. And he relaxed a little further down into his chair. He might have even nodded off in the mid-afternoon warmth …

When Dave opened his eyes again he found the Cruiser's shadow stretching out further beyond his feet, and Nicholas's warm amused gaze on him – and Nicholas's hand resting lightly on Dave's forearm. As soon as Dave stirred, Nicholas's hand lifted away and resettled against the shirt over his chest. Pressed flat over his breastbone. Dave eyed him with a frown, still only half awake.

"Sorry," Nicholas offered, "I thought you'd want to –"

"Of course," Dave agreed. He reached for the water bottle, and poured a bit of life back into himself. "Of course, yeah." He sat up straighter, and checked his watch. Almost five already. Then he thought to look for the butterflies. And found the air was empty for as far as he could see. "Have they –"

"– settled for the night. Yes."

"So should we." Dave frowned in thought for a moment. "One more ten–

click stage," he suggested, "and then we find somewhere to set up camp."

"Only one … ?"

"It's our first camp. It'll take us a while to get set up. Better make sure we have plenty of daylight to do it in."

Nicholas nodded. "All right, yes. I understand."

"Good." Dave drank some more water, and felt revived enough to continue. "I'll pack this lot up, if you're ready."

"I'm ready," Nicholas said. "I'll help."

"Thank you."

Of course the reality was that on a trip everyone had to pitch in and help one way or another. And with only two of them, there was just as much to do in many ways, and fewer people to do it with. Dave had warned Nicholas, of course, and he knew that Nicholas was more than willing to help, but until they got started Dave had been sceptical about how much the Englishman would be capable of. He was the son of an earl who had servants, for a start. He might have gotten away with never having to do much that he didn't want to. Not to mention that the man was slim to the point of scrawny, with pale almost translucent skin.

In the event, Nicholas was tireless, and seemed possessed of a supple wiry strength Dave hadn't even suspected. Not like delicate fine china at all. He cheerfully did all that he was asked, and more, too, when he saw something that needed doing. Well, he was cheerful right through the task of putting up Nicholas's tent. But his face fell when he realised that they were about to put up a second tent for Dave. His face fell, and then resentment sparked in those deep dark eyes.

"Do you really not trust me?"

"It's not that," Dave said uncomfortably.

"I'm not the kind of guy to insist where I'm not welcome. I *promise* I'm not."

"I know," said Dave. "I know."

"These tents are … well, not enormous. But certainly large enough for two."

"They'll sleep four if necessary. I usually allocate a tent for every two or three people."

Nicholas stared at him hard. "Well, then?"

"Don't you appreciate having your own space?"

The stare flickered a little, and some of the righteousness ebbed away. "I suppose. Yes." Nicholas sighed. "Yes."

"I always have my own tent," Dave explained. "*Always*. It's one of my rules. And no one gets to come in. That's my space, d'you see?"

Nicholas sagged a little further. "Yes, of course. I do see."

"It's nothing to do with you. I mean, no more than any client."

"I understand."

"Good." Dave turned away. It's not as if anything would have happened, anyway, whether they shared a tent or not. Such a thing didn't even factor into his calculations.

"I suppose you have a non–fraternisation rule, too. You'd never sleep with a client, would you?"

"Of course not."

A beat of silence. Another.

"Come on, then," Nicholas said with a friendly kind of briskness. "This tent isn't going to assemble itself."

And Dave turned back to the man with an appreciative laugh.

Dave lit a campfire, of course. Partly for warmth, partly for the focus it provided, partly because it was expected. He set a billy to boil over it for bush tea, but otherwise cooked their meat, potatoes and veg on the gas stove. While waiting for dinner to be ready, he pottered about happily, organising everything just so. And he didn't forget to call Denise on the satphone, to give her their coordinates and reassure her that all was well. Dave might have wandered around the far side of the Cruiser before making the call, but that didn't signify anything. In any case, Denise only had time to jot down the details, as Zoe was crying for attention, though she made a point of telling him to take care. Which warmed his heart, even now. Dave hung up, and went to attend to his own charge.

Dinner was a success. Nicholas ate ravenously and gratefully – and, as he finally set his empty plate aside, declared, "That was delicious!"

"Food always tastes better outdoors."

The man laughed, but insisted, "No, it was really great."

"Thank you." Dave measured out the tea into the billy, and added a couple of gum leaves he'd saved for the purpose, then left it to steep. "Come on," he said, beckoning to Nicholas. "Come away from the fire."

Nicholas cast a somewhat nervous look around them. "Are you sure? Why?" He'd stood up, though, and stepped after Dave. "What's out there?" he asked in hushed tones, as if predators could be avoided by whispering.

"Nothing. Don't worry."

But Nicholas's hand had slid into Dave's, just as easily as if Dave had been holding it out in invitation. Trust the gay English earling to interpret his gesture that way! But when Dave turned to tell him off, he discovered a wide-eyed Nicholas, honestly innocent and genuinely fearful.

"If there's anything out there, it's either asleep or it'll avoid you if you give it the chance. I promise. You'll be fine."

Nicholas's hand squeezed his, as if returning his reassurance. "Then what –"

"Just keep your back to the fire. Let your eyes adjust."

They did that, walking away from the fire, with Dave leading Nicholas, hand in hand. Picking their way through the scrub, keeping an intent gaze on where they were putting their feet.

Finally they were ready. Dave came to a halt, and Nicholas settled beside him, watching him trustingly.

"Now," said Dave, "look up."

And rather than take in the wonders of the night sky himself, Dave watched Nicholas's stunned reaction. He gaped, and swayed back for a moment as if he'd find himself abruptly sitting down again. "Oh my ..." he murmured. Dave had let go of Nicholas in order to put his hand to the man's back, keeping him upright. Nicholas similarly grasped a goodly portion of Dave's shirt in one hand, hanging on. Hanging on. Somehow restraining himself from actually touching Dave, though, for which Dave gave him points.

So many more of the stars were visible out here that it seemed like some kind of miracle. Some completely different universe, perhaps, or more than one, intermingling its beauties with the Earth's familiar skies.

"Oh, David," Nicholas murmured.

"I know."

"You don't even guess at all this. Not even from the country, let alone a city. In England, I mean."

"It's just the lack of other lights out here," Dave explained. "We're so far from anything now. This is always there, above our heads. We just don't see it."

After a moment, Dave realised that Nicholas had lowered his head and was staring at Dave with much the same kind of wonder. "That's very wise."

"Is it?"

"Don't you think …" Nicholas slowly began. "That's such a metaphor. For our lives, I mean. The beauty is there – the awesome beauty – but we just don't see it. Most of the time it's right above our heads, and we walk along oblivious."

Dave shrugged uncomfortably. "I was just talking about the stars. I don't know that there's any life lessons to be had here."

Nicholas considered him for a moment, thoughtful. And then he deliberately let go of Dave, and stood alone. Dave let his hand drop, and was almost sorry for it. Nicholas turned his face up to the stars again, and now Dave did, too.

"I'm sorry," Nicholas eventually murmured. "I was making a philosophical mountain out of what should be simply a lovely experience."

"It's all right," Dave muttered uncomfortably.

"Some of us need a little more faith to cling to, that's all."

Dave made a fairly agreeable yet neutral noise, and left it at that. The stars were so very spectacular … He found himself wondering, though, what Nicholas really needed. And why.

Dave woke early, as he usually did – though if he didn't have any particular plans for the day, he was partial to returning to bed for a further snooze. That morning, however, once he'd seen to the necessaries, Dave discovered that Nicholas was already up – and perhaps had been for some while, even though it was still mostly dark. The eastern horizon was just beginning to lighten. And Nicholas was sitting perched on the roo bar of the Cruiser, with a blanket wrapped around his shoulders.

He cast Dave an apologetic smile as he walked closer. "Good morning. I hope I didn't wake you."

"Morning. No, you didn't. This is kinda my usual time." Dave figured

Nicholas must have been very quiet; Dave usually had a sense for what was happening within his own campsite. "How long have you been up?"

"Oh, an hour or more. I wanted to see the stars again. I wanted to watch the sunrise."

"Of course," said Dave, as if this were the most natural thing on earth. Which it was, really. "I'll make us some tea."

"Thank you. Can I help?"

"No need," he easily replied.

Dave put the kettle on, got the tea makings ready, and then took another couple of blankets over to the Cruiser. "Come on, you don't have to sit up there." Dave spread one of the blankets over the bonnet and windscreen, then indicated that Nicholas should get up there, make himself comfortable.

"Are you sure?" asked Nicholas.

"Absolutely. Go on. Just be careful of the windscreen wipers. Like, don't sit right on 'em, or anything."

"I won't. I know what this car means to you … Well, it's not a *car*, is it? This vehicle," he amended. And then he got it right: "Your beloved Cruiser."

Dave guffawed under his breath. "I'm that obvious, am I?"

"To someone who pays attention." Nicholas grinned unapologetically.

Dave didn't deign to respond. "I'll get the tea," he advised. Once they were both settled there on the bonnet, wrapped in blankets and with mugs of tea steaming from their hands, Dave said, "I remembered that story for you. About butterflies … ?"

Nicholas turned to him with the loveliest warmest smile.

Dave cleared his throat, and indicated the eastern horizon, which was starting to glow pale gold. "No, you watch the sunrise, and let me talk."

That lovely smile quirked with humour, and Nicholas turned away again. "All right."

"There's this Aussie singer–songwriter, Pete Murray. He's really good. I'll play you the CDs if you're interested."

"I'd love that," Nicholas murmured.

"Anyway, there's this song of his, called 'Ten Ft. Tall'. He tells the story behind it before he plays it at gigs. And it's about these two friends of his, who were childhood sweethearts. They grew up and got married, and were as happy as. She loved butterflies," Dave continued with a nod at Nicholas. "She always said that when she died, she'd come back as a butterfly."

Nicholas was silent now, staring towards the lightening sky, but also listening carefully.

"Well, she got cancer, though they were all still quite young. And she fought it for a couple of years, but eventually she passed away." He took a breath. "It was about a week after the funeral, her husband and his mates were having a quiet drink down the pub. It was already late, it was almost closing time. And this butterfly flew in through a window, and it headed right for the guy, and settled on his shoulder. And he didn't say anything. He just put down his beer and walked out of there. And the butterfly stayed with him the whole way home."

Nicholas was completely still. The gold grew brighter, and the sky overhead ran from blues, through rich purples, to black velvet.

"And Pete always finishes by saying that it's a true fact that butterflies never fly at night."

Silence.

"It's really awesome. I mean, it's an awesome part of the show. A great song."

Still nothing from Nicholas. Okay, something had evidently gone wrong somewhere.

"Mate –" Dave leaned forward to get a glimpse of Nicholas's face. And discovered that his eyes and cheeks were wet with tears. "Mate, you should have stopped me. It's a sad story, I know."

Nicholas glanced at him with a hint of that same lovely smile, only wobblier. "It's a beautiful story," he amended. "And you're a romantic, David Taylor!"

"I am not!" he retorted.

"No, of course not," Nicholas agreed, though with a catch in his voice. He'd turned away again, facing resolutely towards the sunrise, the breaking day. Either the sight was a distraction or it brought with it a man's fate, whether good or bad. "I'm sorry!" Nicholas said on a gasp. And, all right, obviously he was close to full-on weeping now.

"Ah, mate ..." Dave reached to pat him on the back for sympathy, for reassurance.

And they sat there together watching the sky brighten, and then at last – suddenly – a molten line of gold appeared. Not so long after, the magic was chased away by the new clean day. Dave wasn't sure how much of that

Nicholas had managed to take in, but once it was over the man slipped away with another quiet apology, and disappeared into his tent.

Dave sighed, and went to brew more tea, and make breakfast.

five

The days and nights of the first week of their trip continued much the same. Except for the dawn tears; they avoided any repetition of that scene. Whenever Dave suspected that Nicholas was out there watching the sunrise, he just turned within his sleeping bag and went back to sleep for a while.

They got along well enough. Nicholas was engaged with his hunt, even though he was basically doing no more for now than providing further records for fairly well known phenomena. Dave was patient in assisting his client, and Nicholas was an efficient and uncomplaining member of Dave's camp.

The only time they came near to trouble was on the third evening, after Dave had checked in with Denise. Once he'd ended the call, he headed back towards his tent to put away the satellite phone – only to be met halfway there by Nicholas's puzzled scowl.

Dave almost stumbled a step, half surprised, half defensive.

"Are you going to call her *every* night?" Nicholas demanded.

"What? Yes."

"*Seriously?*"

"Yes. It's a matter of safety. Especially a trip like this when we don't know where we'll end up. I told you, she makes a note of the latitude and longitude, so –"

"I understand that."

So they'll know where to find the bodies. But of course he wasn't mean or unprofessional enough to say that. "Used to be Dad I'd call as often as Denny. Before he – you know. Died."

"But *every* night?" Nicholas returned, as if pleading for reason.

The defensiveness abruptly switched to its opposite. "*My* rules, remember? Life and death? You might be thankful some day that I was careful. Even," he allowed, the anger turning feeble already – "even a bit more careful than I needed to be."

"I think you're using that as an excuse."

Dave's head went back, and a stunned moment welled between them. Then he bit. "What if I am? What's your problem? Jealous, are you?"

Dave regretted that the moment it was out, but Nicholas responded quickly enough, as if he didn't see it as inappropriate at all. "Whether I am or not, I should think that any of your friends would be wanting you to move on by now – more than a *year* after she left you behind."

"Well," Dave started. "Look, she –" But he trailed off.

What could he say? How could he argue with a truth that no one else but for Denise herself had quite dared to tell him.

He took refuge in a rule that he should have remembered before now. "I appreciate your concern," Dave said frostily, "but it's none of your business. Just like your private life is none of mine."

"Right," Nicholas crisply responded, and he glared before turning away.

Still, half an hour later they were eating dinner across the campfire from one another, and they were conversing – a bit stiltedly, but with goodwill. And eventually in a quiet moment, Nicholas murmured, "I'm sorry, David."

"Not a problem," answered Dave. "I was out of line, too."

And he was rewarded with one of Nicholas's beautiful gentle smiles.

The real trouble began at the end of the week. Dave had begun packing up the camp as usual, but instead of pitching in as he always did, Nicholas was loitering, looking dissatisfied.

"I want to stay," Nicholas eventually announced.

"What?"

"I want to stay here at the campsite."

"No. No, we agreed. Once a week –"

"Supplies, I know. But you can go, can't you, David? You've gone alone for petrol and water before."

"Only once!" Dave slid one of the packing cases home into the back of the Cruiser, and then turned to consider the man. "It's not just supplies. It's civilisation. It's other people, and a proper bed for the night, and a proper meal. It's the news, and the internet, and calling home. Aren't you tired of my company yet?"

It was the wrong question, of course. Nicholas put his head down, but tilted one of his wicked little smiles up at Dave from under the brim of his Akubra. He really knew how to work that damned hat already. "No, I'm not tired of you yet. Maybe not ever."

"Right. Well. Don't you think your father would appreciate it if you emailed your butler or whatever, and told him you're still alive?"

Surprisingly, that earned him another scowl. "God, will you stop calling him that?"

"Who? Your father ... ?"

"My butler *or whatever*," Nicholas returned mockingly. "I suppose you think you're being all very egalitarian, but I don't see why you should disapprove of someone getting paid well to do a good day's work. He helps us run that massive old house, which is trickier than you'd think, and he's been part of the family since before I was even born."

"All right!"

"And his *name*, which you'd know if you'd been paying attention, is Simon."

"Yes. All right. Simon. I had a fair bit to do with Simon while he was booking this trip, and I reckon he'd like to know you're alive."

"So, *you* can email him, can't you?"

Dave guffawed. "I think he expects more from me than to leave you alone at a campsite out the back of Bourke ..."

Nicholas glared at him stubbornly, with his hands shoved hard into his jeans pockets. "I'll be all right. What's going to happen? Nothing bad has happened all this week!"

"It's no use pushing your luck," Dave advised. He could just imagine Nicholas blundering about: tripping over his own feet, hitting his head on something as he got back up, and God knows what after that. "Any one of a hundred things could go wrong, it could get really dire, and it would be my fault for leaving you here."

"David –"

"No, I can't do it."

"Can't or won't ... ?"

"Both!"

"David, I might never get back here. I want to make the most of it."

"You've got to know when to quit, mate."

"The simple truth is that I *like* it out here. I want to have a day of peace and quiet out here, instead of –"

"No." Dave cut him off, and walked closer to make his point. "I *can't*, Nicholas. And what I say goes, remember? You promised me you'd respect that."

"For heaven's sake … I'm not asking for much."

"You're asking for far too much. You said you'd trust me."

"David –"

"Mr Goring –"

Nicholas let out an unhappy "Hah!" and turned away. A silence stretched, which Dave was wise enough not to break. "All right. If you're going to *Mr Goring* me, I'll have to take you seriously."

"Thank you."

"Under protest."

Dave sighed. "Would you please pack your bag? I need to take your tent down."

"Of course," said Nicholas quietly. "I'll help."

But that was only the beginning of it.

It was a different town, somewhat rougher than Charleville. Dave had friends there, but he thought of it as more frontier than civilisation. Still … in this day and age, he hadn't thought there'd be anywhere he maybe should think twice about taking Nicholas.

They arrived mid–afternoon, checked into a motel, took their accumulated garbage to the tip, and then went shopping. Nicholas came along, determined to help, despite Dave excusing him from any further responsibilities. Then while Dave was repacking the Cruiser with their new supplies, and filling up with water and petrol, Nicholas went to use the motel's Wi–Fi to connect to the internet.

"I'll say good day to Simon for you," Nicholas said over his shoulder as he headed off.

"Uh, that's *g'day*, thanks, mate."

"What*ever*."

Dave snorted. They were fine.

And they *were* fine together, as they ate dinner in the cafe attached to the motel. It was only when they went down to the town's pub in the evening that disaster struck.

"Day!" someone cried as the two of them walked in.

"Oh God," Dave muttered as he looked around for the source. If the guys were already drunk enough to not even bother with *Dave*, then they were

54 | Butterfly Hunter

well ahead and no doubt closing in on the finish line. "Hey," he greeted the little knot of boozed–up blokes off to the right of the bar. "How ya goin'?"

"Day maaaaate!" was the response, and "Taaay!" Someone managed his full name: "Day Taaay ..."

"That good, then?" Dave queried, glancing back apologetically at Nicholas – who was looking unimpressed, and also a bit weary, as if he'd seen it all before. And surely blokes were blokes the world over, when they were stupid, young and drunk. "What ya' all up to?" Dave asked.

"Celebratin', Daaay! Ce–le–brate–*in'*!"

"Excellent." He didn't see any point in asking what, if anything, had been the excuse for such a session. No doubt he'd get the whole story later. "Right, well, don't let us interrupt you. I'll see ya later."

Unfortunately, however, one of them was still capable of adding two and two together and saying something coherent about it. "Day," the bloke said urgently. "Dave mate."

Dave turned back with a discreet sigh. "Um, yes?"

"Is this –" the man indicated Nicholas, with a wild gesture that slopped beer everywhere. "Is this the English poof, then?"

"Um, *earl*," Dave promptly supplied. "I'm pretty sure I said English *earl*."

"For heaven's sake," Nicholas muttered at his shoulder.

Dave was dying a little inside.

"Semantics," the drunk bloke observed dismissively.

"My, what big words you know," Dave returned, trying to turn it all into a bit of harmless banter. Because he knew these morons would only take such things so far. They might be obnoxious, but they weren't dangerous.

But it was too late. The mood had gotten edgier – and Nicholas had already walked away.

"Thanks, guys," Dave said flatly. "Thank you so much. Apart from anything else, *he's a client*."

"Awww, poor Day squiring around his English poof..."

"Not to mention he's a human being, you Neanderthals!"

They were too far gone to care, of course. Dave turned away, and followed Nicholas to the bar, relieved that at least Nicholas still seemed willing to have a drink there.

Although he might soon change his mind, given that the guys were calling after them, "Sorry, we don't serve iced Chardonnay here!" and,

"Maybe there's some sherry put by for the laaa–dies."

Nicholas was tense with anger, but he had both hands on the edge of the bar, all lined up to order, and when Dave reached his side, Nicholas half-turned to inform Dave with a terse politeness, "They have Cascade on tap."

"Great. That'll be great, thanks, mate." Dave cleared his throat, and before the barman got close, he offered, "Look, those idiots –"

"– are idiots. I know. Forget it."

And maybe that would have been that, if the drunken mob hadn't gotten it into their sodden heads to serenade Dave and Nicholas with a rousing chorus of 'Tiptoe Through the Mulga'.

"Right," said Nicholas. "I'll put up with five minutes of that, but not a whole evening."

"They won't last long. Short attention spans."

But Nicholas shook his head. "I'll see you back at the motel."

"Nicholas –"

But the man was already walking out, deliberately ignoring the idiots who were now going on about someone getting his knickers in a knot. And Dave, of course, followed␉Nicholas out, which prompted hoots about lovers' tiffs.

And then it was over, thank Christ, and Dave was out in the cool night air, with Nicholas striding on ahead with those long legs of his which obviously had far more power to them than Dave might have supposed. Dave didn't call out, but simply followed the man, and finally caught up with him as Nicholas's long pale fingers stuttered with the key at his motel room door.

Nicholas was furious and rightly so, but Dave could see that under the anger there was part of him that was simply hurt – and worse, a bit shamed. The man glanced up, startled and even scared for a moment, until he saw it was only Dave at his side. Nicholas glared at him defiantly. But when Nicholas dropped his gaze away then all Dave could see were those perfect plump lips and how they trembled. And he was pretty sure that if Nicholas were feeling any more confident, if he were at home and not alone round the other side of the world, he would have taken any teasing in good part and given back as good as he got – no doubt better.

"Those idiots," Dave quietly offered, "shouldn't have said any of that. But they *are* all talk, I can promise you that."

"What," Nicholas returned, in a low voice but still with a tremor, "so I shouldn't feel humiliated?"

"They're not worth it. You know you have nothing to feel bad about."

"David – I might never –"

The words halted and the man's head was still down, but Nicholas had turned back towards him, as if there was something he desperately needed to explain.

And the thing was – The thing was – Even if those blokes were mostly harmless, it had still been a horrible experience for Nicholas, and totally undeserved. And the thing was – Dave so wanted to make it up to him, to make him smile again. And the thought of surprising him out of it was a good one, too.

The moment stretched.

Then Dave leaned in and pressed his mouth to Nicholas's. Just for a heartbeat or two. The other man was startled, still. But then he pressed back for a beat. Not deepening it into a real kiss. Not pushing any further. Just returning the gesture. A grateful wistful smile was Dave's reward when he pulled back a moment later.

"Now," said Dave, all brisk yet friendly business. "I want you to get in there," he said, indicating the motel room, "and you'll be fine, but I want to hear you lock the door," he took a step back, in the direction of his own room, "because I want to know you're safe for the night and that you *feel* safe, too – and then I'll see you tomorrow morning for breakfast."

Nicholas was watching him back away with a hint of amusement twisting his lovely smile. He even let out a breath that might have almost been a laugh. "Thank you, David," he said. "Good night."

And then Nicholas slipped inside, and Dave waited to hear the lock clunk and the chain rattle into place, and then he turned and headed for his own room. And really, he thought he'd handled that quite well. He was quite pleased with himself, actually. Points for creativity, definitely. Nicholas was happier, and would hopefully sleep well. Everything was fine.

Except that Dave's heart was tripping over just a little too fast, and he was almost afraid to sleep for fear of what dreams might come.

six

They were quiet on the drive back out into their search area. Dave was conscious of Nicholas sitting peaceably beside him, tall yet comfortable in the passenger seat, still looking about him, happily engaged with all there was to experience out here.

Dave could hardly not be conscious of Nicholas, but mostly he was also paying great attention to the Cruiser. They had spent most of the previous week on sealed roads, but they were going to start exploring the dirt tracks now. There had been no sign of blue clouds or unknown waterholes so far, but it was early days – and Dave even reckoned it would be rather an anticlimax to find Nicholas's blues too quickly. Sometimes it wasn't all about the destination. Even Dave knew that.

The Cruiser handled beautifully, of course. She was going to be such a pleasure over the years …

"Yes, I'm sure you'll be very happy together," Nicholas murmured with a quirk of a smile.

"What?" He hadn't said anything out loud, had he?

"You're not the first man I've known who was in love with his car."

Dave cast him a sidelong look. "Not your chauffeur …"

"The same. Our family has a Rolls Royce Silver Cloud he held a deep affection for, but his real passion was for –"

"You."

Nicholas went pink about the cheeks, but otherwise ignored this gibe. "– an MGB V8 roadster in British Racing Green." A breath whistled out. "I was dead jealous, but I could see what he loved about her."

Dave laughed. "How very reasonable of you."

"He'd take me for a spin of an afternoon, if I'd been good."

"Good at what?"

"Oh shut up!" Nicholas cried, spluttering with laughter. "You ought to watch out, teasing me like that. I'll tell you all the graphic details if you're not careful."

"Quaking in my boots here."

"You should be," Nicholas advised darkly.

Dave just grinned at him, unrepentant. It seemed they were absolutely fine.

"I received a couple of very shamefaced phone calls this afternoon," Denise said when Dave called her that evening.

"Ah, you did, did you?"

"From your mates out at Woop Woop."

"Good. Though I'm amazed they even remember, to be honest."

"Still have a few brain cells intact, apparently." Denise was mystified. "What on earth did they say? I don't think I've ever heard a bloke sound so apologetic."

"Oh, it was nothing much. But they wouldn't let it go. It wasn't great, but Nicholas is all right about it now."

"If you take him back there, I'm sure they'll be suitably embarrassed to the point where even he won't be able to stand it. And no doubt they'll shout you all night, if you want."

Dave laughed. "Last thing we need is another drunken encounter with that lot. But I'll pass on their apologies."

"Think about it. It'll do them good to make amends."

"Well, maybe in a while. I think Nicholas was more ... upset with himself for letting it matter."

"I get that," Denise said. "All right, well, if there's no other news I'll sign off, all right?"

"Talk to you tomorrow, Denny."

"Tomorrow, mate. Stay safe."

And they did indeed stay safe. The Cruiser performed admirably – though, after all, it wasn't exactly challenging terrain for her. The tracks occasionally passed through that fine sand that lesser vehicles sank into, and some tracks were beginning to lose the fight against the encroaching scrub, but Dave found his way through easily enough. His only concern was with the inbuilt satnav, which would occasionally flicker, lose its bearings, and then regroup, but Dave figured that was probably just to do with patchy satellite coverage out here. And it did always regroup. And if the worst came to the worst, he had a good old–fashioned paper map and a real compass packed safely away in the back.

Nicholas continued happily recording anything butterfly–related. They found a group of golden–winged butterflies fluttering about that afternoon, and Nicholas was soon taking notes and photos, his frown of concentration combining oddly with his delighted grin.

Dave watched him, assisting when required. "What do you call a group of butterflies, anyway? You know, like a pride of lions or whatever."

"A kaleidoscope of butterflies," Nicholas informed him, with a quirk of a brow.

"Seriously?"

"I kid you not. Perfect, isn't it? Here," he added, handing his gear over to Dave. "Just be still for a few minutes." And Nicholas stood there near the butterflies with his arms lifted a little, waiting.

"What are you … ?"

"Ssshh …" Nicholas threw him a grin, and then quieted again. And soon enough the butterflies drew near, and started to settle on his skin, on his forearms, and a couple of braver ones on his throat and the hint of chest left bare by his undone shirt buttons. Nicholas was looking as beatific as St Francis on a particularly grouse day.

Well, there was only one thing to do – once Dave had stopped grinning back at the man, of course. He slowly and quietly put everything down except Nicholas's camera, and then started taking photos. A few full–length shots, and then close–ups of the butterflies, and of that beatific beaming smile.

"Here," said Nicholas after a while. "I want some of you."

Dave scoffed a bit, but he was happy enough to let Nicholas have what he wanted. The man approached, pacing evenly, and encouraged one of the butterflies on his arm to shift over to Dave's instead. The thing tickled there, so beautiful and so delicate. Dave watched it, mesmerised, until the click and whirr of the camera shutter caught his attention, and he offered Nicholas a genuine smile to save in pixels.

Now that Nicholas was moving about, the butterflies had mostly lifted away to hover around him, but a few had come to Dave instead. They seemed to be – He carefully lifted an arm to look closer at one. It seemed to be smelling him, or something, with a long probing thing unwinding from just below its head to poke and dab at him. "What's he doing?"

"Drinking your sweat," Nicholas said, in tones that were amused and – it was true – slightly envious.

"Huh. Old pervs, the lot of you," Dave retorted, though more fondly than he'd intended.

Nicholas laughed, and went to sit in the chairs Dave had set beside the Cruiser. "Oh, he's not old. He's newly emerged. And the longest any butterfly has been known to live is eleven months. They know all about seizing the day. They have to!"

"They're gorgeous, aren't they?" Dave offered.

"Yes." Nicholas's smile was back. He picked up his guide, and quickly flipped through to a particular chapter. "Now, let's figure out exactly what he is …"

"I had another phone call for you today," Denise said that evening.

"What, *more* apologies? It's all coming back to them now, is it?"

"No, not that lot. A client. A potential client. D'you think you'll be with your earling for the full three months?"

"Well, I hope so."

A beat of silence.

Dave wondered what on earth he'd just said.

"Do you?" Denise belatedly asked. "I thought you were pretty much dreading it."

"No, it's fine, he's – great. Anyway, hopefully he'll find what he's looking for, and get the chance to study it properly, and –"

"And you like him, don't you?"

"Not like *that!*"

Denise just laughed. "Davey, I wasn't even going there, but seeing as you raised the topic …"

"Oh shut up," he grumbled without an ounce of heat.

"All right, well, I'll tell this guy you're definitely booked for the three months, but you're available after that. He's heard good things about you, Davey. I'm guessing he'll try to reschedule for later in the year."

"Okay, thanks, Denny, that's great." But he found himself watching Nicholas set the campfire, and when he wandered over there after putting the phone away, Dave met Nicholas's affectionate smile with one of his own.

That night, as they sat around the campfire, they weren't around it so much as by it. Because Nicholas had placed his chair close beside Dave's. Well, not *close* close but not far away either. And then Nicholas sat there. With his forearm resting on the chair arm, and his long hand with its pale fingers dangling from that narrow wrist. And he very deliberately *didn't* reach to hold Dave's hand. Dave was watching him warily from the very edges of his gaze, and he could see that Nicholas was holding himself back, almost as if the sheer anticipation of the chance that he *might* cross that boundary was the most delicious thing out.

For once they didn't talk much. Until at last Dave thought it was better to clear matters up now rather than risk any misunderstandings. Because it seemed that, quite inadvertently, and to be honest he really wasn't sure how, Things Had Taken A Turn.

"Look," said Dave into the silence. "Nicholas." Staring hard at the flames dancing on the wood.

"Mmm … ?" said Nicholas in response.

"I'm *not* homophobic. That's not where this is coming from. But I'm *not* gay."

"I think that –"

Dave barrelled on regardless. "It doesn't matter to me that you like men. Honestly. I always thought that it didn't matter whether you loved a guy or a girl. What matters is that you love the *person*. You are in love with the person."

Nicholas was watching him with a guarded kind of interest. "So why can't your person be a guy?"

That flummoxed him. Dave thought about it. "Denny," he said after a while. "There's Denise."

"I know you loved her," Nicholas said, expansive. Reasonable. "You're loyal enough to love her still, which is not such a deal-breaker as your friend in Toowoomba seems to think. But I think you could feel that way for a guy as well. I think if you met the right person, it wouldn't matter whether they were a guy or a girl."

"Well, I guess that's true in a general kind of way –"

"Oh come on!" Nicholas cried. "It's not about theory, it's about practice."

"But I don't –"

"You *kissed* me."

Dave frowned, and wondered if the night's darkness would hide the fact he'd just turned pale. "I did," he admitted. "But just to, like … cheer you up."

"Right …"

"It's not as if it was a real kiss."

Nicholas was merciless with the light scepticism. "You can tell yourself that, David, if it helps you sleep at night."

"Well, that doesn't make a difference, anyway, does it? A guy or a girl. It's still a kiss. It's not like – their bits are involved."

Nicholas laughed hollowly. "Oh, my boy bits got involved, believe me."

Dave threw him a scowl, but then frowned as he tried to think it through. "It's not something I've done before," he eventually continued. "In fact, I've only ever been with Denise. That'll sound pathetic to you, I'm sure, but I've never even kissed anyone else."

The tones in response to this confession were a little softer. "Then I'm honoured, and I'm glad. Thank you, David." After a moment, Nicholas argued as strongly as ever, "But that puts me in a category that consists of only two people in all the world. And I say that a kiss isn't just a kiss. Apart from which, you called me beautiful."

Dave went from pale to bright red in a millisecond. "I did not!"

"You did, too. You were driving at the time. At first I thought you were murmuring sweet nothings to the Cruiser. But you weren't." Nicholas grimaced a little. "I suspect I wasn't meant to hear. You seemed to be thinking out loud."

"Oh."

"Ha! So you're not denying that you've thought it."

"Well –"

"Obviously you have atrocious taste, but in this particular case I'm not going to argue you out of it."

"Look," Dave finally came back at the man with. "Just because I said – I mean, you are, that's all, and I can have an objective opinion, can't I? I can think that guys are beautiful in a purely es – esth –"

"Aesthetic."

"Thank you. – sense. I can appreciate a guy like I'd appreciate … a sunrise!"

"Right. Especially one you've kissed."

"Oh God, shut up, would you?"

"I just don't think that straight guys *think* like that."

"Well, obviously they do. It's self-evident! Cos here I am, thinking like that."

Nicholas was about to retort, but then he seemed to have second thoughts, and closed his mouth again. A moment went by, before Nicholas sighed, and asked, "Why are you fighting this?"

"What! Why are *you*?"

"Because I fancy you, of course! I've fancied you since the moment I saw you at the airport. I fell at your feet, remember?"

"You tripped on the trolley."

"You distracted me, all fit and golden-haired and *beyond* handsome, like some Australian god …"

Dave had no words in response to any of that.

"Since then, I've got to know you a bit. And I like you, David. Very much. I like you very much."

"Well, and I like you," Dave was able to say, "but that doesn't mean –"

"All right, all right!" Nicholas lifted his hands with palms out, as if giving up at last. Or maybe he just couldn't bear to hear any more. "I'm sorry. I'll let you be. Of course I don't want you feeling harassed. I just thought –"

"What? What did you think?"

"That we might have a chance."

Dave looked at him, and saw the very real emotion that was barely hidden by a cool exterior shell. And for the first time in a very very long time, he used the S word. "I'm sorry, mate," he murmured.

And Nicholas quietly replied, "I am, too."

Nicholas seemed to take this final rejection philosophically. He didn't get angry, he didn't sulk. He didn't even get sad, though his happiness felt a shade less bright. Dave found himself missing those hundred-watt grins, though he could hardly change things back to how they were when it had been based on a misunderstanding. He was scrupulous in continuing to be as professional a guide and as friendly a host as he always was, though, and Nicholas likewise continued to be the perfectly equable and helpful client. Perhaps they didn't talk quite as much, but that was all.

And one thing they definitely didn't talk about was the next trip to town.

Dave got up early that day, only to find that Nicholas had gotten up earlier, and was already brewing a pot of tea. Nicholas was sitting on one of the chairs, slumped down into it with a blanket wrapped around his shoulders. And he had his stubborn face on.

"Morning," said Dave.

"Good morning, David," was the reply, more formal than ever.

After dealing with the necessaries, Dave came back and sat in the chair near Nicholas's. Accepted a mug of tea. "Well?" he prompted once the tea was cool enough for him to take a reviving mouthful or two.

"I'm not coming into town with you, David. Not this time."

"My rule still holds."

"I think you can make an exception."

"I'm concerned for your safety. Anything might happen. And you haven't learned enough in two weeks to know how to survive out here."

Nicholas looked across at him, and said very reasonably, "I'm not going. I'm sorry, but I'm not."

Dave let a moment or two drift by. He drank some more tea. He sighed. "We're not going to have a repeat of last week's dramas. You might have noticed, I've been taking us generally north-east. I figured we'd go to Charleville. Nothing bad happened there, did it? And if Charlie's there … Well, he knows who you are, and he welcomed you."

Nicholas nodded soberly. "I shall miss seeing Charles again. But I'm going to stay here. I'm sorry, David," he said again.

For a long while – through that cuppa, and then a second one – a silence stretched, and Dave thought about the situation. Well, he didn't really think about it as such, but instead reflected on an inevitability that didn't make him happy at all. It seemed that Nicholas was determined to have his way. And while the professional David Taylor could pull rank and overrule him, the soft-hearted Davey knew that he was already too involved with this man to do so. But that left Dave making a decision that he knew was wrong, that he already felt bad about.

He thought some more.

"All right," David eventually agreed after Nicholas had quietly gone about setting up breakfast for them both. "All right, you can stay. But I'll only go for the day. I'll be back for dinner."

"You don't have to give up your night in town for my sake."

"But I do," Dave explained in simple tones. "There is absolutely no way I'm going to leave you alone out here overnight. Just *no* way."

"But –"

"No, Nicholas. I'm not happy about this anyway. You've drawn your line, and you're just gonna have to let me draw mine."

Nicholas was staring at him with those deep dark eyes, and there was a storm happening in there, even if the surface was calm. They sat there at the foldout table, neither of them eating. "David, I didn't mean to make you –"

"If I could live my life without rules," Dave blurted, "that'd be great. Well, you know, not without decency, and Do Unto Others, and all that. But out here – you won't live long if you're not careful. There's a reason for every single one of my rules. There really is."

"I know, David. I understand they're not arbitrary."

"So don't go thinking that cos I gave in on this one, I'll start giving in on others. It can't work like that."

"I won't ask for anything else," Nicholas promised. He sounded almost as if he wished he hadn't even asked for this. "I'll come in with you, if you insist. If we both go for the day –"

"No," said Dave, bitterly. Stupidly. "No, you stay, if that's what you really want."

The turmoil was visible on Nicholas's face now. "David –" He reached to rest a cool palm and long fingers against Dave's hand where it lay on the table.

Dave withdrew his hand, and went to fetch the satphone. "I've shown you how to use this. Do you remember?"

"Yes, David."

"The first number programmed in is Denise, and the second is Charlie. I've put my mobile number in, too, now; it's the seventh one. But if you need me, I don't care what for, and you can't get through to me, then call Charlie. If you can't get hold of him, then call Denise. She'll know what to do. All right?"

"Yes, David," Nicholas humbly agreed.

"And you do what they tell you to, even if it makes no sense to you. Even if you don't want to."

"Yes, David."

"You promise? And I mean it. Call about anything. Even if it's just that you can't decide whether to have baked beans or spaghetti with meatballs for lunch."

That won a smile from the man. "I promise. And I appreciate what you're doing. Very much."

"I'm an idiot," Dave said, angry with himself, but unaccountably fond of the man who was making him so idiotic.

"You're the most amazing man in all the world."

"Huh," said Dave. And he went to fetch his shopping list. When he emerged from his tent, he found Nicholas waiting with a thermos of coffee for him. "Well," he had to admit in a mutter, "you're not too shabby yourself."

Dave was out of sorts all day, and he knew well enough why. He'd not only done the wrong thing but he'd done it for the wrong reason. Underneath which was a low–level, fairly realistic buzz of anxiety that he knew wouldn't quieten until he saw Nicholas again, whole and safe.

His thoughts were in a constant fret, going over and over all the advice he'd passed on. *Don't wander so far that the camp's out of sight. You'll get turned around, and head off in the wrong direction, and you'll be lost. Don't leave uncovered food or water out. You'll attract the wrong kind of attention. Don't –* And so on, and so on. How much of it Nicholas had actually taken in was another matter entirely. Dave hoped he wouldn't find that out the hard way.

Charlie came to find him at the grocery store. "I heard you were in town again."

"Just for the day, mate."

After a brief glance around, Charlie asked, "Where's your man, Davey?"

"Nicholas is *hardly* my man."

"Bring him down the pub for lunch. It'll be good to see him again."

"I can't," Dave said. And then he explained why.

"Come anyway, mate. You need to talk."

"I've never done anything stupider," Dave announced once their meals were served. He didn't really feel like eating, though he always looked forward to having a proper meal in town.

"He'll be all right," said Charlie.

"How do you know?" Dave asked, searching Charlie's cheerfully worn face, hoping for even a mystical Dreamtime kind of reassurance – the sort of thing that he wouldn't really believe, but which would feel comforting.

"I have faith … that this isn't Nicholas's fate."

"Faith?" Dave sighed. Faith seemed like little more than blind belief to him. "Do you *know* what a clumsy bugger he is? If anyone could –" He forced himself not to imagine any more disastrous scenarios. "I should never have let him talk me into it."

"Don't be so hard on yourself."

"Someone has to be," Dave said darkly.

Charlie considered him silently for a time, in between mouthfuls of steak, spud and veg. Eventually the man observed, "You care about him, Davey."

"Course I do," he replied a bit scornfully. "I know he's a bit – odd. Nothing like what I expected. But he's become a mate."

"Of course he has," Charlie quietly agreed. "He'll be fine today. And I know you'll take good care of him. But you need to take better care of yourself as well, Davey."

"Uh huh," Dave neutrally agreed around a mouthful of steak.

"How goes the quest for Nicholas's butterflies?"

Dave rolled his eyes. "Nothing. Well, just the sort of grubs and butterflies you'd expect to find, apparently. Which he's happy enough about, and he's busy gathering all the data he can. But no blue clouds, no mysterious waterholes – nothing that's never been seen before."

Charlie nodded for a moment, sagely. "The time has to be right."

"Right time in the right place. I get that. The distances we're covering each day, we're giving ourselves every chance to stumble into it."

"Mmm." Charlie sat back, and mused over his beer. "There's … a strangeness down around there. There's a mystery."

"Right …" Dave warily agreed, wondering if he dared prompt Charlie for more information – or if Dave might even be better off not muddling his head with half-hints of Dreamtime secrets.

"It's reasonable to assume you're not gonna find it the regular way."

"Mmm …"

"Maybe – you have to *not* want to find it."

"What?"

Charlie shrugged. "Maybe you have to *not* be looking."

"How does that work, then?"

Another shrug, and Charlie's gaze slid away.

Dave sighed. Sometimes he reckoned he was just a bit too white and ordinary for the Outback.

As Dave drove back to the camp, the Cruiser's satnav began doing that odd flickering and resetting thing again. Which didn't help his peace of mind, though he had a good sense of direction, and reckoned he could almost certainly find the camp again just on his own instincts. It was a bit of a worry, though, and no doubt he should try to have someone look at it before he and Nicholas really went off-road.

His thoughts were nothing but fretful as the sun started westering. But soon enough he saw the camp in the distance across the flat landscape, and at last he could make out Nicholas standing there waiting for him, and Nicholas appeared to be upright and in one piece, so maybe everything had quite unexpectedly turned out fine. After long moments Dave tore his gaze off that long tall figure in his Akubra and sage green shirt and blue jeans – tore his gaze away to glance across what he could see of the camp, which all seemed to be in much the same state he'd left it that morning. So maybe everything really was fine.

In those last moments before he parked the Cruiser, Dave was abruptly swamped with fury – the sort unleashed in a parent the moment after their child is safe and the danger is past. *What did you think you were DOING?! How could you have been so STUPID?!* But then that ebbed away, too, and Dave was left with a giddy sense of relief, and he knew he was grinning like a loon as he finally turned off the ignition and climbed out of the Cruiser. He approached Nicholas, his grin only broadening even while he felt more and more idiotic – and Nicholas stood there with his hands jammed into his jeans pockets, his grin just as wide as Dave's, and he was kind of shifting about on his feet as if he couldn't quite keep still but he was forcing himself not to – well, not to just grab Dave and hug him, Dave imagined.

"So," said Dave. "You managed not to lose a limb or set fire to your tent or anything?"

"Seems like it," Nicholas agreed. "But I –"

"But you what?" Dave prompted after a pause, though somehow he knew it wasn't anything serious.

Nicholas had his mouth pressed tightly closed, and just shook his head to indicate he wasn't saying anything further for fear of incriminating himself.

Dave had a stab at it. "But you missed me."

Those lips remained pressed together, but widened and quirked into a flat version of the man's wicked grin, while his deep blue eyes danced and his shoulders quivered with laughter.

"You're never going to stay behind again."

Nicholas shook his head emphatically. *Never.*

"Good," said Dave. He let his smile turn affectionate for a moment, risking the man reading that as *I missed you, too.*

And indeed Nicholas's lips parted on a silent huff, and then turned sweetly poignant …

Oh God, thought Dave, *and there's another of The Thousand Smiles of Nicholas Goring. Why on earth hasn't he found a man yet who can see the wisdom of devoting a life to cataloguing them all?*

Nicholas was standing there with his hands hanging free now, standing there so very still, watching Dave. Hardly even breathing, apparently.

It was the first time that Dave had been conscious he might actually be in some danger here. *When did that happen?* he asked himself. *And how?*

There was no answer, of course. The moment lengthened as they considered each other; Nicholas waiting, and Dave's brow beginning to wrinkle with puzzlement.

But Dave soon cleared his throat and turned away. "Right. Groceries. Let's get these unpacked and stowed," he said, heading around the back of the Cruiser. "And then I got one of Billy's homemade meat pies for our dinner. To celebrate, you know?"

"Celebrate?" Nicholas asked in a neutral tone. He was standing there beside him now, uncomplainingly letting Dave load him down with grocery bags.

"Celebrate, yeah. My safe return. You being whole and well. The camp not being destroyed."

Nicholas nodded, as if still not quite trusting himself to speak.

Dave was the opposite, though, babbling on and unable to stop himself even though he knew it was just an avoidance tactic. "So we can continue enjoying our inalienable rights," he said.

Warily, Nicholas asked, "Which would be … ?"

"Life, liberty, and the pursuit of butterflies, of course. What else?"

Nicholas guffawed quite happily, and they were all right again. They were fine. Everything felt easy between them. Nothing need change.

Even though Dave was visually charting Nicholas's post-guffaw contentment, and thinking, *One thousand and one.*

seven

During their third week, they decided, they'd concentrate on trying to find the waterhole where the Barcoo grunter ancestor was dreaming through his long sleep. They had historical maps as well as current ones, and Dave had worked out an itinerary that took in any water feature whatsoever, whether it still existed or not. If that didn't work, they would start exploring any ground at lower levels. The landscape appeared quite flat, but it wasn't really; there were gradual rises and falls, there were folds and creases between them where any rare rainfall would collect and run off. The waterhole might be more myth than reality, but they had to try.

The search was disheartening, though. "I hadn't realised everything was so dry out here," Nicholas commented on the third afternoon, as Dave steered the Cruiser up out of a dent in the landscape and back onto an unsurfaced track. "Butterflies need liquid of some kind, almost *any* kind. It can be quite ghastly what they'll drink, but they need *something*."

"That goes for any living thing, doesn't it?"

"Well, it's just that adult butterflies only drink. They don't eat. But there aren't even any flowers out here for them to sip nectar from."

Dave had to laugh at that. "Sipping flower nectar doesn't sound so gross."

Nicholas cast him a dark glance. "We'll just leave that topic there, then."

"All right! Where to next?" he asked Nicholas, who was navigating from an armful of maps and the handwritten notes they'd both made.

Nicholas sighed, and traced their recent meanderings on the map with one of his long pale fingers. Dave tore his gaze away only just in time to avoid leaving the track and scratching the Cruiser against one of the older gnarled shrubs. It was only that he was interested in their route, of course. And it was only concern for the Cruiser and for their safety that caused his eyes to be drawn to Nicholas gently tapping a fingertip on the satnav, prompting it to reboot.

"That's been playing up again," Dave observed.

"It's as if something is interfering with the signal. Though I can't think what, out here."

Dave glanced at him. "You don't think it's just faulty?"

Nicholas gasped in mock horror. "How dare you! That's one of the

Cruiser's very own instruments you're maligning."

"Hah! I think they call that Stockholm Syndrome, don't they?"

"You'll be loving butterflies next," Nicholas supplied.

"They're beautiful!" Dave protested like a true convert. "What are you saying?"

Nicholas smiled a bit smugly, and left well enough alone. And afterwards Dave thought that maybe that was just as well, for God only knew what else Nicholas might convert him to.

"Do you think it's the satellite coverage?" Nicholas asked a few kilometres later. "I mean, maybe there aren't many that fly over this region."

"Yeah, though it hasn't been a problem before. There's always been enough."

"How about the phone? You're getting through to Denise every evening."

"So far. There were only one or two nights when that was a bit patchy, too."

Nicholas made a non-committal noise of agreement, and turned his attention back to the maps.

Another few kilometres passed, with no variation in the landscape. But they were almost at the top of a long rise now, so when they started heading down again, there would be something to explore.

"The thing I'm still wondering is," Dave said into the companionable silence, "how do you find a blue cloud in a blue sky?"

"It's beginning to seem rather impossible."

"What? No, don't give up yet!" He felt quite alarmed by this sudden turn into negativity.

"I only have so much time …" Nicholas observed, slowly and quietly.

"No, you haven't even been here three full weeks yet. You knew it might take a while. That was the whole idea of the three months, wasn't it?"

A silence stretched. The satnav flickered and went offline.

Then Nicholas said, "Maybe we want it too much. Maybe we have to *not* want to find it."

Dave looked at him askance. After a moment he admitted, "That's what Charlie said."

"What?"

"When I went up to Charleville the other day."

"Why didn't you tell me?"

"Because it makes no sense!"

"I don't care. Let's try it."

Dave rolled his eyes. But he also waited to hear what their next plan might be.

Nicholas sat there thinking furiously. "Maybe we have to let go of the *need*."

"And you could do that, could you? Quit needing your butterflies."

"If I have to."

Dave sighed. At this point, he'd try almost anything. "All right, sure. Let's stop trying. We're just driving along here for our amusement."

Nicholas said with a fair attempt at world–weariness, "I don't even care anymore. Who could possibly give a damn?"

"It was just an excuse for a holiday, right?"

"Right," Nicholas agreed. "Just an excuse to have you to myself for three months."

"Huh." The driest hint of an old creek bed appeared on either side of where the track cut through it. Dave's instincts were to turn right, so he turned left into it, with an odd feeling of abandon.

"Wait, that's the wrong way!" Nicholas cried out.

"There's no right or wrong," Dave argued. "It's not like we're looking for anything, is it? It's not like we're going any place in particular."

Nicholas grinned at him, and settled back in his seat again. "Of course." He looked idly around him, making a great show of not hunting anymore.

They continued on for a while, and Dave's concentration was all for the terrain; there were rocks occasionally, although the ground remained fairly even. But then they topped another slight rise, and there didn't seem to be a mirroring trace of old run–off on the other side. Dave paused for a moment, looking about him at this new territory, which seemed to be a wide shallow basin; the horizon was visibly nearer on every side than they'd been used to.

"Where –" Nicholas began, looking from the landscape to the maps and trying to match one to the other. "I can't quite –"

From the corner of Dave's eye as he scanned around again, he caught a glimpse of something. It was as if a tiny part of the sky had moved.

"What was that?" Nicholas asked in that very moment, in a hushed tone. He'd tensed up again as if an electric current had gone through him.

"What was what?" Dave asked – but his sudden testiness betrayed the fact that he'd seen it, too.

"Like a shimmer, or something."

"Heat haze," Dave said, dismissing the whole thing. But he had turned the Cruiser towards it, and they headed slowly down into the valley.

They were both staring ahead, trying to track a piece of sky that for much of the time looked like any other piece of sky, while Dave was also very conscious of steering the Cruiser safely through the scrub which was slightly denser here than it had been on the other side of the ridge.

"There!" Nicholas cried. "To the left a bit."

Dave corrected his course, having thought he'd glimpsed the flutter, too, even though he'd been mid–blink.

They continued silently on, not seeing any more evidence of whatever it was, but eventually reaching a strange place where a worn old watercourse led out from a sunken piece of ground. Dave brought the Cruiser to a halt a few metres away, and they sat there leaning forward in their seats to stare at this discovery.

It was hard to quite make it all out, but it seemed quite large, this valley within a valley – and there were larger shrubs and trees growing within it, though none of them grew so tall that they stood out from the surrounding scrub. If you were looking across the terrain, chances were you wouldn't even see it.

"I *scoured* Google Maps," Nicholas said in a hushed kind of awe. "The satellite images, you know?"

"It would have just looked like a denser part of the scrub," Dave affirmed.

"And there were a few areas where the images were a bit blurry, a bit odd ..." They both glanced again at the satnav, which seemed to have given up entirely. "Poor coverage," Nicholas tried.

"What you said before, about something interfering with the signal ..."

"Yes?"

"There are huge mineral deposits around here. Australia's known for them. It's such an old place, geologically. So, I was thinking, what if there's a lot of ... something like iron ore here. And it's jamming the signals."

"Is that possible?"

"I don't know. But it would help explain why this wasn't on any of the modern maps."

"It has to be," Nicholas weakly asserted, sitting back to shuffle through the maps again, though he knew as well as Dave that they were all empty around these parts. After a moment, he sat back up again. "Can we drive down into it?" And for once he was actually asking permission, and letting Dave decide, and knowing that Dave might refuse.

Dave thought for a while. And then turned off the ignition. Before Nicholas's face could fall, Dave said, "We'll walk in."

And Nicholas was suddenly just *glowing* with anticipation. This man who didn't think he was beautiful was just ... glowing. And gorgeous.

"We'll leave the Cruiser out here," Dave said, trying to concentrate on practical matters. "Don't know what we'll find in there, and we can't afford to lose it or get it stuck."

"I understand."

"Not that she can't cope with a lot of different situations –"

"Of course," Nicholas stoutly agreed, laying a gently reassuring hand on the top of the dashboard.

"Anyway, if it comes to anyone sending out an aerial search team, she's much easier to spot than either of us – or that ... whatever it is."

"It's the waterhole," breathed Nicholas.

"We don't know that yet."

Nicholas just looked at him. *Yes, we do.*

"The rule still holds. You do what I tell you. All right? If it's a sinkhole of some kind, if it's at all unstable, then we'll –"

"How can it be unstable, with those trees growing in it? It must be at least thirty or forty years old, judging by the size of those gum trees – and older still if it's what I think it is."

Dave just looked at him.

"Sorry," Nicholas said, with honest chagrin. "We'll take it slow, and I'll do what you tell me."

"All right," Dave agreed, with far more severity than he felt he had any claim to.

"Thank you, David."

"Let's go, then."

They paused on the brink of this strange place, to discover what might serve as a track curving down into it along the left wall, which was otherwise quite steep.

"How wonderful," marvelled Nicholas.

"It's bizarre," countered Dave, though he knew he sounded just as awestruck. He checked again that they had what they might need. There was a good length of rope in his backpack, along with a torch, the small first aid kit, and some food. Both he and Nicholas were carrying full water bottles. Chances were they'd need nothing but a refreshing drink once they were in there, but it was a foolish man who relied on chances in the Outback. "All right?" he asked Nicholas again, just in case.

An eager nod was the only reply. Nicholas had his satchel with him, trusting that he would have plenty of discoveries to record. And maybe Dave was just too caught up in the excitement, but he was feeling almost as certain as Nicholas was that they had finally found what they'd been looking for.

"Come on, then," Dave said. And they crossed the edge and walked down into this place, shoulder to shoulder.

Dave was evaluating the track as they went, of course. It seemed wide enough and solid enough for the Cruiser, apparently formed from a harder layer of sedimentary rock that hadn't been worn away yet. The strata that formed the cliff wall above them were reddish with occasional blackish streaks, which hinted at iron ore.

The track lowered them down into the small valley, with one twist that would require a three-point turn, before leaving them on a gently sloping floor. Then the main impediment for the Cruiser would be picking a way between shrubs and trees, but they weren't so closely packed that it couldn't be done.

The temperature was a couple of degrees cooler down here, and there was that crisp feel in the air of a body of water nearby. Nicholas cast Dave an excited look, but he kept pace with Dave, and didn't try to push ahead.

They followed the slope of the ground to eventually emerge from sparse undergrowth and find a pool of still water that was the most astonishing green-blue. The trees provided a light cover over it all, but sunlight dappled around them and sang glints of brightness off the water. It was ... magical.

They stood there staring at the scene for a long while, dumbfounded at finding so much beauty that was so untouched. It seemed that nothing had been disturbed here for years, decades even. Dave couldn't even see any evidence of animals, though why they wouldn't use the only waterhole around for tens of kilometres, he couldn't begin to imagine.

As if Dave's thought of animals had triggered Nicholas's memory, the man cast him a querying look, and when Dave nodded permission, Nicholas looked about him and wandered back along the trees, searching. Dave trailed after him, watching Nicholas, but also glancing around, wanting to get a feel for their surroundings.

And it was Dave who spotted them first. "Flowers," he said – and then had to clear his throat before trying again. "You said they drink flower nectar, right?"

Nicholas looked up, and swung around to see where Dave was pointing. In a dell hidden beyond an ages-old rockfall, a cluster of wattle offered dark gold blooms to the sun. Nicholas gasped a little, and halted. Held out a hand to indicate they should tread carefully. That was all right. Dave knew the drill by now.

Slowly Nicholas approached the plants, bent almost double already to peer in amidst the foliage, keeping an eye on where he was walking. Dave followed him, not deviating from the path he'd set. Nicholas pushed his Akubra back, the better to see.

And then Nicholas had fallen to his knees by the nearest wattle, staring hard, his hands spread on his own narrow denim-clad thighs, fingers white with pressure. Dave waited, keeping his distance. But after long moments, Nicholas reached back, and then turned towards him, that long face both shocked and beatific. "We've found them," Nicholas whispered hoarsely.

"We have?" Dave took the hand that reached towards him, and let himself be gathered in. He crouched carefully just by Nicholas, though still keeping a little further back. He was trying to find blue wings, but couldn't see anything. "Where?" he asked, hushed. "What am I looking for?"

Nicholas laughed, sounding a little hysterical. "Don't you know a pupa when you see one by now? There –" He pointed carefully at … a pupa on a narrow branch of the wattle, that matched so precisely it all looked just like a bumpy branch. Unless you had it pointed out to you. "And there –"

"I see now …" There were heaps, now that Dave could identify them. "How do you know they're yours?"

Nicholas shot him a grin tinged with a delightful kind of madness. "I've never seen anything quite like them. But you're right. We need to make sure." He reached into his satchel for his camera, and took a few photos, carefully focussing in on the pupae. Then he shifted back and refolded to sit cross–legged, before pulling out his field guide and starting to leaf through it.

Dave settled himself in beside the man, and slipped off his backpack. This could take a while, he knew. He took out his water bottle, and swallowed a few mouthfuls; handed it to Nicholas, who did likewise; then Dave drank again. They were long past worrying about things like sharing utensils. Dave pondered that while Nicholas leafed through pages, muttering to himself about form, colour and texture; about tapering spinules, lateral flanges and anal hooks. Which Dave thought sounded rather painful.

"Sorry," Nicholas murmured, shooting Dave a mischievous glance. "That's how they attach themselves to the branches. Well, that or silken girdles!"

"That's so queer," Dave commented. "No wonder you're so fascinated." To which Nicholas just gave him a droll look, before returning to his book.

Occasionally Nicholas would hand Dave the guide and tip forward onto his hands and knees to peer in at a pupa. Sometimes he picked up his camera, and considered the photos on the digital display, zooming in close to see the details. Eventually he announced, "I'm not finding anything that matches."

"I believe you."

Nicholas laughed. "Sounding a bit defensive, am I? Well, I'll keep an open mind, I promise you that, and we won't know for sure until they transform into adults. But this is what I've been searching for, David. These are our butterflies!"

Dave just smiled at the man, and didn't even tease. *So much for an open mind, indeed!* But the last thing he could possibly want was to quench the light in those beautiful bright blue eyes.

Eventually Nicholas was done for now in poring over his bits of stick that weren't. With a sigh he unfolded, and lay back on the ground beside where Dave sat, closing his eyes to let the dappled sunlight bathe his face. After a moment one of his hands found Dave's, and those long fingers dovetailed with his own.

"We're just going to stay here now, aren't we?" Nicholas asked, obviously not dreading the answer.

"Yes. For as long as you need." Dave felt obliged to add, "Other than weekly trips for supplies."

"Of course. Do you think you can bring the Cruiser down into here?"

"Possibly," Dave allowed. When Nicholas opened one narrow eye to consider him, Dave provided a truer answer. "Yes, I could drive her down here, and get her back out again, I reckon. Easy. That's not the problem."

"What's the problem, then?" Nicholas tilted his head back to look at the flat and relatively empty area between the trees and the water. "I was hoping we could set up camp down here."

"I know."

"At least it's a bit cooler down here. It's got to be more comfortable. Quite apart from being close to the butterflies."

"Yes. I just don't know how wise it is."

"What could go wrong?"

"I don't know. That's the problem."

Nicholas lifted up onto his elbows to consider Dave. "Nothing's changed around here for years. Even the water level looks like it's stayed the same."

Dave nodded. "The pool must be fed from the water table."

"Well, then?"

Dave scrunched up his face, knowing he didn't have much to go on other than a sense of unease. "There's no trace of animals coming down here. And why wouldn't they? It's the only standing water in this whole area. No sign of birds inhabiting the trees."

"But our butterflies are protecting themselves from something. They're pretty well disguised."

"Maybe they just haven't bothered evolving. I don't know. Anyway," Dave added. "Charlie said –"

That had Nicholas sitting up beside him, looking a bit disgruntled for the first time. "*What* did Charles say? And what else haven't you told me?"

"Nothing. Nothing, really. He just talked about ... a mystery. A strangeness."

"What did he mean?"

"I have no idea. I didn't want to push. I mean, he's obviously helped us a bit more than he should. We've found ourselves the Dreamtime place where

80 | Butterfly Hunter

the Barcoo grunter ancestor sleeps …"

"The old grunter knew what he was doing, didn't he?" Nicholas agreed with a laugh. "I can imagine worse places to spend eternity."

"Yeah, but I don't know whether Charlie was trying to warn me about something."

Nicholas thought about that for a long moment. Eventually he concluded, "No, Charles would have said if he thought we'd be in danger."

"They can be really secretive when it comes to Dreamtime stuff."

"Oh come on, he's your friend! There's no way he would have let us just walk into danger. He would have found some way of telling you. Or he would have sent us off in a different direction altogether."

"I suppose …"

"Well, then … ?"

Dave sighed. "Not tonight, Nicholas. Give me twenty–four hours. We'll camp up by the Cruiser tonight, and then tomorrow –"

"Yes?"

"We'll see."

Nicholas grinned at him. And then lifted Dave's hand – not to kiss it, thank God, but to caress Dave's palm with his cheek. Which was almost as bad. Maybe it was worse. "Thank you, David."

"Nnn," he said, quite coherently.

As the westering sun left the waterhole in an early twilight, Dave looked at Nicholas, and Nicholas simply said, "I know."

"There'll still be an hour of sunlight up there, but we'd better get the camp set up."

One of Nicholas's gentle smiles blessed him. "I know, David." He was already packing his camera and things back into his satchel. "I'm ready."

"I'm probably being paranoid, but I don't want you coming back down here alone. Not until we're sure."

Nicholas nodded. "I know. It's all right."

"Really?"

"You make the rules, David."

He thought to wonder how long that was going to last. And later on he was relieved, though he hardly admitted it even to himself, when Nicholas without question or remark set up the second tent as if it were still a matter of course.

That evening, Dave had to drive out to the furthest rim of the wider valley before he could get a signal on the satphone or a reading of their location off the satnav.

"We're settled here now," Dave said to Denise. "But I can't call you from our campsite. We must be in some kind of blind spot."

"All right. Just give me the directions from where you are now, in case." When he was done, Denise said, "That sounds pretty incredible."

"It is. But it's like no one's been down there for decades, if ever. It's kind of eerie."

"Beautiful, though."

"Yes. Very beautiful." He thought about that, and about how he *wanted* to feel uneasy while down there by the waterhole, but he couldn't. Not really. The place was weird, but it wasn't *wrong*. "Maybe the only problem is that it's almost too good to be true."

"You should just enjoy it," Denise advised.

"Maybe I should."

"Look, d'you wanna just call me next time you're in town? I won't panic if I don't hear from you in the meantime. It's only another couple of days, anyway."

"Yes, all right," Dave found himself agreeing, although he'd never once let a day go by without calling his father or Denise while he was on a trip. Never once. "That'll be fine."

"Okay, have fun, Davey!"

"You, too, mate," he replied with a pang of parting. And then they hung up, and Dave drove back to the camp where Nicholas waited for him – and even from such a distance away, Nicholas's long tall figure was clear and pale and warm in the last of the evening light.

After breakfast the next day, the two of them walked back down to the waterhole. Everything was exactly the same, of course, with the possible exception of the place being even more beautiful in the cool morning light.

Nicholas was too tactful to ask again about them moving the campsite down there; he simply went to check on his pupae. He took some more photos and made some notes, and eventually came back to join Dave by the side of the pool. The water was clear and inviting, but beyond the jewel–like green–blue surface it seemed fathomless. The Barcoo grunter ancestor had obviously gone *deep*.

"All right," said Dave eventually.

"Yes?"

"We'll pack up camp, and move down here."

"Thank you, David," was the quiet response. But Nicholas was grinning like a madman, Dave knew that even without looking at him. A very fond and enthusiastic and beautiful madman.

"This morning?" Dave asked.

"Yes, please."

Dave sighed, and finally turned towards the fellow. "All right, then. Let's get to it."

eight

It finally happened that afternoon. They'd set up camp, and then eaten lunch together. Nicholas had washed and dried the dishes, and then he'd headed off to wander around documenting the area surrounding the dark gold wattle. Dave spent an hour or so fussing around the campsite, making sure everything was organised as it should be.

Eventually, though, even Dave had to declare himself satisfied. He put a kettle of water on to heat on the gas stove, and ambled over towards Nicholas to ask whether he wanted a cup of tea, even though he already knew the answer would be yes. Maybe it was just an excuse to summon up another of those smiles. Dave pictured it now: the pleasure and happiness and gratitude lighting Nicholas up from the inside, his lovely lips curving and his dark blue eyes glowing ... Dave was beginning to admit to himself that he was not immune to the charms of this man. Which didn't mean that anything need necessarily happen, of course, and actually no doubt nothing ever would, but still. It was kind of an earth-shattering thing for a straight Aussie bloke to deal with, when the only thing he'd dreamed about for all the years of his life was Denise and their own versions of little Zoe.

And that was when it finally happened. Dave was mulling over a few last poignancies for Denise and all the things that could never now be, and Nicholas was walking towards him with just exactly the pleased, happy, grateful smile Dave had imagined lighting him up – Nicholas was saying, "You're making tea? You wonderful man, you must have read my mind!"

When Dave suddenly froze. "Stop," he said quietly, lifting his hands just far enough to insist on stillness.

Nicholas froze, too, and for a moment he was wide-eyed with fear, trying to glance sideways at the waterhole without moving more than his eyes, perhaps thinking there must be a crocodile emerging to stalk them, or something equally dire. "What is it?" he whispered after a moment.

"Stay still," Dave advised. "I'm going to reach for your camera." It was tucked into the top of the open satchel at Nicholas's left hip.

By the time Dave straightened again with the camera in his hands, Nicholas had made a better guess, and was almost quivering with anticipation. "Is it ... ?"

"A scrap of the sky. Yes. On your Akubra."

"Oh, David ... *You* bought me this hat."

He puffed out a silent laugh. "I didn't realise it was a butterfly catcher, too." He took a pace round to his left, and slowly lifted the camera. Zoomed in, and focussed it. Took a few snaps with the butterfly filling the screen. Even while concentrating on photographing it, Dave was astonished by its beauty. A vibrant blue, with black markings, and scalloped curves round the edge of each wing, trailing down to long black tail–like things. Just amazing.

Dave zoomed the camera out a bit, and took a few of the butterfly and the Akubra, and Nicholas's eyes peeking at him from under the brim, wild with excitement and joy. And then Dave slowly handed over the camera, so that Nicholas could scroll through the images on the display.

"Oh, *David* ..." Nicholas breathed in awe.

The man was shaking now, and the butterfly was starting to stir again. Well, Dave knew what he could offer to tempt the thing to stay. He carefully lifted fingertips towards it, assuming it could sense his sweat somehow, get the scent of it, or feel the coolness of available liquid.

"Don't hurt it," pleaded Nicholas. "Oh, *please* be careful ..."

"I will," Dave promised huskily, trying not to laugh at the *Be gentle with me* undertones. Sure enough, the butterfly fluttered and lifted away from the Akubra – Dave drew in a sharp breath, forcing himself to wait for it to resettle rather than risk reaching for it – and then it landed again. On his fingers. That long probing thing unwound, and what with its light feet and its snuffling way of drinking from him – and what with the tension – Dave almost burst into giggles.

But he didn't. He carefully brought his hand down so that Nicholas could see it, and then he stood still while the butterfly drank and Nicholas gaped; the man murmuring things every now and then about the butterfly's beauty, and then muttering about the proboscis, antennae, the thorax and abdomen, and other things that Dave was clueless about – not to mention, "Those *wings*. Those magnificent *wings!*"

Dave laughed, he couldn't help it. He was so damned happy for Nicholas's sake. Nicholas flashed him a grin which was the visual equivalent of answering peals of laughter – and then Nicholas managed to take a photo or two from different angles, before at last the butterfly had drunk its fill, and it gently lifted, and flew a lazy random path around them, and then spiralled up into the dappled sunlight, before heading back towards the wattle.

Nicholas gasped as if wordless, and Dave just laughed some more, wonderful deep belly laughs. They'd done it! They'd found Nicholas's butterflies! Dave expected Nicholas to just turn and go running off after the thing, to watch it, to find where it landed. To *not* let it go.

But, no.

Instead Nicholas shared Dave's laughter for another moment, drawing close, and he lifted his hands, long pale fingers curving out like precious butterfly wings – and then he was cupping Dave's face, still looking awestruck, astonished, jubilant – he was cupping Dave's face, and leaning in close.

And then it happened.

They were in the midst of it before Dave formed another thought, and he could never afterwards say quite how it all came to be, but the truth was that they were kissing, they were each kissing the other, and even in the shock of it Dave knew it was as much his own impulse as it was Nicholas's idea. And those plump pink lips were just as delicious as he'd always known they must be, and Nicholas was masterful and generous and amazing, his waist slim and his shirt cool under Dave's palms.

And then too soon and not soon enough, Nicholas broke away, and grinned happily at Dave, *with* Dave, as if they shared the most awesome secret, the two of them. His cool hands still light upon Dave's skin, his fingertips dragging delightfully as he slowly pulled away. One last press of that wonderful mouth on Dave's, and then with another laugh Nicholas did at last turn to go stumbling off, skipping off after his butterfly, his happiness radiating from him, singing from him – and Dave stumbled after him, to help in all the business of photographing, recording, note-taking, as the giddiness calmed a little but never quite ebbed away, and even though they didn't quite touch again Dave was just *possessed*.

They hardly spoke that evening. Dave cooked dinner and cleaned up afterwards, while Nicholas spent hours poring over his field guide and writing up his scribbled notes.

"I'm convinced they're something no one's recorded before," Nicholas announced as it grew late. "If anyone's even seen them, they didn't realise what they were looking at."

"I'm glad," said Dave with simple sincerity.

"And they're so very beautiful! More than I could have ever hoped for."

Dave just smiled at him fondly. Words were redundant.

"We'll have to watch through a full life cycle, if we can."

"How long will that take?" Dave asked.

"I don't know, it varies so greatly."

Dave just nodded. And after reading and scribbling and thinking some more, Nicholas quietly wished him goodnight, and slipped away to his tent.

Which wasn't what Dave had expected. But a significant part of him was very relieved.

Another part of him was frustrated and yearning, and Dave was certainly honest enough to admit that as he lay awake that night. An hour or more slipped by as he lay on his back in the sleeping bag on the narrow camp bed, breathing, just breathing, and wishing even though he hardly knew what he was wishing for. He could hardly envisage anything beyond that kiss, and the possibility of more of those kisses, and Nicholas's long pale fingers finding him out – and his mind baulked at imagining any more than that, but he couldn't deny that he yearned, he was nothing but yearning and dread.

"David?"

He had the chance then to consider whether the yearning outweighed the dread, or if it was the other way round, for he could make out Nicholas's silhouette just beyond the canvas by the door of his tent. But he couldn't decide. He couldn't decide.

"David ..."

Another whisper, fainter this time. Though the first had been a question, it had been authoritative, but the second utterance of his name allowed for doubt. And after a moment the shadow narrowed and rippled as if turning to go – and Dave's heart was hammering loud in his ears but he managed to say quite clearly, "Yes."

And then Nicholas was slipping inside the tent, striding towards him on those long legs, kneeling by the bed. Those hands cupping his face again, fingertips pushing in to massage the sensitive skin by his ears, and then

Nicholas's mouth on his, masterful and passionate and so damned sweet. Dave groaned into it, he couldn't help himself, he'd been so very hungry for so very long, he hadn't even realised how hungry he was – he groaned again, and then Nicholas's tongue was pushing into him, pushing in, and after a moment's resistance Dave surrendered, and the heat of it swamped him. His head pressed back heavy on the pillow, and he lifted his hands and *clung* to Nicholas's arms just below his broad shoulders, Dave just *clung*.

After a while one of Nicholas's hands started drifting down, the fingertips dragging down sensitive skin to resettle at his chest, a thumb-pad rubbing at one of his nipples through his shirt – and Dave moaned a protest at the spiky sensation, hardly knowing whether it tickled or provoked, but as Nicholas continued regardless, it became clearer that it was pleasure, that it was almost unbearable, but it was *good*. And just as he'd learned that lesson, the hand drifted further still, and this time Dave's moan was encouraging, and Nicholas chuckled into their kiss, their mad mouthing which hadn't broken even once – until now, as Nicholas pulled back to sit on his heels, and he murmured, "Take off your shirt. Don't worry, nothing more than that. Take off your shirt."

Dave found himself obeying, half disappointed and half reassured and wholly confused to find that Nicholas didn't follow suit. They were both in t-shirts and boxers – well, Dave was now in his boxers only, with the sleeping bag still covering his lower half. He lay back again, and waited for Nicholas's next move or next instruction.

"Good," said Nicholas, before leaning in to take up where he'd left off, kissing Dave, with one hand cupping his cheek and then sliding lower to run fingers and palm around the column of his throat, while the other hand crept lower and lower, slipping smoothly under the sleeping bag, smoother still under the waistband of his boxer shorts. And then too soon and an agonisingly long time later, that exploratory hand at last pressed a palm against him, fingertips pushing down to wriggle at his balls, and that palm just grazing flatly against him, a light caress that wasn't half enough even though that would have been all it took if only there were some friction there, some pressure. Dave groaned in need – Nicholas echoed him – and then the caress firmed, that hand encompassing more – and the kiss broke again, though Nicholas peppered kisses over Dave's face and throat, groaning as deeply as if he were the one being touched. And it was so odd and yet so perfect, that hand rubbing up and down, all of that hand mapping his cock and his balls, every slide so random and each touch so unexpected, so intense, though it was nothing like what Dave did for himself, nothing like at all, but infinitely better which should have been impossible. *How did you know?* Dave thought raggedly. *How do you KNOW?!*

Nicholas was shifting, kissing Dave's collarbones now and then lower still to mouth at his nipples and then gnaw at them just roughly enough, and none of this was anything like what Dave had had before, but even though it was strange, he knew it was good. He knew it was good.

"Please," Dave asked, one hand still gripping at Nicholas's arm and his fingers probably digging in a bit hard – the other hand holding firm to the camp bed as if he might fall off. *"Please."*

Nicholas groaned, and the pressure and crazy rhythm of that hand intensified, while Nicholas's other hand slipped away …

Dave waited expectantly, but then he sighed a protest as he realised that Nicholas had reached down to work at himself with his left hand in a mad echo of how he worked at Dave. "No!" Dave cried, shaking at the man's shoulder. "No."

Nicholas lifted his head, and stared at him imploringly, imperiously. "I *need* to."

"I know, but – properly. Both of us." He had no idea what, though. Dave wasn't quite sure whether he was game enough to touch Nicholas yet, and of course he didn't mean – "Not *properly* properly. But not on your own like that."

Nicholas nodded, and glanced about him wildly for a moment. Then he ordered, "Stay still." And he pushed back the rest of the sleeping bag, letting it slide off to the tent floor – pushed down Dave's boxers, exposing him for a long moment – gazed at him hungrily while Dave both revelled in it and died of embarrassment – until Nicholas remembered himself and his need, clambered clumsily on top of Dave. They were lying there together now, and Dave's arms were around the man – it was quite impossible on the narrow bed, of course, but Nicholas lifted up onto one side, just enough to slip his hand down between them, and –

And they came like that, only moments later, with Nicholas wrapping both their cocks up together in one long–fingered hand, tugging arhythmically, and leaning down to kiss Dave like a starving man – until the end, so soon, too soon, when Nicholas lifted his head again and cried out as if his world was ending, and Dave clung on and stayed with him the whole damned way through.

Dave lay there for a long while after, overwhelmed. Cradling this man in his arms, Nicholas, so strong and yet so fragile. So unexpected and yet so inevitable. Nicholas was a wrecked weight upon him, his face pushed close into Dave's throat, and they were warm, pressed too warm together, but God it was good, it was so fundamentally *good*.

Eventually Nicholas lifted his head, cast a discreet glance at Dave, but then kept his gaze averted as he clambered back off Dave and off the bed to crouch beside it. Then he had to gather himself to look at Dave more closely, and it was clear that Nicholas was nervous about what he might find. It was obvious that Nicholas was worried for his own sake as well as for Dave's.

The problem being that Nicholas was supposed to be the one who knew what the hell was going on. Dave felt a flash of fear and insecurity.

Which Nicholas must have seen, for a moment later, his long face cooled into something calmer. "Are you," he said, before clearing his throat and starting again. "Are you all right, David?"

"Yes," he managed in a whisper.

"That wasn't, er …" Nicholas glanced away for a moment, but then his gaze returned. "If I presumed too much –"

"No! No, it was great. You didn't."

"– forgive me."

There was nothing to forgive, of course. Dave reached to gently shake the man's shoulder. *Don't be an idiot.*

Nicholas stood, brisk now. "Let's get you cleaned up." He looked around, but Dave had a towel and face washer, bottled water and a washing bowl, just as Nicholas did in his own tent. Nicholas poured out some of the water, brought it and the face washer over to Dave, and cleaned off their mingled spunk, before setting his boxer shorts to rights again, and lifting the sleeping bag back over him. Then he took the bowl away, and quickly cleaned himself as well, keeping his back to Dave. Rinsed out the face washer, and leaned out the door to toss the water away.

Dave lay still, waiting. Eventually Nicholas returned. But he only leaned down for a moment to take one of Dave's hands and lift it, cradle it to his cheek with both of his own hands, press a kiss to the palm. And then he put Dave's hand back, and said quite formally, "Good night, David. Sleep well."

And he was gone.

Dave blinked, hardly knowing what to make of what had happened. But it had been good. It had been as close to inevitable as made no difference, he could see that now, and it had been good.

He turned over onto his side, facing towards where Nicholas's tent stood only a few metres away. And with a wistful sigh, Dave slipped away into peace.

Dave woke a bit later than usual the next morning. When he emerged from his tent, he discovered that Nicholas was already up and dressed, and sitting on a blanket on the Cruiser's bonnet, leaning back against the windscreen – though there was no point in trying to watch the sunrise while they were down here by the waterhole. The two of them greeted each other silently, with a nod and tentative smiles that soon broadened in response. Dave put the kettle on for tea, and went through his usual routine. Then he took the mugs of tea over to the Cruiser, and needing only the barest hint of an invitation he climbed up to sit beside Nicholas.

"I thought you'd be off with the butterflies," Dave said, tipping his head towards the wattle. They'd deliberately set up camp at as much of a distance as they could, so as not to disturb anything.

"They're not up yet."

"Late risers? Sensible creatures."

"But look at what they're missing," Nicholas said, a hand indicating their surroundings while his eyes lingered on Dave. "It's such a beautiful day ..."

"It is," Dave agreed, and as they sipped the hot tea they contemplated the red rock and the green–blue jewel of the pool, the white–grey of the tree trunks reaching tall and the grey–green of the foliage. "It's *really* beautiful," Dave murmured, wondering if he just hadn't looked properly before, or whether all his senses were heightened, because –

"David –"

He turned towards Nicholas – and those long fingers were plucking the empty mug from his hands, Nicholas was reaching to stow their mugs on the edge of the roof rack behind him – and then Nicholas was taking Dave's face in his hands again, kissing him, *kissing* him, and they were making out – Dave was lying back, with Nicholas close beside him, Nicholas with those long legs curled under himself as he leaned in over Dave and *kissed* him.

Dave reached a hand up to grasp Nicholas's arm again, to anchor himself. The pleasure didn't inundate him as quickly this time, but that was all right. He still wanted this in the clear light of day, and he really didn't mind if they eased their way carefully into it. They kissed for long moments, for ever, and at last Dave let his hand slide down to find Nicholas's narrow waist again. He thought – Today, he thought, he could touch the man. Today, he was pretty sure, he could cope with that.

Nicholas murmured agreeably as he pulled away and sat up. Shucked off his shirt to reveal a pale chest with virile dark scatterings of hair, the man slim enough for his ribs to undulate down his sides, yet strong enough for those surprisingly hefty shoulders to impress.

"All right?" the man asked as he reached to start unbuttoning Dave's shirt.

"Yes."

The fingers stilled, as Nicholas apparently sensed a doubt. "David?"

"Let's … just take our time. If you can."

Nicholas looked at him drolly. "Haven't I already proved that I can control myself?"

"Yes. Mostly," Dave added with a grin.

"Well, then." Those long fingers continued, and Nicholas quirked a smile at Dave. "We'll take it slow, and I'll do what you tell me."

Dave was lying back, wallowing in being taken care of, having long since handed over control of all this. "I don't wanna tell you," he argued peaceably. "I just want you to – do stuff."

The smile turned wry and wonderful. "It will be my pleasure to – do stuff to you," Nicholas replied. "But then … along the way … you must tell me if there's anything you *don't* want. Will you promise me that?"

"Promise."

Nicholas helped Dave out of his shirt, then let him settle back before leaning in to press kisses across his chest, to suddenly rasp his tongue against a nipple. Dave's breath hissed, and Nicholas sinuously wound up to kiss him again. Against his mouth, Nicholas murmured, "Do you think we might get naked this time?"

"Reckon we could." So, it would be a first, but they were well past worrying about that, weren't they?

"My boy bits won't put you off?"

"Didn't seem to last night."

"But you didn't have to *look* at them …"

"Felt them, though. Against mine. No mistakin' 'em for anything else."

Nicholas chuckled filthily, and he sat up again, his fingers already working at his own jeans. "David, you are a constant revelation to me."

"Likewise, I'm sure."

"Oh …" Nicholas happily murmured.

And moments later Nicholas was straddling Dave's thighs, his hips shifting rhythmically as he rocked his cock hard along Dave's, both of their cocks wrapped up together again in one of Nicholas's beautiful hands – just like the night before, except this was daylight and they were naked and there was no question anymore about who they each were and what they each wanted. Dave's hands wandered boldly of their own accord, sliding up Nicholas's long thighs, feeling the muscle work below the cool skin, then shaping themselves to the man's sharp hip–bones, before finally easing around to fit up against the subtle curves of Nicholas's rear.

So different to what he was used to, and yet reassuringly the same in some ways, as Denise had liked to take a turn on top, and often she'd have him sit up against the pillows like this so she could lean in and kiss him when she wanted – just as Nicholas was doing now, swooping in to mouth at him hungrily – though Nicholas was undeniably different, and he seemed to have this habit of not just kissing but *caressing* Dave's face with his own, and it felt odd but amazing to have Nicholas's cheek slide along his own, the tip of Nicholas's nose gently rub across his closed eyelids, Nicholas's forehead roll against his, then those teeth carefully gnawing at the corner of his jaw before pushing lower to worry at his earlobe …

Dave had been without for too long to last – and he had too few defences against the surprises of a man loving him. In the end it wasn't any one particular thing that tipped him over the edge, but a combination of Nicholas curling in to bite at a nipple, and his own back arching deliciously in response, and Nicholas moaning his appreciation so that the sound vibrated through Dave's chest, and a stutter in Nicholas's rhythm followed by a twisting tug of their cocks – and Dave was shaking and shouting, and just *fountaining* out a week's worth of spunk – and Nicholas was laughing in joy – and the bastard waited, saw him through it all right to the last shudder, and didn't let up in the slightest, but kept going, rubbing his own cock against Dave's softening sensitivities which was just excruciatingly exquisitely wonderful – until Dave couldn't bear it anymore, and growled, grasping that narrow rear in his hands, hauling the man to him, insisting *"Now!"* – and Nicholas came with a howl right in Dave's ear which was both pleasure and punishment.

And when he was done, Nicholas fell back to lie against the Cruiser, but took Dave with him, so that Dave unexpectedly found himself curled against the man, holding and being held, in the utter comfort of completion.

He must have dozed off.

Dave came to a while later feeling a bit too cool, a bit too stiff in the thigh muscles, a bit too itchy where the sticky patches were drying on his stomach. "Ngh," he grumbled, shifting back a little, and reaching down to scratch.

"*Stop!*" came an urgent whisper – and Nicholas grasped Dave's wrist with iron strength.

"What … ?" he complained, even while he obediently stilled again. And then he felt a telltale tickle down amidst the wet spots. "Oh fuck …"

Nicholas chuckled – though he warned, "Don't you *dare* hurt it."

"As if." Dave had managed to open his eyes, and now peered down to find exactly what he'd feared. Nicholas's butterfly was drinking from his skin. And this time it wasn't sweat. "Fuck's sake!" he exclaimed, not knowing whether to be appalled or amused. "They're as queer as you!"

A happy guffaw met this declaration. "You are *so* lucky my camera isn't in reach."

"Oh God …"

"How could I resist? My three favourite things: cocks, balls, and butterflies."

Dave sank back, letting his head thud against the Cruiser. "That's four things."

"My four favourite things in all the world," Nicholas lightly confirmed. "Your cock … your balls … our butterfly …"

Dave laughed. He had to laugh, or he'd cry. "This is *way* too weird for me. You didn't tell me I'd be participating in butterfly porn!"

"Tit for tat," was the tart response. "You can't tell me this hasn't always been a fancy of yours ... being debauched atop the Cruiser."

Some kind of *too much* sound bubbled out of him, and Dave stirred himself to flap a hand towards the butterfly – though not too close, so it probably wasn't any use. "Shoo!" he tried. "*Shoo!* Go on! There's a whole damned waterhole over there for you to drink from."

"Oh, but I'm sure you are so much sweeter," Nicholas murmured, curling up against him, and watching the butterfly but also snuggling his head in against Dave's shoulder. "I'm envious. I want to taste you."

"Not safe, I suppose," Dave said, after a moment's thought. The weird thing being that he hadn't ever had to worry about such things before. "Um ..."

"It's all right, I realise you're probably a fine healthy specimen, and as far as I know I am, too, in that regard – but I won't do anything that isn't safe."

"Thanks."

Nicholas fervently burst out, *"God,* I want to get my mouth on you, though ..."

"I want that, too," Dave had to admit. "It was your mouth ... It was your mouth I noticed first."

"Yes ... ?"

"Your smiles. I like the way you smile. And, um ... your lips are pretty. No offence."

"None taken," Nicholas immediately replied. He tilted his head for a moment to frown up at Dave. "Do you really think I'd mind you finding my lips pretty ... ?"

Dave had to grin, though he felt rather sheepish. "No, I don't suppose you would." They looked at each other for a long moment. And then Dave leaned in and pressed a kiss to those pretty lips, because that was only fair and right, and the contentment in Nicholas's smile afterwards was ample reward if any were needed.

Sweet still moments passed.

Until at last Dave couldn't bear it anymore. "I've got to move," he said. "Sorry to interrupt the feast and all that, but I want to clean up."

"It's all right. You've been very patient."

"If I just start shifting off the Cruiser …"

"I'm sure he'll get the idea and drag himself away. We know we have to let you go sometimes."

"Huh," said Dave, as he gingerly started sliding across to the side of the bonnet.

Nicholas was off the Cruiser and on his feet a moment later, his hands out to offer support if needed. "Could we have a dip in the pool? Did you test the water?"

"There's an idea!" Dave finally lowered himself to the ground, and at last with his dining table vertical the butterfly lifted off, and started fluttering around just over their heads. "Let's see if this one will come along, too. I think a change in diet is required."

A gurgling laugh from Nicholas, before one of his cool hands slid into Dave's. "Come on, then!"

"I don't want you drinking any of the water, mind," Dave lectured him as they walked down to the waterhole, both of them still bollocks–naked. "It seems safe, but there's no point in taking any risks we don't need to."

"Yes, David."

"And no diving in or anything. At least not until we explore a bit and make sure there's nothing hidden under the surface."

"No, David."

"Just a quiet dip, like you said."

"I might have to kiss you while we're in there, though," Nicholas said very seriously. "I'm giving you ample warning."

"Fair enough," said Dave quite stoically. And when Nicholas finally slipped into the jewel–like water to join him, Dave let the man gather him into his arms, and he suffered himself to be kissed.

nine

Nicholas had hardly said anything all morning, but it was perfectly obvious that something was going on with the butterflies. If the increase in activity hadn't clued Dave in – with photos being taken, notes being scribbled, and comments being muttered as Nicholas riffled back and forth through the field guide – then he could hardly be immune to the tenseness of suppressed excitement.

Still, the butterflies were Nicholas's concern, and Dave was happy enough pottering around the campsite, or sitting back with his feet up and *Clarissa Oakes* in hand, contemplating the sun gentled by leaves and pouring down softly on the water. The pool was as quiet as it had always been, though Dave had often thought to wonder whether there were actual Barcoo grunters in there. He found that he kind of hoped so.

Late morning, Dave took a mug of tea over to where Nicholas sat cross-legged by the wattle. "Here you are," he said.

"Thanks," Nicholas replied. He scratched his head through that thick thatch of dark hair, and belatedly tipped a sweetly distracted smile up at Dave. "Thank you."

"No worries." Dave let a beat go by before asking in a tone he was careful to make no more than mildly interested. "What's happening?"

"Well …"

Dave didn't push – but he noticed that Nicholas had been frowning over the manual for his video camera, not the field guide as Dave had assumed. "Um … Can I help with that, at least? Isn't it working, or are you just trying to figure out –"

Nicholas was nodding. "– whether it can do time–lapse photography, whether there's *any* kind of timer, or programmable thing …"

"Oh. I think that's gonna be a bit outside its specs." Dave sank to sit beside Nicholas, and took the manual when it was offered. "Why d'you need it? We're here now. If we set up the camera on its tripod, we can just take a shot ourselves every hour or whatever. We can work out a schedule, or –"

Dave ground to a halt.

Nicholas just looked at him, kind of both wide–eyed and glum at the same time.

"You want to set it up for tomorrow," Dave concluded, "when we're due to go into town."

"They're emerging," Nicholas whispered in hoarse intensity. "Some of the pupae are beginning to break open. The butterflies are starting to emerge from the chrysalis."

Dave nodded. He understood. God, he had it bad for this guy. "Obviously you'll have to stay."

It was perfectly plain that Nicholas wanted that more than almost anything. But he said, "I can't. I promised you –"

Dave gusted a sigh. "I think, under the circumstances, we can break that rule one more time."

"No, I don't want to take advantage –"

Dave just had to scoff at that. "Bit late to be worrying about that, mate!"

"Oh, David …"

"And how stupid was I?" he added rather disgustedly. "I thought you'd be wanting to have your way with me in a real bed!"

Nicholas became nothing but grin. "You'd share my bed in town? We'd share a room … ?"

"I should have known better. It's always the butterflies with you."

"David –"

"Well, all right. Maybe in a town where nobody knows me."

"*Is* there a town around here where no one knows you?"

"No."

"Oh."

Nicholas sounded so forlorn that David couldn't help chuckling. "Don't fret. I'm sure the discreet shared use of a double bed is somewhere in our future. Just not tomorrow night."

"Are you sure … ?" Nicholas actually seemed quite torn between the two prospects.

"Of course I'm sure. I can wait a week, and so can the bed. But it sounds like the butterflies can't. They wanna become fabulous, and they want it right now!"

At which Nicholas was just *glowing* at him …

"Um … But I'd better go in myself. Just for the day again. I promised Denise I'd call her, and she'll worry if I don't. I mean, we could get by for a while on the food we have, but I think I'd better go anyway. Denise will –"

"Yes," Nicholas said, cutting him off.

"I *do* understand, you know," Dave said, heading off down another path, which for some reason felt just as aggressive. "This is what it's all about for you, isn't it? The change from one thing to another. From a grub to something beautiful."

Silence.

Dave felt like an utter bastard. Though he couldn't have even explained to himself why. He let a few beats go by, and then started again in friendlier and more professional tones. "Is there anything you need? Anything you want me to do?"

"Send a Tweet," Nicholas replied readily enough, "to Charles and to Simon. Tell them … Nicholas has found his butterflies."

"I will."

"And then come back to me."

"Well, I'm *hardly* gonna leave you out here!"

Nicholas cast him an enigmatic look. But then he unwound and knelt tall beside Dave. Cupped Dave's face in both hands again, and bent his head to kiss him. His usual masterful style seemed undercut this time by a hint of wistfulness. "Come back to me," he murmured again, with his lips against Dave's.

Dave headed for Cunnamulla, and for once he was all business. He left the Cruiser at the mechanic's for a quick check–over and tune–up, dropped off their clothes at the laundromat, did the grocery shopping, ate a hamburger at the best of the takeaways while considering the other items on his list. Although the first thing he'd done, of course, had been to use his mobile to send the tweet as Nicholas had asked him.

Almost an hour later, he received his first response: *Takes a lot to make old charlie speechless. You found it didnt you?*

Yes we found it, Dave tweeted back, assuming Charlie meant the waterhole.

Come see me next week and tell me all. Both of you if he will come too.

Sure. I'm sure he'll be happy to. See you then!

And then in the late afternoon, just as Dave was getting into the Cruiser to drive back, the second response came through: *Excellent news to wake up to. Please give our congratulations and love to Nicholas. Thank you, Mr Taylor.*

To which he replied, *You're welcome, and I will pass that on. It will make him smile one of those big beaming smiles.*

It was only after he'd thumbed the Tweet button that he thought, *Too much!* But it was also too late. Dave quickly turned the phone off before he was forced to face just how easily he could be seen through.

The satnav gave up on him again, of course, but based on the distance he'd driven that morning Dave knew he was within five kilometres of the waterhole. He kept driving, quite confident that he recognised the landscape, that he was in the right place. He'd get there on instinct, he'd simply head straight there, no problems. They'd laugh about how easy it was to find after all. He'd crest that long rise and head back down again, turn left up the old creek bed, and he'd be back with Nicholas before the sun was even close to setting.

Except that rise never quite appeared, the road seemed level all the way to the distant horizon, and there was no sign of any dusty old water courses.

"Fuck," Dave eventually muttered, chewing at his bottom lip. He'd done almost ten kilometres now, which meant he had to have passed it. After another hopeful minute or two, he stopped the Cruiser, and got out to look around and see if he could get his bearings.

Nothing. He had a good sense of direction, but there was nothing to go on, nothing distinctive to see.

"Right." He got back in, and turned the Cruiser around. He was sure he hadn't gone wrong already, so he slowly retraced his trail, looking for the creek bed again, remembering how it had crossed the road. Once he'd done another ten kilometres, he stopped again, and tapped at the satnav, wondering if it would come back to life. It didn't.

His belly was this hollow stone sitting heavy within him, but he refused to give in to the dread. There was no point in being anything but calm and thoughtful. He had to find his way to Nicholas before it got dark, that was all. And he'd do it, too. If not, he was sure that Nicholas would be fine for a night, and so would Dave. He could sleep in the Cruiser. Nicholas would trek out to the rim of the wider valley the next morning to use the satellite phone, but he was perfectly capable of doing that, and by the time he'd returned to their camp Dave would have found him again anyway …

Dave sighed. No, he had to get back that evening. He *wanted* to. He was desperate to. Nicholas would be fine, really. But Dave couldn't bear to risk it.

He wondered if he'd gone wrong somehow and ended up on a different track. Although he was sure they'd been heading west when they first found the valley, so perhaps this road ran parallel to the one they'd driven before. Which meant that from here he needed to turn left, and strike out across the countryside, hoping to come at the valley from the opposite direction.

It was a wrench. It took an actual physical effort to force himself to turn against his instincts, to deliberately head what felt like the wrong way. "Oh God," he muttered under his breath. "Maybe I have to *not* want to find him …" It was impossible. His every instinct clamoured against such a notion. "Don't ask that of me."

There was nothing. For a long time, which was probably only a moment or two, there was nothing.

And then a bit of the sky moved, off to his right – almost exactly where he least expected it – and his heart tripped as he realised he was driving up across a slow rise.

"Thank you," he breathed.

He turned the Cruiser, and soon was looking down across the wide shallow valley, and there was the slightly denser foliage that hid their waterhole – a few bits of sky were dancing low over it in the last of the sun, and Nicholas was waiting for him. Nicholas was standing there where the track led down towards the waterhole, and his figure was tall and pale and fine and *glowed* in the sunshine.

Dave felt as if he'd found home.

But *hell*, he'd almost mislaid a client. He'd broken the rules, and he'd almost been badly caught out. And Nicholas – Oh God, Nicholas –

The thought wouldn't quite come, but what if the man had …

Dave was a bit shaky by the time he got down there, and he was almost grateful for Nicholas's firm hand grasping his forearm as Dave climbed down from the Cruiser.

"Are you all right?" Nicholas asked, apparently concerned.

"I'm fine. Are you?"

"Yes, it's been a quiet day. A wonderful day. Thank you."

"Good."

Nicholas considered him for a long moment. "For once you look paler than me! Are you sure you're –"

Dave cut across him hoarsely. "I think I had to *not* want to find you."

"Oh."

"I couldn't do it. I couldn't do it. It was sheer bloody luck –"

"David," Nicholas said in hushed yet fervent tones.

"Don't ask me to leave you alone here again."

"I won't, I promise. *I won't.*"

"Yeah?" Dave asked, wondering if it would really be that easy.

"Yes. I'll come with you. I'll stay with you." That hand shook at his arm, and Nicholas gently scoffed, "Just try and be rid of me. See how far you get."

"I don't want –" he said brokenly. Unable to finish.

"It's all right," Nicholas whispered, "I know. David, I know …"

And Dave couldn't resist any longer. He hadn't wanted them falling into each other's arms and kissing passionately and all that nonsense. He hadn't wanted them to make anything more of this than what it was. But he'd gone long enough now without a kiss, he'd denied Nicholas long enough, so somehow he signalled that he was ready, that he wanted – and Nicholas, awake to every little nuance, kindly obliged.

They drove down to the waterhole, and Dave cast a glance around the camp to find that it was all, of course, in good order. He smiled at Nicholas as he turned off the ignition, and before they climbed out of the Cruiser he asked, "How are the butterflies?"

"They're fine. They're fabulous! There's a few of them emerged today."

"I saw some over the treetops."

"They'll be settling for the night now."

"Show me," Dave said. As he got out, one of the butterflies fluttered over and landed on his forearm. The thing just sat there; it didn't even start drinking from him. Dave tried not to disturb it as he walked around to meet Nicholas in front of the Cruiser.

Nicholas laughed. "It's your old friend! He's taken quite a fancy to you …"

Dave peered down at the thing. "How can you tell it's the same one? Does he have particular markings on his wings … ? Or is he bigger than the others? He was the first to emerge, wasn't he?"

More laughter, and Nicholas took his other hand as they walked towards the wattle. "No, I was just teasing. Or identifying, or something. Actually, butterflies don't get any larger once they're out of the chrysalis. They emerge full-grown."

"Oh."

"They were good ideas, though. I like the way you think. You should be a scientist, too."

Dave cast him a sardonic look.

"You have an enquiring mind," Nicholas explained with light sincerity.

Dave was saved from any need to respond to that by the simple fact that they'd arrived. He watched as Nicholas crouched and peered into the wattle. His own butterfly lifted up and flew about for a moment before disappearing somewhere in the midst of the dark gold blooms.

"There," Nicholas eventually said, indicating where Dave should look.

He bent down and leaned his head in close to Nicholas's. Stared hard – and saw nothing.

"It's difficult to find them, but that's the point. They don't want to be preyed on."

"They close their wings up flat, right?"

"Right! And the underside is quite a neutral shade, sort of a slightly bluish grey. Well, you've seen the colouring on our friend. Maybe if you try a different angle …"

He would have thought the wings were still large enough to show up easily, even when folded up tight, but apparently not. Eventually he thought he got a glimpse – of a butterfly or a shadow, or a butterfly that camouflaged itself as a shadow – and he reckoned that would have to do. The twilight was drawing in.

"I think maybe … maybe next time you can show me properly," Dave said.

"All right," Nicholas replied, with a delighted smile, as if Dave had just asked him out on a date or something.

"Let's get those groceries unpacked!"

Nicholas chuckled, apparently almost as happy with the practical aspects of their camp as he was with anything butterfly-related.

They worked together well. Once they had the food stored away, Nicholas offered to get dinner started. Dave was grateful for the offer, as he had other tasks he needed to do. He began by unpacking the goods on the Cruiser's roof rack and sorting them onto a tarpaulin. Then, some he stowed in the back of the Cruiser – the things that needed more protection, or simply the things that fit. The rest he began stacking away neatly in his tent. They had still been each retiring to his own tent at night, and Dave figured they'd both be grateful if they could still have space of their own. But he had other plans for their sleeping arrangements now. Once the tarpaulin was clear again, he began working on those plans.

Nicholas had been humming away quite contentedly to himself, but he finally came over when he realised what Dave's grand purpose had been. "Is that … ?" he asked, with a wicked glint in his eye.

"Yeah." An inflatable double mattress.

"For … ?" Nicholas warily pointed to the top of the Cruiser.

"Yeah." Dave quit pumping for a moment, and considered the man very seriously. "But only if you can promise me you won't fall off in the middle of the night."

Nicholas cast a searching glance over him from top to toe. "Well, that depends on how hard you try to buck me off, I suppose."

Dave snorted. "Let's assume that's not an issue. Are you gonna roll off the edge in your sleep?"

"No …" He sounded a bit doubtful, though. Which was honest of him, for Dave assumed that Nicholas wanted very much for them to share a bed.

"It might not be an issue, either," Dave reassured him. "You know how the sleeping bags unzip, so you can lay them out flat?"

"Yes." He'd already got it, and that glint had turned into the first smoulderings of a fire.

"You can put one on top of the other, and zip them together to make a big double bag."

"Then I'm only going to fall off the Cruiser if you do, because I'll be sleeping all night with my arms around you, and maybe my legs, too, so you'll take me with you if you go."

Dave resumed pumping, looking down and hoping the gathering twilight hid his face. Because he'd been missing that. He'd been missing that simple comfort so very much, for so very long. "It's going to be fine, then," he concluded when he could be sure of his voice.

"It's going to be *wonderful*," Nicholas countered, before heading back to finish preparing their dinner.

Dave had passed on the messages from Charlie and Simon as they sat at the campfire with their dinners, and Nicholas had been suitably delighted. But after that they fell silent, both contemplating yet another step they were about to take which felt trivial in some ways and madly significant in others. Dave supposed that anyone else might feel they were rushing things, but for him it felt so comfortable, so easy. Sinking back into a happiness and a belonging that he'd wondered if he'd ever find again.

It did occur to him that maybe he was fooling himself, and he reminded himself occasionally that he didn't really *know* Nicholas yet. Although, on the other hand, after twenty years of thinking that he had gotten to know Denise, she still managed to turn around and do the shockingly unimaginable. So there might be something to be said for going with the flow, and having a holiday fling with someone who certainly seemed decent enough to trust. With Nicholas, at least, Dave knew ahead of time that he was going to be left behind again. They'd have their three months, and then he'd take Nicholas back to Brisbane airport, watch him disappear through the security gates – maybe Nicholas would turn for one last poignant smile – and that would be that. But at least this time there was no pretence, no promises either spoken or implied ...

Dave sighed, and put the rest of his dinner aside.

"Not hungry?" asked Nicholas.

"Not really. It was great, though. Thank you. I like your cooking," he offered quite genuinely.

Nicholas eyed him for a moment, as if doubting him. But when he finally spoke, it turned out he'd had something completely different on his mind. "Did you buy condoms today?"

"What?"

"Along with the double mattress. I was just wondering if you'd –"

"I heard you!" Dave took a moment, wondering why that had thrown him so. Finally he answered, "No, I didn't."

"Ah." Nicholas's gaze slid away, and then he turned his head as well, so that it was impossible to make out his expression.

So far they'd done very nicely without. Dave had been perfectly happy with all the myriad ways Nicholas used his hands and his own cock to bring Dave off, not to mention Nicholas lying over him, rubbing off against Dave's cock or his hip, and driving Dave quite wild with it. The simple pleasures could be profound pleasures, too. But then Nicholas had expressed the wish a few times to get his mouth on Dave, and who on earth was Dave to argue against such an idea – but even the preliminaries of Nicholas going down on him were starting to cross the line, from what Dave understood of safe sex.

Eventually Dave said into the silence, in uneasy tones, "Look. I have a couple of boxes of 'em here. If you want –"

If he hadn't already come to a halt, Nicholas's sudden glare would have stopped him in his tracks. "Oh, right," Nicholas sardonically responded. "So much for your non-fraternisation rule. I'm not your first exception at all, am I?"

"Yes, you are," Dave countered, a bit mystified. "They're not for me, they're for clients. I like to be prepared, is all. With anything they might need."

"Oh." Nicholas quickly sank again, looking sheepish. "Sorry."

Dave shook his head. *Don't be.* He was a bit disappointed, to tell the truth. He'd have thought Nicholas knew him well enough by now to have figured that out on his own.

"Look," said Nicholas after another long moment. "Really I was just asking to … sound you out. See what you're thinking … about what we can be doing."

"You'd know better than me." Dave shrugged. "Whatever. Anything. I'm in your hands."

"Really … ?" Nicholas seemed flabbergasted.

"Well, I trust you. You know … Just not – Not going the whole hog, yeah?"

"Yeah," Nicholas echoed faintly.

"Not yet, anyway," Dave found himself saying – at which even he sat up and raised his brow in surprise. "Um, or not *ever*," he mumbled, probably fooling Nicholas about as well as he fooled himself.

"David ..." Nicholas breathed.

"Yeah, mate?"

"David, I think we'd better get the washing-up done. As soon as possible."

"Sure," he amiably agreed, standing up and collecting his plate. "Could do with an early night," he added with a yawn.

"Me, too," Nicholas fervently agreed. "Oh yes. Me, too."

He felt both strange and safe, lying there atop the Cruiser, with nothing between his skin and the stars but the foliage above and then Nicholas shifting over him, Nicholas's mouth roaming all over, those plump pretty lips dragging kisses across him, those teeth nipping and gnawing, that tongue swathing any small hurts and then rasping across sensitivities – *all* over, making even the most mundane places sexy, until Dave's whole body was just *singing*, was just *thrumming* with need.

"Please," he said at last when he didn't think he could take any more – he didn't think he even *wanted* the pleasure continuing. And he never used the S word unless he had to, but he wasn't so proud that he wouldn't beg. "Please ..."

Nicholas lifted up from where he'd been grazing up the inside of Dave's thighs. Nicholas lifted to kneel up tall, and he looked down upon Dave a bit remotely, as if measuring him, as if assessing. As if Nicholas could keep doing this all night, he wasn't even properly started yet.

Dave lay there spread before him, heavy with heat, boneless with pleasure, shamelessly open. He hadn't known there was a nakedness that went far beyond being naked. He'd never quite lost himself like this. "Please, mate ..."

At last Nicholas nodded, as if what he saw was satisfactory. He reached for the condoms, and carefully, deftly rolled one down onto Dave's cock. Dave groaned as even the brief brushes of businesslike fingers threatened to undo him. But Nicholas said, "Not yet," so Dave tried to hold on, or at least tried not to strive for the end. He wasn't sure whether, if he relaxed and let things happen, it would simply then unfurl within him without any further provocation at all, or if that would postpone it beyond any kind of reason.

"Not yet," Nicholas said again, admonishing him this time, warning him

– which was fair enough, for Nicholas bent down again, and then he was taking Dave's cockhead into his mouth, and gently suckling on it, and Dave was groaning and crying out some kind of gibberish that was mostly vowels, and he hoped Nicholas took that naked nonsensical noise as a fitting tribute to just how awesome a lover he was.

Just when Dave thought he couldn't bear it anymore if he couldn't *come*, damn it, Nicholas pulled away again. When Dave almost, well, *whimpered* a plea and lifted a heavy hand to reach up for him, Nicholas murmured, "Stay still. It's all right. Just wait a moment." And he seemed to be doing something with the lube that Dave had bought with the condoms, which sent Dave's thoughts spiralling off into fear and need and he had to chant to himself to make himself keep still, *I trust him, I trust him, I trust him.*

As Nicholas bent down over him again, he caressed one hand around Dave's waist, and then his forearm followed, sliding in underneath, forcing Dave to arch up the small of his back, and he whimpered again, there was no other word for it, and he had no pride left at all – he whimpered to feel the arch and the way his thighs opened for Nicholas, the way his cock and balls yearned towards the man –

And that mouth was on him again, suckling not as gently now – so gorgeous so gorgeous – that tongue doing clever swirly things – and it was all intended to distract him of course from Nicholas's other hand which was delving fingertips down down along that ridge behind his balls, and Dave was just *all* of him so sensitised that of course that felt good, too, so good, and he groaned in surrender, knowing what was happening to him, and not really even wanting to stop it. He groaned as those fingertips ran down further still, and were sliding across the most sensitive skin of all, each dipping in against the pressure, just the finger-pad, there was no question of more – but of course that's what he wanted, he wanted more. As one of those finger-pads returned to rub against him, Dave grunted an assent, an incitement, arching up further, and –

Nicholas intensified his efforts; Nicholas *hummed* around him. Dave cried out wildly – and suddenly he was coming, he was coming, and it was fucking *marvellous*, and that finger slid into him, it was just that easy, one of Nicholas's long pale fingers slid into him like that's where it belonged, and it felt odd but awesome, and the pleasure rolled through him again, heavy and intense, and a third time, and then at last he sank down again, babbling something grateful in the wake of it.

Gently, oh so very gently, Nicholas disengaged his finger, withdrew his arm from under Dave's back. Lifted up to deal with the condom. And then he folded back down again, crouched over Dave, his arms bracketing him, and his face pressed against Dave's soft and tender cock.

At last as the pleasure ebbed away and the world returned around him, the night air, the foliage, the stars – at last Dave sighed his poignant satisfaction.

Nicholas lifted his head, and grinned wickedly up at Dave. "Good, huh?" he said, knowing the answer.

"Yeah, wasn't bad," Dave agreed.

Nicholas chuckled – or, rather, gurgled in appreciation.

And Dave couldn't do it. He couldn't do the wry Aussie humour. He was going to have his citizenship revoked, but it had to be said: "It was so bloody good … It was fuckin' fantastic!"

"I'm glad," Nicholas said.

And the man still hadn't moved to take his own pleasure, but was instead letting Dave wallow in his … Well, fair was fair. Dave sighed again, satisfied, and resigned to the worst. "And you?" Dave prompted.

"Mmm …"

"Your turn now."

"Yes." Nicholas slowly lifted a little, and shifted up, sort of stalking up Dave on his hands and knees. Watching him with hunger and need and just a hint of cool remoteness.

"If you want –" Dave said. They both knew what he was offering.

"Hush," Nicholas said, admonishing him again. "There," he continued, shifting his weight over onto one side. "Put your legs together."

"Bit late for that," he joshed, even as he obeyed.

Nicholas rumbled an agreement, a laugh, but he was beginning to focus within himself now; he was beginning to lose himself, too. The man moved back over Dave, his legs straddling him – and then he lifted up for a moment, arranged himself – and pushed down, his cock sliding hard and hot between Dave's thighs.

They both groaned in reaction, and then Nicholas settled himself, lying close over Dave. He began a slow but unrelenting rhythm, working himself off, Dave's hands settling on the narrow curves of his rear, feeling them flex as Nicholas rocked and shifted up and back, up and back. And to be honest Dave was too raw for this now. Nicholas was pressed so close to him that Dave's cock and balls were rubbed up and down in an action mirroring Nicholas's – and he could see that would work so nicely if he were still up for it. Well, maybe next time. For now it was the kind of exquisite that was almost painful.

But he bore it, because he sensed Nicholas wouldn't take long at all, and anyway the man deserved something in return for his generosity and his self-restraint. He could be having Dave now, and they both knew it.

Instead he was groaning again as the end approached, and he was letting his head fall to gnaw at Dave's nipples, each in turn, and beyond his mess of dark hair, Dave could see his shoulders and back wrought up and tense – until at last with a guttural cry Nicholas came, and wet warmth spread between Dave's thighs, easing Nicholas's way.

"Good?" Dave asked in a whisper, long afterwards, with Nicholas still lying hot and heavy upon him.

"Oh, mate …" was the only faint reply.

ten

Dave thought he was in for a great comic episode the next afternoon.

Nicholas had spent the morning happily observing and recording the butterflies as more and more of them emerged from their cocoons, their wings folded and damp, but slowly drying and spreading out into magnificence. The creatures were such an awesome bright beautiful blue and such a rich velvety black that it almost felt impossible they were natural; it felt more as if they'd been created, and the designer had gone just a little bit over the top. Once they could move, they settled on the dark gold wattle blooms, and sipped away at the nectar. It was pretty awesome.

Dave spent most of the morning watching Nicholas, who seemed as if he were in his idea of heaven. The only times Dave managed to tear his gaze away were when he went to make tea, or Nicholas had a task that Dave could help with.

After lunch, Nicholas reappeared from his tent rather self-consciously carrying a butterfly net. The kind with the long pole and the white cone of netting that Dave had thought belonged in the past along with Enid Blyton books and safari suits.

"You're kidding me," Dave said.

"Um ... no, I'm afraid not."

And Nicholas, after one last pink-cheeked glance, went off stalking his quarry. It was all very amusing watching this gawky gorgeous guy pit himself against the grace and guile of the butterflies. Dave got a good few chuckles out of that, despite Nicholas's increasingly pithy requests that he be quiet.

But eventually, with a swoop and a surprisingly efficient twist of his wrists, Nicholas caught one.

And that's when Dave finally realised what the man was doing. What the purpose of all this was.

Nicholas was very carefully placing the net over an open jar on the ground, and gently encouraging the butterfly down into it. When this was finally done, he screwed the lid on firmly, and lifted it to watch with a cool eye as the creature fluttered about for a while, settled onto the white cloth bunched at the bottom – and then rose in a panic that was all too brief.

The thing was dead.

111

It lay there with folded wings the colour of shadows, hiding the only beauty it was left with. Nicholas reached in with those long pale fingers, picked it up by the body, and transferred it into a semi–transparent envelope. He was gentle now, but there was no pity in him. No regret.

Dave watched, kind of horrified. Though he couldn't really work out why. He'd known this would be part of the deal, even if he hadn't really thought about it. He'd known that Nicholas, during all those long days back in Brisbane, must have been examining hundreds of such specimens. And Dave wasn't a hypocrite. He ate meat, and loved it. He'd killed fish and animals – not many, but enough – and prepared, cooked and eaten them. He waged a perennial war on the pests that threatened to invade his home back in Brisbane. And yet there was something about this …

Maybe it was the simple contrast. Not so long ago, Nicholas had been standing amidst a storm of butterflies, his arms out in welcome, in celebration, in love – and his happy smile just *beaming* like it could light up the whole world. Like a sexy St Francis, in a black shirt and blue jeans. And now he was systematically killing them.

Not all of them, of course. Probably only a handful of samples, for himself, for the museum and university in Brisbane, and perhaps for somewhere equivalent back in England.

Nicholas shot him a defensive glare as he came back with another one in his net. *"Death comes equally to us all,"* he muttered.

It sounded like a quote – but whether it was or not, Dave could find no reply.

His own reactions puzzled him, but it made some things clearer still. Dave actually had to make an effort to give himself over to Nicholas's seeking hands that night. He really had to push himself past a wayward sense of reluctance. It was ridiculous. And yet that's what made it clear to him what was happening here.

He was giving himself over to Nicholas, he was letting the other man take charge. And he'd been happy to let Denise take the lead in all kinds of ways, but he'd seen that as equality and fair's fair. This … this was something more.

This was trusting someone else enough that he didn't need to be Dave anymore; he didn't even need to be one half of Denny–and–Davey. Instead, he became nothing that didn't belong to Nicholas Goring – even if it was only within these very limited circumstances, within this sleeping bag for an hour or two and no more. And he got such a fucking *charge* from it.

Nicholas began his attempt to win Dave over with gentle kisses, just pressing those lips against Dave's mouth and cheeks and forehead and chin with no expectation of response. His penitent hands stroked Dave's hair, and then his throat. Nicholas lay close against him, overlapping him, one leg bent so that Nicholas's thigh angled across both of Dave's, holding him there. And it didn't take much to keep him there, accepting these soothing caresses, even at the beginning. By the time Nicholas's free hand had stroked its way down to rest over Dave's heart as if feeling the beat of it against his palm – well, by then Dave had surrendered, and he was Nicholas's again.

"I won't hurt you," Nicholas whispered, when it was clear that he could have his way again.

"Yeah, you will," Dave responded evenly, "but I don't care."

And Nicholas bent his head to claim Dave's mouth in a full–blooded kiss, and gathered him up close in his arms. A hand began slowly caressing down his backbone, languorously pursuing its goal, knowing it wouldn't be denied.

Later, much later, Dave was finally allowed to come, held pressed close to Nicholas with his hips rocking helplessly between sensations, both of them otherwise still, and Nicholas murmuring, "That's it … Yes, that's it …" Rocking between the rough graze of his sensitive cock against virile dark hair and the rub of Nicholas's spent cock, the roll of his balls against Dave's thigh – and one of those long pale fingers deep inside him, not moving, but only letting him feel the slide of it as he rocked up and back, up and back. It was like nothing he'd ever imagined for himself, but Dave didn't mind the possession. Already, it felt sweet.

It was astonishing how many hours in the day Nicholas could devote to his butterflies: watching them, recording them, writing up his notes longhand in a journal. Nicholas had initially planned to type up his notes on his laptop, but of course that required power – and while they would put the generator on for a short while when necessary, it created too ugly a noise for their haven. While Nicholas was so happily engaged, Dave tended to the camp, and cooked for them both, or spent an hour or two reading. And the rest of the time – especially once twilight fell, and the butterflies settled for the night – was theirs to share.

"Pleasure can be learned," Nicholas asserted once, before rasping his tongue across a place it had no business being, following this with soothing little licks that tickled at first. When Dave laughed, and tried to squirm away, Nicholas had hushed him, and firmed his hold on Dave's hips. "Be still, relax. Pay attention. *Learn* this."

"Nicholas –" he protested. "You can't –"

But the man just bent his head and continued, and eventually the tickles became uneasy shivers and then provocative shudders, before at last it became too much, this sensation whatever it was, it was too much, and he groaned distraught and Nicholas took pity on him, wrapping palm and long pale fingers around Dave's cock, knowing just how to bring him off now, all the while lapping at him, lapping at him, until Dave shook to an exhausted halt, his nipples hard and all his nethers tender.

One afternoon, Dave saw that Nicholas was watching something particularly intently, and filming it with his video camera. Whatever it was was on the ground, and continued for a while. At least long enough for Dave's interest to be piqued, and for him to wander over there.

"*Don't* say anything inappropriate," Nicholas advised. "I'm filming this for posterity."

Two of the butterflies were flat on the ground with their wings spread, overlapping each other but facing in opposite directions. There was much fluttering and bumping about, almost as if they were trying to take off in this unlikely configuration. "What are they doing?" Dave asked – and he realised the truth even as he suggested rather pathetically, "Wrestling?"

Nicholas chortled, and replied in hallowed tones, "They're mating!"

Dave had to laugh. "There you go again with your butterfly porn."

"Yes. It's a beautiful thing."

"I'm sure it is." Dave considered the logistics. "Their tails … ?" It was all going on underneath the spread wings, but he couldn't think how else it would work.

"Yes. Their genitalia are in the last few segments of their abdomens –

what you think of as their tails. And they ... engage back to back."

Soon it was over, and after ... disengaging, the butterflies gathered themselves, and eventually flew lazily off back to the wattle. Nicholas followed them with his camera, but once they'd settled he turned it off and came back to where Dave still stood.

"Well," said Dave.

Nicholas was favouring him with a lascivious grin. Dave never had been able to resist that one.

In between, there was time enough to talk. They'd while away hours around the campfire, or sitting on the Cruiser's bonnet, or lying atop the roof watching the stars wheel about the sky. If they were close together, then Nicholas almost invariably had his arms around Dave, or at least a hand resting upon him, as if he just couldn't get enough.

"It's just as well you have a thing for the hired help," Dave commented at some stage. "An earl would hardly deign to notice me otherwise."

"I'm not an earl," Nicholas argued, "and what do you mean? You're a friend, not the help."

Dave felt a smile bloom in response to that, but he kept it to himself. "Your first was the chauffeur, your latest is me ... Like a bit of working–class rough, do ya?"

"Idiot," Nicholas said, kissing and nibbling at the tender skin just beyond Dave's ear. They were curled up together on the Cruiser's bonnet and windscreen, and the night air was soft upon them. "I have a thing for gorgeous hunky men. Can't blame a fellow for that."

"Of course not, sir. You just have your way with me, sir, and then discard me, that's all right."

"Oh shut up!" Nicholas cried with a laugh. "I thought you Australians didn't believe in class."

Dave shrugged a little. "Not as much, maybe. It's a pretty egalitarian place. There's still rich and poor, though."

Nicholas finally sat back a little – not far enough to let go of Dave, but to consider him. "Why do you even care? I'm *not* an earl, and never will be. I'm the youngest son of an earl. Which hardly means anything at all."

"It means you've got the money to come over here for three months chasing butterflies."

That earned him a scoffing laugh. "The family's money came from my grandmother: a commoner in the grocery business. Our fortunes had sunk pretty low before she came along."

"She's a grocer?"

"Well. In a rather large way."

"Oh." Dave reflected on that for a while, and Nicholas returned to nuzzling him. There was so much he didn't know about Nicholas, and probably half the things he thought he knew were wrong. Dave turned away a little and settled in more comfortably, hoping for a long story. "Tell me about your chauffeur," he prompted.

"Mmm ... Don't know that there's much more to say."

"Did you and he ... you know ... do stuff?"

"Oh yes," was the ironic response. "It was *that* romantic."

"Come on ... What aren't you telling me?"

Nicholas sighed, and settled in behind Dave, his mouth against Dave's nape. "I've kept the secret all these years. Why should I tell you? The man's still associated with our family. And he married later; he has a family of his own. I'm not going to embarrass him now."

"So, you did, huh?"

"Idiot ... Well, don't let your imagination run away with you. There might have been a kiss or two. It all seems so innocent now. So harmless. But it felt delightfully wicked at the time. And I really wouldn't want to embarrass him, David. He was only being kind, and maybe he's forgotten all about it. This has to stay between us, all right? Please."

"Of course," he stoutly agreed.

Then Nicholas asked, "So ... tell me about Denise, then. When did that start?"

Dave huffed a laugh. "The very first day of school. I was five years old. Totally out of my depth. And she took pity on me. Took my hand, and led me about all day. She made me ... She made me smile when all I wanted to do was cry. She was brave enough to face dragons, you know?"

Nicholas was still and hushed. Though when he finally spoke, it was only to lightly say, "Do you even have dragons in Australia?"

"Bunyips," Dave insisted. "She'd have faced a bedevilment of bunyips for me."

And Nicholas quietly commented, "You really have been in love with her your whole life."

"Yeah, it was just … Well, I never questioned it. She was always there. I assumed that … when she was ready to get married, she'd ask me. Or – not married. I figured that when she was ready to have kids and do that whole shebang, she'd let me know." He thought about that for a moment, and then added, "Which she did, I guess. Except it wasn't gonna be with me."

Nicholas's arms tightened around him, and they wriggled in a bit closer still until the fit between them was perfect. The stars wheeled overhead until at last the sense of loss was overtaken by the sense of belonging.

"David," Nicholas whispered, with his lips and his breath damp and warm against Dave's skin.

"Mmm?"

"Will you let me …"

"What?" he asked mildly, though he figured he knew. Of course this was where they'd been heading all this time.

"Will you let me fuck you? I want to – so badly."

He guffawed under his breath. "Not if you're gonna do it badly, no."

"Don't tease. I want to have you. I'm pretty sure you want that, too."

He let the minutes drift past. Eventually he said, "I'm game to try, all right? But not out here."

"I'll be careful," Nicholas assured him. "And anyway, it won't hurt as much as you think it will."

"No, well … that's not what I'm worried about. Or only a bit."

"*What*, then? I mean, why not out here?"

"Because –"

"Where better? This is *our* place. We're safe here."

"But if something goes wrong –"

Nicholas shifted up on an elbow so he could look at him properly. "Like what?"

"I don't know."

"*I* do. I know what I'm doing, David."

"I'm sure you do!" He wondered how many lovers Nicholas had had over the years. Obviously they would outnumber Dave's tally by *far*. None of which was the point.

"What's the point, then?"

"I just – Look. I don't have a backup plan for this one."

And apparently this made sense to Nicholas, or at least he was used to Dave by now, and all the care he took about their travelling, their camps, their safety. The fail-safes and backups and redundancies.

"All right," Nicholas agreed, leaning in to press a kiss to Dave's temple. "Next time we're in town?" he asked hopefully.

"Yes," said Dave. "Next time we're in town. We'll go to Charleville. We'll get a proper bed for the night."

Nicholas sighed with satisfaction. And for now they made do happily enough with bold hands and mouthy kisses.

eleven

They reached Charleville early in the afternoon. And their first task, Nicholas insisted, was to secure a room for the night. Or, more to the point, a bed.

Dave refused to be a coward about this, but oh God he really had to screw his courage to the sticking place. He fronted up at his usual hotel. Marge was at the reception desk, for which he didn't know whether to be thankful or not.

"G'day, Dave," she greeted him in her usual laid-back friendly tones. "Hello, love," she added to Nicholas who was quite naturally there at Dave's side.

"G'day, Marge," Dave responded, and Nicholas said, "Hello."

"Two singles?" she asked, though it wasn't really a question. She was already scanning down that night's register, and had picked out the rooms before Dave managed to force out a reply.

"Actually. One double, thanks, Marge."

She looked up with a carefully schooled face that didn't quite manage to hide her surprise. A glance flickered over both of them, before she evenly replied, "Of course." And she bent her head to run a finger down the register again.

Dave felt like dying would probably be an easier option than dealing with this embarrassment. But to be fair to Marge, she was probably more surprised that Dave the one-woman man was interested in anyone other than Denise; that Dave the scrupulously professional guide was sleeping with a client. She probably didn't really give a toss about Dave suddenly deciding he batted for the other team. She might actually, Dave told himself, find it hardest to forgive him for taking up with a Pom.

"Here we are, love," Marge eventually said, handing a key over, and taking the opportunity to pat Dave's forearm with kind reassurance. "Twenty-three on the first floor. It's an en suite. Usual rates for you, Dave, but it's our best room."

Right. Well, if his face hadn't been as red as a waratah before, it certainly was now. "Thanks," he managed to say – or squeak. He cleared his throat, and managed a rather more manly, "Thanks, Marge."

Nicholas smoothly added, "Thank you very much."

And there was no way in hell Dave was heading up there now, even if it *was* only to unpack. He turned to Nicholas. "Pub."

"Excellent idea," Nicholas agreed. "We'll see you later, Marge."

"See you, boys!"

And they headed off out the door, shoulder to shoulder, and Dave said, "Oh God, I am just going to *die*."

Charlie didn't even need telling. He was already sitting there, on his own at the same table as last time, as if waiting for them. He took one look at Dave and Nicholas as they walked towards him, his gaze encompassing *all* of them, and he *knew*, damn it. He knew they were together. In response, bless him, Charlie grinned like a particularly happy loon.

They had barely sat down when, in this pub with emphatically *no* table service, Rosie brought over three Cascades. "Here you are," she said, setting them down – and she *winked* at Dave. "On the house, boys."

The other two said their thanks very nicely, while Dave sank down further in his chair and just withered. God. It must be written all over him. *This man is in sexual thraldom to a queer English earling.*

He wondered how long it would take for the news to spread from the hotel and the pub on outwards. He was gonna be losing the very last shreds of his tattered virginity that night, and the whole damned town was gonna know exactly what was going on. *Dave Taylor is taking it up the arse ... and loving it!*

Really. Dying would be so very much easier.

"You two have had a busy couple of weeks," Charlie eventually observed.

Nicholas laughed. "We have," he agreed quite happily. "The butterflies, Charles: they're so beautiful! More than I could have ever hoped for. Last week I got to watch them emerge, watch their wings drying out and spreading – and then flying for the first time! Well," he added with a chuckle, "that's never going to get old, but with these particular beauties ..."

"And you're the first white fella to find them?"

"I think so, yes. Or the first to really identify them, anyway. There's nothing quite like them in the CSIRO field guide." Nicholas was looking pleased and proud, but he attempted to turn the conversation. "All that's for later, though. For now it's just a privilege to have all this time to spend with them."

Charlie persisted. "What white fella name you gonna give them?"

Nicholas's cheekbones turned pink, and he turned towards Charlie, shielding his mouth as if telling him a secret – but Dave was certainly meant to hear his loud whisper. "Actually, I think I'll name them after David." At which Dave went waratah red again. "But don't tell him! I'm mortifying him enough already."

That drew a rumbling chuckle from Charlie, who considered Dave for long excruciating minutes. But eventually all Charlie said was, "So, you found old man grunter's waterhole."

"Yes," Dave replied, feeling the ground a little firmer under his feet. "It's an odd place. But there's no sign of any fish there, so I don't know if it's really –"

"Yeah, you found it all right."

"There's nothing there but the butterflies. It's beautiful, but there's no birds or animals, no fish, no insects. Just the butterflies. Isn't that kind of weird?"

Charlie shrugged. "How does it feel to you?"

Dave sighed, and looked away.

"He feels like it *should* feel wrong," Nicholas supplied. "But it doesn't."

"Of course it doesn't," Charlie stoutly agreed. "You don't go drinking the water, though. You know that much?"

"Yeah, we know," Dave agreed. "We swam a couple of times, but we were careful." And now he thought about it, they had instinctively avoided bathing very much, when really he'd have expected them to be taking a dip every afternoon in that gorgeous jewel–like water.

Charlie nodded. "There's a mystery, a strangeness. My compass didn't like the place. It kept pointing me away."

"The satnav doesn't like it, either."

"Minerals," they concluded. "Heavy–duty mineral deposits."

Nicholas contemplated this. "Would that keep the birds and animals away from the water? But the butterflies have managed to adapt somehow?"

Charlie nodded. "Could be … Could be."

After a moment, when it seemed that they'd said all that could be said about that, Nicholas nudged Charlie with a friendly elbow. "If I have

Butterfly Dreaming, what kind of Dreaming does David have?"

And Charlie considered Dave again for long long moments. "I don't know, Nicholas," he eventually said. "I look at him now, and all I see is you."

Nicholas squirmed in pink-faced delight, giggling like he was still in high school, while Dave muttered, "Yeah, yeah. You always know just what to say, don't you, mate?"

"I always do," Charlie complacently agreed.

A while later, Dave decided that if Charlie knew, then it was only fair to tell Denise as well. And she would be expecting him to call anyway, in line with their new routine. He took the three empty glasses back to the bar, and speed-dialled Denise's number while he was waiting. Rosie was wise enough to leave him be for the moment.

The first thing Denise said when she picked up the call was, "Davey! I missed you!"

Even now his heart skipped a beat to hear her greet him so. "Yes. I'm used to talking with you every day. I missed it, too."

"How's the trip going? Are you all right?"

"Yes, everything's fine. Denise –"

"Are you still camped at the waterhole?"

"Yes. Look," he said. And he sighed. She knew enough to wait now, when in many ways he would have preferred her to insist on doing all the talking. He was sure she would have gotten to the truth in the end. "Look. Denny ... I'm, uh –" he wasn't sure what verb to use, so he left the word incoherent. "I'm *nnngh* ... with Nicholas."

A moment of silence. Then she burst out, *"Seriously?"*

"Yeah."

Another beat resounded before, "Oh, Davey, that's *marvellous*."

"Um. Really?"

"Yes. Yes, of *course*. God, I've hated that you've been alone all this time."

He laughed a little, under his breath. *Well, whose fault was that?* he thought. But all the heat of it had gone. All the bitterness had left him.

"Davey, I'm so happy for you."

"It's not too weird?"

"No, of course not. Love is love, wherever you find it."

"Oh. Uh, no one's using words like that, Denny."

She laughed. "Then a fling is a fling is a damned fine thing, Davey. Enjoy yourself, and I'll hear from you in a week's time, all right?"

"All right." And once she'd ended the call, he murmured, *"Goodbye."*

"You right, Dave?" Rosie asked, once she'd finally worked her way down the bar.

Dave smiled at her. "Three Cascades, thanks, mate."

The three of them spent quite some time poring over various maps, but they were really no closer to pinpointing the waterhole, or working out whose land it was on. There was a large Aboriginal reserve in the area, and the edges of two different privately held properties. But where the waterhole sat in relation to these seemed almost impossible to fathom.

"It's almost as if," Dave said, feeling idiotic but saying it anyway – "as if it's in–between."

"It's in the interstices," Nicholas said, as if he were agreeing.

Charlie just contemplated them both for a while, and then drifted off in thought.

After scratching their heads over the maps for a while longer, Nicholas and Dave left him to it.

Pretty much as soon as it was decently dark, Dave and Nicholas snuck up to their room with their overnight bags, managing to avoid Marge's notice – though Dave suspected that was more due to her tact than their own cunning.

Then it was just the two of them, which felt so familiar these days, it felt so safe. Nicholas wandered into the room while Dave locked the door. They put down their bags, but neither of them turned on the light – which was hardly needed, as there was a street light nearby pouring a block of cool light in through the net curtains. It was certainly enough to help them see what they were doing.

Nicholas must have realised that something needed sorting out, for he didn't kiss Dave or even touch him, but simply heeled off his shoes and sat on the bed, his back against the pillows and the iron railings of the bed head, and his legs stretched out long. And he waited patiently with his hands held loosely together in his lap.

Dave picked up the straight-backed chair and turned it around so he could sit facing the man, and then he thought about what he needed to say and how to say it. But in the end, of course, he just blurted it out. "Does everyone know what we're doing tonight?"

"Well, it seems that most of them have the general idea by now."

"I mean you fucking me. Is it really obvious? It feels like it's really obvious."

Nicholas took a moment with that, as if determined not to let this faze him – or not to freak Dave out by showing that it fazed him. "I would have thought," Nicholas eventually said, "if they *are* speculating about the details, they'll assume it's the other way round."

"Really?"

"Yes, what with me being gay and you being otherwise straight. I think that tends to be the assumption."

"Oh."

Nicholas let a silence drift by, before asking, "What bothers you: the fact that that's what we had planned, or the idea that everyone knows about it?"

Of course it was the latter, but Dave was too ashamed of his lack of courage to say so.

"I don't care what we do, David," Nicholas said, sincerely but also a bit coolly. "You can fuck me, if you'd prefer. I really don't mind."

"Yeah?" Dave had hardly even thought about doing that, but now that he considered it, he reckoned he could.

"Of course. We can save the rest for some other time. Or we can just do the things we've already done. Then again, we don't actually have to do anything at all." Finally he added, a bit more warmly, "David, I'll do anything you want."

The problem was, however, that Dave wanted to be fucked. He sighed. "How did you know? That this is what I'd end up wanting. Is it that obvious?"

"Not at all."

"I feel like it's ... blazoned across my forehead, or something. In neon lights."

Nicholas settled in a bit, and began comfortably telling his side of the story. "When I first saw you, I assumed it would all be the other way round. I like to be in charge when it comes to sex. Doesn't say a lot about me as a person, but in bed, that's what works best for me. When I saw you ... You're gorgeous, David. I don't think you realise how bloody gorgeous you are. I fancied you like nothing else. And you were this tough strong Aussie hunk of a man. And that first morning!" Nicholas laughed at the memories. "You were so efficient, so in control. You were laying down the rules, telling me how things would be, and I was following you around like a smitten little puppy with my tongue hanging out. I thought, well, nothing's going to happen, because you're straight, but if it ever did ... then you'd be the one in charge. And I thought, that's how it must be when you holiday Down Under, everything goes topsy–turvy."

"So when did you realise?"

"It took me a while. I'm not usually that slow, or I hope not, anyway. I realised that a lot of the efficiency was about you being the best tour guide you could be, about you knowing the dangers, and making sure that no one in your care ever got hurt. There was another David underneath that, a more private man, who was happier to just go with the flow. There were times I felt as if you were ... waiting for me. Then I'd tell myself that was just wishful thinking. It was only when we began ..." He paused. Apparently Nicholas wasn't sure of the right verb either. "It was only when I kissed you properly for the first time that I started feeling the lure of you ... the tug of you ... inviting me in."

Dave let out a breath that definitely *wasn't* a gasp. But it was as if those last phrases were poetry, they were so true. Dave himself could feel the draw of the notion ... of lying back and inviting Nicholas in. Not just in the obvious ways. And in that moment, he knew that it was going to happen that night – even if all of Charleville did know it, too.

"Nicholas," he said a bit brokenly, standing and letting his sense of direction guide him. His knees bumped into the side of the mattress.

And Nicholas was shifting towards him, his arms wide in welcome, and those pretty lips pursing for kisses and smiling in delight as he murmured, "My beautiful man ..."

Dave had never had pretensions to poetry. As he turned within those strong affectionate trustworthy arms, letting gravity take him back down onto the bed, he said, "Fuck me. Nicholas, I want you to fuck me."

"Oh, I will, my darling David. I will – but all in good time."

"Close – getting close now – hurry up, for God's sake –"

"Mmm," Nicholas agreeably remarked, not stopping what he was doing, and not easing off or intensifying it, either.

"God's sake – *fuck me* – gonna go off any *minute* now –"

Nicholas removed his mouth from Dave's condom-covered cock for long enough to say in friendly tones, "As you wish. In your own time."

"*No!* No," Dave insisted.

Nicholas gurgled a delightful laugh around Dave's cock, and lifted his head again to hush him. "Stick to *yes, yes*, would you? Unless you *want* half of Charleville dashing in here to protect what remains of your virtue."

Dave groaned in frustration, having lost the sweet fine edge he'd been balancing on. Maybe that was just as well, though. This way they could take it careful and he could really concentrate on it. Dave lifted his head to stare at Nicholas, who'd inexplicably remained exactly where he was: between Dave's thighs, which was great, but penetrating him with nothing more than a long narrow finger.

"What the hell are you waiting for?" Dave demanded. "I'm good to go here! Fuck me already!"

"Not the plan."

He almost spluttered in indignation. How on earth could Nicholas get this so very wrong? "No. Obviously. I wanna come while you're –"

Nicholas was shaking his head. "Not the first time," he advised.

"Not – ?!"

"I need you relaxed for that. Post-orgasmic works just fine."

Was this really not clear? "No – No, I want to come while –"

"Coming involves tension," Nicholas argued implacably. "Which is not conducive to enjoying your first thorough rogering."

Dave glared at him and sank back, thoroughly disgruntled. And hard. Thoroughly disgruntled and ball-achingly hard. "Fuck's sake," he muttered.

"Enjoy this, you gorgeous thing, and then I promise you'll have a fair chance of enjoying the rest."

"But I wanna …"

"Next time. If you're up for it, having survived the first time, then next time we'll try for the whole nine yards."

Dave wanted to sulk for a while, but how could he when the oh–so–reasonable Nicholas set himself up so very perfectly? "Oh, now you're just trying to show off," Dave complained, "when I know very well it's not even nine inches."

Nicholas stared at him blankly for a long moment – before finally twigging, and the two of them burst into giggles. Not for long, of course, but it was enough for them to regain their equilibrium.

The mood had kind of ebbed away, so Nicholas – leaving his finger in place – shifted up far enough on an elbow and knees to lean in and kiss Dave – to mouth at him hungrily, to bite at his lower lip and suck it in and chew on it – and then to press his tongue into Dave's mouth, stiffly miming his ultimate intentions, echoing the slow relentless rhythm his finger maintained. Dave groaned around the luscious intrusion, and then tried chasing after when that bold tongue eventually withdrew.

"All right, my darling man?" Nicholas whispered with his lips brushing against Dave's – and Dave didn't want to lose that, he loved the intimacy of being in each other's faces when they came – so he answered by nibbling in turn on Nicholas's pouty lips, and reaching down a hand to shuck the condom and bring himself off. Which took hardly any time at all, with Nicholas lying over him, connecting randomly skin–to–skin as well as that mouth and that finger, and his pithily crooning encouragement …

Glorious.

And then – at last, before the glory faded – Nicholas got down to work, and for a little while Dave took himself away. He wasn't afraid anymore, he didn't think it would hurt, he wasn't even embarrassed now, but he figured he needed a time-out to see it through, to let it happen.

Which was probably completely unnecessary because of course Nicholas knew just what he was doing, and he'd prepared Dave so thoroughly … Far sooner than Dave had anticipated, in barely a few moments, Dave was surfacing again, eager for the full experience.

He was breathless with it. He was breathless, he was full of Nicholas, there was no room for breath in him. He was breathless, he was curled up below Nicholas on the bed, on his back with Nicholas over him, within him. His right hand clung to Nicholas's knee where it rested on the bed below Dave's hip, clung on tight, for he was so breathless he was dizzy with it, or was he simply dizzy with sensation –

He was capable of thought, of small regrets. Wishing he hadn't come already, though he understood why now; he knew Nicholas had been right, it would have been impossible. Wishing he was on his front, on his knees, so that he could feel that delicious arch in his back as he tilted his rear up for Nicholas to plunder –

And this was what it felt like, this plundering, this was what he'd craved, to be part of someone else, for them to be a part of him. "Want more of this –" he said. "I'll want more –"

Nicholas let out a laughing sob, as if happy and relieved and overcome all at once – which Dave supposed he was, really. "Oh my darling man," Nicholas said, reduced to endearments. "My darling David …"

"I want to *know*, I want to learn this."

Nicholas had no words for that, but only gazed down at him, damp-eyed. Meanwhile, his hips maintained a steady rolling rhythm as relentless as the waves on the ocean. Nicholas was almost kneeling upright, one arm tautly stretched before him, the hand clasped around an iron railing of the bed head, his lean bicep a lovely long curve. He was strong, his slim frame and his usual loose clothes were deceptive, though the wide shoulders gave him away. He was strong, and everything a man ought to be. Not who Dave had expected at all. Nicholas's other hand reached down to clasp Dave's hip, keeping them both grounded as he pounded steadily in – careful, but he'd soon realised Dave was coping well enough.

"Next time –" Dave said, each word a pant of precious breath, "wanna be – on hands and knees –"

"Do you … ?" Nicholas seemed to grasp at the conversation now, as if needing distraction. "I'm sorry, I'm selfish, I wanted to be able to see you, to see the gorgeousness."

"You didn't – explain it – that way."

"No," the man admitted with a laugh.

Dave was curled up so far that his shins were against Nicholas's chest, the idea apparently being that he could push Nicholas away if he needed to. His thighs were his strongest muscle group, he knew that, but to be honest he didn't feel strong anywhere right now, he was just heaviness and heat and a whole lot of contradictions such as wanting this to be over and never wanting it to end, or at least not until he had learned it. He was fascinated by the sensations, though he'd hardly call it pleasure, not yet. One day, though, he reckoned. One day he'd grasp it, he'd understand it, and it would make sense, and –

And it would be spectacular.

"I'm sorry," Nicholas was murmuring. Englishmen were always apologising, Dave had found.

"What the fuck for? I was – just thinking – *spectacular*."

Nicholas's colour was already heightened, but he still blushed very prettily about the cheekbones. "I'm sorry you don't have a gorgeous view, as I do."

"You're mad –" Dave told him. "You're beautiful –"

"Oh …" Nicholas groaned raggedly, and sank towards Dave, and struggled a bit, obviously trying to last, but he was overwhelmed. His hand loosened its grip on the railing and dropped to the bed as he leaned in further, and Dave parted his thighs to let him in close, leaned up to meet him as Nicholas drove deeper still with him – and Nicholas came like that, quaking with it, and groaning gutturally as Dave whispered kisses across that beautiful face.

Dave felt that he hardly slept that night. He was happy and delightfully sore, and Nicholas was wrapped close around him, deeply slumbering – and how on earth could Dave sleep? He didn't even need to, he was so happy. The main curtains had been left hanging open, so the first hints of dawn glowing through the net curtains woke Dave from a doze. He lay there contemplating the world and all that was right with it –

And jumped a mile when his mobile went off. Dave reached for it, scrabbled to pick it up from the bedside table, while Nicholas grunted a protest, still mostly asleep. "H'lo?" Dave managed once he'd answered the call. "Denny?"

"Nah, it's Charlie, mate."

"Charlie? God! What is it?" Dave's heart was still thudding in shock, and he had to assume – If anyone was gonna be asked to break bad news to him, it would have to be – *"Charlie. What's wrong?"*

"Nothing. Nothing's wrong. Just need to talk with you."

Dave let a beat go by, wondering if he was actually dreaming this. None of it was making any sense. "What … ? *Now?*"

"Come on down. I'm outside. Bring your man, if he's awake."

Dave turned to look at Nicholas, but of course he *was* awake by now. His embrace was as encompassing as ever, but he'd lifted his head to listen in. When he caught Dave's eye, he smiled with a soft warmth. Which was very enticing.

"Davey … ?"

Nicholas nodded encouragement, so Dave answered, "All right. Just give us a few minutes."

"You wouldn't make an old man wait while you two got distracted, would you?"

Dave chuckled. "Charlie, we were *asleep*. Give us a few minutes, all right? And I'll try to restrain myself."

"I make no promises," Nicholas added darkly – and Dave ended the call on the sound of Charlie's groan.

But ten minutes later they were walking with Charlie through the cool of early morning towards the Warrego River. After greeting them, Charlie lapsed into silence, so they followed suit. They crossed the river on the Willis Street bridge, walked north–east along the riverbank for a short distance. And then when Charlie indicated, they all settled cross–legged on the ground, underneath a red river gum and beyond that the rich blue sky.

Dave and Nicholas remained quiet, while Charlie thought some more. And then eventually Charlie let his story slowly spill forth.

"That waterhole," said Charlie. "An old friend of mine, he was the last of his tribe to know the songs, to know the story of that place. It has strong magic. Strong."

Well, Dave was on board so far. He exchanged a glance with Nicholas, who obviously agreed.

"He passed those songs on to me, or they would have died with him. So much has been lost already, so many songs forgotten, so many Ancestors go unacknowledged. The power of the land, she's slumbering, but who knows what she will do if the songs aren't ever sung? So it was better that he pass those songs on to someone in the wrong tribe, from the wrong place, than let it all be lost."

They nodded their understanding – though if Charlie was still feeling

130 | Butterfly Hunter

qualms about it all, then the reassurance of two white guys was hardly going to count for much.

"I went out there," Charlie continued, "I couldn't find it. I walked for days, I couldn't find that place. I was walking round in circles, and old man grunter was having a big laugh."

Into the saddened silence, Dave said, "It's in this wide flat valley. I thought – maybe it's an old crater, you know, formed by a meteorite. But really old, so it's mostly worn down again. Maybe you never saw into the valley, but it's not like it's surrounded by hills or cliffs or anything."

"You found it," Charlie said to Dave.

"Me? Well, both of us."

"Nah, Nicholas found his butterflies. You found the waterhole."

"Well –" But Dave stopped. Nicholas was looking at him intensely, and Charlie was obviously very very serious.

"Long time ago," Charlie mused after a silence had passed, "this was all one land. Gondwanaland. We were all one people. We still are. I'd forgotten that." Another silence, and then Charlie announced, "I'm thinking, I'm still thinking about this, but maybe I need to pass the songs on to you, David Taylor."

He was absolutely astounded. "No … No, that's too much."

"Too much to carry?" Charlie asked, as if testing him.

"Too much honour," Dave protested. "I'm just an ordinary bloke."

"Do you know where you were conceived?"

"Well. Somewhere out here, actually. Mum and Dad had been trying for a while, and she came with him on one of his trips – I guess he was gonna be away for, you know, *those* days. Anyway, he said by the time they got back home they knew already."

Charlie nodded, as if this confirmed it all for him.

"And I was born in Cunnamulla," Dave continued. "Though I wasn't meant to be. Mum didn't come along on many of Dad's trips, but she thought it would be her last chance for a while. And I arrived early."

"Old man grunter chose you," Charlie said, as if there were no point arguing. And maybe there wasn't.

"But, Charlie, it's never done, is it? No one's ever actually passed the really sacred stuff on to a white fella."

"I'm thinking," Charlie said again. "That's all. I haven't even told you the

Ancestor's real name yet. But you should know what I'm thinking."

"Of course," murmured Nicholas. He reached to grasp Dave's hand for a moment, as if to convey his faith.

"I'm gonna talk to the elders about it. They might say no, they might say it's not the Ancestors putting these thoughts in my head. There might be more and more talking, long time arguments. But I won't even start with telling them if you're not willing."

Dave thought about it, but even in the midst of his astonishment he could hardly consider denying Charlie's request. It would mean going back to the waterhole, maybe once a year, maybe more. Learning the songs to sing there, the rituals to perform. He'd make a fool of himself for a while, but there'd be no one to see except Charlie. And in return, there would be a place where he belonged. There would be land that needed him, a song that needed him, no matter how useless he was otherwise.

"If you really think I'm worth it," Dave said.

"The land needs us all," Charlie said in an uncanny echo of Dave's thoughts — and Nicholas took Dave's hand in his again, and this time he didn't let go.

"All right. I mean, of course. Yes," Dave said. "Thank you," he added. Which wasn't anywhere near enough, but was all he had.

He and Nicholas walked back to the hotel together after that, and Dave was so stunned he didn't even realise until they got there that they'd been holding hands the whole way.

twelve

"Can you find your way back there?" Nicholas asked once the satnav flickered and died.

"I'd hope so," said Dave. "I've done this often enough now."

"And it's your land. You have a connection with it."

He quibbled, driving further along the road by instinct. "It's not *my* land. More like, I'm its human. If Charlie's even right."

"I think he's right," Nicholas said. He was obviously still rather awestruck by the whole thing.

So was Dave, come to that, though he retained a scepticism, too. Or a sense of reality, maybe. He suspected the Aboriginal elders Charlie consulted would soon put an end to such notions, and it would all come to very little – well, very little beyond the honour Charlie had done him to even consider such things.

"What do you think?" Nicholas asked, looking around them at the endless scrub. "I feel as if we're close already, but then nothing looks familiar."

"Most people think it all looks the same out here."

"No, there are subtle differences, if you're open to seeing them..." Nicholas turned to grin at him. "You'd know that better than me."

He returned the grin, but had to shrug. "It's a weird place; it seems to change every time we're here. I have to go on instinct."

"Go on, then."

But actually he had to go against his instincts. It seemed to work if he did the opposite of whatever his sense of direction was telling him. So Dave turned right instead of left off the track, feeling completely mad – and ten minutes later they crested a rise, and drove down into the broader valley.

"You're brilliant," said Nicholas.

At which Dave blushed. He was doing way too much of that lately.

All of Nicholas's clumsiness disappeared when he was having sex, all his uncertainties, and he seemed to completely lack any kind of self-consciousness. The man just took charge and went with it. And Dave found himself more than happy to go along with it, too.

One afternoon Dave found himself on his back on the mattress atop the Cruiser, and his arms were over his head, his hands each wrapped around the roof rack railing. It's just as well he'd chosen the steel, for it was taking all the tension of his flexed arms and stomach as he took most of his own weight. Nicholas was supporting Dave's hips, to an extent, while he knelt there with his thighs wide, powering into Dave as if there were no tomorrow. It was awesome. And the stamina of this guy! This slim Englishman, who had at times seemed so delicate, could come in a moment or last *forever* – and by choice, too.

Afterwards, Dave found that his grip on the railing had kind of locked into place. Nicholas leaned in to help gently prise his fingers back into some semblance of human shape. He pressed a kiss to each one as it was freed.

"Mmm," he murmured as one hand was done and they began work on the other. "Maybe next time I need to tie you down instead."

"Mmm," Dave agreed, finding that he liked the notion – as long as it was understood that Nicholas would then have his thoroughly wicked way with Dave. "Not a chance, though," he had to add.

"Ah, come on," Nicholas chided. "I heard that note of interest in your tone."

"Not while we're out here, mate."

"Why not?"

Dave's hands were both free now. He tentatively stretched them out, and then cradled them on his chest while the blood circulation recovered. "What if something happened to you?"

"I hope something would!" Nicholas retorted.

Dave laughed. "I mean, what if something bad happened to you, and I couldn't free myself? Chances are, you'd fall off the side of the Cruiser, hit your head, and by the time we're found I'd have lost my tackle to sunburn."

Nicholas pondered this disturbing notion. Considered Dave's well-used and well-loved tackle. "Well, we can't have that, can we?"

"No, we can't."

A winsome look turned his way. "So maybe in town … ?"

"Maybe," he agreed. And thought with a rush, *Definitely.*

Even the butterflies seemed to shift to second priority for Nicholas now. The butterflies had laid their eggs – neat rows of little prickly pale green spheres – and Nicholas had taken umpteen dozen photos, but then they just seemed to get on with living. As did Nicholas and Dave.

The two of them spent all their time hanging out together, talking or silent or both of them reading; having ridiculous amounts of sex or lying around idly, randomly touching or sitting quite separately but so very *aware* of each other. They shared the chores around the camp, the cooking and the cleaning and the organising, because no matter how self-indulgent Dave was being otherwise, he wouldn't let such things slip. Nicholas had learned all of Dave's routines by now, and helped without being asked or expecting to be thanked. They worked together well. They did everything together well.

"I know we do," said Nicholas, with the happy kind of smugness that no one could possibly take exception to.

"Oh. Am I thinking out loud again?"

"It's one of your most endearing traits."

"My most idiotic, you mean."

"No, not at all." They were lazing about on the ground near the pool, staying just within the dappled shade provided by the eucalypts. Even so, over time Nicholas's skin had turned a delightfully pale gold colour. All over. Dave dragged his gaze away from the man's narrow rear when Nicholas looked across at him and continued, "I feel that I can always trust you to be yourself. There's never any pretence. None at all."

Dave couldn't help sulking a bit. "Don't wanna be simple …"

"Oh, you're not. You're as complex as anyone. But you're honest, and open. That's marvellous, to me. I think … I suspect it's an Australian thing."

"Dunno." He thought about that for a while. "I guess, maybe. Denise was always – very direct."

"What about your parents? Were they like that?"

"Well, actually my dad was English."

Nicholas sat up with a surprised laugh. "He was?! So you're half English … I didn't know that."

"I've never thought of myself that way. I mean, not that there's anything wrong with that," he added with a grin that Nicholas shared. "But Dad just totally fell in love – with Australia, with my mum, with the Outback. He never went back, not even for a holiday."

"And your mum?"

"Australian. Well, you know. I think the family were originally English and Irish, but they'd come to Brisbane yonks ago. I don't know how many generations, but back into the great–greats, yeah? So what with all of that, I just think of myself as Australian."

Nicholas was nodding emphatically. "And you are, and that's great. But it's cool that we have something in common, isn't it?"

Dave grinned at him, and reached to stroke his fingers across those cheekbones, to push back across his sensitive ears into that thick dark hair. "It's cool that I'm a bit English, too," he agreed. "You're kind of a bit Aussie now."

And they just watched each other for a while, as if they'd never quite get enough.

Eventually, though, Dave cleared his throat. "Um, which town d'you want to go to this time for supplies? I was thinking, maybe we should go back to Woop Woop, so those guys can apologise to you."

Nicholas twisted up his mouth. "Not necessary."

Dave thought some more, but said it anyway: "We can get our own back. We can walk into Drongo Central, holding hands. They won't know *what* to do with themselves."

Nicholas offered him a momentary grin. "Tempting, but no." Then he said, "Why don't we go to Cunnamulla? Your birthplace. You can show me where you were born. Was it at the hospital, or – ?"

"Sentimental idiot," Dave said fondly. At which Nicholas just smiled a bit mysteriously, and winked at him. And Dave found he didn't mind very much at all.

After the Cunnamulla trip worked out, Dave came up with a bolder plan still. "Not the next trip," he suggested while they were still sitting around after dinner one evening, "but maybe the one after? We'll have been out here seven weeks. You'll be just over halfway through your three months. Why don't we do something crazy, like go to Brisbane?"

"Brisbane!" Nicholas repeated, clearly startled.

"It's not so far, if you're up for a day's drive. It's about ten hours from Cunnamulla. We could drive there one day, stay for two nights, then drive back again."

"Oh," the man said. He sat up a bit straighter, and thought about it. "I suppose … I've got used to being out here. It didn't occur to me to go back to the city."

"We could stay at my place," Dave said, suddenly finding that he couldn't quite meet Nicholas's gaze. "I've lived there all my life. My mum and dad bought it when they got married."

"I'd love to see it."

"Won't be anything fancy like you're used to, but I like it. Bit big for one person, mind. It's built in this architectural style – an Australian style called Federation Bungalow. Which isn't as dire as it sounds. It was a bit of a wreck when they bought it – I've got the old photos – but we did it up over the years."

Nicholas was watching him, mouth slightly agape. He stirred himself to say, "I'm sure it's lovely."

"Yeah, well. I belong there, you know?" Dave looked about at their secluded surroundings. "If Charlie's right, and I belong here, then it's as well as there. Cos that's my home."

Nicholas said, with a full heart, "I'd love to stay there with you, even if it is only for two nights."

"*And* … you can meet Denise, maybe."

That earned him a droll look.

"I was an only child, and so was Mum, and so was Dad. So Denise is all the family I have, even if she did drop me."

"I'll be happy to meet her. She sounds – well, like no one I've ever met before."

"Yeah, she is that." Dave laughed. "There. That's what you two have in common. You're like no one I've ever met before, too."

Nicholas sniffed. "I'm sure she'll understand if I think she did an idiotic thing, letting you go."

Dave glared at the man. "Well, that's what you're gonna do, too, isn't it? When you fly back to England?"

Nicholas's head went back, and he turned kind of wild–eyed for a moment. Then: "Yes," he blurted. "I suppose that I will."

Had Nicholas not been thinking that far ahead? Dave sighed. "Well, come on. Might as well make the most of it."

"Carpe diem," said Nicholas after a silent moment. "Seize the day."

"That the Goring family motto, is it?"

"No, actually. Just mine."

Dave knew a joke he could tell, so he played it through once in his head to be sure he had it, then nudged Nicholas's foot with his own to get his attention. "What's the motto of the Fat Poets' Society?"

"What?" Nicholas asked, with a smile dawning.

"Seize the Danish."

"Idiot!" Nicholas said, though he was laughing. He stood, and came over to collect Dave's plate. "Right. Time to do the washing-up."

"Can't it wait this once?" Dave asked, having had other things on his mind.

"Certainly not! David Taylor, I'm shocked at you, letting your standards slide like that."

"All right, all right," he grumbled.

It wasn't long, though, before the chores were done, and they were safely tucked away in their double sleeping bag. Nicholas grabbed at Dave, and dragged him closer. Dave went willingly, letting himself be configured as Nicholas desired.

"Time to make the most of it," Nicholas murmured, and his mouth captured Dave's.

thirteen

Dave didn't think anything of it when he found one of the butterflies lying dead on the ground one afternoon. He supposed that every now and then one would die, just as humans died, naturally or by accident. He felt quite strongly that it should be left to rest in peace at the waterhole, though, and not be added to a collection somewhere, pinned to a board and left in a drawer for months at a time until some stranger came to peer at it. So, feeling a bit guilty and very idiotic, he took it over to the sandier ground by the pool, and quickly scooped out a shallow grave. He laid it quietly within, and pondered for a while the brightness of the blue wings against the reddish soil. But then he heard Nicholas moving about the camp behind him, so Dave quickly covered the butterfly up, and for good measure placed a flat stone over the spot as a mark of respect.

"Sleep well," he whispered. "Go find old man grunter, wherever he's dreaming now …"

"What are you up to?" asked Nicholas in all innocence on Dave's return.

"Just pottering about," said Dave. "Putting things to rights."

And that was so very Dave Taylor that Nicholas didn't question him any further.

Things took a grievous turn a couple of days later. Dave woke rather later than usual, and stretched luxuriously to work the kinks out. He was alone, which was also unusual given that Nicholas tended to just snuggle up even closer if he woke earlier than Dave. He stretched again, senses alert and seeking the scent of tea, the roil of boiling water. Nothing. Nothing, except …

Weeping. Muffled, and resigned rather than distraught, but crying it was. And of course Dave knew who it had to be.

Dave grabbed his shorts and t-shirt, and quickly tugged them on, then swung down the back of the Cruiser, not bothering with the ladder. He'd already spotted Nicholas, on his knees over by the wattle, with his face in his hands. Dave headed over there at a jog.

And he didn't have to ask what the matter was. It was immediately obvious. A drift of dead butterflies, their blue and black wings still deceptively vibrant, trailed across the ground from the wattle back to the edges of the surrounding cliffs. Dave's heart clutched in grief and guilt. "What happened? God, what did we do?" For, despite the fact that he was careful to always wrap up their garbage and take it back to town with him to dispose of, and despite the fact that he always used biodegradable *everything*, Dave assumed that they'd caused this tragedy.

But Nicholas was shaking his head. "Nothing," he managed. "Nothing. This is what happens. Some species barely live even a few days …"

"Ah, mate …" Dave murmured in sorrow and fellow-feeling. He crouched down beside Nicholas, and caught a glimpse of his white tear-sodden face. And Dave forgot about this being a bloke, and thought only of what he'd do when Denise was upset. He shuffled closer, shifting so that Nicholas was bracketed by Dave's legs, and then Dave tugged him close so he could hold him.

Nicholas, unsurprisingly, collapsed against him, and Dave sat there cradling him for a while, stroking gently at his back and shoulders and hair. Dave had time to remember how cold-blooded Nicholas had seemed when taking specimens of his beautiful butterflies; so different to how he was now, confronted by natural mortality. Perhaps Nicholas could explain that, or perhaps not. Dave knew all too well that death and grieving could affect people in such different ways.

Eventually Nicholas quietened, but he didn't seem to want to move, and Dave was hardly going to make him. So Dave had time to remember the lone dead butterfly he'd found, and he wondered if that had been *their* butterfly, the first to emerge, the one that welcomed them to the waterhole and had seemed so keen to drink from Dave's skin. Of course it would have reached the end of its natural lifespan sooner than the rest.

When Nicholas finally stirred and sat up, Dave offered him a gentle smile, and received a wobbly one in return. "Shall I make some tea?" Dave asked. "Or … anything. What would you like to do?"

"Tea." Nicholas nodded. He glanced away for a moment, chewing on his lower lip in thought. Then he looked back at Dave. "I'd like to tell you something. If you don't mind."

"Of course. You can tell me anything." Dave shifted, and stretched out his left leg which had gone to sleep. "All right for now, mate?"

"Yes. Thank you." Another watery smile. "I'll be along in a minute. I'll wash my face. I must look a sight."

"Beautiful as ever, I'm afraid," Dave said stoutly. "You are *so* bad for my peace of mind." And Nicholas even laughed a little under his breath at such a ridiculous notion.

"I have – I have a brain aneurysm." Nicholas's face was long and chalk-white. "I'll save you from all the details of what's happened, and how they found it, but –"

"*Oh Nicholas!*" Dave quietly burst out once he'd regained his voice.

Nicholas blinked, and carried on. "– but I could drop dead at any time, or have a stroke, or what have you. There's no predicting it, and very little preventative treatment available. The risks of surgery are about the same as the risks of not doing anything, so I decided not to. Do anything."

A stunned silence grew.

Dave struggled for something to say. Eventually he came up with: "Is that what the medication's for?"

"Yes. It's nothing exotic. It controls my blood pressure. Which should reduce the risk of –" But apparently he couldn't bring himself to say it twice.

"This is awful," Dave managed, which was horribly inadequate, but what else was there to say? Nicholas was only two or three years older than Dave himself. Otherwise healthy men in their twenties shouldn't have to face this kind of thing. Dave tried to think it through. "Is that why –"

"Yes," Nicholas said, cutting him off. "I expect it's the explanation for a lot of things."

Dave felt at a complete loss.

Then suddenly it was far far easier to feel angry. It helped him ignore the great gaping chasm that had opened up right under his feet. "Why the hell didn't you tell me?" he asked – not loud, but furious. "You might have died out here, and I wouldn't know why, or what to do –"

"There's nothing you could do," Nicholas crisply replied. "Or not that you wouldn't have done anyway. Simon made sure that you're qualified to apply first aid. You would have called for an air ambulance, and tried to resuscitate me."

"Yeah, thanks," said Dave, laying on the irony.

"I left a letter – with the medication. You or the medical personnel would have looked for the medication, and found the letter. There's nothing more you could have done."

"I don't believe you. Telling me might have made the difference between you dying and … and you *not* dying."

"Well," came the tart response. "Under some circumstances, I think I would actually rather die."

Dave just stared at the man, infuriated by the situation he could have – he could *still* find himself in. But he understood, too. Reluctantly, he had to admit that a part of him did understand. Nicholas didn't want this condition to define his life.

"Exactly. I was tired of – of being taken care of. In relation to my health, anyway. And – well. I might live until something else gets me, or I might not have much time. I don't know. But I wanted to do this, to find the butterflies. I didn't want to risk you deciding that you couldn't bring me out here."

And he really did understand. Dave hated that. It went against all his rules, but he couldn't help thinking he'd have probably done the same.

"Thank you," Nicholas said stiffly. "I do appreciate the position I might have put you in."

"Thanks," said Dave, very quietly, but he meant it this time.

"And once you've forgiven me, I can assure you …" Nicholas caught Dave's eye, and glanced towards their bed on top of the Cruiser. "Regular exercise is to be encouraged."

"Oh, *Nicholas*," Dave said brokenly. He was breaking apart inside from anticipated grief.

And as with their first real kiss, Dave couldn't say now who initiated it – but what did that matter? A moment later they were sitting on the ground between the two chairs, and Dave was cradling Nicholas again, who curled up within his arms and clung on. It seemed that Nicholas was done crying for now, but of course he still needed the comfort.

All Dave could think was that, no matter what Nicholas was to Dave, whether he was a client or a friend – and no matter if they never saw each other again after this trip – Dave liked the world a whole lot better for knowing that Nicholas was in it.

"Thank you," Nicholas said again, almost gasping.

"Is this why –" Dave dared to ask. "Is this why the butterflies?"

"Tell me."

"They make you feel long-lived."

"Positively ancient," Nicholas agreed. "And … ?"

But he was all out of wisdom. "Tell me," said Dave.

Nicholas sighed. He was almost calm again now. "Because … you can hibernate a very long time in that chrysalis. But once you emerge –"

"You become fabulous," Dave supplied.

Nicholas shifted around so that he could see Dave properly. "But then the clock starts ticking."

They took it slow. They drank the tea, which had remained warm in its pot. And then Dave took Nicholas back to their bed. This time, Dave made love to the man. And he treated him as gently as he knew how.

"There," said Nicholas afterwards, sounding philosophical. "We hit the high point."

Don't, Dave wanted to say. But who was he to deny Nicholas anything?

"It was one of those dangerous moments," Nicholas said, obviously quoting something, *"when feeling, running high above its average depth, leaves flood-marks which are never reached again."* He sighed again. "Denise would recognise that."

Don't. Dave hid his face against Nicholas's throat, cheek against the steady thrum of his heartbeat, and he held on to the man with tender strength.

"Do you know what the name David means?" Nicholas asked a long while later. When Dave shook his head, Nicholas answered, "Beloved."

"What does Nicholas mean?"

"Virile," the man claimed.

Dave stared at him for a long moment, before bursting into laughter. "It does not!"

"It does, actually."

"Prove it!"

"I'd love to." And Nicholas rose up from the mattress like a whale breaching the surface of the ocean, and then he turned, and took Dave under.

fourteen

They reached Dave's house around seven–thirty one evening. Dave smiled as he walked in the front door: he liked being home. And his smile broadened as he welcomed Nicholas in.

"There's a side door off the garage," he explained inconsequentially, "but I thought you'd better see it properly. At least the first time."

"It's lovely," Nicholas said as he trailed along behind Dave, gazing about him as Dave turned on the lights in the hallway, then the living room. Dave himself looked about at the colours with fresh eyes – the dark green, and rich cream, and occasional scraps of rusty red – before leading Nicholas through into the family room and kitchen. "Now, *this* is nice," Nicholas added appreciatively, as he took in the room that ran along two–thirds of the width of the house.

"Wait until you see it in the morning," Dave said. "There's a veranda out the back there, and then the yard. This is the best room …" He grinned, and then pointed in the direction of the other third of the back of the house. "Well, this and the master bedroom, anyway."

Nicholas's smile curled wickedly. "I trust you'll give me the full tour later." And he didn't mean the house.

"I'll just check the fridge –" Though why he even said that, Dave had no idea. He knew he could rely on Denise, and there was no point in pretending to Nicholas that she wasn't an intrinsic part of his life. "We've got the essentials here, Denise said she'd make sure of that. Thought I'd make an omelette for dinner, if that's all right."

"That's great."

Dave started fetching out the eggs and butter, mushrooms and capsicum, bacon and cheese. "D'you wanna get cleaned up, or anything?"

"Later," Nicholas said. "Is the shower big enough for both of us?"

Dave went pink. "Maybe …"

"Then the shower can wait for afterwards. I'll make a pot of tea, if I may. You do the sustenance, I'll do the antioxidants."

"Going to need them, are we?"

"Oh yes," said Nicholas. And once the tea was stewing, he sat there at the breakfast bar, watching Dave with a wickedly content smile.

They weren't expected at Denise's until twelve-thirty, so after coffee and muesli, and a wander around the lushly planted backyard, the two of them seemed to gravitate quite naturally again to bed.

"Making the most of it?" Dave asked as he backed towards the bed, with Nicholas's hands sliding up under his t-shirt.

"Seize the Dave," Nicholas whimsically agreed.

Dave laughed – but then Nicholas turned serious, reaching around Dave to tug at the doona and then fling it off the bed and onto the floor with a strong twist of his wrist. Dave was pushed back to fall against the mattress, the cotton sheet cool against his skin. Nicholas eyed the wooden slats of the bed for a moment, before turning back to Dave. "What can I tie you down with?"

Dave let out a gasp, and he instinctively wriggled away on his elbows and rear – until Nicholas caught him again with one long pale hand wrapped around Dave's ankle.

"What can I use?" Nicholas demanded.

"Dad's dressing gown belt," Dave blurted.

"Good," said Nicholas. And he headed for the wardrobe that Dave indicated with a nod. "Good," he said again, once he'd found it.

Nicholas walked back towards the bed, his gaze pinning Dave down. And Dave's cock kicked into full-blooded life.

It was nothing like he'd expected.

Dave found himself naked and face down on the bed, the wrong way round with his head towards the foot, and his arms free. His ankles, however, were bound together and then the tie was secured to the bed head. Nicholas was sitting there against the pillows, just looking at him lying there. Nothing else seemed to be happening at all.

"Uh ..." Dave started uncertainly.

"Hush," said Nicholas. One of his cool hands wrapped again around Dave's ankle, and caressed him through the binding. "Let me see you," he continued.

Dave shifted to look at him over his shoulder. "What?"

"Shush … Put your head back down. Then arch the small of your back the way you like to. Show me that *delicious* arch in your back."

"Oh …" he groaned. He was sure he'd never talked about that. Nicholas must have really been paying attention. After a moment Dave shifted back a little so he could do as Nicholas requested – which of course meant that his rear was poking up in the air. He assumed that was the intention.

"Further," said Nicholas. "I want you to really feel it."

He did so, forcing the curve until it was just the right side of painful.

"Good." That hand patted at his calf in reward. "Now show yourself to me. No, keep your knees together, but turn your thighs and your rear out. I want to see everything you've got."

Dave mumbled something that was half a protest, but he did his best to obey, though it felt to be an infinitesimal move. Nicholas, however, again expressed his appreciation.

"Now," said Nicholas. "Don't move. Not even a twitch."

"But –"

"What did I tell you?"

"Don't move," he said with a sigh. He didn't know how he'd go with that, though. Even when he let Nicholas do all the driving, Dave still liked to participate, and he still liked to be working his hips when he came.

"Good."

"I'll try –"

"You won't move. You will, however, give thought to coming like this. Without me touching your cock." Nicholas continued on, overriding anything Dave was about to say: "I'm going to be rimming you and fingering you, and sucking on your balls, and fucking you – and you're going to come."

"But –"

"Hush …" Nicholas was shifting, and apparently stalking down the bed until he could straddle Dave's legs on all fours without touching him – until he bit gently at the curve of Dave's butt.

Dave's breath hitched. And thus began an endless time of torment.

At the last, Nicholas took mercy on him, and reached below to take him in hand, to end it with three masterful strokes. Which triggered an orgasm almost too intense to be pleasurable.

"I'm sorry," Dave was mumbling afterwards, as Nicholas unfastened him. The man didn't make Dave move, but brought a pillow down with him and tucked it under Dave's head, tugged the doona up over them both, and then wrapped himself around Dave as if he'd never ever be pried off. "I'm sorry."

"What for?" Nicholas asked, sounding immensely satisfied. "*God*, that was good."

"I'm sorry I couldn't come like you wanted."

"Oh, my darling man! You didn't have to. It was just an idea. I'm sorry you felt you had to."

"I wanted to. I wanted to cos you wanted it."

"I know, you gorgeous thing. Hush now. Let's have a nap, and then we'll get cleaned up again. All right?"

"All right," said Dave. And he sank away into warm velvety darkness.

Of course they were late for lunch, and of course Denise knew exactly why. She greeted Dave with a smirk and an unexpected kiss on the cheek. "Hello, Davey." She took a moment to look him over, before handing him Zoe. "You're looking well. Not to mention well-shagged."

"Jeez, Denise!" he grumbled, feeling his face flame up again. He sought refuge in a much safer topic. "How's little Zo?" he asked, cradling the sleepy warm figure in both arms. "She's, like, twice as big as when I last saw her."

"Yeah, she's doin' great. You must be Nicholas," Denise added, reaching past Dave to shake Nicholas's hand.

"I'm pleased to meet you, Denise."

"Oh yeah, sorry," Dave said. But they were taking care of the introductions without him, which was just as well.

But then when Dave started drifting towards the family room, he found that the others weren't quite done yet. Denise and Nicholas were actually standing there in the hallway, sizing each other up.

"You know," said Denise, "I don't want to make you feel uncomfortable or anything, but I only invited you around to make sure you're good enough for him."

Nicholas scoffed a laugh in a manner befitting an honorary Australian. "That's all right. I only accepted to make sure you know he's not yours anymore."

148 | Butterfly Hunter

"Guys –" Dave said, heading back there. Zoe was stirring in his arms, as if picking up on the tensions.

But eventually Denise simply said, "I know that."

"Do you?"

"Well, I do now," Denise replied with a laugh. She offered to shake hands again. "You'll do, Nicholas."

"Thank you, Denise."

Dave sighed. "Right. Thank God that's over."

Luckily Vittorio seemed nothing more than amused by these two squaring off over Dave – and Dave had long ago realised that Vittorio wasn't the jealous type. As Denise and Vittorio headed for the kitchen, Dave and Nicholas followed after to settle at the table in the family room. Vittorio brought them a bottle of Cascade each. And Dave had time to belatedly feel flattered. No one else in all these years had ever thought Dave worth challenging Denise for. But still. They weren't in high school anymore. Dave hoped that was that.

Denise brought a warmed–up bottle of milk over for him to feed Zoe with, and got him properly started. The baby gazed up at him solemnly as she settled into it. Meanwhile, Denise and Vittorio were finishing off their preparations for lunch, and asking Nicholas about his trip; Nicholas was telling them about the butterflies as if he were a relatively sane person. Everything was going suspiciously well.

When Zoe got to the end of the bottle, Dave put it down, and then considered her for a long moment. She wriggled a bit uncomfortably, and he knew he was meant to do something else with her at this point, not have her lying back in his arms. "Is this the bit when I chuck her over my shoulder, or something?"

Denise had her hands full of crockery, and quickly spun about to put it back down – though Vittorio was inadvertently in the way. "Hang on," she said. Zoe scowled forebodingly.

"Not *over* your shoulder," Nicholas was advising. "A bit more civilised than that." He was standing by Dave now, laying a hand towel over Dave's shoulder – and then, with his hands cradling Dave's, showing him exactly how to hold Zoe upright against his chest, with her head lightly supported. "There you go. Now pat her back gently."

Denise was just watching them, obviously approving. "Kids of your own?"

she asked Nicholas.

"Oh no," he answered with a smile. "More nieces and nephews than I can count. It's only my eldest brother living at home now, with his wife and children, but we see a great deal of the others." He sat down again as he rambled on. "If there's a good kids' movie on, I get to borrow whoever will come with me to see it at the cinema. Or they'll stay over on a Saturday night, and I get to babysit while their parents go out – which really means I just get to hang out with them. That sort of thing."

Denise smiled. "You'll do very nicely indeed, Nicholas Goring."

A remark seconded by a resounding burp from Zoe, and backed up with a great deal of laughter.

The two of them walked slowly back to Dave's place, Nicholas looking as adorable as ever in his Akubra.

"I'm glad I got you that hat," said Dave.

"I am, too," Nicholas answered with simple sincerity.

They wandered on, watching each other a bit skittishly. Dave began to fear another hand–holding incident was imminent – and was relieved when his phone chimed to announce the distraction of a text message. Though he groaned when he read it. *You're in love with your earling.* Denise, of course.

Dave made sure the display was hidden from Nicholas. *I am not. Go away!*

Are too. Can't fool me, Davey.

He turned the thing to silent, and shoved it back in his pocket. Cleared his throat and said to Nicholas, "Shall we go do the grocery shopping for next week? Get that done?"

"It can wait for tomorrow, can't it?"

"Guess so. If you don't mind it being a long day, with the drive as well."

"Don't worry about that. I'm feeling rather like seizing the Dave again."

"Oh," he said, unable to prevent a pleased smile giving everything away. It was just as well no one was about on this warm afternoon, for surely this was worse than holding hands.

As it turned out, Nicholas didn't seize him at all, but instead treated him sweetly and gently, as if Dave needed seducing. It was lovely.

Later that evening, after they'd eaten dinner and were sprawled on the lounge watching TV, Nicholas said, "Don't worry about tomorrow. We're not going back."

Dave was so startled, that all he could do was repeat, "We're not –"

"No," said Nicholas very evenly. "I've changed my ticket. I'm flying back to England tomorrow."

Dave's hand was clutching painfully at Nicholas's, but the man didn't flinch or indeed show anything much. "What?" Dave managed. "No ..."

"I'm no good at farewells. At this point, I'd rather take the coward's way out and go home."

"No. No, you *can't*."

"I am, though. At least I'm telling you today. It's hard enough living with the goodbye for a few hours. I can't do it for a few weeks."

"But –" It wasn't just about Dave. It was about the whole trip. "You haven't finished with the butterflies yet! The trip's barely half over!"

Nicholas cleared his throat. "The balance of your fee will be in your account by now. Simon's taking care of it."

"God, d'you really think I care about the money?"

"No, I don't suppose that you do. But I care about upholding my end of a deal."

"Is *that* what you think you're doing?" Dave demanded – immediately continuing, "You haven't finished with the butterflies. You haven't seen the caterpillars yet."

"But we don't know when that will be. They might only go through one life cycle each year. Even if the eggs don't have a dormant phase, they might take weeks to hatch. We could go back and spend over a month doing nothing but watching the eggs."

"Doing nothing ... ?" he protested.

"David, it's done. My flight leaves around one in the afternoon. I'll take a taxi to the airport, if you'd prefer. In fact, I'll take a taxi now, if you like, and stay at a hotel for the night."

"Don't be ridiculous!" Dave burst out.

"Well, don't make this any harder than it needs to be."

Dave fell silent, and let the man's hand go. This was horrible. Dave felt as if he'd ruined everything. But he also felt that Nicholas had wilfully let it be ruined. Though the man had enough to be dealing with already, and no doubt he was doing the best he could. They were both just doing the best they could, weren't they? Dave sighed.

"I don't understand," he said. "What do you mean about not being good at farewells?"

"Just exactly that. I don't have the art of saying goodbye. Not gracefully. Normally, I don't let things start – not really – so that I don't have to say goodbye at the end." Nicholas reached to take Dave's hand in his again. "I broke all my rules for you."

"Then we're even, aren't we," said Dave. "Just … talk to me. I want to understand. And give it to me straight. I reckon I already have abandonment issues, so don't worry about that."

"Oh, *David,*" Nicholas said with a wry fondness.

"Is this about … the last goodbye? The final one?"

"Well. Yes. I almost – don't want to start living, because I can't face it ending. Being alone – other than my family – It makes the prospect of letting go – easier."

"Ah, no … No, mate."

"Tell me another way. There is no other way. It can't be another way."

"I get it," said Dave. "I do. But it's too late. You *are* living. You've transformed. You're the fabulous butterfly now."

"Because of you," Nicholas suggested with a half-sceptical half-pleased little smile.

"No, you already were when you met me. You just didn't know it yet."

"Oh God," Nicholas said, with his breath shuddering for a moment. "David. This has been –"

"I know," said Dave, cutting him off, terrified that they'd both end up bawling like babies. "I know."

And Nicholas pushed over to kiss him, and then he really did seize Dave, and they fucked, right there on the lounge. Frantically.

They eventually made it to Dave's bed, and Nicholas abruptly fell deeply asleep. He was exhausted, and perhaps taking the coward's way out in this as well. David didn't blame him at all, even while he lay awake, already feeling lonely.

The following morning, they were polite to each other, in a friendly enough way. They didn't fuck again. Nicholas took his time repacking his gear, which didn't really need it. He'd obviously been at least half intending to do this all along. Dave helped him, and fed him, made him coffee, and watched him, keeping his distance, as required.

He found himself wishing that Nicholas would say something – any little thing – to indicate that they might meet again. A hint of plans for another trip next year to see the butterflies. An invitation to drop by if Dave should ever find himself in England. Anything like that. But no. Nicholas talked about practicalities, but was otherwise quiet – not reminiscing about the trip, and not looking ahead to anything beyond his flight.

Soon enough, they had to leave so that Nicholas had time for all the international check-in procedures.

Soon enough – too soon – it was time to part. Once Nicholas was beyond the security barriers, then he was as good as out of the country.

"Just tell me you don't hate me," Nicholas said as they stood there together.

"For what?"

Nicholas shrugged. "Just tell me. Lie if you have to."

Dave looked at him, steady and true. "I don't hate you."

"Thank you," Nicholas said. And there in Departures, with everyone milling around them, Nicholas pressed one last kiss to Dave's mouth. And Dave didn't hate him for that, either. "Goodbye, David."

"Goodbye," he whispered.

Nicholas turned, and resolutely headed for the security entrance. He turned left into the corridor with his head high and one last glance that barely even made it halfway towards Dave. A moment later the man was gone.

fifteen

Dave felt at a total loss. He took care of the Cruiser and its contents that afternoon – clearing everything out, cleaning it, reorganising, noting what needed restocking, and all the rest of it. He bought himself some groceries, and caught up with his laundry.

He gave hours of serious thought to going back out to the waterhole by himself. Surely he owed it to Nicholas to go and record the hatching of the eggs, and the … the crawling of the caterpillars. Even if it was taking a while, he could probably go back every couple of weeks or so, just to keep an eye on developments. After all, if Dave hadn't broken his own rules, then Nicholas would still be here, they'd be client and tour guide – with some tensions, perhaps, and probably not friends as they'd become – and his client wouldn't have felt the need to cut his trip short, and maybe could even have extended it if he'd needed to. If the butterflies really weren't cooperating.

But the thought of going back there right away on his own just filled him with reluctance. He felt an almost physical resistance to the idea. Dave had been alone for so long that he'd gotten used to it. Before his unexpected English earling had turned up, anyway. Now he thought that hanging around that waterhole without Nicholas to share it with would crush him with loneliness.

Not that hanging around home was going to be much better, he supposed. He'd have to start calling around the travel agents and tourist centres, and let them know that he was available again for short or long trips. He'd have to get used to the notion of having other people to take care of. He'd have to relearn how to keep a professional distance.

Dave sighed, and headed back inside. The scent of Nicholas and sex still lingered in his bed, so Dave grabbed a pillow and took it through to the lounge with him. Wore away the night hours with television. Which wasn't an answer, but it got him through the first day.

Or maybe, he found himself reflecting on the second day, he could have broken his fraternisation rules but handled it all better so that Nicholas hadn't panicked and felt the need to leave. There must have been some way to reassure the man that they could part with a laconic Aussie 'see ya' rather than a solemn English 'goodbye'. That way, they could have had five more weeks of sex and friendship and – well, Dave had to acknowledge the truth – affection. Surely he could have managed that.

He was obviously totally useless at relationships, whether short or long.

He lay low for most of that first week, pottering about the house and working on the garden. Reading *The Reverse of the Medal* and *The Letter of Marque*.

And then he finally went around to see Denise.

She was astonished, to say the least, to find him on her doorstep. And all the more so to find him alone. "Davey! Why aren't you out at your waterhole? And what have you done with Nicholas?"

He explained, as best he could, at the dining table over a mug of coffee. He kept his voice low, and avoided both dire curses and airy denials, because Zoe was asleep in a bassinet just around the corner in the living room. Not that he needed to curse or deny. It had ended badly, which was probably to be expected given that he'd made so many mistakes. But that was that, and Dave just had to get used to being alone again.

"Oh, *Davey* ..." Denise said in sorrowful tones, reaching to wrap his hand in hers.

He didn't need sympathy. He took his hand away and drank his coffee.

"Nicholas was trying to do the right thing by you," she said rather more coolly.

"Yeah, absolutely ..." he said, voice heavy with sarcasm.

"You probably made it clear to him that it was only a holiday fling."

"It *was* only a holiday fling."

"Oh, for God's sake!" she said, sitting back and rolling her eyes. "So what's with all the moping now?"

Dave glared at her. "Cos he just left! Five weeks early! And I stuffed everything up, I ruined his trip for him, I should have known better than to break my rules, and he was bloody-minded enough to pay the fee for the whole three months as well!"

Denise sighed. "From what I saw of Nicholas, I'd say he had the time of his life out there with you. Perhaps he wanted to end it on a high note."

"I don't see how that's doing the right thing by me."

"Oh you idiot, do you really not get it? You're such a loveable sort, Davey. We all want to take care of you. Your dad, me. Nicholas. We try to do what's right for you."

"Leaving wasn't right for me." He frowned, and amended that: "Not yet, anyway. Obviously he was going to leave later."

"If you were really so determined that it was only for the three months and no longer, then you can hardly blame him for ending it on his own terms. Poor sod."

That earned her another glare. "I should have known you'd take his side in this."

"Davey, don't be any more idiotic than you have to be."

"Look," he said stiffly. "I have found that … nothing lasts forever."

"If that's the only thing I taught you, Davey, then I'm more sorry than I can say. But it's not, is it?"

He set his face against her at the time, and in a thoroughly disgruntled mood Dave left and walked home again. Wondering what the hell to do next.

But it didn't take him long to back down a bit. Fair's fair, he thought. So he texted her: *Not the only thing.*

Charlie called the next day, and was almost totally convincing in claiming that Denise hadn't put him up to it. "Nah, mate, I'm coming up to Brisbane for a few days. Thought we should have a beer."

"Come and stay," Dave offered. "The house is too big since Dad died."

"So … what have you done with your man, Davey?"

"He's gone back to England. As I'm sure you know already."

"Then you're going, too?"

"No." Dave frowned over that. Of course he'd thought about it. He just figured there wasn't any point. If this was the way that Nicholas wanted it, then who was Dave to argue?

"Davey … ?" Charlie prompted after what must have been a lengthy silence.

"Look," said Dave. "I reckon you know he thinks he doesn't have long, right? Well, I think he just wants to live his life his way, the best he can."

"His way would be with you, mate."

"No, I think he wants to keep it easy. I think he wants to spare himself, and whoever else ... the grief." God, even saying it brought an intimation of the weight of it down upon him.

"We're all going to die, Dave my man. No reason not to live while we can. There'll be time enough in the Dreaming for the rest."

"Well, then," Dave argued, "it can wait. Can't it?"

"No, what you have with Nicholas is a part of life. The kind of thing you *do* get to take with you when you go, if you live it right. Next thing I want to hear about you, my man, is that you're in England."

"But I don't think he really wants –"

"I never knew you for a fool, David Taylor."

"Oh." After a moment he rallied again. "Well, I can't, can I? What about the waterhole? And the songs?"

"You'll come back," Charlie said, in his confident way. The man had such faith! "I'm thinking both of you will be back, and you'll be looking after that place for us, Nicholas will be looking after those butterflies. And the grunter and his love will be together again."

Dave sank a bit, overwhelmed. Minutes went by, but "Oh" was all he managed to say. And then, weakly, "I can't."

"All right," Charlie said easily. "Well, I'll see you in a week or so. If you come to your senses, though, just call me. I can find somewhere else to stay."

"You won't have to."

"We'll see."

Right. He really hated it when people said that.

And of course, Denise wouldn't leave the subject alone. "You're not *that* embarrassed about being with a guy, are you? Life's too short, Davey."

He almost laughed at that. "His motto was Seize the Day."

"Well ... ?"

"It's not that I minded being with a bloke as such ..."

"You minded being his bitch."

Dave went bright red, and thanked God or the Ancestors that Vittorio wasn't around. "Denise!"

"If that's how things are between you –"

She meant the sex, he assumed. "It's not *that* I mind so much as –"

"People knowing."

"Yes."

"Everyone knew you were my bitch, Davey, and you lived with it."

All right, that gave him pause. "Yeah, I did, didn't I?" The endless jokes about who wore the trousers in their relationship had been so much a part of his life that they'd never bothered him. As a child he'd always wondered what on earth could have been so wrong with enjoying Denise taking care of him. As a man, he'd understood better, but still he felt that most people who'd teased him about it had just been jealous.

"So what's different?" she asked.

He thought about it some more, and couldn't come up with an answer.

Denise realised, of course, that she was finally making some headway. She came to sit next to him, and just spoke very gently now. Not pushing at all. "I almost bought what you said at first, about it being a short–term thing. But I don't anymore."

He looked at her doubtfully. But underneath, his whole world was shifting.

"Maybe he was wrong, but he was trying to look after you, Davey. Now it's your turn to look after him – and yourself, too. *You* have to seize the day this time. He can't do it all on his own."

"Denny –"

"You've got to go find him again. You've got to go get your man!"

"That sort of thing," he said a bit shakily, "it only happens in books. Movies."

She emphatically disagreed. "No. You go make it happen in real life, too."

And in that moment, he knew he would. He wasn't quite ready yet. But he knew.

"And send me an invite, won't you?" Denise added.

"For what?"

"Your wedding."

"What?"

"You can get married over there, you know. I want to be – I *demand* to be your best man."

"Denny –"

"You were mine."

"Oh God ..."

And so once he'd escorted the Americans around in their quest to wrestle crocodiles, the next trip that Dave prepared for was to Buckinghamshire in England. He decided it had better be a surprise. If he was going to be dropped all over again, it had better be made clear and done in person. He wouldn't know what to do if he contacted Nicholas and then received an ambivalent email in response that could be interpreted a hundred different ways. Dave didn't want to lose what little certainty he had.

He knew for sure he was doing the right thing before he flew out, though. Because he was browsing the internet on his mobile while hanging around the departure lounge at the Brisbane airport. And he happened to Google 'Nicholas Goring'. And the first entry in the search results was from the website of *The Australian Journal of Entomology*, announcing an article that would appear in the following month's issue. It was about an Englishman, and the new butterfly he'd discovered in the Outback.

And he'd called the butterfly *Ogyris davidi*: David's Azure.

sixteen

Dave was standing at the massive doorway to a manor house, feeling somewhat overwhelmed. Definitely about to change his mind and take the coward's way out. It was a gentle English summer afternoon. Somewhere there were children laughing in irrepressible delight – perhaps in the gardens. Which was lovely, and brought this imposing old house alive. They were some of Nicholas's nieces and nephews, Dave assumed. The sound was magical, but it also underlined the fact that Dave didn't really belong there.

His hand, which had been about to ring the bell again, fell loosely to his side.

Dave had just turned away when the door finally opened – and the very proper butler, after a long moment, softened into a happy smile. "Mr Taylor … ? Yes, it is, isn't it? I recognise you from your photo. I'm sorry to have kept you waiting."

"Hello, Simon," Dave replied.

"Please, do come in. You'll be very welcome, sir."

"David."

"Thank you, David. I'll take you through to the conservatory. You'll be able to surprise him there."

A blur of rooms, and then they were there already, before Dave had even had time to catch his breath.

"Nicholas? You have a visitor."

Dave just stood there, still within the darkness of the house proper, a little way behind Simon, unable to really take much in. Nicholas was there in the gentle plant–filtered sunlight, sitting cross–legged on a tarpaulin on the tiled floor, potting orchids. With someone beside him. A child. That was all right. Dave's heart was pounding.

Nicholas stared for a moment, and then unfolded to stand with his usual inelegant grace. "David?" he said, in a hushed tone – not confirming who he was, of course, but really asking The Question. *Will you … ?*

"Yes," Dave answered huskily. *For better or worse, as long as we both shall live.* "Will you … ?" he asked. *Come live with me and be my love – in Australia.*

"Yes." Then Nicholas closed the remaining distance between them with two shaky strides, and Dave was deep in his arms, and holding on with all his might, and they were kissing kissing *kissing*, and it was just the most *awesome* thing ...

Until they were recalled to their surroundings by the giggle of a child and the clearing of a butler's throat.

"Oh," said Nicholas, stepping back a little. "Well. How are you?" he asked, running a caressing hand back over Dave's hair. "Did you come straight here? What a long journey you must have had, that flight is hellish, isn't it – I'm sure you're parched. Simon, please would you bring us some tea?"

"Yes, sir, of course."

"Here, come and meet my nephew Robin," Nicholas continued, taking Dave by the hand and leading him out into the conservatory. "We're just re-potting these orchids, but we'll be done soon. You can help us, if you like."

"Sure," Dave said, starting to let go and relax into the flow of it. Nicholas would take care of him, he knew that now. He could trust this man with *everything*.

"Robin, this is my friend David, from Australia."

"Pleased to meet you, sir."

"You, too, Robin."

"I should warn you that *everyone's* here," Nicholas said as he sank back down to the tarpaulin. Dave sat down beside him, infinitely comfortable despite everything. "A gathering of Gorings. It's the summer holidays, you see. But you don't have to meet them all yet. We'll have tea first, and get you unpacked ..." Nicholas's gaze caressed him, top to toe, adding the promise of *undressed ... debauched ...* "Not that you should worry. Everyone's going to be so glad you came."

At last Nicholas was quiet again, and after a while Dave felt he should offer something more. "I'm glad, too," he said, his voice still rusty as if he hadn't used it, not properly, for so very long.

"How brave you've been. How incredible!" And Nicholas took one of Dave's hands in his, and lifted it to caress Dave's palm with his cheek. "Thank you, David. Thank you so much."

"Nnn," he replied, quite coherently.

What with one thing and the other, it was a couple of hours before they headed back down to meet everyone. As they reached the top of the stairs, Dave asked, "Are you sure I'm dressed well enough?" He was in a new pair of washed-out blue jeans, and a white button-down shirt in a textured cotton which he wore loose, and brown leather sandals. The outfit had cost him so much that he winced to remember, but now all he could think was that he must appear too casual.

"How someone as gorgeous as you can fret about what he's wearing, I have no idea," Nicholas grumbled. "As if anyone is even going to notice! And anyway, it's not like we do the whole white-tie-and-tails thing for dinner."

"Oh God. You know, I've never even *worn* a suit in my whole life … ?"

"All right, now *that's* a deal-breaker, if ever I heard one." They'd reached the landing, from which the staircase swept down into the main hall. Nicholas stopped, and tugged gently at Dave's hand to bring him round to face him. "Let me have another look at you, then …" His gaze caressed Dave once more from top to toe, making Dave blush yet again. "You look *perfect*: you look exquisitely yourself."

He mumbled something grateful, and then they continued on down the stairs …

Only to find that they must have been overheard, for two men were sitting on the pair of sofas either side of the fireplace down there, apparently talking quietly between themselves. They stood as Nicholas changed tack and approached the men.

"My father and brother," Nicholas had a moment in which to murmur to Dave – and then they were there, and Dave was being formally presented. "Father, may I introduce my friend David Taylor, from Australia. David, this is my father, Lord Goring."

"It is a great pleasure to meet you, David, and to welcome you to our home."

"Thank you, my lord," he managed smoothly enough as they shook hands. "It's a real honour to be here."

"Please call me Richard; we don't stand on ceremony with friends." And he certainly seemed to be a delightfully avuncular figure.

"Thank you," said Dave, half of his fears melting away already.

"Robert," Nicholas continued to the other man, who looked like a rather less beautiful, rugby-playing version of Nicholas himself, "this is my friend David. David, this is my eldest brother, Robert."

Again they shook hands, and did the "Very happy to meet you, David" –

"Thank you, my lord" – "Thanks, but please call me Robert" exchange.

As the three Gorings chatted briefly about some household business or other, and as the happy sounds of a large family gathering floated faintly through from elsewhere in the house, it occurred to Dave that the earl and his heir had deliberately positioned themselves here in order to greet Dave, and ease him into this whole meet–the–family thing. Which was beyond considerate. Dave relaxed a little more, beginning to anticipate that he faced nothing worse now than confusion about which names belonged to which newly met faces. But he had Simon and Robin, Richard and Robert sorted out already, and Nicholas of course. Always and forever Nicholas.

"Shall we go in?" Richard asked. "If I introduce David as your friend, Nicholas, is that acceptable to you both?"

"Of course. That will be fine." But Nicholas held back as the rest of them turned away to head off. "Wait a minute, though." His hand slipped into Dave's, and squeezed in reassurance or maybe in a plea. "Just between us for now, Father, but I think we're more than friends."

The earl had turned back readily enough, and now he hesitated for less than a blink before saying, "I'm sure we all understood as much, Nicholas, and we're very happy to have David here with us."

"No, I mean …" Those dark blue eyes searched Dave wildly, glowing with a tentatively grasped hope which increased in certainty every moment. "I mean, I think I proposed to David earlier, in the conservatory. Didn't I?" he asked.

"Yes," said David.

"And … I think you accepted me. Didn't you … ?"

"Yes."

"Oh!" Nicholas cried before leaning in to press a kiss against Dave's mouth. "I was hoping it was so."

And then Richard was shaking Dave's hand again, heartily expressing his delight, and welcoming Dave to the family, before gathering his obviously beloved son into his arms and offering congratulations. "You couldn't have made me any happier," the earl said as they all tried to regroup. "Nicholas, this is the last wish I had for you that remained unfulfilled. Until now."

"Thank you, Father."

But there was no way to keep it secret of course. Nicholas and Richard were as damp–eyed as Dave, and Robert couldn't quite suppress his pleased, proud smile. Within ten minutes of them entering the family living room, just about everyone had twigged. And Simon didn't even need to be asked; five minutes later the adults each had a flute of champagne, and the kids had flutes of lemonade. Robin was standing there holding Dave's hand, and gazing devotedly up at him and Nicholas, though he seemed a bit young to really understand what was happening. Given that Dave's other hand held his champagne glass, Nicholas had taken the opportunity to wind an arm about Dave's waist, which was great because Dave feared he was so giddy he might teeter and fall otherwise.

"I don't think Nicholas will mind me acknowledging," the earl said to the gathering, "that I was anxious when he decided to travel to Australia on his own, and planned to spend so much of his time there far beyond our ken. It seemed too bold an enterprise, full of dangers. I was afraid of losing this young man who is so very precious to me. But Nicholas didn't only find his butterflies there. I'm sure those of you who've spent time with him since he returned will agree that he found his own best self. And now, to complete the whole, we discover that he has found a loving partner as well. His future husband. And so I'd like to propose a toast …"

Richard looked across the room to nod to Simon. "Yes, please. Bring everyone in. This is for all the family."

Dave watched as six or seven others filed in, remaining tactfully out of the way, but each with their glass of champagne, and each smiling happily at Nicholas, while considering Dave with an inquisitive friendliness.

"To Nicholas and David," the earl at last said, lifting his glass. "May they enjoy the long and happy life together that they both deserve."

"To Nicholas and David," everyone responded.

And Nicholas leaned in to kiss him again, and Dave gave himself over to it, blushing only with a painful kind of pleasure now. Whooping and cheers, laughter and the clinking of glasses rang in his ears, but that all faded away when Nicholas murmured with his lips brushing Dave's, "You're mine now, you gorgeous darling man."

To which Dave replied, "Yes, I'm all yours."

And it was done.

❖

Of Dreams
and Ceremonies

wedding

one

Dave slept late that first morning, and when he woke he was alone. Nicholas's bedroom loomed large and empty around him. It was on one corner of the house, so there were two big windows on each of two walls, and the curtains were hanging wide open – which was apparently Nicholas's habit – so the place seemed full of light and air. The room contained an odd collection of furniture, some of it apparently very old, but all of it comfortable. Almost everything that wasn't wood was blue – upholstery, carpet, curtains, ornaments and oddments. And then there were books, a whole heap of books scattered everywhere.

There was also an en suite bathroom, thank God, which he promptly made use of, but then Dave headed back to the four-poster bed. He didn't get in again, but hefted up to sit on the side of it with his feet hanging some distance off the floor, and he looked around him quietly, still a bit dazed with jet lag. Well, with jet lag and with the enormity of what he'd done.

He, David Taylor of Brisbane, Australia – a quite ordinary bloke who'd spent almost all his conscious life in love with his best friend Denise and assuming he was straight – had fallen in love with Nicholas Goring, the youngest son of an English earl, while acting as his tour guide during a seven-week journey in Australia's Outback. Yesterday evening, having flown halfway round the world to belatedly follow Nicholas to his home in Buckinghamshire, Dave had even agreed to marry the man.

"Well," Nicholas had explained a little later, once his dauntingly large family had finally quit congratulating them, "it's a civil partnership, not a marriage. It's a civil partnership ceremony, not a wedding."

Which all sounded like far too many tongue-fumbling syllables for Dave. "How do you think about it?" he'd asked.

Nicholas had grinned so wide and so happy it was almost impossible to believe that one person could feel so ecstatic. "I'm getting married!"

"Good," said Dave. "Then that's what it is."

Now that he was alone in Nicholas's natural habitat, Dave took the opportunity to consider his surroundings. Though the room was full, it didn't seem cluttered so much as well lived in. There was the bed, of course, a free-standing wardrobe, and three assorted armchairs loosely arranged around a low coffee table. There was a serious-looking desk with a laptop computer and a scatter of papers, magazines and the like. Beside it, a bookcase reached towards the high ceiling, full to overflowing with books. The books were really the only thing that didn't fit in with the blue colour scheme, and so they made random rainbows along the shelves, in a couple of piles on the desk and the table, and in a smaller stack on Nicholas's bedside set of drawers. A couple of paintings on the wall were of landscapes and therefore introduced some green into the room, though really they were mostly sky. There was also a glass case on a side table, containing the pinned remains of various butterflies – at which Dave didn't look too closely.

A large chest of drawers stood by the bathroom door with a tall mirror beside it. Dave leaned a little to the right so he could peer at himself, wondering if he looked as vague as he felt. Yes, he did. It was the different time zones, maybe. Despite his long night's sleep, he thought that maybe his body was still on Australian time – and no doubt as far as his body was concerned it was still the middle of the night.

As Dave sat back up again he noticed four framed photos standing on top of the chest of drawers, and he went over to investigate. There was one of what must be Nicholas's parents – a much younger Richard than the man Dave had met the previous day, formally posed beside a rather smart-looking woman with Nicholas's dark hair and pale skin, his long face and unusual beauty. Another photo was a far more informal close-up of Nicholas and his nephew Robin, all hugs and laughter.

The other two photos had been taken in Australia, at the remote waterhole where Nicholas had discovered a new species of butterfly. The photo of Nicholas was one that Dave himself had taken – the first of their butterflies had alighted on Nicholas's Akubra, and there was a wickedly joyous look on the face peeking up from under the brim. The photo of Dave was one he hadn't even been aware of Nicholas taking. In it, Dave was sitting back reading one of his Patrick O'Brian books, lost in the long-ago maritime world. Another of the blue butterflies had settled on his shoulder, and seemed to also be contemplating the novel.

Near the framed photos was a glass cube in which one of the blue butterflies had been preserved. Dave considered it, remembering.

He and Nicholas had spent three weeks as friends, and four weeks as lovers. It wasn't much, perhaps, on which to base a marriage, but once Dave had gotten past his initial resistance, there had been a certainty about the relationship. Though he hadn't admitted it to himself at the time, even his resistance had felt as if he were fighting the inevitable. So it hadn't taken very much to push him into finally following Nicholas back home to England. Maybe it was just the way that Dave did these things: after all, he and Denise had been inseparable since the day they'd first met. Maybe Dave was just an all-or-nothing kind of guy.

Dave sighed, and reflected that it was time for a cup of tea – or coffee if he could get it. Wherever Nicholas had gone, it seemed he wasn't coming back soon, and it was eleven-thirty already. Dave had a quick shower in the en suite, and pulled on a clean t-shirt and pair of jeans. He was probably hopelessly under-dressed for an English manor house, but his self-imposed budget had only allowed for a couple of new nicer items, and he thought he'd better save them for best.

It was only as he collected his watch from the low table on his side of the bed that he realised Nicholas had left him a note.

Good morning, David – or good afternoon! Take your time, and come down when you're ready. Simon will keep an eye out for you, and I'll be somewhere around. Try the conservatory?

Nicholas x

There was an arrow pointing to the kiss, and a promise: *To be delivered in person ASAP.*

Dave grinned, took a breath, and headed out of the sanctuary of Nicholas's bedroom.

As Dave walked down the main staircase into the hall, Simon – the family butler – did indeed put his head out of a door concealed in the wood panelling, and then came out to offer a smile and a good morning. "I hope you slept well, Mr Taylor," he added without even a hint of innuendo, when Dave was all too conscious that everyone must be assuming he and Nicholas spent a fair amount of time and effort the previous night in … getting reacquainted. And their assumptions would be right, too.

"I slept very well, thank you, Simon."

"I'm glad to hear it –" After a moment's pause he finished with "David" rather than Mr Taylor.

"Actually, I know I said David yesterday, but is there any chance of you calling me Dave? You're probably the only person here who will."

"Dave, then," Simon obligingly agreed. "You're probably in need of tea or coffee, and perhaps a late breakfast of some kind?"

"Please, yeah, coffee would be great. And something to eat – though I guess it's almost lunchtime?"

"Come this way, Dave, and I'll show you the family kitchen. You can make your own drinks there at any time. Mrs Gilchrist – our cook and housekeeper – will be serving lunch to the family at one, but of course we'll make sure you have something to tide you over until then."

They'd gone through the concealed door, past an office which Dave thought must be Simon's, and then headed down a very plain staircase to the basement level, where they proceeded along an unadorned corridor. Dave had watched enough British TV to realise that this must be the servants' domain.

"Thanks," Dave said, following along. "I have to say, I am kind of hungry." It was the long sleep and irregular hours, he thought. Never mind the exercise he'd had both yesterday afternoon soon after he'd arrived and last night as well, all in the cause of getting reacquainted. At this point he needed sustenance just to cope.

The family kitchen turned out to be a room off the main kitchen – perhaps it was an old walk-in pantry or storage room converted – with a water cooler, an urn and a fridge, work benches and cupboards, and a high table with stools. Simon gave him a quick tour. "There will always be supplies here for you to make a hot drink and a sandwich, whenever you have need. And we tend not to serve formal lunches if it's just the family. By which I mean the family who live here."

"I get it," said Dave, his attention more on the sandwich Simon was making for him, and his hands wrapped warm around the mug of coffee Dave himself had already made while Simon was showing him round. "Thank you." He was rather relieved to know he'd be expected to fend for himself at some stage during an ordinary day.

Mrs Gilchrist came through from the main kitchen for a moment to be properly introduced; Dave stood and shook her hand before she headed back into the bustle.

"With everyone here," Simon explained, "that's twenty family members to cater for. Twenty-one now," he added with a nod towards Dave. "You'll understand if we're a bit stretched."

"Yeah," Dave said with a wry half-grin, in between bites of the sandwich. "Should have known it would be bad timing."

"On the contrary, it's excellent timing. Everyone is glad of the opportunity to meet you." Simon lowered his voice to confide, "The family are very happy that you came, you know. We all are."

"Thanks," he replied, hoping he had even a small chance of measuring up to whatever these people expected of him.

Simon tactfully changed the subject. "On most days I'm sure you'll be glad to know it's a great deal quieter than this! Nicholas and his father Lord Goring live here, along with Nicholas's oldest brother Robert and his family – his wife Penelope, and their children Robin and Isabelle."

That made him grin properly. "I actually have faces for all those names already."

"Well done," Simon said with a smile that bore not the faintest hint of irony or condescension. "You'll be fine, Dave. There's not a person here who doesn't welcome you."

Dave couldn't help but wonder how that could be. His scepticism must have been plain to read.

"Everyone adores Nicholas, and it's been rather obvious since his return from Australia that you're what makes him happiest."

Dave coloured up, and muttered something about Nicholas having found the butterflies.

"Yes, sir – but he also found you."

Two mugs of coffee, a sandwich and an apple later, Dave was feeling rather more human. "I'm sure you have things you're busy with," he said to Simon. "I shouldn't keep you."

"That's perfectly all right, Dave. I'll take you to Nicholas, shall I? I believe he's in the garden."

"He said something about the conservatory."

"Ah, he and Robin were finished in there by about ten-thirty."

"Right! Garden it is."

Simon led him down another corridor, and then up a narrow staircase to reach a cloakroom at the back of the house – which contained an extraordinary collection of different gum boots, a row of coats, and a laundry-style sink. From there, a door opened onto a large paved area. The basement had been rather a warren, but Dave's sense of direction hadn't quite failed him yet.

"I think you'll find that Nicholas is talking with Frank, who helps tend the garden," Simon said as he ushered Dave out onto the terrace. "He used to be the chauffeur, and he still maintains the cars, but he no longer drives."

"Ah," said Dave. The infamous chauffeur. Nicholas's first love. "Did he get too old to drive? Lose his licence?"

"No, sir. There was an accident. Nothing of any real account, but there was nerve trauma which affected his vision. He felt it best if he gave it up. A matter of safety for himself and the family."

"I thought – Nicholas spoke of him as having retired."

"Well, I suppose that's how we all considered it, in many ways, though it wasn't due to age." The two of them were strolling along the terrace very slowly now. Simon cast Dave a discreetly querying look.

Dave nodded. It was perfectly obvious what wasn't being said. "Nicholas told me about … how he felt for the man. Frank."

"Frank Brambell."

"Right. But I thought it was meant to be a big secret. Nicholas didn't tell me much – not even Frank's name. Didn't want to embarrass anyone. Does he know that you know?"

"I shouldn't think so."

The two of them came to a halt, and Dave considered Simon for a long moment. "You know pretty much everything that goes on around here, don't you?"

"You've nothing to fear from me on that account, Mr Taylor."

"No, of course not. I just meant – Well, can I talk to you? Sometime soon. I need to ask you about something. Nothing to do with Frank."

"Of course. Shall we say eleven tomorrow morning? I usually have a quiet hour or so before lunch."

"Perfect. Thanks." Dave added, "You really don't have to call me Mr Taylor, you know."

"Habit, sir, I'm sorry – long ingrained!" Simon led them off again, and they headed down some steps onto a lawn. He murmured, "David, I'm very glad that Nicholas told you about Frank."

And then, before Dave had time to even think about how to respond to that, Simon gestured towards the middle distance where a man was on his knees by a flower bed – and Nicholas was sitting cross-legged on the grass nearby wearing his Akubra but otherwise soaking up the sunshine. He looked so utterly relaxed.

"Thank you, Simon," said Dave. And Simon nodded his acknowledgement and headed back inside.

Dave took a moment to breathe in the fresh air and turn his face, as Nicholas was, to the sun. It was so much gentler here than in Australia. He liked it well enough, but figured it would take some getting used to. He set off across the lawn, watching his … whatever it was he and Nicholas were to each other. He doubted there were any words. Or none that wouldn't make him wince. Or blush.

Australians weren't meant to blush. They were going to put something in the Preamble to the Constitution about it.

Meanwhile, it seemed clear that Nicholas was basking in not just the sunshine but in Frank's presence, and in his own happiness, too. Dave liked to think that he himself might at least have something to do with the latter.

Nicholas finally saw him when Dave was about halfway across the lawn. He grinned impossibly bright, and scrambled up to his feet, jogged lightly over to meet him. There was confusion for a few moments of the most delightful kind. They were reaching for each other's hands and fumbling, not hugging but still drawing near and nearer; Dave was grinning like an idiot himself, they were both grinning too much to kiss, so they settled for resting temple against temple under the brim of Nicholas's Akubra and then twisting around, trying to see each other more clearly while staying in contact … It was ridiculous, really, and at last Nicholas just let out a joyous laugh, wrapped both of his arms tight around Dave's shoulders and gathered him in, and Dave wound his own arms around Nicholas's waist, and they just kind of clung and swayed together there as if they were utterly mad.

Which Dave supposed they were, really. In the best possible ways. This was love. If Dave had still had any qualms or questions, there could be no doubting the answers now.

Eventually Nicholas laughed again, and they broke apart – except that Nicholas kept one of Dave's hands in his, and tugged at it. "Come and meet Frank," he said, with a complete lack of guile.

"Sure," Dave replied easily. He didn't know if he was supposed to realise who Frank was, but that was fine. There was no need for any drama or fuss.

Frank was apparently weeding, grasping each invader in one gloved hand, and levering it out with a gardening fork in the other. He stopped what he was doing as Nicholas and Dave drew near, and stood, taking his gloves off. When Nicholas introduced them to each other, Frank shook Dave's hand with both of his own – and he called Dave 'sir' with a friendly smile. It seemed to be as Simon said, that everyone was happy to welcome him as Nicholas's … whatever. Future partner. There was no hint from Frank that there was anything particular about his relationship with Nicholas, but while the three of them exchanged inanities about the garden and the weather, Nicholas seemed both proud and bashful. And finally, when Dave happened to be turning to look back towards the house, he caught a glimpse from the corner of his eye of Frank winking broadly at Nicholas, as if to say 'Well done!' – and Nicholas gurgled a happy laugh in reply. Dave manfully pretended not to notice.

"*Anyway,*" said Nicholas rather heavily, as if needing to change the subject, "poor David has had to leave his beloved Land Cruiser behind in Australia –"

"Are you joking? I'm having it shipped out."

"So, *Frank*, I thought maybe you'd give him a tour of the cars sometime, and see if there's something that might distract him from the grief."

"Of course, Nicholas," Frank replied. "Tomorrow morning, perhaps, sir?"

"Um, after lunch would be better. If that doesn't get in the way of your work."

"Plans already?" Nicholas commented with a slightly quirked smile.

"Plans … jet lag …" Dave gestured vaguely: Who could possibly know?

They agreed that Nicholas would accompany Dave to the garage at around two–thirty the following afternoon. And then Frank added that if there were any motors that Dave took a shine to, there'd be no problem with him using them, working on them, driving them …

"Thanks," said Dave, quite genuinely. Though as he and Nicholas finally took their leave of Frank and started heading back towards the house, Dave complained, "I can't believe you want me to cheat on the Cruiser!"

"Aw, don't think of it like that … The Cruiser won't mind you having a meaningless holiday fling."

"Yeah, well, look how that worked out for you! And anyway," he continued, "if we're getting married or whatever, don't you want me to be the loyal type?"

"If … ?" Nicholas echoed, with a quiet little edge to it.

"Well, we are, aren't we?" Dave confirmed. "Getting married." He found himself literally scratching his head in puzzlement. "And I'm the loyal type. Whether that's Denise, or the Cruiser, or you … Wasn't that one of the first things you knew about me?"

Nicholas took Dave's hand, just very lightly, and stopped them both somewhere on the lawn between the flower beds and the terrace. "This got rather serious," he said with a solemn kind of humour. "I thought you'd enjoy seeing the cars, and maybe driving them. That's all."

"Yeah, that's fine," Dave replied, though he suspected there was more to it than that. "That's good."

"I really didn't mean it about you cheating on the Cruiser, you know."

Dave smiled. "That's even better."

Nicholas took a tiny step closer, suddenly seeming a little breathless. "I like you being loyal. I even liked that you were loyal to Denise – and still are!"

"I know." It was fine. He squeezed Nicholas's hand, and they turned to continue slowly on their way.

A long moment passed before Nicholas asked with deceptive lightness, "How long were you planning to stay?"

"Well …" He hardly knew how to answer that.

"I mean … you have a return ticket … ? Is it an open ticket, maybe?"

They hadn't talked about the future in anything but the most general terms. Dave cleared his throat, wondering if Nicholas could pick up on how nervous he was. Knowing that he probably could. "No, I don't."

"You don't – ?"

"Have a return ticket. But I *do* want to go back, right? I want – I'd really like it if we lived there. Nicholas, if you –"

"No, I want that, too. To live in Australia with you. In your home … ?"

"Yes. Please. Unless you –"

"No, I loved it there. I really did. Your family home."

"Good." Not that Dave had family any more, but it was the house in which he'd grown up. The house his parents had bought when they married. The house which, between the three of them over the years, they'd fixed up and made into something pretty special – though nothing to compare to an English manor house, of course.

"And – Well, if –" Now Nicholas cleared his throat. "Um – I don't understand. They let you into the country without a return airline ticket?"

"No. I, um – Well, I applied for a British passport before I left. I mean, I'm still Australian, but Dad was English, yeah? So I can be both, and I thought –"

"Oh, David!" Nicholas had stopped again, and was standing there staring at him with his eyes glowing. "That's marvellous!"

"It's one of the reasons I didn't come over right away. To be honest, it took me a while to realise I should, and then it took a few weeks to get the passport, but that was okay because I had to get things sorted out with the house. I did one trip I had booked, but there's another I'm meant to be doing in September."

"So we have until September?" It wasn't quite August yet.

"No, I've got – Well, there's a couple who help me out with the larger tour groups. They're gonna do this one for me."

Nicholas asked, kind of hushed, "How long were you planning to stay?"

"As long as it takes, I guess."

"Oh *God* ..." Nicholas looked almost more overcome than he'd been when they'd been announcing – in front of Nicholas's entire family – their intention to marry. "Thank you. Oh David, *thank you*."

Dave cast a look about him as if there'd be some answer to the nervousness he felt. He hadn't counted on this meaning so much to Nicholas. Except he'd known that it would, hadn't he? "I figured the passport – I mean, having British citizenship or whatever – would make things more straightforward."

"It will. Oh, I'm sure it will. And you'll stay while we're planning the ceremony and everything?"

He sighed, and ventured, "We're not talking about just swinging by the registry office next time we're in town, are we?"

Nicholas shook his head very solemnly. No. No, they were not.

"How long are we talking about?"

"Six months?"

"All right," he said stoically. Six months of – he assumed – living in a mansion house with an Earl, with nothing to do all day but plan a big gay wedding and be tempted to cheat on the Cruiser. Well, he didn't suppose that was so bad.

"Can you do that? Do you have other trips planned for later in the year?"

"No, most people want to head up north – to places more like Kakadu, you know? But once the Wet starts, there's no point."

After a moment, Nicholas said a bit brokenly, "Can we go sit down? Inside?"

"Of course. Are you okay?" Dave asked in concern, following Nicholas towards the nearest door while managing to usher him in at the same time.

"Yes. Yes, I'm fine. I just – need a cold drink. I don't like to get too hot."

"You never said … How on earth did you cope in Australia, then?"

"I don't know. I don't know. That was different. And it was winter there!" Nicholas led the way into the family living room, and headed for the discreet little bar area while swiping off the Akubra.

Dave watched carefully as Nicholas put together two tall tumblers of ice, bottled water and lime juice. He needed to learn this kind of thing, for both their sakes. Though he reflected that he'd never had to push Nicholas to drink enough water in Australia, as he'd often had to with other clients from cooler countries. Now he guessed something of why.

Nicholas brought the drinks over, and collapsed to sprawl on a sofa, glancing at the seat beside him to indicate Dave should join him. A moment passed during which Nicholas cooled down, and even Dave sipped appreciatively at his drink. Eventually he asked again, "All right?"

"Yes." Nicholas nodded gently, not lifting his head from the back of the sofa. "It was different in Australia. It was an adventure – and I was so happy! And it'll be fine when we go back there."

"Brisbane, though," Dave said with fresh misgivings. "It was still pretty warm, wasn't it? Compared to the kind of winters you're used to. And you don't know what it's like in the summer. It can be pretty tough, even for those of us who are used to it. It's not just the heat, it's the humidity."

"Don't let's worry about that for now."

"What, then? What was the matter?"

"I just –" Nicholas gazed at him, more utterly vulnerable than beseeching, though it had the same effect. "Three months, if you want. Not six. But – you know what I'm talking about. Once I've gone, I might not get to come back. And I've *loved* it here, David. I *love* my family, I've *chosen* to stay here, it's not because I had to –"

"Oh God," he muttered, distraught.

"It's all right, though," said Nicholas. "It's all right, because I love being with you even more."

Dave just reached to hold his hand.

"So we'll do this, all right? But let me have this time. Share this time with me, be part of it with me. Let me make a bit of a fuss. I'll say goodbye properly. And then we can start our new life together, and it will be fine."

"Will it?" he asked.

"Yes," Nicholas replied with great certainty. "It will be *perfect*."

Dave groaned a little, completely out of words. And then he put the drink down, and crawled along the sofa to lie by his love with his head on Nicholas's chest listening to that strong patient heartbeat. Praying that it would never ever stop.

Late that night they made love in Nicholas's bed with the lights out, but with the curtains and windows open letting in the moonlight and the fresh night air. Soon – as he had a few times already in the past thirty-six hours – Nicholas was kneeling between Dave's thighs, rolling a condom onto himself. "We're getting married …" Nicholas mused. "We'll get the tests done. We won't have to use these any more." After a moment he added, "I've never fucked without one."

"You'll like it," said Dave.

"Will I?"

"I'm guessing … it'll be intense."

"Guessing?"

Dave shrugged. "Me and Denise – there was never anyone else. Didn't need them. I liked the – skin against skin. No barriers. Me and you –"

Nicholas belatedly understood. "You haven't had the chance to find out." He sat back on his heels, considering Dave with a bit of a sour twist to his mouth. "You want to fuck me, David?"

"Wouldn't be many men who'd say no to that. But not if you don't want to."

"I've never – I've never actually done that." Nicholas drifted further into thought, his brow wrinkling in a frown, though his cock still stood proud and rubber-wrapped between them. "Don't know why, really ..."

Dave wondered if he was misremembering. "You offered once before, didn't you? In Charleville, the night you first fucked me."

"Did I ... ? Well, I suppose ... it felt like a night on which *something* significant should happen." Nicholas appeared rather troubled by the recollection.

"Hey, if it's not your thing, it's not a problem," Dave assured him, shifting up onto his elbows and reaching for the man. "Come on, don't leave me hanging here."

Nicholas's attention returned, and he slowly eased forward into place, shifting over Dave as if he were prowling, his focus becoming curious, engaged. "You like this, yes?"

He shivered, already losing himself. "Yes. Already lost count – since I got here –"

A gut-deep groan wrenched itself out of Nicholas. "I'm – Oh God! Maybe I shouldn't –"

"You bloody well should," Dave insisted in a vehement whisper.

"Shouldn't overdo it," Nicholas was muttering, even as they both moved into place. They already knew this so very well. "Don't want to hurt you."

"Don't care if you make me feel it, Nicholas. Never thought about it before –"

"Before ... ?"

"Before there was you." His thighs gripping either side of Nicholas's waist, his stomach muscles curling him up, lifting his hips, ready to receive the man. "Before you made me such a slut for it."

Nicholas groaned again, and surged forward. "You're sure?" he asked, hesitating at the last possible moment.

"Do it," said Dave. And they both cried out as Nicholas impaled him.

two

Dave woke at a far more reasonable hour the next morning, and shared a late breakfast with Nicholas, before making his excuses and heading off to meet Simon at eleven. He figured he'd tell Nicholas about it afterwards.

Simon was waiting for him in the main hall, and showed Dave through to the neat little office just beyond the hidden door. "How may I help you, David?" he asked in a warm yet professional manner once they'd both sat down.

"It's about Nicholas," Dave blurted out.

Simon didn't even blink. "Yes, of course."

"It's about – He told me about – about the brain aneurysm, you see. And I wanted to make sure that I understood. I figured – you'd have made it your job to know what to do, what to be careful of. I want to make sure I know that, too."

About halfway through this stumbling explanation, Simon had begun smiling softly, and after a brief pause he said, "Nicholas has made a very good choice in you, hasn't he?"

Dave coloured up, and remained silent, though to himself he fervently swore, *'God, I hope so.'*

"If I know anything about you, Mr Taylor," Simon continued, "I would guess you've already done your homework."

"Yes. I know that only one in twelve- or thirteen-thousand people have a ruptured aneurysm each year in England."

"And in Nicholas's case, it's a small aneurysm, sir. A diameter of less than seven millimetres."

"Oh. Good." He hadn't known that. Cerebral aneurysms could measure even five centimetres or more, and of course the larger they got the more dangerous they were.

"He has it monitored, and he's on medication. I'm sure you'll support him in that, though Nicholas takes the matter quite as seriously as you'd wish him to."

"But he hasn't had surgery to fix it."

"The balance of risks doesn't make surgery worthwhile – under present circumstances. It might become more desirable later. But I'm afraid that even surgery wouldn't entirely fix the problem, David; it would only reduce the likelihood of rupture."

Dave nodded. Things weren't quite as bleak as he'd feared, though it was bad enough. "The problem is …" he slowly continued, "if something happens, if it ruptures, there probably won't be anything I can do about it. And I hate that."

"Of course there'll be plenty to do, sir," Simon briskly replied. "You'll need to immediately call for an ambulance. The emergency number is 999 here in England."

"Yes."

"He will be – I'm sorry, sir, but you'd best be prepared. Nicholas will probably be in a great deal of pain. They describe it as … beyond the most excruciating of headaches. You'll need to take care of him. He'll be disoriented. He might lapse into unconsciousness. And he might vomit, so you'll need to make sure his airways remain clear. But I know you have a current first aid certificate, so you'll know what to do."

"Of course. Yes." Dave swallowed, not liking at all to think of Nicholas in agonising pain, and probably terrified as well. But Simon was right – it was better to imagine it now, and not be shocked or panicked into being good for nothing at the time. "The – the recovery position. Will be useful."

"Just so. He'll be in good hands with you, David, until the medical personnel arrive. I have no fears for him on that account. And I'm sure he'll find your presence a great comfort."

He asked, "Is there anything else I should know?"

"I don't think so, sir. It seems you're aware of the important matters, and I'm sure your research has detailed far more."

Dave was quiet for a time. Mentally girding himself. Hoping that such preparation would never be called on. At last he thought to say, "If his family are concerned – Would you reassure them? I'll do my very best for him. I really will."

"They know as much, sir, but I'll tell Lord Goring that we've spoken, if I may."

"Of course."

Another pause lengthened. Dave must have been looking a bit lost, as Simon softly said, "Don't worry unnecessarily, Dave. Nicholas leads a healthy life. He does what he can to minimise the potential for problems. And he's still young. There'll be time to worry more when he's older."

"I hope so. Yes."

"There's every chance that he'll enjoy a long life. Whatever happens, though, if he's shared his life with you, then he'll want for nothing more. He'll have no regrets."

Dave had coloured up again, but he glanced at Simon and nodded his thanks.

"And you, sir?" Simon asked lightly. "Are you all right? It can't be easy for you. Nicholas isn't the only person for us to worry about."

Which Dave appreciated, he really did, though he brushed off Simon's concern. "Oh, *I'll* be all right. Like you said: nothing more. I don't want for anything more."

"Then bless you, Dave, for being your own good self."

At which point Dave stood, muttered his thanks, shook Simon's hand, and made himself scarce.

There didn't seem to be any order in which the extended family sat down for meals, with three exceptions: Richard, the earl, always sat at the head of the table; Robert, his eldest son and heir, always sat somewhere around the middle; and Robert's wife Penelope always sat at the far end. Dave assumed that Penelope had become the lady of the house after Nicholas's mother died a few years before.

Otherwise, people sat quite randomly, depending on whim or on who they were already having a conversation with. It had felt a bit disorienting at first, but Dave soon decided he liked the informality – especially when contrasted with the dauntingly old dining room, where they were surrounded by the sort of tapestries and paintings Dave associated with the dustiest museums. There was a great long table set with fine china that put the set he'd inherited from his grandmother to shame, and glasses that were probably crystal or something – different sizes and shapes for different drinks – and cutlery that was probably real silver. Still, everyone seemed far more concerned about having fun – and talking over each other and making sure the kids were okay – than bothering over whether Dave was using the right knife.

As they gathered for lunch that day, Richard came into the room just after Dave and Nicholas, and murmured, "Perhaps you'd sit by me today,

David."

"Oh. Sure. Thanks." He looked at Nicholas's father, and saw at a glance that Simon must have already told Richard of his conversation with Dave. Richard looked back at him with solemn gratitude, and nodded. Then a sweeping gesture invited him to sit at the earl's right – which even Dave knew was a place of privilege. He'd been invited to sit there for the first family dinner he'd attended, as well.

Nicholas didn't seem to make anything of it, other than perhaps accepting this as Dave's due. He followed Dave, though chatting away to his sister Lilibet, and claimed the seat to Dave's right by standing there with his hands on the back of the chair. Young Robin made the most of Nicholas's distraction, however, by nipping in to sit down beside Dave.

"Oh! Cheeky!" cried Nicholas – who promptly made sure to claim the next chair along. Lilibet sat on his far side, and picked up the briefly interrupted conversation.

Robin chuckled in glee, and grinned winningly at Dave. Robin was all of ten years old, and the most delightfully innocent flirt. Dave smiled back at him, and winked, which made the boy chuckle again.

"Robin," said Richard, "perhaps you'd let Nicholas and David enjoy being together for this little while. I suppose it mightn't mean very much to some, but they recently became engaged."

Nicholas glanced at Dave, though he must already know that Dave didn't mind. It wasn't as if Dave didn't have plenty of Nicholas's undivided attention at other times ... "It's all right, Father. I can share. *To a point*," Nicholas added in ironically severe tones to Robin.

"You'd think Robin would be jealous," one of the other adults commented. A sister–in–law, Dave thought. Which would make her Amanda or Christine.

"You'd think he'd hate him," someone else down the far end of the table muttered under his breath.

Robert commented, "Oh, I think Robin saw pretty quickly that he'd lost that one – and if you can't beat 'em, join 'em!"

And Robin was still beaming at Dave almost as broadly as Nicholas did, apparently perfectly used to being teased about his partialities. Dave laughed, and chucked him under the chin – and wondered if Robin mightn't faint with happiness.

Once they'd all been served and were more settled, Richard asked Dave and Nicholas, "Have you two made any plans?"

"Uh – Tour of the garage this afternoon," Dave supplied. Too late, he realised what Richard really meant, and feebly concluded, "I hear you have quite a collection of cars."

"We do. Rather an indulgence in this day and age, I'm afraid, but please make yourself at home there, if that's where your interests lie."

"Thank you. I will."

After a moment Nicholas answered the real question. "I know it's not much time to organise everything, Father, but we thought we'd hold the wedding in three months, if that's all right –"

"Six months," Dave quietly put in. "We talked about *six* months."

"No, it's fine," Nicholas reassured him. "Three months. Apart from anything else, I'd like to have the reception in the garden, and late October is probably doable, but winter certainly isn't!" Upon which thought he got distracted by his own fancies. "Although what if it snowed … ? That would be amazing! A real white wedding! Like in *Camelot*, you know? With the sled and the furs …"

"A *white* wedding," someone muttered, and someone else snorted – and Dave felt like hitting them, family or not. He remembered Denise once remarking, '*Everyone* deserves to wear white on their wedding day, if that's what they want.'

Penelope said, rather more reasonably, "Nicholas, I don't think even you could stage manage the weather, I'm sorry, and a slushy wedding would be so *dreary*."

Nicholas laughed under his breath, though it sounded a bit forced. "All right, the end of October. Reception in the garden, if we can."

"And the ceremony?" Richard asked.

"Just a few of us in town, I thought – the two of us and witnesses – and then come back to everyone here." He turned on his seat towards Dave. "We haven't talked about this yet. You'd better tell us what you'd like."

"It's fine," Dave said. "Sounds good so far." Though he took the opportunity to lean in closer over Robin's head and mutter, "Don't have to wear white, do I? Or *do* I … ?"

Nicholas laughed more genuinely, and answered so that everyone might hear him. "No, we'll wear morning suits. You'll look very dapper, I promise."

"*Mourning* suits … ?"

"No, uh – I –" Nicholas gestured at himself, as if about to launch into an explanation, before realising it was hopeless. "We can talk about that later. I'll show you mine – though of course I'd like for us all to have new ones."

"Right," said Dave, a bit shortly. Hadn't he already told Nicholas that he'd never once worn a suit? If he hadn't worn one for his dad's funeral, then he didn't see why he should wear one now.

The pause threatened to become a difficult silence, until Richard smoothly asked, "Wouldn't you like to hold the ceremony here as well, Nicholas? That would seem appropriate."

"Ah, but we'd have to apply for a licence to hold weddings and partnership ceremonies, and that would mean *anyone* could get hitched here, so – unless you want to go into business as an event venue … ?"

"Ah. Maybe not. What a pity! It would have been nice to have it all here."

"It'll be nice in town, too. Do you remember they have rooms set up at the old courthouse?"

"Yes, of course."

"There's the Disraeli Room on weekdays," Nicholas chattered on, "and Midsomer Court on Fridays and weekends. Midsomer Court has the nicer name, but it looks kind of plain judging from the photos. Though there's this terrific light coming in through the high windows … The Disraeli Room is older, and more what I imagined. Like I said, though, it depends on the exact day we're doing this …" He finally trailed off, seeing that everyone was watching him in amusement. "What?"

"You've researched this, then," Robert commented.

"Yeah."

"Wondered what you were both doing up there in your room for all those hours …" This was greeted with guffaws from various adults around the table.

Nicholas sniffed and said primly, "David was sleeping off his jet lag, so I had to occupy myself *somehow* …"

"All right, all right," said Richard, quite amicably. "That's enough of that. Simon, perhaps it's time to clear the plates?"

"Oh!" Nicholas exclaimed as they were walking through the house after lunch. "I can show you …" He took Dave's hand and led him round a corner and into what seemed to be a study or maybe even a small library. A profusion of framed photos covered a great deal of one wall. Nicholas only took a moment to find the one he was looking for. "See? This was Robert and Penelope's wedding. We're all in morning suits. It's what's expected, it's traditional, but really I just love it. Everyone looks so smart!"

"Well," Dave admitted, "you *do* look smart." All the men in the photo looked very – whatever that word Nicholas used was. Dapper. They were very dapper – and especially Nicholas with his tall slim frame and his broad shoulders. But even Robert looked great, despite the fact he tended to appear as if he'd just been hauled backwards out of a rugby scrum – and the rather sturdy Richard was every inch the Earl.

"I jump at any excuse to wear Morning Grey, to be honest – I prefer that to the traditional black jacket and striped trousers like Robert and my father are in here, and I figure it's our wedding so we can just go with the grey if we want to – but we can add a bit of colour to things with the ties and waistcoats, if you like. Hey! Maybe, like, a rainbow of colours – subtle colours, I mean, but each of us in a different colour of the rainbow." Nicholas nudged him with an elbow. "Gay pride, you know?"

"Yeah. I get it."

After a pause that became a bit too lengthy, Nicholas said, "Well, we don't have to wave the whole Gay Pride flag thing, but *God* you'll look gorgeous in a morning suit, David. I promise you will."

"They have *tails*," he complained.

"A cutaway skirt," said Nicholas.

"A skirt! Like *that* makes it better." Dave sighed, and took a step back. Considered Nicholas, and tried to judge just how important this was to him compared to how important it was to himself. They seemed equally determined at this point. "I think I told you already," Dave eventually said, "I've never worn a suit before."

"There's a first time for everything," Nicholas remarked – and he made his point by complacently patting Dave's rear. "As well you know."

"Nicholas. I just don't do suits."

"But –"

"You look great," Dave said, indicating the photo again. "You really do. But my idea of dressing up is the white shirt and jeans I wore on the first day I came here."

Nicholas's mouth pinched up unhappily. "You're not suggesting," he slowly responded, "that you wear *jeans* for our wedding ... ?"

"Well, no," said Dave, privately thinking that actually he'd be perfectly happy with the kind of wedding where *everyone* wore jeans. "I don't know, all right? Not jeans. But ... not a suit either."

Nicholas let out a gusted sigh. "All right. Well. We'll have to think about that, then."

"*You* can still wear a morning suit, can't you? If that's what makes you happy?"

That earned him a smile, tiny but genuine, and Nicholas reached to hold Dave's hand again. "All right. Come on," he continued rather more robustly. "Let's not keep Frank waiting."

Dave was given a tour of the old stable block which had been converted to, among other things, a working garage and a display area for an impressive range of cars. Frank led the way, while Dave followed with Nicholas tagging along after him. Dave and Nicholas held hands the entire time. Perhaps they needed the mutual reassurance. Frank seemed like a fairly quiet man by nature, but it didn't take much to get him talking. He provided a potted history for each car, and lovingly listed both their strengths and their weaknesses. He had polishing cloths stowed in a pocket, and at the slightest provocation would haul them out, one in each hand, and buff the paintwork and chrome.

When they reached the Rolls Royce Silver Cloud, Dave was way more impressed than he thought he'd be. "That's something," was his verdict.

"Yes, sir, it is."

Dave turned to Nicholas. "You said we'll be going into town for the ceremony ... ?"

"Yes. We'll be going to Beaconsfield."

"Will we go in this ... ?"

Nicholas was suddenly beaming again. "*God*, yes!"

"There you go. Got that sorted."

And with a pealing laugh, Nicholas slid his arms around Dave's waist, and clung on, tucking his head in beside Dave's like they'd never be parted again.

"And for the honeymoon, sir?" Frank smoothly asked after a moment or two. "Will the two of you be driving somewhere?"

"I don't know! Nicholas? I haven't had much of a chance to think about any of this."

"Because I thought, sir, that you might like to take the Jaguar XJ."

"Oh!" Dave looked back down the line of gleaming bonnets to where the Jaguar waited, ready to prowl. "In that case, yes, I think we *will* be driving somewhere, absolutely!"

"I'll have you added to the family's insurance policy, sir. Shouldn't take more than a phone call."

"Thank you. Really, thanks. That's great."

Nicholas clung on even harder, and Dave found himself pressing a kiss to the man's dark hair, just instinctively and without embarrassment.

"So, then you have *that* sorted out as well, sir," said Frank with a certain sense of satisfaction.

It seemed, for now at least, that the wedding was the main topic of conversation for the entire family – though Nicholas was no doubt the only one of them to find it so endlessly fascinating. Over dinner that evening, Richard said, "David, forgive me for not asking before. I assume you'll be inviting guests from Australia?"

"Oh. Yes." They'd already established that Dave had no 'real' family any more, being the only child of parents who'd died – his mother when he was just a boy. But that didn't mean he didn't have *family*. "My friend Denise," he said, "and her husband and daughter. Well, Zoe is still a baby, but she can travel, can't she?" He looked about him, figuring that someone in the Goring family would know the answer to that. "She'll be … getting on for six months old in October."

Penelope said, "I'm sure that'll be fine, David."

There were other assenting murmurs around the table. Someone chipped in, "Prudence came to Germany with us when she wasn't even *three* months." – "Oh, that explains it," someone else teased.

"Zoe is a healthy baby … ?" Penelope asked, smoothly ignoring the repartee.

188 | Of Dreams and Ceremonies

"Yes. Well, as far as I know," he added, though he figured that Denise would have told him if there was anything very wrong. Zoe was his godchild, after all – on an informal basis anyway. "She seemed to be thriving last Saturday!" God, he thought … was it really less than a week ago that he'd been in Australia?

"I'm sure she'll be fine. It will be lovely to meet your friends."

"And there's Charlie, as well," Dave continued. "I'd like to invite Charlie. I don't know that he'd want to bring anyone. And that's probably about it."

"Excellent," said Richard. "They'd be very welcome to stay here with us, if that's what they'd like. There's plenty of room, certainly for another four."

"Oh. Thank you. That's very good of you."

"Perhaps you'll let them know. You must phone them whenever you like. Nicholas, we really ought to be sending out invitations, as soon as you've decided on a date."

"I'm on it, Father!"

There was some wry chuckling and comments such as "Of course he is" from around the table.

Nicholas ignored them, and was instead contemplating Dave. After a moment, he asked, "Who'll be your witness?"

"Denise." This was met with a nod, as if Nicholas had known the answer all along. Dave asked, "Who'll be yours?"

"Robert." Nicholas looked across the table at his eldest brother. "If you will … ?"

"I'd be honoured," said Robert in low fervent tones. The two of them each stood, and shook hands across the table. Such an honestly felt moment moved everyone, and there was a respectful silence for a while as the brothers sat back down again.

Dave sighed, and reflected that if it was evening here in England then it must be early morning in Australia. He'd see Simon about phoning Denise once dinner was over, though he'd have to figure out how to cover the costs of the call. Denise hadn't heard his news yet, though he knew she wouldn't be surprised. And in any case … he missed her.

"You little beauty!" was Denise's reaction to his announcement. "I knew it!"

"I know you knew it. And you were right."

"Still. That was fast work."

Dave could hear his own chuckle echoing down the line. "Mate, I was engaged within about five minutes of walking into the house."

She made some more jubilant noises, and hollered out the news to Vittorio, before at last saying rather more seriously, "Davey, I'm really happy for you, mate."

"Thanks, Denny." He smiled, imagining her smiling. Not that he had to imagine it, really, as he could hear it in her voice.

"And you're happy, right?" Denise continued.

"Yeah. Yeah, I am."

"So, have you, like, started talking about dates and things … ? I suppose it's a bit soon to be getting into all that!"

Dave snorted. "*Yeah*, we've been talking dates … The ceremony's at eleven a.m. on the thirty-first of October, in the Disraeli Room at the old magistrate's courthouse in Beaconsfield. Which is somewhere near here, in Buckinghamshire. We haven't formally registered our notice, or whatever it is, but Nicholas called to make sure the time was available, and we're going in to fix it up as soon as we can. Apparently we can't do that until I've been here for nine days, or whatever."

There was a brief pause, before Denise said, "Oh."

"After the ceremony, the reception's in the garden back here at the house." Then he burst out, "God, *tell* me you'll be here, Denise. Tell me you'll come. With Zoe and Vittorio, too, of course. I'm gonna ask Charlie as well. You can all stay here at the house – Richard said you should. The Earl, I mean. My future father-in-law! Denise –"

"Of *course* we'll be there, Davey. Of *course* we will."

"And you'll be my witness, like you said."

"Oh, Davey mate," she said quietly, almost sorrowfully, "of course I will. I'll *always* stand beside you. That's what I said, and I meant it."

"Good," he said. "Good."

Another pause lengthened. Eventually Denise asked, "Are you all right, Davey? I mean, I know you're happy about Nicholas, but … are you all right otherwise?"

"I guess."

"Now, come on, don't clam up like a big dumb Aussie male on me now. You're made of sterner stuff, mate."

In almost no time at all, Dave was confessing, "I just don't like being the centre of attention, you know? I mean, if I'd been marrying you, *you'd* be the centre of attention, cos you'd be the bride! But here –"

"Are you telling me you feel like you're the bride in this, Davey?"

"*No. God*, no. I'm not. And I'm not talking about what goes on in bed or anything –"

"Uh huh."

"Just … God, they're *all* here. The entire family. Not to mention the servants, for God's sake. Servants! And everyone's curious, and when they're around Nicholas hardly talks about anything other than the wedding, and –"

"Are they treating you okay? Is anyone giving you grief?"

"No grief at all. They're all really happy about it. They're *staggeringly* open-minded about the whole gay thing."

"Well, look. Don't you think it will be, like, a seven-day wonder? If they're that cool, then it won't take long before you just fit in, and you're part of the family already. Then it won't be such an issue, right?"

"Right," he agreed, though doubtingly.

"Just give it a few more days, love. Once the planning's properly underway for the wedding, and once people are used to having you around, I bet it'll be fine. And in the meantime, maybe you and Nicholas could go do some sightseeing, or something? Find an excuse to get out of the house for a while, you know? With just the two of you."

Dave grinned down the phone. "Denny, you're brilliant. Of course that's what we'll do. That's just *brilliant*."

"Any time, mate."

"So, look," he said. "Seeing as you're such a genius, you have to help me find something to wear for the wedding that isn't jeans and isn't a morning suit."

"A *mourning* suit?"

"I know, right? That's what I said!" And he explained the situation, and how he didn't want to let Nicholas down, but he just couldn't wear a suit, and eventually Denise said very seriously, "Let me think about it, all right? We'll come up with something, I promise. But give me a few days to think about it."

"God, thank you *so much*," he said. "Love you, Denny."

"Love you, too, mate. Always."
And finally they said their goodbyes and hung up.

three

The next day, with Nicholas happily curled up beside him in the passenger seat, Dave carefully drove the Jaguar XJ out of the garage and down the gravel driveway. Frank stood there watching them go – Dave glimpsed him in the wing mirror – Frank's smile happy yet with a slight poignancy to it which Dave wondered was more about Nicholas or more about the car.

"Okay. Where are we going?" Dave asked as they reached the road that ran past the mansion house.

"You wanted sky –"

"Well, just a bit more of it. You know what Aussie skies are like." England's skies were mild and pleasant but seemed so much smaller. Which was probably impossible, but also undeniably true.

"It's all right. I can give you sky. Turn left," said Nicholas. Once Dave had done so, Nicholas announced, "We're going to Ivinghoe Beacon."

Which didn't mean anything at all to Dave, but between the satnav and Nicholas's supplementary guidance, he got them there safely – and the Jaguar proved to be a sinfully smooth way of doing so. Ivinghoe Beacon turned out to be the last hill of a long curving range. Once they'd climbed the chalky paths to the top, then all of Buckinghamshire and probably a fair bit beyond it lay spread before them like a patchwork quilt in greens and browns. Importantly, there was plenty of sky, and with their backs turned to the other hills, it felt as if the earth had risen beneath their feet and thrust them halfway up into the air.

The two of them ended up sitting on the grassy slope just beyond the edge of the hilltop, just before it got steep. Nicholas lay back to dream up into the sky, while Dave simply gazed at the horizon, so very much more distant than the other English horizons he'd encountered so far.

After a while, Nicholas's hand slipped into Dave's, and they continued there connected in a companionable silence, not caring if they startled the nearby model plane enthusiasts who were making great use of updrafts on the north side of the hill. Occasionally a plane swooped past them or circled above. Not exactly butterflies, but they'd do!

Eventually Nicholas asked, "What d'you think?"

"It's great. Thanks. Just what I needed."

A brief pause before Nicholas continued, "This is one end of an old path called the Ridgeway. It leads down across England all the way to Avebury in Wiltshire. There's a stone circle there that you've probably heard of, or seen pictures of. Though I think the path originally continued on right down to the coast in Devon or Dorset or somewhere. It's been used for thousands of years."

"Cool," said Dave.

"I know it's not anything like your Australian songlines – it's more of a practical road, really – but I thought you'd like it."

"I do." He clasped Nicholas's hand tighter for a moment, as the man seemed to need reassurance. "And you know, songlines were practical, too."

Nicholas abruptly sat up. "God, you've only been here a few days, and you're already finding it a bit much, aren't you? I mean, my family and everything."

"Well," he started slowly … "I guess I am used to living on my own. And in my own house. But that's okay."

"It's not usually like this. Even when we try to all get together, it's rare that everyone's there. But it won't be for much longer. Lilibet and her lot are heading home tomorrow, and Michael is, too, because of work, though Amanda and the kids are staying on for an extra couple of days. It won't be long before it's just, well, the six of us – seven, with you – and Simon and so on. I suppose even that's going to be too much for you at times!"

"It'll be fine," Dave insisted. "Just maybe if we can do this sort of thing every now and then. If it can be just us two sometimes."

"Of course. Of course. We can go chasing butterflies, while the weather's still warm."

"Sure. I'll drive you wherever you like. See a bit of the country."

"What else d'you want to do?"

"You," said Dave in his best deadpan. "I want to do you."

Nicholas snorted. "And in between times … ?"

"Whatever you're doing. Planning the wedding and all that. Potting orchids. Teasing Robin. Housework! I'm used to looking after my own place, remember. Do the servants do *everything* for you?"

"Not everything, no."

"So I'll help with that – or the cars, or the garden. And otherwise we can just hang out."

"For three months?"

Dave shrugged. "Well, we just hung out at the waterhole, didn't we? That wasn't so bad."

"It wasn't, was it?" Nicholas sighed. "And what you said before? You must know … I want it to be just the two of us."

"I know you love your family, Nicholas. I know you need to be with them, too. It's obvious you all get on really well." He sighed. "I really get that, you know. I don't remember much about my mum, but I know we were happy. And I adored my dad. He was my best friend." Dave confessed, "I don't know that I'd have been willing to leave him behind. Even for you."

"Oh, *David*." Nicholas leaned in closer, and wrapped a firm arm around Dave's shoulders. "It'll break my heart to leave my father, like I know it would have broken yours. But there's one major difference."

"What's that?"

"Your father only had you. It was just the two of you, and Denise. Of course you couldn't have left him. My father has three other sons and a daughter, and all but one are married or as good as, and they've all got children. He'll hardly even notice I'm gone."

"You know he will," Dave said roughly, "cos you're the one he loves best."

Nicholas echoed in a forlorn little voice, "I'm the one he loves best."

"But he's a really decent guy, isn't he? He wants you to be happy. More than anything."

"And I'm happy with you, David. I'm happiest with you."

"I know." And they sat together there, hand in hand, halfway up in the sky.

Dave wasn't sure what woke him up that night. Nicholas was at his computer with the desk lamp on, but that wasn't anything very unusual. What with the last lingering effects of Dave's jet lag, and their spontaneous bouts of sex and napping, neither of them were keeping regular hours. But Nicholas wasn't just reading or surfing or answering emails – he was upset about something. Dave could tell from his edgy posture, if nothing else.

"Hey, what's up?" Dave murmured, shifting onto his elbows and trying to focus properly. "Nicholas?"

"Nothing. It's fine." Nicholas turned his head to offer a smile which was patently false. "It's fine, David. Go back to sleep."

Bugger that for an idea. Dave hauled himself up out of the bed, and padded over to rest his hands on Nicholas's shoulders, to lean in and find out what had troubled his love. He wasn't very surprised to discover an Australian Government website on the screen, and specifically a page titled *Visas, Immigration and Refugees*. "Ah. That's something I haven't looked into yet, I have to say. Except I worked out that at least they treat us like any other de facto couple. They'll give us a fair go, Nicholas, even if they don't consider us married."

The man looked up at him woefully, with his hands knotted together in his lap. "They want us to have lived together for twelve months before I can apply for a visa as your partner, and I doubt they'll count the time we spent together in Australia. I'd been thinking we could go live there right after our honeymoon, but if – Well, I know you can't stay here with me for a whole year. You have a business to run! Not to mention a life."

"Nah, there has to be a way. Look –" Dave glanced around, but he already knew there wasn't another straight–back chair in the room. "Look, bring that over here and sit with me. We'll work this out."

Dave ended up tucked into an armchair, with Nicholas curled up beside him with his thighs across Dave's lap, and the computer balanced somehow between them. "Okay," said Dave. "So, you need a Partner visa, right?"

"Yes. I can apply for a temporary one either while we're here or while we're in Australia, and it lasts for two years, and then if we're still together –"

"Which we will be."

"– which we will be, they'll consider making it permanent."

"So far, so good."

"We have to prove that we have a real relationship."

Various untoward thoughts drifted through his head. "Um …"

Nicholas shook with a weak chuckle. "Mind out of the gutter, David Taylor. I'm talking statements from friends, and a joint bank account."

"We'll go open one tomorrow."

"But there's still this twelve–month rule. I can't ask you to stay here with me, and my current visa only lets me stay in Australia for up to three months at a time … I don't see how we're going to even make this work at all!"

"I realise there are going to be hoops we need to jump through, but they can't have made it completely impossible!"

"Can't they?" Nicholas asked darkly.

"Show me the page." And Dave watched as Nicholas clicked through a number of screens before he settled on *Eligibility*, and scrolled down. "So … there's a waiver of the twelve months if we have children, if your partner – that's me – holds a humanitarian visa – which obviously I don't – or … if we've registered our de facto relationship."

"But that's in Australia. The civil partnership doesn't count!"

"All right," Dave said soothingly. "No worries. Let's see if we can do this registration thing as well." He freed his arm from around Nicholas's waist, opened a new tab in the browser, and soon found the right pages on the Queensland Government site. He read through them – silently this time – and concluded, "This will work. Only one of us has to already live there, and there's nothing to say we couldn't apply right away. And that means we can see about waiving the twelve months."

Nicholas was still gazing at him rather woefully, as if convinced it was never going to happen.

Dave gathered his thoughts. "Tell me why this won't work, then: We go ahead with the civil partnership ceremony. That's got to count as proof of our commitment, if nothing else. After the honeymoon, we travel to Australia. You still have your short–term visa from when you came out in May, right? So you can travel on that. As soon as we're settled, we register our relationship. Then you apply for a Partner visa. And we get on with life."

Hope was dawning on Nicholas's mutable face, though he warned, "It costs almost four thousand dollars to apply."

Dave didn't even blink. "So? I've got the money – and I'd pay a damned sight more than that to keep you with me."

Nicholas began smiling helplessly.

"It'll work!" Dave insisted.

But then the dawning smile faltered. "No, it won't. I can't stay longer than three months on my tourist visa, and they take up to six months to process a Partner visa application!"

Dave's face fell, too, for a moment – but then he rallied. "Look, if they're going to take that long, that's not our problem, is it? Surely there's a way of applying to extend your visa, or getting some other kind of temporary visa – all completely legit – while we're waiting for the outcome."

The outcome.

The words hung between them for a long moment. Nicholas whispered, "What if they don't approve it?"

"They will."

"But what if they don't?"

"Well, I'm a British citizen, too, remember? I'll come live here with you. Maybe not *here* here," he added, casting a glance at the huge old mansion house surrounding them. "But, you know. *Here*."

"You'd really give up Australia … ?"

"For you, Nicholas," Dave said, in deceptively light tones, "I'd even give up Australia."

They stared at each other solemnly. Nicholas's eyes grew damp, and Dave's started prickling a little.

"So," Dave continued rather more robustly, "the Department of Immigration doesn't scare me. It'll cost a bit, and take a bit of work, but we'll jump through the hoops. And in the meantime we can have fun gathering evidence to prove our relationship. Like …" He cast around him, but didn't have to look far. There was a tiny camera lens in the lid of the laptop. "Like photos. We can take a photo of us here together right now, and it'll be date-stamped and everything. And we already have a couple of others, don't we? Lilibet took photos of us on that first night with your dad, and you took one of us with your phone when we were on the Beacon today."

By this time Nicholas was grinning in delight. "We'll take a photo every day!" he said. "You know, one a day, but at different times and places." His long pale fingers were calling up the laptop's camera even as he spoke. "And I could start up a blog! Yes, that's what I'll do. I'll blog every day, about us, and about all of what we're going through. That'll be proof, won't it?"

"It sounds *perfect*."

Nicholas tucked his head in beside Dave's, adjusted the angle of the computer, and they both grinned while the camera faked a shutter sound. There wasn't enough light in the room for a quality photo, but their happiness came shining through sure enough. "That really is perfect," said Nicholas, so quietly that he himself might not have been aware of it. He carefully saved the photo, and then closed the laptop's lid. "Let's go to bed," he said, in rather more normal tones.

"You," said Dave, "always with the good ideas …"

"Ah, but in this case, it definitely takes two."

It wasn't that night but on another one not long after, that Dave felt like rewarding Nicholas. Dave was supposed to be the organised one of the pair of them, but Nicholas had been as good as his word; he'd set up his blog on wordpress.com, chosen a theme he liked, and diligently made an entry every day, each featuring a photograph of the two of them. He'd even created extra entries to cover the preceding few days, though being absolutely scrupulous about not fudging the date and time stamps on either the photos or the posts – and he was planning to also start a sequence of posts telling his story about how they'd first met and got together. His writing style was charmingly chatty and easy to read, no matter whether he was talking about Dave or their wedding plans or the visa rigmarole, describing where they'd gone that day, or waxing lyrical about butterflies. Dave figured that only an immigration officer without a soul could possibly remain unmoved or unconvinced. Dave himself was so moved that he'd had to force himself not to comment on the posts, for fear of making a complete arse of himself. About which he just couldn't tell any more.

On a more pragmatic level, Nicholas had realised they couldn't open a joint bank account until Dave could provide proof of where he was living. So Nicholas had made an appointment to introduce him to the family solicitors in order to ask for a formal letter to confirm matters. In response to which, Dave had said, "I should see about making a new will. I guess we can get things started on that while we're there, as well, yeah?"

Nicholas had gaped at him and then frowned in thought for a long moment, before tentatively asking, "What were you intending to … ?"

"Well, right now, it would all go to Denise or Zoe. But you should be my main beneficiary, shouldn't you?"

Nicholas still seemed surprisingly unsure about something. "Because it will be evidence of us being in a committed relationship? For the Department of Immigration, I mean."

"No, because that's the way it should be," Dave corrected him. "We're getting married, aren't we?"

"Yes, we are." Nicholas finally broke into a big happy grin. "I'll do the same."

"But getting married doesn't change the fact that Zoe's kind of my godchild, right?"

"Of course not! It means she'll be kind of mine as well. If Denise and Vittorio don't mind."

"They won't mind," Dave said, very lightly. So once things were finalised and signed and witnessed, other than a substantial bequest to Zoe, Nicholas would receive all Dave's worldly possessions when he died.

Nicholas did likewise, though he chose to leave some personal gifts to Robin rather than money. "It's not like he won't have plenty anyway," Nicholas explained to Dave. "He's in line for the whole shebang one day. So you might as well have what's mine. And there's a fair bit, you know. I haven't had my own family to raise, like the others, and I've never had my own home to pay for."

"As long as you know that's not why I'm marrying you."

"No, it's for the sex, isn't it?"

"Yes, Nicholas. It's for the sex."

Well, whether it was or it wasn't, Dave wanted to offer something to Nicholas as a reward. Late one night as they drifted together down the river that was making love, Dave with Nicholas, this wondrous river already so familiar – just as the current started to tug them into deeper stronger waters, Dave murmured, "What d'you want to do? Nicholas? What do you want that we haven't done yet?"

"Oh God," Nicholas complained half-seriously against Dave's throat, "you're bored with me already."

"You *know* I'm not." He tried to explain while Nicholas resumed the lovely distraction of his mouthings and gnawings. "I just thought ... if there was something different ... you might want ... as well as, I mean. Not instead of."

Nicholas finally pulled back a little to consider him, and they gently floated back into relative calm. A long serious moment later, Nicholas asked, "Anything?"

"Anything," he promised with perfect confidence.

Another long moment passed by before Nicholas finally lowered himself again to pepper sweet kisses across Dave's cheekbones and nose, mouth and chin. Then, close by Dave's ear, Nicholas tentatively asked, "Would you wear something?"

He pulled back again to see Dave's reaction. Dave frowned, not really knowing what to think. They usually had sex naked – and why not? Naked allowed for the complete experience, with no hindrances or frustrations or distractions. The only times they didn't get naked were when they were too frantic to bother completely undressing. Which wasn't a sex thing, but an urgency thing. So what did Nicholas mean? "Wear something … ?" Dave eventually echoed. "Like what?"

Nicholas flushed a little, which suggested a few horrible ideas to Dave.

"No, not like a … you want me to dress up as a …"

"Not necessarily."

"Or like a costume or something?"

Nicholas scrunched his face up. "I'm open to the possibilities, but that's not what I had in mind."

"Look," said Dave, struggling to sit up a bit and really face his lover. "I'm a man, all right? I know you fuck me a lot, and you usually do the driving in bed. But that doesn't make me –"

"Of course not!"

"I am *not* going to play the drag queen for you. I'm not a woman. I'm not going to pretend to be anything I'm not."

"That's *fine*, David," Nicholas said, starting to sound a bit exasperated.

Dave took a breath, and then sat up further against the headboard. Nicholas was kneeling between Dave's bent legs, but they weren't touching any more. Finally Dave managed, "Not that there's anything wrong with that for those who want to. But I don't. Want to."

"I get that," Nicholas remarked tartly. Then he softened a little. "For heaven's sake, David, I *like* that you're a man. You're all man even when you're getting fucked, I *promise*. And that totally works for me. I don't want to change anything about you."

"But you do, don't you? You want me to be gay, and I'm probably stuffing it up badly."

Nicholas groaned in frustration and annoyance. "I have news for you, David. All you have to do to be gay is love me. And actually you're pretty much a genius at that."

After another long moment of bullheadedness, Dave took a breath and tried to be more reasonable. "All right. Then, what is it you want me to do?"

"Nothing at all, if you don't want to – honestly."

"Yeah, *all right*, I trust you. Just tell me!" A silence stretched, and Dave belatedly reflected that no doubt Nicholas was now feeling as vulnerable and misunderstood as Dave himself had not a minute before. "Hey," Dave joshed. "You want me to wear a chauffeur's cap and call you sir? We can do that. Just don't … don't call me Frank in the middle of it, and we'll do fine."

Nicholas cast him a flat look. "I said it wasn't about costumes. And I so do not have a sense of humour about how I used to feel for Frank."

"Of course not," Dave offered softly. He sat forward, and let both his hands settle on Nicholas in a gentle caress. "Come on, tell me. If I can, I will, I promise. Even if I don't understand." That earned him a fond glance. "Be patient with me. I'm just a dumb Aussie who never had to think much about this sort of stuff. But I'm not a *totally* lost cause."

"No, that's the very last thing you are," Nicholas declared. Then he finally shifted forward so he was sitting with his legs curled under him, and one hand resting on Dave's thigh. Eventually he said, very quietly, "I like naked, I like skin. But I like silk, too. Would you wear something made of silk while we're in bed?" He dared to glance at Dave and then swiftly looked away. "Doesn't have to be feminine or anything. It's the … texture that counts. Not what it actually is."

Dave swallowed, not sure what he was really getting into. But he couldn't find anything to protest about in what Nicholas had just asked. "Well," he replied, both firmly and cautiously. "That sounds okay."

Nicholas shot him a grateful look – and then suddenly he was looking directly at Dave, directly *into* him, his gaze shockingly level and intent. Dave let out a breath that was almost a gasp, exactly as if Nicholas had just penetrated him. Nicholas drew closer – and Dave couldn't help but draw back, at least for an inch or two until his head collided *thunk* against the headboard.

"You know what I like best of all?" Nicholas asked.

Dave shook his head. No.

"I like looking into your eyes, your beautiful blue eyes, and they're so clear and you're so open to me, like an infinite sky, like a pool that sinks down *forever*. There are no barriers – not like there are at the moment. There's no confusion or doubt or pain or fear, there's just *you* … there's you letting me in … and me inside of you … there's just *us* together … and then there's the air and the sunlight and the pleasure, until at last – at last –"

"Oh God," said Dave roughly. "Silk or not, I don't care – just fuck me. Just fuck me now."

And that's what they did.

four

Denise called back a couple of days later, and chatted briefly with Dave before asking, "Who do I talk to about our clothes for the wedding, you or Nicholas?"

"Am I going to hate them?" Dave asked.

"No, you are *not* going to hate them!" she retorted in mock exasperation. "Don't you trust me any more, Davey?"

"Yeah, you know I do. Well, unless it's real simple and obvious, you'd better talk to him, right? Or I'll just confuse the issue when I pass it on."

"That's what I thought."

"Huh. Okay, hang on, and I'll get him for you. I'll just be a mo." Dave carefully put the phone down, and then jogged on through to the family living room where Nicholas was stretched out with a book.

Nicholas had been out of sorts from the moment Dave woke that morning, and Dave wasn't sure why – though he assumed it had something to do with the fact they were due to have lunch with a group of Nicholas's friends that day, most of whom were either former university friends or gay – or both. Dave himself was dreading it, and he imagined that Nicholas was, too.

Once Dave had conveyed what Denise wanted to talk about, Nicholas got an intent look on his face, and without saying a word in reply headed off to pick up the call. Dave figured he'd be better off leaving them to it, and settled on a sofa before taking up Nicholas's book and examining it. Which was about butterflies, of course, which meant that at least Dave could appreciate the pictures.

About fifteen minutes later, Nicholas came back into the room and stood looming over Dave with a thunderous scowl. "Did you tell her about the silk thing?" he demanded.

"No! What?" Dread fell through Dave and settled uneasily in his gut.

"Are you *sure*?"

"Of course I'm sure! I'm not gonna be talking sex stuff with Denise!" Which wasn't actually the point. The point was: "God. What does she want me to wear?"

Nicholas relaxed a fraction. "You'll like it. It's all right. A silk shirt and linen trousers. Maybe a waistcoat, too, silk or linen. You'll be fine."

Dave looked at him closely. Nicholas was still thoroughly out of sorts. "What about you?" Dave asked cautiously. "Are you okay with it?"

"Yes. Yes, I am." Nicholas at last folded down onto the sofa opposite Dave, and sat there hunched forward with his elbows on his knees. "You'll be smart–casual, while we'll be formal, but the colours will work together perfectly." He added with a humourless smile, "There's no point trying to dress you up as something you're not, is there?"

"No," Dave agreed, very quietly and very cautiously.

"Actually, I suspect Denise has just managed to rather creatively save the whole thing. I mean, it would have been good. Now it's going to be perfect."

"Well," said Dave, still rather cautious, "that's great. Isn't it?"

"Yes."

A silence threatened to drag out into something unbearable. "Look. Are you going to tell me what's bothering you? It's about me meeting your friends, isn't it? But, you know – I figure they'll be happy for you. Even if they don't like me."

"What?" Nicholas scowled again, this time looking honestly mystified. "Why on earth wouldn't they like you?"

"Because I barely made it through high school, and because I'm not, you know … gay enough."

"Oh, for God's sake, not *that* again."

"So," Dave retorted, "if that's not the problem, why don't you tell me what is, then?"

Nicholas stared at him as if Dave were a pinned butterfly that refused to be properly identified. "How would you describe yourself now? If asked. Gay? Straight? What?"

"See, I never had to think about it before. Because I had Denise."

"So why are you suddenly so keen on labels now, then?"

"I dunno. I guess because everyone else seems to be."

"Well … ?"

Dave let out a sigh. "Well, I suppose I'm … bi. Bisexual." He coloured up a bit. It was the first time he'd ever said the word aloud, and he had the horrible suspicion that some people would interpret bi as indecisive or maybe just lacking courage. "I mean, I loved Denise. That was real. But this is real, too. So I guess that makes me … both?"

"Exactly. And why the hell do you think my friends – whose business it so totally isn't, anyway – Why do you think they'd have any kind of problem with that?"

"I guess they wouldn't. But I just don't know how to … be."

"Fuck's sake! Just be yourself. You have no problem doing that when it comes to whether you'll wear a suit or not, do you?!"

Dave just stared back at the man, trying to scramble through all the confusion back to its source. "Um. Okay. So you think it's gonna go all right? Lunch, I mean."

Nicholas heaved an exasperated sigh. "Of *course* it is. Just what kind of idiotic friends do you think I have, anyway?" he added in a grumble.

A moment passed. "Right," said Dave. "So, what have you been unhappy about today? If it's not that."

Another moment passed while Nicholas just considered him, his annoyance at last dwindling away into something cooler. Eventually he said, "We have to go soon. There's not time to get into it. We'll talk about it later this afternoon, all right?"

"All right." Dave let out a breath, and made himself ask what Denise would have wanted him to ask if it were her. "Is it something – between us? Something I've done."

"No …" Nicholas gusted a breath and fell forward onto his knees, at last softening, warming, pushing into Dave's embrace. "No, not at all." They took each other into the deepest of hugs. "Nothing like that."

"You gonna give me a hint?"

"Just – I found another hoop. In the visa process."

"Ah, well. Hoops are for jumping through."

"And that's why you're the hero in the story of my life."

"Oh *Nicholas*," he groaned. And they held each other tightly there, prepared to deal together with all the world might throw at them.

The accord between them was wonderful, but it didn't last. Despite the fact that Nicholas's friends greeted Dave as if he were already their friend and had been all along – and despite the fact that Dave quickly relaxed in their company as if he'd just walked into a pub in Charleville rather than Beaconsfield – Nicholas was soon out of sorts again.

"I should have brought the Akubra," Nicholas grumbled. A table had been set for them outside in the beer garden along which ran a canal. There were willow trees on the other bank, and everything was idyllically English – but Nicholas grimaced fretfully up at the sunshine despite being under a broad canvas umbrella, and said, "I don't want to get too hot."

"Shall we see if we can move inside?" Dave asked – though they'd walked through the pub when they arrived, and it had been clear it was one of those really old places with rooms far too small and cramped to cope with even ten or twelve people all sitting together.

"No, it's all right."

"Drink, Nicholas?" someone asked.

"Still water with ice and lime," he said, squinting up at whoever it was. Dave hadn't managed to attach a single name to a face yet.

"David?" the someone continued. "I think they have Foster's on tap."

Dave suppressed a shudder, and decided the affronted lecture on what a Queenslander was prepared to drink could wait. "I'll have the same as Nicholas, thanks."

Nicholas looked at Dave, his expression scrunched up with concern now. "You can have a beer."

"I know. But I'll keep you company."

"Well. You might not want to start *that* habit. I should warn you I hardly ever drink."

"You drank beer in Australia," Dave remarked.

"Only ever one or two, not very often – and when in Rome …"

"You drink beer in Rome?"

"No! Idiot …" Nicholas guffawed with genuine humour, which made Dave smile. "I'm sorry," Nicholas said very quietly after a moment. "I'm just paranoid about getting headaches. Even … ordinary ones."

"I get it," Dave said, matching his tone. "D'you want to take a couple of your pain killers, just in case? Prevention being better than the cure."

Nicholas smiled at him fondly. "No, it's all right. I'll be all right."

"You go inside the moment you want to, and I'll get everyone else moved in as well, I promise. It won't be a problem."

The smile broadened, and Nicholas finally relaxed. "I like you looking after me."

"Just trying to return the favour," Dave asserted, endeavouring not to turn self-conscious and betray himself. When he finally turned away from

Nicholas and sat back, he discovered that those people nearest him were regarding the pair of them very very fondly. It took every single ounce of his Aussie brashness to face them down – and even that didn't seem to dent their affection, not one little bit.

Late that afternoon Nicholas lay stretched out on their bed, unwinding and cooling down. They had all the windows open so the room was full of fresh air, and Nicholas lay there in just his jeans and a t-shirt. Dave sat beside him, up against the headboard, simply idling away the time. They weren't touching, for the sake of Nicholas not wanting any of Dave's body heat, but that didn't mean they weren't close.

Eventually, once Nicholas seemed to have reached something more like his usual happy demeanour, Dave asked, "D'you want to have a nap? I'll get out of your way, if you like."

"Maybe," said Nicholas, "and only if you want to."

"All right." After a moment, Dave said, "D'you want to tell me about the thing with the visa? If we get that sorted, then maybe you'll feel better."

A long quiet peace stretched, though it was clear to Dave that Nicholas hadn't slipped away into sleep. Eventually Nicholas said, "It's about my health. I guess I'd read it before, but it hadn't quite sunk in."

"What about it?"

"It's a serious condition, David. They're not going to like it. They might refuse me the visa."

Dave took a moment with that, then asked, "On what grounds? It's not like it's catching or anything. It's not like you're endangering anyone."

"No, it's about the fact that at some point – maybe not for years, decades – I'll probably need surgery. Brain surgery."

"So … ?"

Nicholas threw him a frustrated look. "It's the cost and resources involved. Why would they want to take me on? I can't even promise to pay my way in the meantime, unless I get really lucky with the right kind of work."

"Ah." Dave thought about all of that, though the answer seemed clear to him.

"I guess …" said Nicholas very slowly, "I could have the operation done here. Before we go."

"No!" cried Dave, his heart thudding painfully.

"But then it's not such an issue," Nicholas doggedly continued. "Of course, things could still go wrong later, but at least I'll have done what I can in the meantime."

"No," Dave firmly replied. "The risks aren't worth it. There's no point in you going through something so serious."

"There is a point if it means I can be with you."

Dave shifted down onto the bed and turned towards Nicholas. "I've got a much better idea, anyway."

Nicholas reached to take his hand. "What's that, then?"

"We don't rely on Medicare. That's like the NHS here – and that's where the cost to the government comes in, right?"

"Oh! Of course!"

"We'll take care of ourselves. We buy private health insurance, whatever it takes. It's not like we can't afford it – and then there's no financial risk involved to anyone else. Problem solved. Right?"

"Right," said Nicholas with a watery smile. "God, you're amazing!"

"Not too shabby, I guess."

"I just – I didn't think of that. Of course I already have health insurance as part of the family policy, and it covers me worldwide. I checked that before the trip. God! Why didn't I add that up myself?"

Dave smiled, and offered somewhat weakly, "Two heads are better than one."

"I am definitely better with you," Nicholas fervently replied – and he turned in against Dave, and Dave held him, cradled him for a while. Dave's shirt got suspiciously damp where Nicholas pressed his face against it, but then Nicholas finally drifted off into a restful sleep, and when he woke again he was his own best self.

Dave kind of adored Nicholas's blog entry for that day.

The Real Thing
It's true love. When Stef offered to buy David a Foster's at lunch today, David refrained from violence and didn't even swear, but only politely replied that he'd

have what I was having. All for the sake of not causing an irreconcilable rift with his new partner's old friends. It was remarkable.

Having quizzed David about the significance of all this, we decided that offering a Queenslander a Foster's was equivalent to putting Coca Cola in a Scot's whisky. So, you see how very remarkable this is ...

True blue love, I tell you. Fair dinkum, mate.

five

'Yes, I'm all yours,' Dave had said to Nicholas on the first day he'd arrived in England – and in front of Nicholas's entire family as witnesses, not to mention their loyal retainers as well. There was many a time over the following weeks when Dave wished that had been all it took to be married. And of course in many ways – at least for the two of them – that had indeed been the moment in which they'd really committed themselves. That was never in question. Later on he'd followed that up with, *'For you, I'd even give up Australia.'* There was no doubt about Dave–and–Nicholas. The problem was all the other stuff that went on and inexorably on.

After the first couple of weeks which seemed plagued by upsets, Nicholas had – thank God – regained his equilibrium and dived into the wedding preparations with his usual cheerfulness. But he wanted the ceremony and reception to be absolutely perfect, which was pressure enough, never mind the business surrounding Nicholas's move to Australia and the visa requirements. Never mind him saying goodbye to his father and the rest of his family. And Nicholas had never been good at farewells.

One of the things Nicholas was good at was gifts. Within about a week and a half of Dave's arrival in England, Nicholas presented him with a new Kindle device on which was loaded all the Patrick O'Brian books. Given that Dave had only brought a couple of the paperbacks with him, he felt almost overwhelmed with gratitude. Jack Aubrey and Stephen Maturin had been his constant companions for so long, and their adventures provided inspiration or a failsafe refuge whenever needed. Right now, there was plenty to be doing and helping Nicholas with, and of course hanging out with Nicholas was always a good thing. But there was no denying that wedding plans and visa applications weren't quite as involving as planning and leading a trip in Australia's Outback. And there were times when Dave – so used to living on his own – needed an escape into the more solitary pleasures of reading.

As September turned into October, the level of activity in the house and its surrounds heightened. Mrs Gilchrist was responsible for the catering at the reception and was baking fruit cakes and accumulating crockery at an alarming rate; Frank was responsible for the cars they'd use and was also helping the head gardener add what seemed like hundreds of new plants to the flowerbeds so they looked as lush as possible; Simon was assisting Nicholas with the logistics. As the only surviving parent of either of them, Richard was taking his role as host – and as father or stand-in father of the grooms – with great gravity. New morning suits were being made and fitted by a tailor in Beaconsfield, but that was the province of Nicholas and Robert – apparently Dave and Nicholas weren't to see each other's outfits until the day of the wedding itself, despite Nicholas's nervousness about what Denise was organising for the Australian half of the wedding party.

"You can trust her," said Dave. "She knows far more about these things than I do. And I have to say she looked *great* when she married Vittorio." Denise in a simple elegant white wedding dress with her long blonde hair done up in a casual twist had been a revelation ... Dave's heart had broken all over again.

"I have complete faith in her," Nicholas said – though his long pale fingers skittered away as if daring to disagree. "I loved her ideas. I honestly did."

"I believe you!" Dave asserted.

"Yes, I know," Nicholas replied rather miserably. "Thousands wouldn't."

Despite Dave not having any direct responsibilities other than being Nicholas's mainstay and willing assistant in all things, the stresses must have started to show. One evening, Richard happened upon Dave as he came down the main stairs into the hall, and took the opportunity to invite him into the study, the room where all the family photos were hanging on a wall. "Nothing to be alarmed about," Richard assured him as he took a seat in one of the leather armchairs – Dave had discovered that there were comfortable armchairs in just about every room in the house! The earl gestured an invitation for Dave to sit opposite him. "I was simply concerned for you, David."

"For me?" he blurted in surprise. "I'm all right."

Richard nodded as if genially agreeing. "You've been here a couple of months now, and I feel we've come to know something of you. David, it's clear that you're exactly the sort of fine, responsible young man any parent would wish for a son-in-law."

"Oh. Oh, well. Thanks." Dave was blushing again. Which was one thing he'd be glad to see the back of once he and Nicholas were married and it was all settled and accepted and *done*.

"I'm sorry to make you uncomfortable, but I want you to know how pleased and proud we all are."

"Thanks," said Dave again rather pathetically. He tried not to squirm.

Luckily Richard started talking about Nicholas instead. "Of course Nicholas is determined to live his life, and with good reason. He's an inspiration to us all, really. He sets the example for how to approach life."

"Yes."

"And we hope – we *fervently* hope – that it will all come to nothing, and Nicholas will outlive his own generation as well as mine."

"Yes," Dave agreed, though in rather muted tones.

"In the meantime, however, it's true that Nicholas ... has a tendency to sweep all before him in his enthusiasms."

And Richard left a pause.

Eventually Dave offered, "But with what Nicholas is facing ... I think seizing the day is the only answer. He's brave enough to do that."

"Yes, he's almost always faced this with courage – but he's been braver still since he met you, David. I was afraid he'd never quite let himself really love someone."

Dave couldn't possibly respond to that, but he stored it away for future comfort and somehow managed to sail blithely on. "It's like you said, seizing the day is something we should all do, really. Make the most of what time we have."

Richard nodded, but continued, "I am ... only concerned, David, that you may have been swept up in something that you possibly now ... regret."

"Regret?" he exclaimed, frowning at the man. "No, I'm not sorry about being with Nicholas. Are you?" he added, perhaps a bit too belligerently. "I mean, are you sorry I'm with him?" Dave clarified in more reasonable tones.

"Not at all – though we shall miss him a great deal when you're living on the other side of the world. We will miss both of you."

"I'm –"

Richard lifted a hand to stall whatever Dave had been going to say. "I realise that's what you both must do. No, what I was trying to say was that it's a significant burden to take on – a partner, a husband who might not live to see your first anniversary."

Dave swallowed hard at the thought, but of course he'd faced this already. He'd faced it for Nicholas, and he'd faced it in all kinds of other ways, too.

"We all live with that, though, don't we?" he said. "Like you said, Nicholas might outlive me. If he doesn't – Well, my mother died when I was young, and my father not so long ago. Any trip I take into the Outback might be my last, no matter how careful I am. We all live with death, Richard. Nicholas already knows what the only answer to that is. Sometimes I – Well, there have been times I needed to be reminded of that." He took a breath, and firmly concluded, "I don't have any regrets, Richard. I'm grateful. With Nicholas around, I'm never going to forget again – I'll never forget to *live*."

It seemed that Richard was moved, and he needed a long moment before he could be sure of his voice. Eventually he said, very very lightly, "I once asked Nicholas how he knew you were the man for him. Do you know what he said?"

"No. Actually, I don't." Dave cringed a little inside, just in case.

"He said that right from the day you first met, he felt utterly *safe* with you."

"Oh." That wasn't so bad. Dave relaxed again.

"He added that maybe I'd been hoping for a more passionate answer."

"No, actually that's kind of perfect, isn't it?"

"Yes, David," the earl replied with great warmth, "actually it kind of is."

His Imagination
David apologises for reading – as if I could possibly mind. He says he feels bad for ignoring me, sometimes for hours at a stretch. He doesn't seem to realise I love him all the more for being a reader. Our best selves are readers.

And look what he has chosen for his other world! Books as clever and clear–eyed as they are kind and courageous. Who wouldn't fall for a man who shares his imagination with Jack Aubrey and Stephen Maturin?

At last it was mid–October, and Denise was due to arrive at Heathrow early one morning. She and Dave had of course spent time apart before, but never for so long, and never with half a world between them. He didn't expect her to have missed him as much as he'd missed her, but still. Dave anticipated a damp–eyed reunion in the grand tradition of airline ads everywhere. And of course it wasn't only Denise, but Charlie, and Zoe, and Vittorio.

Dave and Nicholas were up at five, and on their way by half past. Dave was driving Robert's Renault Espace, which had room for everyone. Frank had fitted a baby seat for Zoe. There was almost no traffic at that time of the morning, of course, so they made it there in about twenty minutes – and then it was a matter of Dave anxiously waiting by the barriers, while Nicholas went to fetch them coffee.

At last Dave's disparate little family appeared, and he beamed like an idiot as they saw him and headed in his direction, all of them obviously tired and a bit frumpy, but all of them just as obviously happy. Soon Dave and Denise were holding onto each other tight, as if they were two halves of a whole that had been too long sundered. Then wonderful Charlie must have a great warm hug, too – and then even Vittorio claimed one – and Zoe, who was strapped to her father in a carrier, lifted her hands and yearned towards Dave as if she might even remember him. "She's, like, doubled in size again!" Dave exclaimed, quite astounded by the changes. He was ashamed to realise he wasn't quite sure if he'd have recognised her.

"She's thriving," Denise said, quite complacently. "Though she'll be all the better for seeing you again, Davey."

"I'm all the better for it, too."

Before Dave could completely let the side down with sentiment in excess of the standard Aussie limits, Vittorio got them all moving towards the exit, with him and Charlie pushing the trolleys of luggage, and Nicholas leading them to the car park. Soon they were on their way back to the Goring family home, and the sun was rising into what promised to be a perfect English day. Denise sat up the front with Dave, catching him up on all the Brisbane gossip, while Charlie sat in the back with Nicholas, and Vittorio took care of Zoe.

Then they were home, and Simon and Frank were helping with the bags, and Richard was there to welcome everyone and show them to their rooms, and invite them to come back down for breakfast as soon as they'd settled in and freshened up. All was glorious chaos for a long while, except that in the midst of it, Dave got to sit at the breakfast table holding Zoe and feeding her, and the two of them gazed at each solemnly, and remembered anything about each other that they might have forgotten.

There was a quiet half hour with Denise late that morning as well, as she showed him the clothes she'd had made for the two of them for the wedding, and for Charlie as well – and she also had some news. "I'm pregnant again, Davey. So, if you're up for another irreligious godchild …"

"Always," he vowed. "Me and Nicholas maybe? As godparents?"

"Yes, absolutely. You and Nicholas. For Zoe, too." Denise laughed fondly, and whispered, "But mostly you, Davey."

He reached instinctively to rest a reverential hand against her stomach – and thought better of it just in time. But Denise took his hand and held it against her warm belly, still flat yet full of possibilities. "I've missed you, you know."

"It won't be long now, and I'll be home again."

"And your man with you, where he belongs."

Dave grinned at her, no doubt a bit lopsidedly. "Where we both belong, yes."

Denise turned away, busying herself with the unpacking. But she quieted after a moment, and said, "You're still sure about this, are you? Getting hitched, I mean."

"Yes. Why?"

"It's all happened pretty quick, that's all."

"It was quick for you and Vittorio, too. You just know, don't you? You know when it's worth trying, anyway."

"Yes."

"And this whole 'Seize the Day' philosophy has a lot going for it."

Denise laughed a little under her breath, and shot him a glance. Apparently if she'd really had any worries, he'd just convinced her as easily as that.

He watched as Denise carefully hung up the wedding clothes in one of the wardrobes, and then he dared to say – now while they were still a bit punch drunk with jet lag or the reunion or the early start to the day. He dared to say, "Nicholas has this thing, you know …"

"So I gathered."

"Ha ha." And he was blushing already. Dave sighed, and continued anyway because he knew Denise wouldn't let him get away with changing the subject now. "He asked me if … if I'd wear something silk. To bed. And I guess he wasn't talking pyjamas."

Denise came and sat beside him, and considered him seriously. "What d'you think about that?" she asked.

216 | Of Dreams and Ceremonies

He shrugged. "I'm not meant to tell you. In fact, I said I wouldn't. He was – When you talked to him about the silk shirt for the wedding, he was mad at me, cos he thought I'd told you."

"So why are you telling me now?"

"I want you to help me. You did good with the wedding clothes. I figured you could help me with this."

Denise reached to grasp his hand for a moment, and then let him go before asking very matter-of-factly, "Are we talking lingerie? Something a woman would wear?"

Dave's face was waratah red, he could feel it, but he pushed on. He could trust Denise, and he wanted to make Nicholas happy. "I don't know. He said it didn't have to feminine, he just liked silk. But then he said actually that didn't matter, and he started talking about how he likes it best when I'm – um ... When there's no barriers, yeah? Does that make sense? When it's just him and me ..." He gestured, helplessly, with both hands miming the gates over his heart opening – and then flitting to and fro between their mutually engaged gazes.

"Davey –"

"Mmm?"

"He's not into ... humiliating you. Is he?"

"No! God, no, nothing like that."

"You trust him?"

"*Totally.*"

"He wants to ... really *experience* that, I guess."

"Yeah, I guess so. And it's good, you know? When it's intense like that." Dave looked at her. "I need your help, Denny. I need you to figure out what I could wear – I mean, what it would take – to go far enough for him – and not too far for me."

"If you really trust him," she said very carefully, "then what would be too far?"

"Well, you know. If I just ended up feeling ridiculous. Would be kinda counter-productive. Don't you think?"

"Yeah, I get it." She frowned over all of this for a long moment with her head down, and then reached to hold his hand again. "No worries, mate," Denise said softly, her gaze meeting his with no judgement. "No worries. We'll figure it out."

And Dave let out a breath he'd barely known he'd been holding.

On the following Saturday night, Robert and Penelope took Denise and Vittorio out for dinner, and left Nicholas and Dave at home to celebrate a joint buck's night – not only with Charlie, but also with Zoe and Robin and all the other Goring children. They took over the family lounge room and played games, watched *Monsters, Inc.* and generally had a wonderful time. Nicholas read aloud from a Roald Dahl book chosen by Robin, and Charlie told a Dreamtime story that had all the kids enraptured – and the adults, too.

Dave thought the whole thing was hilarious. "I never thought I'd be over-indulging in *ice cream* on my buck's night!" But it was also completely perfect. "Best night ever," he quietly commented as he accompanied Nicholas carrying a sleepy Robin up to his bedroom once all the other kids had finally been reclaimed by their parents.

"Best ever ..." Robin echoed. "Love you, Nic'las."

"Love you, too, my darling boy."

And Robin clung on with his arms around Nicholas's neck, and had to be gently prised off before at last he curled up on his own in his bed and fell heavily into sleep.

Dave knew just how the young fellow felt – though he realised now that unlike Robin he'd never once declared himself. He'd never used the L word to Nicholas. Though perhaps at this point he didn't really need to. Dave figured maybe it was understood.

It seemed that no decision relating to the wedding could possibly be straightforward. There was probably some kind of law about it. The current topic was cars. As there were only five people attending the actual ceremony – Nicholas and Dave, Robert and Denise, and Richard – Robert's idea was that they would all just go in one car and he would drive. Richard, however, thought that Nicholas and Dave should have a little time alone together after the ceremony, and therefore they should travel home separately, and Simon could drive them. Robert seemed to find this a bit unnecessary, though he didn't seem to have any particular reason why. Nicholas seemed to like the idea, but was concerned about Simon already having enough to do that day with organising the reception and helping Penelope to welcome the guests.

Robert and Richard were amicably arguing the matter back and forth between them when Dave noticed that Robin had sidled up to Nicholas and was whispering in his ear. When Nicholas pulled back a little to consider him, Dave could see that Robin was upset about something.

Nicholas made up his mind and settled the dispute. "It'll have to be two cars," he announced, "because Robin's coming, too." On which Robin clung to him, and Nicholas hauled the young fellow up onto his lap for a cuddle.

"Would there be room for Charlie as well, then?" Dave asked.

Robert still seemed a bit disgruntled over something, but everyone agreed that yes, there'd certainly be room for Charlie. And so that, at least, was finally sorted.

six

Early on the morning of the thirty–first of October, Dave woke nestled deep in the bed, with Nicholas curled around him pressing sleepy kisses to his nape. "Good morning, husband," Nicholas murmured with his lips brushing against Dave's skin.

Dave shivered in delight – and snorted. "Not yet, I'm not!"

"Mmm … Our last chance for a bit of illicit fornication …"

"You don't want to save yourself … ?"

"At least a decade too late for that!"

"Tart!"

"And you can't resist a fine tasty tart."

"That's true."

So they made love, just as they were, still warm and blurred with sleep, Nicholas thrusting gently against Dave's rear and each with a hand overlapping on Dave's cock echoing the same sweet rhythm. They spilled over with sighs, and still wrapped up close they snoozed again for a few minutes, before at last the alarm went off.

"Good morning, husband," Nicholas said again.

Dave chuckled. "Come on, then. Let's make that happen!"

They each had a quick shower and dragged on the nearest casual clothes, then headed down to join the rest of the family for breakfast. The general mood was cheerful yet busy. Everyone made a point of greeting Dave and Nicholas, and wishing them well.

Dave found that he wasn't very hungry, so after he'd drunk his coffee he made his excuses and wandered outside for some fresh air. He must have been looking pensive, for when Simon popped his head out of the front door to find Dave pacing back and forth on the driveway, he asked, "The not unexpected cold feet, sir, or is it serious second thoughts?"

He managed a low chuckle in reply. "Neither, really. And today of all days, you can call me Dave, can't you?"

Simon came out to join him in the cool morning air, closing the door behind him. "We're a bit more formal here in England than you're used to, I imagine."

"Just a bit," he replied, bunging on the irony.

"You know, … Dave. You must always ask if you need anything."

"Thanks, Simon," he said with a nod. "I will. And – likewise."

"I mean, sir, that I would consider myself to be serving the ultimate good of the family, if there was something you wanted … even if you felt they wouldn't agree. I would be happy to serve you, sir."

Dave eyed him narrowly. "Are you encouraging me to make a run for it?"

"Not encouraging, Mr Taylor. Merely making sure that you know it's a possible course of action. If you wish to take it."

"I don't. But I appreciate the thought." They paced back and forth together companionably for a while, before Dave confessed, "I've been thinking that I've never said – those three little words to him."

"I am sure that Nicholas is very much aware of how you feel for him. We can all see it."

"Yeah? Then why do people keep asking me if I want to get out of this?"

"Ah." Simon considered the gravel at his feet for a moment. "Nicholas does have a way of carrying all before him. Everyone here loves him dearly, and he's too sensitive a man to deliberately hurt anyone. We have, however, learned to speak up on the few occasions when we've needed to." Simon tipped his head towards Dave. "I suppose there might be some concern that you have yet to learn that."

"No, that's all right. I can fend for myself. Australians are rarely backward in coming forward."

"Of course, sir. Dave. Well, if I may, I would like to wish you every joy today and in all the days to come."

"Thank you, Simon. You, too, mate." And Dave went back inside and drank another coffee.

Soon it was time for Dave to head off with Denise and their little family to get formally dressed. Nicholas kissed him on parting, and told Dave how beautiful he was going to be. Treating him just like a bride! "God, shut up," Dave grumbled. "Anyway, you know no one's gonna outshine you."

Nicholas chortled in surprise. "Oh, I do believe you have it bad, Mr Taylor."

"I do, sir," he murmured in reply. "I have it very bad indeed …"

And they were parted, not to meet again until they were suited and groomed, and ready for the ceremony.

Dave got dressed in Charlie's room, under Denise's supervision. She was stunning in a dress of heavy silk that looked as if it had simply been draped snugly around her figure but might slip off again at any moment. It was coloured the grey–green of eucalyptus leaves. She'd had a shirt made for Dave in the same material, along with dark grey linen trousers with a slightly rough weave.

There was also a silk waistcoat of a hazy dark green–blue. It was a simple design, without any collar and with rather discreet buttons, but it was nicely fitted – and a step or two more formal than Dave was really comfortable with.

"You don't have to wear that," said Denise. "Just the shirt, trousers and proper shoes are enough."

"Nicholas would like it, though," Dave responded. "Wouldn't he?"

"Yes, I think so."

"Okay, then." Dave had had his way about the morning suits, after all, so he could make a gesture in return.

Charlie, meanwhile, was dressed in the same kind of trousers, and a shirt of the same silk but coloured a dusky version of pink eucalyptus flowers. He looked absolutely magnificent.

"Jeez …" Dave complained. "Just as I'd gotten used to being the centre of attention for once, you two decide to go and look, like, *ten* times more gorgeous than me!"

"As if," Denise returned.

"And it's *my* wedding day, thank you very much!"

"Don't worry about it, mate," Charlie said with some fervour. "You look about as beautiful as a white fella can."

Which made Dave turn about as pink as Charlie's shirt – and then he went red as Denise pressed a kiss to his cheek that was warmer than any she'd bestowed on him since they'd broken up.

And maybe she'd done that deliberately, for he didn't manage to raise a protest as she fixed a buttonhole corsage to his waistcoat. It was made of creamy–white eucalyptus flowers and leaves. "How d'you manage that?" he asked in a subdued kind of voice.

"They're silk," she replied.

And there it was again: silk. Dave sat down on the nearest chair, and tried very hard to pretend that he didn't feel rather dizzy.

Charlie was shrugging into a grey–green silk waistcoat, which unfortunately toned down the effect of the pink, but it did turn them into a proper coordinated wedding party. Dave shook his head, thinking that Denise had worked some kind of miracle – and praying that Nicholas recognised it as such. There was a buttonhole corsage for Charlie, and then a silk shawl and a wrist corsage for Denise – all in pinks. And they were done.

Denise was considering the three of them with pride. "Not too shabby for a bunch of colonials, if I do say so myself!"

"It's marvellous, Denny," Dave said.

Charlie was beaming happily. And then Vittorio came in with Zoe wrapped in a carrier across his chest, and told everyone how wonderful they looked – though it was true his gaze lingered longest on his wife. Which was as it should be, Dave figured.

"They're bringing the cars around now," Vittorio continued. "Nicholas said he'll be away in about five minutes, and then if you follow when you're ready."

"This is it, then, Davey," said Denise.

He had to clear his throat before he could speak, but that was just the expected jitters. "I'm ready," Dave said. "I'm ready now."

Simon drove Dave, Denise and Charlie to Beaconsfield in the Rolls Royce Silver Cloud. When they got to the old courthouse and parked behind Robert's Renault Espace, Dave was amused and touched to find Frank there in his full chauffeur uniform, despite the fact that he knew Robert had done the driving. Apparently Frank felt the need to also give Nicholas away, or shine up the cars, be available to deal with any breakdowns, or some such thing. Dave went to shake his hand, and received a solemn nod in return.

Then Dave headed inside with two of his very best friends at his shoulders. His third best friend gaped in wonder for a moment on seeing him – and then beamed more brightly than he'd ever smiled before. Nicholas strode across the lobby to meet Dave, and to take both of Dave's hands in his own. "God, David – you look – you look *beautiful* ..."

"So do you," he offered perfectly genuinely. Nicholas wore a grey morning suit as if it had been designed for him, for his tall, lovely figure with his slim waist and strong shoulders. There was a creamy–white rosebud on his lapel, and under the grey suit was a sage–green waistcoat, an ivory shirt, and a dusky–rose cravat. Dave was grinning at his husband-to-be for the sheer delight of seeing him, but he was also beginning to see that between them Nicholas and Denise had come up with a genius solution to the clothes problem. The away team were certainly far more casually dressed than the home team, but the shades of grey, pink and green – while very Australian on one hand and very English on the other – made the whole thing work together perfectly. "God, this is brilliant!" Dave exclaimed.

"Denise," said Nicholas in heartfelt tones – though he didn't let Dave go. "Thank you. *Thank you.*"

She was happy, too. "My pleasure, Nicholas."

"And as for you, Charles," Nicholas continued. "How gorgeous are you in pink! You almost make me wish I hadn't seen David first."

Charlie guffawed under his breath. Richard and Robert had come over by then, and each shook Charlie's hand, and kissed Denise on the cheek, with much murmured admiration. Robin was standing there looking somewhat overawed by the whole thing – and also utterly charming in a perfectly tailored morning suit of his own.

Dave, who'd been dreading so many aspects of this day, found himself declaring, "I can hardly even wait to see the photos!"

Nicholas laughed. "Hey, let's get married first, though, eh? Seeing as we're here."

"Yes, let's," Dave agreed. And they turned, and walked together hand-in-hand into the Disraeli Room and down the aisle, with their beloved friends and family following along behind.

"I declare that I know of no legal reason why we may not register as each other's civil partner. I understand that in signing this document we will be forming a civil partnership with each other."

Those were the formal vows, such as they were. Even Dave thought they lacked poetry. But then they each said a few words of their own, and they exchanged rings.

Nicholas said: "From the first day I met you, David, you made me feel safe. You made me realise that I could unfurl my wings and be myself and simply live. I'm not afraid any more. I'm not afraid. No matter how long or short a time we have together, I want you to know – I want you to always remember – that no one has ever been happier than how I am with you. David, I want to spend the rest of my life with you."

And Dave replied, "Then that's what we'll do."

Dave said: "We were friends first. Even though I turned you down, and it took me ages to realise what we could be together, you were a real friend to me, and I was a friend to you. We took care of each other, right from the start. And we still have that, that's still the bedrock, even though we have so much more as well now. We take care of each other, and we'll go on looking after each other for all the years to come. And that means the world to me. Nicholas, I want to spend the rest of my life with you."

And Nicholas replied, "Then that's what we'll do."

Everyone was so happy, and the whole thing felt so charged. Robin finished off the ceremony by reading out a poem by A.A. Milne called *Us Two*. Dave had originally thought Winnie-the-Pooh a rather bizarre choice for a wedding ceremony, but hearing it on the day, when they were already bubbling over with joy, he felt it was absurdly apt.

Even then, though, he wasn't quite done because there was something more he had to say – now, for the record, and with witnesses. Just as the registrar was about to call time, Dave said for them all to hear, "I love you, Nicholas. I *love* you."

And Nicholas said, "I love you, too, David Taylor."

And they were married.

honeymoon

seven

Dave and Nicholas spent their wedding night in an old manor house turned hotel about a half–hour drive from the Goring family home. Their room was large and seemed to date back centuries. It was all rich worn reds and wood panelling, tapestries and velvets, with an enormous four–poster bed. The en suite bathroom seemed to date back no later than yesterday, though the style of it all was old–fashioned.

Dave didn't take much of this in, however. They were both quiet, and only had eyes for each other, though Dave was growing more and more bashful at the thought of what was ahead, while Nicholas seemed to be calmer and more confident by the moment. They ate a very light supper in the hotel restaurant – both drinking plenty of water with lime juice, which seemed to be becoming a firm habit despite all the teasing about Dave being at risk of forfeiting his Australian citizenship.

Soon it was time to head upstairs.

The room was dark and mysterious now, with only a bedside lamp glowing and a wood fire burning in the large fireplace, throwing light and making the shadows dance. Dave wandered in, feeling a little lost, while Nicholas locked the door securely behind them.

Then Nicholas was there before him, taking his hands, and pressing a gentle kiss to Dave's mouth. "I thought I'd go and have a shower. Or do you want to go first? I want to be – perfect for you."

"You go first," Dave managed to whisper.

Another kiss, and then Nicholas headed off, humming to himself quite happily.

Dave sorted through the gear in his overnight bag, and then just sat on a chair and waited. It felt like forever and like not long enough, but then Nicholas reappeared, damp and flushed and dressed only in his favourite blue robe. "Your turn," Nicholas said brightly.

Dave grabbed his gear, and headed for the bathroom without a word.

The Big Day

He said 'I love you' today. Is it weird that we hadn't said that before? It's not like we didn't know. If there were any doubts, then him coming to England pretty much put those to rest.

We got married today, and he said 'I love you'.

He's in the shower now, and when he comes out –

Well, I have so much to write about, what with the ceremony and the reception. So many photos to share. Our wonderful family and friends. Thank you. If you were a part of today, and you're reading this: Thank you. It was astonishing.

But I think I'll keep this post short. I am just about to have better things to do ...

He said 'I love you'.

Dave took somewhat longer getting ready than Nicholas, though eventually even Dave got impatient with himself, and he cautiously opened the door and stepped through into the bedroom.

Nicholas was waiting for him, sitting on the side of the bed. A lovely smile dawned on Nicholas's face as he took in the sight of Dave's new cream silk robe. Dave just stood there, pinned by Nicholas's gaze. After a moment, Nicholas asked in quietly appreciative tones, "Is that silk you're wearing for me ... ?"

Yes. He couldn't find his voice, so he just nodded. He knew his cheeks were glowing pink, and not from the heat of the shower.

"Come here, you gorgeous thing ..."

He walked a little closer and then tilted his head away, not wanting to refuse. But wanting to get this over with. He took a breath, and then lifted a hand to the robe's belt; pulled at one end, and let the knot fall away. The robe sighed open, and revealed what he wore underneath.

Nicholas gasped, and fell to his knees on the floor, staring.

It was only a plain slip in the same cream silk, though shaped – on the bias, Denise said – to be slightly snugger around his waist. It wasn't much, but it was enough to make Dave feel exquisitely self-conscious.

"Oh, *David* ..." Nicholas lifted reverential hands to shape around the front of Dave's thighs. Staring. Still staring.

Dave wasn't quite sure how much Nicholas could see, but the slip was barely long enough, and he thought his cock must be peeking out below the silk hem. He felt more naked than naked.

He let the robe slip back off his shoulders and down his arms while Nicholas watched, and then he let it go so it slid right down and pooled on the floor about his feet.

"You are so very beautiful," Nicholas said in hushed tones. He pressed his face in against Dave's cock and balls, caressing them through the silk, his hands slipping around to Dave's rear.

When Nicholas sat back on his heels again and looked up, Dave offered the gold silk ribbons he'd held clutched in one hand. "I didn't know –"

"Oh, my darling man …" Nicholas pressed a kiss to Dave's hand and took the ribbons – after a moment he tied one around Dave's right thigh, about midway down, finishing it off with a bow. He pressed a kiss just above it. "All right?" he asked.

Dave nodded. He felt … adorned. He felt as if he were worth adorning. Worth adoring. Such a notion had hardly even entered his head before.

Nicholas took another ribbon, and tied it around Dave's left wrist, taking up the long ends and tying bow after bow with them until the ribbon became a golden corsage. Then Nicholas put the other ribbons aside, and simply spent forever and forever suckling at Dave's balls and rubbing his nose at the base of Dave's cock until it stood proud, jutting out from under the silk – until Dave himself only remained upright in the warm haze of pleasure because of Nicholas's hands firmly holding onto his hips, and his own hands resting on Nicholas's shoulders.

"Come to the bed," Nicholas eventually said. He stood, bringing the ribbons with him, and he led the way despite it only being a few steps. He climbed up onto the sheets, kneeling there and carefully bringing Dave after him, carefully laying him down, arranging him there on his back with his knees bent. Nicholas showed Dave the ribbons. "I'll tie you down, if you like – or you could promise me not to move unless I say so."

"I promise," said Dave, his voice as rough as if he hadn't used it all day. He wasn't sure it was a promise he could keep, but he was already dealing with enough without being bound as well. "I promise I'll try."

"Good," said Nicholas. "That's so good. I love you so much …"

"I love you, too," he replied. And he watched as Nicholas arranged him, he watched Nicholas and let himself be arranged. His feet were slid up close to his butt, and his knees gently pressed as wide apart as they would go. His arms were stretched out to each side. There was nothing for his hands to hang onto, but he figured he could cope with that, he could keep them there.

Nicholas knelt between Dave's spread thighs, and slid his hands around Dave's waist; grasped him either side just above his hipbones, and gently encouraged him upwards. "Come on … arch your back the way you like to."

He did – happily, obediently – feeling that delicious curve shaping his backbone, feeling his thighs widen further still, his head tilt back and press into the pillow. He felt glorious, and then there was the silk shifting against his skin – Nicholas had been so right about that – and the ribbons adorning him, Nicholas adoring him …

"Now, stay exactly there, my darling man …" And Nicholas bent to take Dave's cockhead into his mouth, and suckle as sweetly as he'd treated Dave's balls; it was the only contact between them, and it held something of the divine.

Dave moaned raggedly, loving the feel of Nicholas's mouth on him with no barriers, no protection. They'd had the tests done weeks ago, but then with nothing being said, they'd taken a step back, somehow agreeing to save this experience for this night, to help make it all really count. Which meant that soon – soon – not soon enough – Nicholas would be fucking him for the first time without a rubber, there'd be Nicholas and Dave and nothing between them. Dave groaned in need, and arched up just a little more, opened his thighs, opened himself a little more, pushing the boundaries a little further. Nicholas chuckled around his cock, and the tremors made Dave *shake* …

Then a well–lubed finger slid into him and he was lost … lost … lost in warm golden darkness and a pleasure so intense. He tossed his head and a moan reverberated through him. He wasn't sure – he'd meant to ask, but he had no words – he wasn't sure if he was allowed to come yet – but the pleasure went on forever, for impossibly ever – and with no warning the end was upon him, and Nicholas rumbled appreciatively around him which meant it was permitted, it was approved – and the pleasure surged through him, making him quake so that even though he grabbed at the sheets with either hand, he couldn't help himself, he shook loose and lost the pattern he was meant to keep – his feet planted firmly and his thighs pushed him up – but that was all right, for Nicholas was holding onto his hip with one strong hand, staying with him, Nicholas's mouth and finger drawing every last ounce of pleasure through him and then returning it tenfold.

"Oh ..." he groaned, collapsing back at last, sprawling back ... "sorry, I'm sorry ..."

"You beautiful man," Nicholas said fervent and low. "God, you're incredible, you taste like the purest nectar. No wonder the butterflies couldn't get enough!" Then he was kneeling up between Dave's thighs, pushing in close and hauling Dave's rear onto his own thighs – intent – but not so intent that he didn't take care to ask, "All right? David?"

"Please," he said. "Please."

Dave's legs were too heavy with satiation to move, but Nicholas lifted one to hook a heel on his shoulder, bent the other leg around his waist – and then was pushing in, his cock lubed and *hot* and hard and it was so fucking intense, so fucking good – Dave cried out as if sundered, his eyes closing, his hands clutching, but Nicholas was wise enough to hear that right, to read that, to know that Dave was feeling it and *loving* it. And Dave gasped, and opened his eyes, opened himself further, let Nicholas's gaze pour down into him, and fill him, so they were two made one.

And they didn't last long, how could they possibly last – Nicholas's guttural groans rolling through them both, his long pale fingers digging into Dave's flesh as if hanging on for life itself – and then Nicholas was crying out and coming, his seed pulsing deep within Dave, a wet blessing deep inside him, Nicholas's seed becoming a part of him now – and the pleasure impossibly surged through Dave again, just once in an aftershock, leaving him weak and dazed and wonderful –

At last Nicholas collapsed down beside him, and they managed to shift, to hold each other near, Nicholas peppering kisses to whatever of Dave he could reach, until eventually the giddiness ebbed away and they both quietened, and then slipped away into a peaceful doze.

eight

Their wedding night had been spent in the luxuries of the best room in a manor house; their honeymoon would be spent in an isolated cottage on the Lizard Peninsula of Cornwall. Not that they were exactly roughing it, as the cottage belonged to a friend of Robert's and had been done up in a suitably traditional style but with no expense or mod-con spared. Also, Dave had to laugh at the English definition of 'isolated', as the village of Lizard was no further away than a ten- or fifteen-minute stroll.

Still, they had a magnificent view all to themselves, with the only other human construction in sight an old circle of standing stones on top of a steep rise to the north of them. Otherwise there was grassy moorland, with a sheltering hill close behind them, and in front – to the west – nothing but the edge of a high cliff, with the ground to the north descending to craggy rocks, then continuing on until eventually curving round to the west. Beyond all of that was the ocean. The beautiful, powerful ocean stretching all the way to a distant horizon. The place was quite breath-taking.

"Stunning," was Nicholas's muttered verdict on their first evening there as the sun began westering. "Stunning." He was, unnervingly, loitering almost right on the cliff edge, and with his hands jammed in his jeans pockets, too, so he wouldn't be able to grab onto anything if he tripped over his own clumsy feet or lost his balance.

"Mate," said Dave, easing up near him – though not too near. "Come back here, would you? I am *not* going to lose you when we've only been married a day. And especially not over a cliff. It would make me seem – a bit too laid-back."

"But take a look down here! It's like we've got our own little private beach."

First Dave had heard of it. He sidled a little closer, and carefully peered over. A long way down – a *long* way down at the foot of the cliff, there was a crescent of pure white sand between two sharp dark outcrops of rock, with gorgeous turquoise water lapping gently on this mild day. "Beautiful," he said. And he'd thought Australia had cornered the market on beautiful beaches. But then he looked at the surrounds, which were mostly sheer cliffs. "We're never getting down there, though. I don't know if you'd even want to land a boat. They have pretty high tides here, don't they?"

"Not as high as South Wales, but two or three metres on a regular basis."

"And all those rocks," Dave continued, figuring he'd better quash any of Nicholas's whimsies before they turned into wants. "Not the place to go taking chances in boats."

"No," Nicholas agreed. "This area is known for its shipwrecks. All the 'romance' of the high seas!"

"Right. Not exactly the sort of romance we're after just now." Dave turned away, and looked for alternatives. "We could go explore those standing stones."

Nicholas obligingly came away from the cliff edge, but cast him a wry look. "Now who's being reckless … ?"

"Reckless?" Dave considered the stones, which had obviously been standing there for hundreds if not thousands of years. "Well, you'd be pretty unlucky if one of them happened to fall on you, after all this time."

Nicholas laughed, but followed along as Dave started ambling in that direction. "Where's your imagination, David Taylor? You – maybe one day the custodian of a Dreamtime site!"

"Oh." All right, that had probably been pretty stupid. "I don't know anything about standing stones. I guess they're full of religious significance, then?"

"We don't know. They were made so long ago that their purpose has been forgotten. The knowledge hasn't survived like it has for the Aborigines in Australia. All we have are theories. And superstitions."

That didn't sound like so much fun. Not that Dave really believed in any of that kind of stuff, but here they were, alone in an isolated cottage with nothing but a circle of standing stones for company. And a very high cliff just beyond their front door. Dave was beginning to wonder if it would actually be a very good idea to spend the entire honeymoon in bed. He was just about to suggest this notion, when Nicholas continued, "There's probably a ghost story or two about these stones. We should ask around."

"Or not," said Dave. "Don't you think it's better not to know? Then we can just admire them as … as a feat of engineering. Something kinda beautiful, created by people who were probably every bit as smart as us. Or most of us, anyway … Certainly a lot cleverer than me!"

They were almost at the stones, and both remained silent for the last short climb up the steep rise. Then they were in the circle – what must have been at one time a pretty much perfect circle of tall stones, a total of –

"Don't count them!" blurted Nicholas.

"What?" Dave scowled at him. "Too late, anyway. There's –"

"*No!* Don't tell me!"

"Oh, for God's sake …" Dave rolled his eyes, while Nicholas either looked at Dave directly or at their general surroundings rather indirectly as if not even letting his subconscious pick up the pattern. "Right." There were nine stones in the circle, with their surfaces worn but most of them standing true, and only one looking as if it had been broken off at some stage. Then there was a tenth stone, squarer than the others and lying flat in the centre. There was a margin of bare dirt around the latter, as if the grass had been worn away by visiting feet. Dave wandered up to it, and propped his own foot on one edge. "So, what was this for, then?"

Nicholas shrugged. "We tend to think of them as altars, and I suppose they probably were. That's where some of the stories come in, anyway. People were sacrificed or executed or murdered on that, and their ghosts remain to haunt us."

Dave squinted at his partner, who was standing there with his hands shoved in his pockets and his shoulders hunched as if his hackles were up. "D'you believe in ghosts, then?" Dave asked, trying not to sound quite as sceptical as he actually was. "I thought you were a scientist!"

"I don't know … Not really …"

"You *do*, don't you!"

"Well, everything's made of matter and energy. *We're* made of matter and energy. When we die, where does that energy go? If it's a good death, a peaceful death, maybe it just … transforms into other, entirely natural forces. If not …" And Nicholas actually shivered. "If not, maybe it lingers."

Dave considered him for a long moment, then walked back over to him and ran a hand down the underside of his bare forearm. "You know what?"

"What?" Nicholas looked at him, unsmiling.

"This is our honeymoon, remember? I reckon we should just head back to the cottage, and get settled in. And then we can climb into bed, and seriously try spending the entire two weeks there."

That earned him a grin, though Nicholas still seemed a bit shaky. "Sounds like a plan."

"It *is* a plan. Nothing and nobody is going to bother us there. Everyone knows a blanket will protect you against anything, ghosts or otherwise."

Nicholas laughed. They had already left the stone circle, and were ambling back down the hill. "Will you let me have one afternoon out of bed, though? Just one?"

"Dunno. Depends."

"I just want to –" Nicholas looked about him. "The coastal path must run round the back of the hill behind the cottage. If we pick that up and head north and then west for a mile or so, there's this place called Kynance Cove. It's meant to be really gorgeous. All dramatic rocks and pale sand and green sea water."

"All right," Dave agreed with a great show of reluctance. "As long as it's just one afternoon."

"They say it's very *Famous Five*, you know? That's –"

"Enid Blyton, yeah. Read the books as a kid."

Nicholas was back to glowing happily and walking freely, rather than being hunched and spooked. "This is just the place for an adventure, isn't it? All smugglers and spies, and great long hikes with bars of chocolate in our backpacks."

Dave laughed. They were almost back at the cottage. "I've got the perfect adventure in mind right now."

Nicholas's grin grew broader still. "Does it take place in bed?"

"It does."

"Will there be chocolate?"

"Yeah, I think we can manage some chocolate. You'll need your sustenance, after all."

Nicholas laughed, like a joyous peal of bells. "Then lead the way!"

The following morning Nicholas and Dave ambled into the village to say hello to the woman who acted as housekeeper and caretaker for the cottage when the owners weren't in Cornwall. Along with her mother and daughter, she also ran a small grocery store and news agency. Nicholas and Dave introduced themselves, and she shook their hands with a pleasant smile. "Margaret Widgery. This is my mother Joan, and my daughter Maeve."

The older woman smiled on them benignly from her comfortable chair placed directly in the sun pouring through the front windows. The younger woman said "Hiya" and finished tapping out a message on her smartphone before slipping it away into a pocket and returning to the task of shelving new stock. She had a flower – a white daisy – tucked into her abundant curly red hair.

"I hope you found everything shipshape at the cottage," Margaret was continuing. "It's just as Mrs Brett and her family like it, but you must say if there's anything you want done differently."

"No, it's great," Nicholas said. "I'm sure we'll be very comfortable there."

"I stocked the fridge, of course, but I wasn't sure whether you'd be wanting to eat dinner out, or cook for yourselves …" She paused, and confided with a hint of a blush. "I understand this is your honeymoon, but other than an extra bottle or two of champagne I didn't know –"

"We'll be fine," Nicholas assured her. "We can fend for ourselves, if need be!"

"And may I offer my congratulations, as I should have done before." She shook their hands again, and Dave saw that the daughter was grinning at them, while the grandmother seemed mostly oblivious.

"Thanks," Dave said. He was starting to wonder when he'd encounter someone who *didn't* approve. He wasn't entirely sure how he'd handle it.

"Thank you very much, Mrs Widgery. We're very happy about it, I must say. It's been a *marvellous* few days …"

Before Nicholas could launch into a detailed account of exactly what he was so very happy about, Dave smoothly cut in. "We were wondering if you knew anything about the circle of standing stones near the cottage. Like, the history, maybe."

Margaret looked rather taken aback. "I can't say that I do. It's local stone, as you've probably seen, and they say it dates back well over two thousand years. But more than that – I don't know."

"Any stories, then?" he tried. "Like, what happens if you count the stones? Nicholas said I shouldn't."

"Ah!" Maeve put in rather cheerfully. "If you manage to correctly count the stones, then the Devil pops up and drags you back down to Hell with him."

"And yet," said Dave, "here I am."

"*Why, this is Hell,*" Nicholas muttered, "*nor am I out of it.*"

Margaret looked from one to the other of them – but surely fretting more over the maintenance of their happiness rather than anything real relating to the stones. "It's nothing but tall tales. I'm sure there's nothing at all to worry about."

Then Joan spoke, proving she wasn't so oblivious after all. They all hushed to listen to her quiet voice. "If you see someone up there, sitting on the altar stone …"

"Admiring the view," put in Dave. "It's a great view from up there." Not that they had really looked, now that Dave thought about it. They'd been more concerned with the actual stones.

"I wouldn't go disturbing them, my lad."

"Why's that?" he asked. Though he knew he didn't want to hear the answer.

"Because sometimes it'll be folk having a rest while walking along the coastal path. And sometimes it'll be folk who aren't resting at all."

At which Nicholas was looking decidedly spooked.

"Right," said Dave. "I think that's probably enough hair-raising stories for now."

"Pay it no mind," Margaret urged. "They're just stories."

"Exactly. And we're on our honeymoon. To be honest, I plan to spend most of it safely tucked away in bed." At which Maeve guffawed appreciatively – and Dave abruptly blushed crimson, realising that not only had he managed to set Nicholas's imagination working overtime about the stones but he hadn't avoided the honeymoon-related embarrassment after all. "Oh *God*," he grumbled. "One day I'll learn when to shut up."

At least Nicholas was looking at him fondly, ghosts forgotten for now. "I think that's our cue to leave, taking what little is left of our dignity with us."

"Absolutely."

Margaret kept them long enough to press upon them another business card with her phone numbers, despite them having already found a stack of such cards at the cottage – and to assure them at disconcerting length that she wouldn't be dropping by without phoning first, so they should feel free to *do whatever they liked at any time* without fearing *any surprises*. Soon enough, however, they were out of there.

"I think," said Nicholas, "we should go and do … exactly what they think we're going to go and do …"

"All right," Dave gamely replied. It wasn't as if he could feel any more embarrassed.

"Or ... maybe something wickeder still."

Dave grinned at him. "You're on."

They had lunch at a pub in Lizard the next day. It was cold but sunny, so they sat out the front under a canvas umbrella, taking in the view to the south. The land fell away until it reached the southernmost point of mainland Britain. "We should do that, should we?" asked Dave in admittedly lazy tones. "Are we doing the tourist thing?"

"We could wander down there ... if I've left you with the necessary energy."

Dave thought for a moment, and chuckled. "There's no right answer to that, is there?"

"No," Nicholas smugly replied.

"Have you done the other points? I mean, north, west, east ..."

"No, and I'm not likely to now, am I?"

"Maybe we should do this one anyway. Seeing as we're here."

Nicholas scrunched up his face a bit. "Have you done that in Australia?"

"No ... Byron Bay's pretty cool, though. That's the easternmost point. That's worth a visit, anyway. Pete Murray lives there, though he's really a Queenslander."

Nicholas was grinning again. "Will we go on holiday there, do you think?"

"Yeah, maybe." It was Dave's turn to scrunch up his face. "I dunno. Some years, I'm so busy with the tours that just hanging out at home is enough of a holiday."

"I can understand that."

Their conversation might have ambled on forever, if a couple of blokes hadn't come out from the pub with their pints, and sat themselves down at the next table along. And they obviously weren't there for the ploughman's lunch. One was an older man with a white hair and beard, who seemed well–weathered and well–salted. The other was maybe forty or so, with black hair and a devilish glint in his dark eyes made all the more attractive by his narrow sinuous hips.

"Afternoon," the two blokes said in greeting.

"Afternoon," Dave said – and Nicholas responded rather warily, "Good afternoon."

"I heard you young fellows were interested in our stone circle," the older bloke said.

"Well –" said Dave, wondering how to head this off at the pass. Nicholas's face had gone as blank and cold as if the shutters had come down.

"I could tell you some tales, and that's the truth."

"Tell 'em, Bert," the thin one encouraged.

"That really won't be necessary," said Nicholas. He added rather pointedly, "We're on our honeymoon, you see. The two of us – fellows."

Old Bert wasn't put off, but blessed them with a genial smile and actually winked before launching into his story. "My mam told me, from when I was a boy –"

"*Really*," Nicholas continued, "we're far too busy fucking to care about stone circles. And when I say fucking, I mean *each other*."

"Oh aye, I heard that, too," the fellow quite amiably replied, winking again.

Dave couldn't help but let out a laugh. It seemed that Nicholas had been silenced and maybe even a little shamed, so Dave said, "Go on, then. Tell us your tales." And he reached across the table to squeeze Nicholas's hand and then hold it as a gesture of support.

"So, my mam used to tell me, right from when I was a boy, that those stones used to be witches who were dancing around in a circle one May Day, and they was cursed by the local priest for their heathen ways, and turned to stone."

Nicholas was unimpressed. "I thought the stones were over two thousand years old. In which case they're a bit early for priests and heathens."

"*I* heard tell," said the other bloke, "they were maidens of the village who refused the, er … the *attentions* of their local lord and master, and it was him that damned them."

"Right …"

"I heard there are times when the local maidens still dance there," he added with a knowing wink. "Either way, witches or maidens, once a year at midnight every May Day they are freed from the stone for an hour – but still they must dance, though they are weary unto death."

"*And* once a year at midnight," Bert contributed, "when the altar stone hears the church bells ring, it turns over, it turns right the way over."

"Is that also on May Day?" Nicholas asked, in full sceptical mode – though he looked rather paler than usual. "I'm sure no one in the cottage would get any sleep, with all that going on."

They were saved from any further stories when their lunch arrived, and the barkeep chased the two locals back inside with mock threats of never serving them again if they drove away the visitors. Perhaps the barkeep had read Nicholas's discomfort, because he came back to say, "I'm sorry. Bert is mostly harmless, and he can be great company, but Vincent does egg him on rather."

"It's fine," said Dave. "Honestly, it's fine." Then, once they were alone again, he said to Nicholas, "These stories … Don't think about them, if they bother you."

"They don't bother me," Nicholas replied a little remotely. Then after a moment he smiled, and said rather more sincerely, "They don't bother me at all."

Late that night, however, Dave woke in the small hours to find Nicholas standing at the bedroom window, having drawn one of the curtains open, staring pensively up towards where the stone circle must be. "Hey," said Dave, bleary with sleep.

"Hey," Nicholas softly replied. "Sorry. Didn't mean to wake you."

"'S all right …" Dave got up out of bed despite the bed being perfectly warm and comfortable, and went to stand behind Nicholas, wrapped his arms snugly round his narrow waist. He peered over Nicholas's shoulder to see the stones fitfully lit by moonlight. "What's going on up there?"

"Nothing. Nothing, really." Nicholas sighed. "Those are just cloud shadows."

"Not ghosts, then?"

"I think we're going to lose the fine weather."

"All the more reason to stay tucked up safely in bed."

Nicholas huffed a laugh, and then sighed again. "Just what I always wanted … a husband with a one–track mind."

"Come back here, then." Dave took the man's hand and tugged, stepping back towards the bed. Nicholas followed him willingly enough.

239

It was true that Nicholas generally took the lead when they had sex, but every now and then Dave felt the need to take care of his lover, and this was such a time. He encouraged Nicholas into the bed, lying on his back, and then lay near, leaning over him to kiss him and sooth him with gentle hands until Nicholas finally forgot about the fretting, and thought only of Dave.

Slowly still, Dave knelt up and undressed them one item at a time – first his own t-shirt and then Nicholas's, next his own boxer shorts and then his lover's. His husband's. They were both so very ready, but he didn't rush. He reached for the lube in the bedside cabinet, spread some on his palm and then caressed it onto Nicholas's cock and balls, and his own. Then he lay over the man, matching them up with their legs interleaved, and his hips almost by instinct started an easy rocking motion as he thought about the strong slow surge of the sea.

Nicholas's hands came up to run back over Dave's hair, to shape themselves to his nape and encourage him down for a kiss, and then slowly slowly those hands slid lower down Dave's back, those palms and long cool fingers moulding themselves to every inch of his skin in turn, until at last they were firmly spread on Dave's rear, and Nicholas eventually in desperate need grasped him hard, dug his fingertips in, begged with those midnight-blue eyes …

Dave spun it out for a few moments longer until at last even he felt it was the perfect time, and then he slid a hand down under Nicholas's rear, and they crushed themselves even closer together, each thrusting against the other like mad things – until the end came, and they quaked with it, and clutched at each other, and mouthed kisses over anything of the other they could reach.

Afterwards, as Dave was drifting drowsily, Nicholas said, "I think you should fuck me."

"Mmm?" he managed.

"Not *now*. I mean, sometime. While we're here on our honeymoon."

Dave opened one eye and then the other to peer at his lover in the dark. "If that's really what you want."

"It is. I really think we should."

"All right," he said, though it was more an acknowledgement than an agreement. "Sleep now?" he asked.

"Yes. Sleep now." And Nicholas turned to him, and they snuggled close as they usually did when they slept. But Dave was sure he slipped away first.

nine

The following morning was rainy, so they took the opportunity to laze about, indulge in a full cooked breakfast, and then put their feet up in the front room with a book for Nicholas, the Kindle for Dave, and a large pot of coffee between them. The rain cleared in the early afternoon however, so they decided to walk the coastal path around to Kynance Cove, even if the overcast sky meant they wouldn't be seeing the countryside at its best.

As it was, the place was pretty spectacular. The cove was fairly small, but the rocky outcrops were huge and dramatically shaped, and the sea was running high with milky–turquoise waves dashing white spray. Dave kind of loved the wildness of it. They took a while to watch the waves crashing in, but it wasn't long before the cold wind coming off the sea started biting a bit too deep. Luckily there was a café just inland from the cove, so they headed there for a warming cuppa.

Dave placed their order while Nicholas went to use the facilities. He took the opportunity to ask the guy at the counter if there were any butterflies around at this time of year. The guy consulted with a young woman who happened to be making a delivery, but unfortunately the general consensus seemed to be that there weren't, and certainly not now the weather had finally turned cold. "Thanks anyway, mate," Dave responded.

"What's up?" Nicholas asked once he returned.

"I was just asking about butterflies in the area. I think we're out of luck."

Nicholas smiled at him with a glowing kind of softness. "I know. It's far too cold for them by now, I'm afraid, and not enough flowers to drink from."

"I guess I figured you'd plan any trip like this around butterflies."

The smile grew fonder still. "It's our honeymoon, David," Nicholas said, reaching to hold Dave's hand across the table. "I wasn't thinking of anything but you."

Dave tried to suppress a pleased grin, but didn't succeed very well. He hung onto Nicholas's hand when Nicholas would have withdrawn it. He might be putting his Aussie citizenship at risk for being demonstrative, but Denise had trained him too well over all their years together. She'd had no patience with the restraint of affection beyond what was required by decency.

"But you know," Nicholas continued, his smile turning a bit cheeky, "if you really can't get by without a butterfly sighting, David Taylor – tart for them that you are – we could try at The Eden Project."

"Ah. The place with those big bio domes or whatever they are?"

"That's the one. Just in case I'm not enough for you, and you want a butterfly drinking your nectar, too."

Dave chuckled, and unleashed his best grin. "You know you love that they love me. You don't mind sharing."

Nicholas growled in reply, and his hand tightened possessively around Dave's. "In very rare circumstances … and only with butterflies. Don't you go getting any ideas."

He didn't tease any more, but leaned in against the table edge to murmur, "I'm all yours, Nicholas. I promised you that."

They gazed at each other intensely for a lovely charged moment – but then had to sit back when their coffee and tea were brought to the table. "Sorry to interrupt, guys," the guy said. "Thought you'd like it hot, you know."

Dave guffawed and Nicholas just about hooted with laughter at the hint of innuendo. "Thank you," Nicholas managed. "You're right, we *do* like it hot."

Once the guy headed off again, however, Dave saw that not everyone at the café approved of his and Nicholas's involvement with each other. 'At last!' part of him cried. Someone to challenge them. Someone to face down. Dave needed the practice, he figured, before he went home to Oz and became the subject of teasing and taunts.

There was an older couple sitting at a table nearby; the man was scowling and the woman looked disgusted. They didn't say anything, but they stared in disapproval at Nicholas and Dave as if they expected this would force the two men to quit holding hands so very obviously.

Nicholas hadn't noticed yet, being too busy checking on how his tea was brewing in the teapot. Dave, however, took the opportunity to direct a big uncomplicated beaming smile at the couple. And he leaned towards them a little to confide, "We're on our honeymoon!"

The woman had been about to drink more of her tea, but now she put down the cup as if having lost her taste for it. Nicholas, having finally taken in the situation, lifted Dave's hand and pressed a kiss to the back of it as reward and further provocation. The woman stood up and stalked out, leaving the man to belatedly stand and then grumble a complaint at the café guy on his way out – which was politely shrugged off.

When he came over to clear the couple's table, Dave said, "Sorry. Didn't mean to chase away your customers."

The guy shrugged again. "Who needs them? You two enjoy yourselves. You deserve it."

"If they didn't pay, I'll cover the bill."

"They'd already paid, don't worry about it." And he nodded politely before taking the abandoned tea things away, and leaving them alone.

"My knight in shining armour!" Nicholas murmured, caught between admiration and laughter. "Will you tilt at *all* my dragons … ?"

"Yes," he fervently vowed. "*Yes*. For all my life."

Late that night Dave woke to again find Nicholas standing at the bedroom window staring up at the standing stones. Even taking into account the eerie effect of the moon's cool light, Nicholas appeared pale and spooked. "Hey," said Dave, waking up quite quickly this time. "What are you up to? Come back to bed."

Nicholas glanced at him before returning his gaze to the stone circle. "There were lights up there. I swear I saw lights up there."

Dave frowned, and slowly got out of the bed to go stand beside Nicholas. "What kind of lights?"

"I don't know. Just a couple of dim lights, or maybe a few. Bobbing about."

It took a moment for Dave to focus properly on the stones, and then he stared hard for a while, but there was nothing up there now. "What, like torches, maybe? Or do you say flashlights?"

"We say torches. Could be, but they weren't very bright."

"Fireflies … ?" Dave tried.

Nicholas cast him a look. "*Very* unlikely."

"Well, you're the scientist," Dave responded, a little sharper than he'd have liked, but what could anyone expect from a man woken in the middle of the night? "What do *you* think they were?"

"Will–o'–the–wisps," Nicholas said, just as sharp but with a touch of whimsy.

"Which are … ?"

244 | Of Dreams and Ceremonies

"Pixies carrying little lights trying to lead you astray."

Dave let that be for a moment. Then he said, "You know, if you just left the curtains closed, they'd protect us. Like the blankets do. We're perfectly safe here in our bedroom. It's like a fort."

"You think this is all in my imagination, don't you?"

"Whether it is or not, as long as you don't go out there and try following the lights over the cliff or whatever, we'll be fine."

"There really were lights, you know. Though I'm assuming people, not pixies."

"Promise me you won't go investigate in the middle of the night."

Nicholas just looked at him rather flatly for a long moment. But eventually he said, "I promise."

"Good. Now, come back to bed, and let me hold you, and maybe we can get some sleep. You'll be perfectly safe."

"I know," said Nicholas, following Dave to the bed with a sigh, as if merely humouring him. Though when Nicholas climbed in after him, he wriggled deep into Dave's arms, and that felt entirely genuine – as did his remark. "I'm always perfectly safe with you."

The next morning after they'd eaten and cleared up breakfast, Dave found Nicholas at the table again poring over their map of Cornwall, measuring things off with a ruler. "What, are you working out distances or something?" Dave asked. "Are we going for a drive today?" He had to admit that taking the Jaguar out for a spin hadn't gotten old yet.

Nicholas looked at him a bit shamefaced for a moment, but then metaphorically girded his loins and announced, "You can draw a line on the map that runs from Lizard Point, through St Michael's Mount, to Gurnard's Head – which looks like a pretty significant promontory on the north coast of Cornwall. And as far as I can make out, the stone circle is right plumb on the line."

Dave let out a sigh. "So, what does that mean?"

"Do you know about ley lines … ?"

"They've been debunked as random coincidence, haven't they?"

Nicholas seemed almost too astonished to be outraged. "I never realised what a sceptic you are! How did you find our waterhole in the Outback? And why on earth does Charlie think you have a Dreamtime connection with the place?"

Dave shrugged. "Dunno. I just think you've got to be careful with this kind of thing. Cos the human imagination is pretty damned powerful, and you can project anything you like on things that don't actually mean anything at all."

"Right," said Nicholas, obviously unimpressed.

"Anyway, if it *is* real – the Dreamtime thing, I mean – then that doesn't necessarily mean I'm gonna feel a connection with other places, too, does it? In fact, maybe it means that I *won't*."

Which Dave thought was an entirely reasonable point, but Nicholas directed a mighty scowl at him, and Dave decided he might as well go get some fresh air before they ended up really arguing. Which he assumed was an activity to be avoided if possible while on honeymoon. "Just heading out for a wander," he announced – and once Nicholas had acknowledged him, he did so.

He didn't go far, but just rambled around in front of the cottage with his hands shoved in his jeans pockets. He didn't go near the cliff edge, as Nicholas was wont to do, but he watched the endlessly changeable sea which was steely-blue today under an overcast sky. Eventually he looked inland, and with a start realised there was a figure sitting on the altar stone in the middle of the stone circle.

For a moment his heart raced as he remembered Joan saying, 'I wouldn't go disturbing them, my lad.' But then the figure waved, and once Dave squinted to focus properly in the diffuse light of the day, he saw that it was actually harmless old Bert.

Dave waved back in a friendly manner, thinking that would be that. But then Bert waved again, somewhat more urgently than might be expected in a greeting between acquaintances, and Dave twigged that Bert wanted him – or them – to go up and talk to him. Dave shrugged, and tried to indicate with another wave, 'Wait there, and I'll be up in a minute.' Well, it looked like Bert wasn't going anywhere for now, so Dave headed back inside.

Nicholas had put the map aside for now, and was on his laptop. "I'm just starting up my blog for the day," he said. "Do you want to go visit the Eden Project? We could take our photo there, with some butterflies maybe. Could be cool."

"Are you writing about us disagreeing?" Though that wouldn't necessarily be such a bad thing. "I suppose that makes it seem all the more real, doesn't it? I mean, no relationship is all plane sailing."

Nicholas sniffed. "It *is* real. But no, I wasn't. Though I may write about us *discussing* the matter. It's not as if either of us is entirely convinced one way or the other, is it?"

Dave grinned at the man, hugely and stupidly relieved. He went over to drop a kiss to the top of Nicholas's dark-haired head, and then said, "You remember old Bert from the other day at the pub? He's up there at the stone circle. I think he wants to say hello."

"Okay. Is he coming down?"

"No, I think he wants us to go up. Is that all right?"

"Yes, of course," said Nicholas. He offered Dave a wry smile. "I promise I won't get spooked."

"Good man," said Dave. And they headed out to meet Bert.

The old fellow beamed at them genially as they reached the stone circle and walked up to the altar stone. He didn't get up from the stone – which was flat and low enough for his booted feet to be firmly on the ground – but he seemed happy enough that they'd come.

"Hello," said Dave. "It's Bert, isn't it? I'm Dave and this is Nicholas."

"Hello," Bert replied. His smile when it turned to Nicholas – as so many people's smiles did – grew sweeter still.

"How are you today?" Dave continued. "Are you taking in the view? It really is a great view from up here." He took the opportunity to finally look at said view himself, which was much the same as the one from their front door, though with added magnificence due to the higher ground. Their cottage looked snug and peaceful from here, tucked away in a rounded dell at the foot of a steep rise.

"Oh aye, I'm well enough," Bert said a bit bashfully, glancing at Nicholas again.

"What do you do around here?" Nicholas asked. "Are you a fisherman?" Which was what Dave would have guessed, too, given Bert's reddened weather-beaten skin.

"Used to be. But my boat – Well, I crew sometimes, for the *Alice May* out of Mullion, during the main season. But my boat, the *Fortune Teller*, is at Cadgwith – and I take tourists out for trips. Cash only, mind. Scenic trips." Bert looked hopefully at Nicholas. "Aye, maybe you'd like to come out, if the weather holds."

Nicholas looked at Dave with a querying brow, but it seemed clear he was interested. "Sure," Dave answered for them both. "If it's safe, you know?"

"Sure," Bert echoed, and his eyes slid away mischievously. "If you can spare the time away from … what you said you were doing here."

Nicholas snorted a laugh. "Sorry about that. I was being horribly obnoxious."

"You're on your honeymoon!" Bert protested. "What else should you be doing?"

"Okay," Dave said, trying to steer the conversation back to smoother waters, "we can probably fit a boat trip into our busy schedule. But only if it's safe. I don't want to be losing Nicholas already when I only just found him, I'm sure you can understand that."

"I know these waters like a landlubber knows his garden. And no one's ever been hurt on board the *Fortune Teller* – aye, nor lost off her, neither."

"Sounds like it could be fun," said Nicholas. "It would give us another perspective on the coastal scenery, at least."

"But I hear there's a lot of shipwrecks off Lizard Point," Dave persisted. "I don't want to add to them, and it's not like we're talking about taking a rowing boat out on a pond, is it?"

Something fired within Bert, though he also seemed confused, even a little uneasy. "Sure, and there's Spanish galleons down there with treasure, and old British frigates! I take people out diving for treasure." He frowned, and then squinted up at Nicholas. "Maybe you'd like to go diving, if the weather holds?"

"No. No, I can't." Nicholas was now looking even edgier than Bert. He appealed to Dave: "I can't. The pressure, you know?" He lifted a hand to his head, though Dave had already understood. Nicholas didn't want to subject his aneurysm to the compression and decompression involved in diving even in shallow waters.

"That's all right," Dave reassured him, though there was a part of him that was sorry to lose the opportunity. "We won't be diving. Is that something you used to do, Nicholas? I haven't even gone snorkelling before,

248 | Of Dreams and Ceremonies

though I wouldn't have minded learning."

"No, I never have – and now I can't."

"It's all right, I understand. We definitely won't be diving," Dave repeated to Bert. "But we'll think about the boat trip, all right? Especially if we have another nice sunny day."

"All right," Bert said, watching Nicholas with both curiosity and anxiety. They were all silent for a long moment, until at last Bert stood up. "It's gonna get blowy soon, but if we have a nice day, Mrs Widgery will know where to find me."

"Thanks, Bert, that's great. Either way, we'll see you soon."

Nicholas remained silent, despite Bert looking at him again, wanting something, even if it was simply acknowledgement.

Then, unexpectedly, Bert said, "You don't come up here at night, do you?"

Dave frowned. "No … No, we don't." He looked at Nicholas, who was likewise frowning, and no doubt remembering staring out their bedroom window at the stones at all hours of the night. "Why?" Dave asked. "Why shouldn't we?"

Bert shrugged, and started sidling off. "There's the cliff and the ground so uneven as can be treacherous and the – the – stones. And well, you don't want to be losing him already, do you?"

"All right," Dave equably agreed. As soon as Bert was out of earshot on his way back to town, Dave grumbled to Nicholas, "What the hell was all that about?"

"I don't know." Nicholas was pale again, though he didn't seem spooked so much as unsettled. "I don't know. Let's head back down and make a pot of tea."

Dave guffawed a little. "That's your answer to everything. You're so English!"

"And you love me for it."

He laughed again, fondly. "Seems that way!"

On the way back down the slope towards the cottage, Nicholas asked a bit edgily, "Are we going to go for a boat trip at least?"

"Not without consulting Margaret Widgery first," Dave said very firmly indeed. "Did you hear that about cash only? Doesn't exactly inspire confidence."

And Nicholas visibly relaxed. "Sometimes," he said – "just sometimes, mind you – I think you're an even better answer than a cup of tea, David Taylor."

Dave grinned at the man, for whether he agreed with it or not, he knew a man's truth when he heard it.

ten

They walked into Lizard the following morning, and headed for the grocery store. Margaret Widgery was there; her mother Joan was sitting in what must be her usual place, and this time Maeve was sitting by her, reading a book, with a white rosebud tucked into her thick red hair. While Dave explained his qualms to Margaret and asked her opinion, Nicholas browsed the postcards.

"Bert knows the sea and the peninsula as well as anyone," Margaret said in response. "He wouldn't take any risks with the tides or the weather. However, he's not an official tour operator. You'd be trusting him as an individual. An acquaintance."

"Do you know if his boat is licensed?"

"Well, I can't say for sure, but I should think so. He takes better care of the *Fortune Teller* than of himself. But he may not be fully insured for passengers, and so on." She caught her lower lip between her teeth, obviously unwilling to either recommend they take the trip or be unfair to Bert.

"I don't care so much about insurance," said Dave, "as about nothing bad happening in the first place."

"Well, there are always risks in taking a boat out to sea. But then there are risks in driving a car along the road – probably more! It becomes about what you're used to." Margaret sighed. "If you'd trust me to drive you to Penzance in my car, say, then you can trust Bert to take you out in his boat for a couple of hours. I suppose that's what it comes down to."

Joan put in, "Bert will bring you safe home again, no need to worry about that. He sails these waters by sun and by moon and by the stars."

"Thank you," Dave said to them both, nodding his appreciation.

"You'll let us know when you go out, though?" Margaret asked. "And let me know once you're safely back."

"Yeah – if we go. I'll have to think about it some more."

Margaret smiled at him. "I'm sure you'll make the right decision."

"And I think I finally have, too," said Nicholas, coming over to the counter with ten or twelve postcards and a pen, which he bought along with stamps. "This will surprise everyone! They'll wonder how we found the time, what with us being on our honeymoon and all."

Dave huffed a laugh, and turned away before he could blush again.

They headed for the same pub to have lunch, and sat outside again, in the sunshine close to the wall so they were out of the wind. There was a wood-burning brazier near them, which helped provide a little warmth and a lot of atmosphere.

Nicholas started writing out his postcards with fluent ease. Apparently he could be just as charming in writing as he was in person. "Take a couple," he encouraged Dave. "I bought plenty. I thought you'd like to send them to Denise and Charlie. They'll be home again by now, won't they?"

"All right," Dave grudgingly agreed, sifting through the remaining pile to pick out the two he found most appealing. However, there was only one pen, so for now he was excused from having to come up with actual words. He hadn't had much practice in the writing of postcards.

The barkeep came out with menus, made a point of welcoming them back, and then took their orders for both drinks and food. As he headed back inside, Dave glimpsed Bert hovering in the shadows just inside the doorway, peering out at them anxiously. When he realised Dave had seen him, Bert withdrew a little further – but it was obvious he was still there. Dave said to Nicholas, "I think Bert wants to come and say hello again."

Nicholas looked around, and waved cheerily – though he turned back to Dave and muttered, "I'm sorry if this bothers you. Rotten timing and all that, given that we just got hitched. But I'm afraid he seems to have taken a bit of a shine to me …"

Dave just stared at Nicholas for a long moment before guffawing. "Are you serious? *Everyone* falls for you, Nicholas. It's a wonder I had any chance at all."

"Oh," said Nicholas, apparently rather nonplussed.

"You just don't get to do anything about it any more. Not with anyone but me. All right?"

"Right," Nicholas agreed, promptly though a little vaguely. "Well, can he come and say hello, at least?"

"Of course." Dave laughed. "It's all right, I'm not the jealous type. But I'm loyal, remember? We're going to be loyal, aren't we?"

Nicholas nodded. "Of course we are. That's what I want, too." And after a moment in which they acknowledged this fundamental agreement,

Nicholas turned around again and beckoned for Bert to come and join them.

Bert shambled over and stood there looking a bit shyly at Nicholas. "Hello," he said.

"Hello, Bert," Nicholas replied. "We're still thinking about the boat trip, I'm sorry. I'm sure we'll make up our minds soon, though. It's not like we're here for very long. Hardly more than two weeks, really."

"That's all right," said Bert. Then after a brief pause, he blurted, "But you don't go up to the stone circle at night, do you?"

"No," said Nicholas with a frown. He glanced at Dave before asking, "Why? Why do you keep saying that?"

"It's not safe, it's not good."

Nicholas seemed spooked, but also intrigued. "Why, though? Does something happen up there? Some kind of ceremony, maybe?"

"No, that's not it. That's not it."

"But –"

"Bert! Are you bothering these fellows again?" It was slim, sinuous Vincent who'd come out of the pub to lay a restraining hand on Bert's arm. He seemed just a little too familiar with Bert, as if he knew he could presume. "Remember we got told not to bother these good fellows … ?"

Bert remained silent, but was alternately glancing at Vincent and looking rather imploringly at Nicholas.

"It's all right," said Dave, puzzled by the whole thing. "He's not bothering us."

"Nah, come inside, Bert," Vincent insisted. "You don't believe his tall tales, do you?" he asked Dave and Nicholas even as he tugged at Bert's arm.

"You were telling us tales about the standing stones as well," Nicholas pointed out.

"Fairy stories. Nothing but rubbish."

"Right …" Nicholas sounded sceptical, as well he might. If it was all rubbish, then why did Bert seem so unsettled?

"Come *on*, Bert," said Vincent – and after another tug at his arm, Bert followed Vincent back inside the pub, casting one last longing glance back at Nicholas.

Dave and Nicholas looked at each other. "What the hell?" said Dave, rhetorically.

After a moment, Nicholas ventured, "It's like … there's something Bert isn't saying. Something he's trying to tell us about."

"Something he wants from us?"

"Maybe." Nicholas cast a worried look into the pub. Not that they could see anything inside, given the relative brightness of the day.

"D'you think he's trying to ask for your help?"

Nicholas guffawed, but answered, "Maybe. And maybe Vincent doesn't want him to. But then, why wouldn't Bert ask you? You're the heroic one, David."

Dave smiled despite himself. It was sweet that Nicholas thought so, though Dave himself had to disagree. "No, I'm not."

At least this new topic successfully distracted Nicholas from fretting over Bert and the mystery of the stone circle. "I've told you before: you're the hero of my story," Nicholas insisted.

"And there I was, thinking that you're the hero of mine …"

They gazed at each other with amused fondness – or maybe it was fond amusement – until their lunch arrived.

It had been on Dave's mind that Nicholas had asked Dave to fuck him while they were on their honeymoon, and he hadn't yet done anything about it – so as they made love that afternoon, as they stretched tall and pressed close and kissed wild, Dave let his hand slip down Nicholas's long backbone, his fingertips trailing down each knob and dint, until at last he touched the man somewhere he'd never touched anyone before. Nicholas shuddered in reaction – and, remembering as vividly as if he were touching himself, Dave shivered, too. It was a strange dark glorious kind of intimacy that Nicholas had introduced Dave to. It was certainly more than time to repay the favour.

As Dave teased his fingertips back and forth across that tender pucker of flesh, Nicholas pushed further into Dave's embrace, he moaned and his kisses became ragged with hunger, his thigh slid up higher so that he was more exposed … That all seemed promising. Dave settled in, and slowed his pace to something more deliberate. He rubbed a fingerpad against Nicholas, and pushed gently, feeling the tension and the slight give, remembering that he himself had never really had a problem with this. Not physically. He suspected Nicholas might find the act a little more problematic, but it was Nicholas who wanted it … It was Nicholas who wanted to be fucked. They'd take it slow, that was all. They'd take it steady.

Dave reached a long arm for the bedside table and the lube.

"No, wait," said Nicholas, his voice husky with need.

Dave left the lube where it was, and met the man's heated gaze. "I was just gonna finger you," he carefully explained. "Nothing too serious. Not yet."

"No – No, I'll –" Nicholas was actually so far gone as to be having trouble with words. He was also, however, adamant. "*I'll* prep myself. Trust me?"

"Yes."

"I'll do that. I want our first time to be full on. I want it to be –" Nicholas groaned gutturally – "*elemental*."

At which unexpected word Dave groaned, too. And they had a fair go at 'elemental' right then and there, twisting and turning, holding and pinning, to rut hard against each other as if it were the natural order of things. Which Dave supposed it was.

Afterwards, as they lay there sprawled heavily in each other's embrace, even as they were still panting with the exertion, Nicholas commented, "If we can't go up to the standing stones at night, like Bert says, and we can't do it during the day cos anyone might walk past along the coastal path, then it'll have to be first thing in the morning. At dawn. That's appropriate."

Dave frowned over that for a moment, but had to ask, "We'll have to do what at dawn … ?"

Nicholas replied, as if it were perfectly obvious, "You fucking me for the first time."

"What – ?"

The matter-of-fact tones continued despite the outrageous notion. "I want to sacrifice my virginity to you on that altar stone."

Dave was kind of horrified. He shifted his head a little so he could stare at Nicholas. "You can't possibly be serious."

Nicholas blinked, but said "Maybe" in the way that meant he actually was. Then he added, "Aren't you man enough to do that for me?"

"Don't try to out-macho me," Dave grumbled. "You said you felt safe with me! And your father trusts me to take care of you. So you have to let me have a say in things like this. The last thing I want to do is hurt you!"

"Like I said, I'll prep myself. It'll be fine."

Dave let out a sigh. "Yeah, all right, I trust you to do *that*. But outside? On a *rock?* I dunno, Nicholas …"

"We did it outside at the waterhole. Any number of times!"

"That was Australia, out the back of beyond – and on a mattress, mostly. This is England, five minutes from the nearest town – not to mention the fact that it's almost winter!"

Nicholas hauled himself up onto his elbows so he could talk more directly to Dave. "I want it to be – primal. I want to – You said it once. You said you wanted to *feel* it. It hardly counts if it's too easy."

Dave considered the man. Lifted a hand to run a wary, curious finger down that long, determined face. "In the middle of a stone circle …" Dave said rather more quietly. "Don't you think that's just asking for trouble?"

"I thought you didn't believe in all that supernatural stuff."

"Supernatural or not, it seems a bit … risky to me. And did I mention the cold?"

Nicholas was reduced to using his imploring face.

Dave couldn't help but chuckle in response. Nicholas usually got what he wanted, Dave had found. But then even Simon had advised Dave to stand firm – or indeed, run away – when necessary, in his own interests or in Nicholas's. "Let me think about it," Dave eventually conceded. He assumed the answer would have to be no, but maybe he could come up with a half-decent alternative.

Nicholas immediately agreed, "All right," and there was a slight smugness to his smile, despite an attempt at demureness. It was perfectly obvious that Nicholas assumed the answer would end up being yes. Sharing his life with this man might prove to be even more of an adventure than Dave had realised!

During a lull in the cooking that night, Dave caught Nicholas gazing at him curiously. It was so plain that Nicholas had something he wanted to ask that Dave wondered why he couldn't already read the words spilling from those perfectly plump pink lips. Dave laughed, and prompted, "What?"

Nicholas's gaze slid away, and he turned bashful. Which was getting to be a rarity. These days Nicholas was too happy to be shy; confident in all the right ways. Dave took that as the best compliment he'd ever been paid.

"Come on," Dave insisted, unable to prevent himself grinning. "What's going on in that tricksy mind of yours?"

Another pink–cheeked hesitation dragged by until at last Nicholas said, "At lunch? You said that everyone falls for me …"

Dave guffawed. "Well, they do. Everybody *adores* you. Do you honestly not know that?"

"Everyone likes you, too, David."

"It's not the same thing. I get on all right with most people, if I try. And I do try. You don't have to. People just fall for you, no matter what you do."

Nicholas sighed, and grabbed the cloth to wipe down the already clean counter. Eventually he asked, "Why was I alone for so long, then?"

"Were you?" Dave scrunched up his face in thought. "I kinda assumed … I dunno. I guess I assumed you got around a bit. Plenty of boyfriends."

Nicholas seemed to be finding this conversation excruciating, and yet equally seemed determined to see it through. "Well," he said. "I suppose I had my share of … friends with benefits. And … um … acquaintances with temporary privileges. Probably rather too many of the latter," he confessed. And then Nicholas looked at Dave with shocking directness. "But you're only the third guy I've really loved."

"The third? Me and Frank and … ?"

"Oh, a guy at uni. It only lasted a couple of years. Not even that, really. Not properly. I think Frank spoiled me in some ways … It was only ever really friendship, no more than that for him – but he was very … steadfast … in his affection."

"That's not spoiling you. You're entitled to expect steadfast."

Nicholas smiled at him softly. "It's one of the things I love most about you."

"You already know you're only the second person I've ever loved," said Dave in his turn. "It's only been you and Denise for me. And I'm not planning for that to ever change. Not now."

Nicholas nodded vigorously, but his head was down again. Apparently they hadn't quite got to the point of the conversation yet. Dave glanced at the oven timer; they had two minutes, maybe. Though in reality, they had the rest of their lives.

"Hey," said Dave softly, going over there to wrap his arms around

Nicholas's waist and push close. To get right in Nicholas's face in the most loving of ways. "Hey, you have to know I reckon I'm the luckiest guy in the whole world, to get lucky with you – when you could have had absolutely *anyone* you ever wanted."

And at last Nicholas lifted his head again, and those deep dark eyes looked clearly into Dave's own. "And you should know, David, that I feel exactly the same way. *Exactly*."

"Do you … ?" Even now he found that hard to believe.

"Yes. You should have more faith in me."

"I have complete faith in you. Not so much in myself, I guess."

"It's the same for me," Nicholas insisted again. "What you just said. It's exactly the same."

"Well, then," said Dave, feeling something within his chest at last relax and warm into utter happiness. A tension he hadn't even known was there was now gone.

"Well, then," Nicholas agreed. And his smile perfectly reflected how Dave felt.

eleven

Dave figured that more research about the boat trip was called for, so he and Nicholas walked around the coastal path to the village of Cadgwith one morning. It took them about two hours, which included time to gaze in awe at the rugged scenery – though they didn't linger anywhere for very long, as the weather was cold and windy. The seas were running high, with waves crashing spectacularly against the rocks and cliffs. Which was all very well to look at, snugly bundled up as they each were in padded coats. This was Dave's first proper coat, and he was certainly beginning to see the merit in it. However, "Right now I'm thinking no about the boat trip, Nicholas."

"I don't think Bert would even consider taking us out on a day like this," Nicholas agreed. The path widened a little, and Nicholas settled into step beside Dave; took his hand in his. And Dave would have hung on no matter what, but on that day he had to admit to himself that he was glad there was no one else about. He still got a bit too self-conscious sometimes about being gay, about having a husband. It was something he knew he had to work on.

Eventually the path took them down a steep hill into the fishing village, and they saw that the weather must be even worse than they'd thought. All the boats were drawn up out of the water onto the stony shore, with a couple apparently battened down for the winter season. Another boat was being hauled up by winch even as they arrived. As luck would have it, the boat turned out to be Bert's *Fortune Teller*. Nicholas and Dave stood out of the way and watched the goings on. Vincent was with Bert, dealing with scuba gear and with his slim figure still snugly encased in a wetsuit, so it seemed he'd gone diving while they were out there. The other boats all appeared to be working fishing boats, and there were the usual sights and strong smells involved in dealing with a catch, including a flock of hovering seagulls. All very vivid and picturesque!

Dave took the opportunity to cast a critical eye over Bert's boat, but he soon had to admit that to a landlubber it looked as sturdy and serviceable as any of the rest of the fleet. Perhaps, if it weren't for the weather ...

When Bert was finally free to come over and say hello – casting bashful glances at Nicholas whenever he dared – Dave commented, "There's a storm coming, then?"

Bert looked amiably confused, and for a moment frowned up at the overcast sky. "Um, no ... ? Maybe some rain later, and a bit of a blow. Wouldn't call it a storm."

"Oh. I just thought, with you going to all the trouble of hauling the boats up onto the shore ..." Dave didn't dignify it with the term 'beach'. He had his standards.

The confusion vanished. "No, we always haul them up here. The sea gets too rough to moor offshore, and the cove's too small to hold even one boat at anchor."

"I see!" It seemed like an awful lot of bother to be hauling boats in and out of the sea, but who was Dave to argue? He noticed that Vincent was nearby, still fiddling with his scuba gear and looking at them a bit edgily. Maybe the man didn't like Bert wasting time on taking tourists out on the water. Maybe he just didn't like Bert paying so much attention to anyone else. "Look, Bert –" Dave began.

"I know. You're still thinking about it."

Dave laughed, and Nicholas offered a shrug with one of his most charming smiles.

"I wouldn't take you out today or tomorrow, it's going to be windy tomorrow, but we're looking at a couple of calm days after that," Bert said. "You just let Mrs Widgery know if you decide."

"Will do. Well –" Dave turned to Nicholas. "Shall we grab some lunch here before we head back?"

"Sure. Thanks, Bert!"

They had offered their farewells and turned away when Bert called after them. "If it rains, Vincent can drive you back home."

"Oh, that's all right," Dave said – for Vincent didn't look very pleased at being volunteered. "It'll hold off, and anyway we'll go cross–country this time. We came the long way round."

"No, go on," Bert insisted. "You really should." After a dramatic pause, he added, "Vincent has a Maserati."

"What?!" Dave exclaimed, thinking that Bert must have got that very wrong. Could he have possibly meant a Mazda ... ? But when Dave glanced at Vincent, he received a cool nod of confirmation. A Maserati it was.

Nicholas let out a breath which sounded like '*Wow* ...'

"Don't you go getting any ideas if he drives us," Dave cautioned, though quietly so only Nicholas would hear. "You and your thing for chauffeurs," he grumbled.

"Never!" Nicholas took Dave's hand again, and Dave bore it manfully.

"Have your lunch, and come back down in an hour or so," offered Vincent. "I'll run you home before I drop Bert off."

And so they agreed.

The Maserati hardly had the chance to shine in the five minutes of country roads that took them back to the cottage, but Dave and Nicholas were stirred enough to decide on taking the Jaguar out for a spin that afternoon. They headed for Penzance, then drank a takeaway cuppa while considering St Michael's Mount, drove back home again – and then made out in the car until the windows steamed up. The evening played out the way that honeymoons are supposed to …

Late that night Dave woke, and was unsurprised to find that one of the bedroom curtains was open. Nicholas, however, was nowhere to be seen. Dave would have assumed he'd gone to the bathroom, if only Dave didn't have a lingering notion that it had been the noise of the front door quietly closing that had woken him up. Dave cursed under his breath, and hauled himself out of the soft warm bed. He was already dressed in his usual t–shirt and boxer shorts, so he simply grabbed his coat on the way, and made his way outside.

Nicholas was out the front of the cottage, standing on the cliff edge. Dave's heart pounded in fear. From the cottage door, it looked as if Nicholas was *literally* on the edge, and dressed in little more than his dressing gown, too. There was a stiff wind coming in off the sea, so at least that was pushing him back in the right direction – but then Nicholas seemed to be leaning into it as he peered down the cliffs, and what if there was a moment's lull in the wind's resistance, and Nicholas was leaning just a little too far to keep his balance?

Dave walked closer, quietly, not wanting to startle the man, and he veered off at an angle so that he wasn't coming up directly behind him. Once he was about two or three metres distant from Nicholas's left shoulder, he said the man's name in tones that were calm but would carry. "Nicholas. What's up?"

Nicholas didn't seem surprised to find he had company, thank God. He cast Dave a scowl, and said, "I thought I heard something. I'm sure I saw lights."

"Where? At the stone circle?"

"No, on the beach down there."

Dave wasn't quite game enough to get that close to the cliff edge, but he looked to see if he could make out any light that couldn't be explained by natural causes. There was nothing. "Nicholas. No one would bring a boat into that bit of beach with this wind, even in daylight. It would be far too dangerous. They call it a lee shore," he added, drawing on the seamanship he'd learned from Patrick O'Brian. "They'd be driven onto the rocks."

Nicholas was absolutely adamant, of course. His jaw set mulishly.

"There's no other way of getting down there."

"I wasn't imagining it."

"I know. But if they're gone now, we're not going to solve the mystery tonight, are we? Come back inside, Nicholas."

A long moment dragged past while the wind buffeted them. Nicholas seemed to be shaking – though whether from cold or fear, excitement or anger, Dave didn't know.

"Please, Nicholas. Come back to bed with me."

That earned him a reluctant glance, and a protest half–shouted against the wind: "Don't humour me!"

"I wasn't! I'm just frozen through to my marrow, is all." Dave waited until Nicholas glanced at him again, a little more sympathetically this time. "I can't warm up properly without you. Not any more."

Nicholas huffed as if still suspecting that he was being played. But after another long moment he turned away from the cliff edge, and stepped towards the cottage, holding out his hand to invite Dave along with him. The ever–clumsy Nicholas simply turned and stepped away from the edge as confidently as a tightrope walker. And Dave stumbled towards him, took his hand, and hung on.

They didn't talk about it. Nicholas obligingly disrobed and got under the covers and wrapped himself around Dave – not that Nicholas felt much warmer than Dave himself, but with the doona and an extra blanket tucked in around them, they warmed up soon enough.

Despite all of which Nicholas felt tense, as if he wasn't prepared to forgive Dave nor ask for forgiveness himself. Eventually Dave asked, "Why d'you go out there?"

After a brief pause, Nicholas gave a succinct answer: "Curious."

Dave persisted. "What did you think you'd find?"

"Dunno." Nicholas shifted as if shrugging, but seemed to finally relax a little.

"Witches? Maidens? Pixies?"

"Smugglers," was the reply. "This is a *Famous Five* adventure, not a ghost story."

"Oh, *Nicholas*," Dave chided.

Luckily Nicholas saw the funny side of it, for a chuckle bubbled out of him as if he just couldn't help himself – and then Dave laughed under his breath, and soon they were giggling, and wriggling in closer together, and they were warm and happy. Nicholas yawned, and then Dave did, too – and soon they had smiled and snuggled themselves back into a peaceful sleep.

Nicholas wandered out for a breath of fresh air the next morning, while Dave got breakfast ready. Within moments, however, there was a cry of "David!" and then Dave heard Nicholas at the front door again. "David, come out here, will you?" Nicholas called in urgent tones. "Can you leave that? There's something at the stone circle."

Dave had already covered up the food – an Australian habit, apparently, as flies seemed almost non–existent in England – and for good measure he switched off the kettle, though he hadn't known it not to automatically cut off when it was done. "What is it?" he asked as he met Nicholas at the door and then followed him out.

"I don't know yet. I didn't go up."

Dave didn't cast the man a sympathetic look, but instead took his hand as they walked up there.

"See?" said Nicholas almost before they'd even left the cottage behind.

Dave squinted up at the stones. The wind was strong off the sea, so he had to push his hair back to get it out of his eyes. There was something – small. Not a witch nor even a hiker, but something small and yellow or white, apparently tied to one of the stones. The one most directly opposite the sea.

"What —" His mind raced, but didn't come up with any ideas at all.

Nicholas kind of went 'Huh huh' under his breath as if forcing a laugh. "Not a sacrifice!" — as if trying to convince himself.

"Well," Dave reasoned, though perhaps not helping anything, "if it was a sacrifice, it would be on the altar stone, wouldn't it?"

Nicholas just glanced at him, perturbed.

When they got up there, it seemed both relatively harmless and curiously weird. They stood there together still hand in hand, staring a bit gobsmacked at a small bunch of silk flowers bound to one of the stones with a long yellow–gold ribbon. The flowers were yellow and white and —

"Wattle," said Nicholas. "Which is Australia's national flower, isn't it?"

"Yes. And a rose … ?"

"Which is England's." They stared some more in silence before Nicholas observed, "That's you and me. I mean, okay, you wore eucalyptus flowers for the wedding, but otherwise — that's you and me."

"And the gold ribbons —" Dave said a bit faintly, remembering their wedding night. Which no one but Denise and possibly Vittorio could have any idea about. Surely.

"They're not exactly the same kind of ribbons," Nicholas cautiously offered. "Gauze rather than satin."

"It's still kind of creepy," said Dave. He looked about them, but the countryside seemed deserted, the coastal path was empty. "I suppose," he tried, "it could be meant nicely. Kind of … done in our honour. If you see what I mean."

"Could be," Nicholas agreed. "Do you think maybe … Bert?"

Dave laughed. "If it was Bert, he wouldn't have bothered with the wattle. It's you he fell for, Nicholas."

"Oh. Well, I guess that takes us back to creepy instead of nice."

"Maybe that's our imaginations working overtime again," Dave added, diplomatically going for *our* rather than *your*.

"Maybe."

"Well," said Dave at last. The sky was clear, but the wind was cold, and he was dressed in nothing warmer than a light sweater. "Let's have breakfast, anyway. No harm in breakfast, eh?"

"No harm at all," Nicholas agreed. And they walked back down to their snug, safe little cottage, hand still clasping hand.

twelve

Dave woke alone in the small hours again, and saw that the curtains were half open – again. He sighed, and waited in the blissfully comfortable bed for a moment or two, just in case Nicholas had got up for the bathroom. But of course that wasn't it. Eventually Dave sighed once more, and grumbled to himself about broken promises, before climbing out of bed and padding barefoot through to peer out of one of the front windows. Nicholas wasn't out at the cliff edge. Dave went back to the bedroom and looked out to check whether he could see anything happening up at the stone circle. Something seemed a bit off–kilter up there, but there was no Nicholas.

Right.

Dave quickly hauled his jeans on over his nightgear, then his boots, and shrugged on his coat. He picked up his mobile phone and – despite the fact it was a clear moonlit night – he collected the torch from the kitchen on his way out for good measure. It was one of the heftier Maglites.

The wind seemed to have blown itself out at last, and the night–shrouded countryside seemed quiet and still. There was no sign of Nicholas. Dave felt anxiety settle like a stone in his stomach.

He didn't have much of a clue about where to start looking, but he figured the standing stones were as good as anywhere. Also, there had seemed to be something a bit odd about them, though looking up at them now Dave still couldn't quite pin down exactly what or why.

As Dave walked away from the cottage towards the stones, however, he thought he heard something from beyond the cliff edge. A voice, perhaps, shouting out angrily. Certainly something, though he could be projecting human qualities onto a bird's cry or a wave's crash.

He headed towards the cliff, not too proud to lower himself to hands and knees once he got close, and cautiously shifted forward until he could at last poke his head over the edge just far enough to peer down.

One thing was immediately apparent, and that was the boat moored just off the little beach at the foot of the cliff, a boat that was of much the same shape and type as Bert's *Fortune Teller* and the other small fishing boats they'd seen at Cadgwith. There was also a dinghy drawn up on the sand. The beach seemed empty otherwise –

Until a figure stepped out from the cliff's foot, collected something from the dinghy, and cradling it in both arms took it back to where he'd come from – not breaking his stride even once as he neared the cliff, so Dave thought there must be some kind of cave down there, even if not an extensive one.

There was the sound of a voice again, and then an answering one. So that was at least two people involved. And Dave couldn't help but fear that Nicholas had got himself mixed up in this somehow. He had no idea what was going on – though it was hard not to think smugglers – but if Nicholas was down there, then Dave had to go fetch him back. That was all.

How Dave was supposed to get down there himself was another matter. He didn't have a boat, and it would take too long to try tracking down Bert in the middle of the night; Dave had no idea where he lived. The cliff was obviously impossible for him to scale; the rock face wasn't even, but all the ragged folds and edges ran vertically.

Dave scrambled backwards, got up to his feet, and looked around. There was nothing. No clues or hints as to how to proceed.

But his attention was again caught by the stone circle. There had been something odd, he remembered … That would have to do as a starting place.

Dave headed up to the circle as fast as he could – and was gobsmacked for a moment by what he found.

The altar stone in the centre of the circle had been shifted by about half its width towards the sea, to reveal a hole in the ground with crudely–hewn stone steps leading down into the dark. Dave stared at it for a long moment, then switched on the torch to see what else he could make out.

There wasn't much. The steps – some man–made and some raw rock – continued down into what otherwise looked to be a natural fissure. There was also a rope running along just overhead, which reached the entrance and then doubled back. Dave's first guess was that this was to provide handholds, but changed his mind when he realised the rope seemed to follow its own route directly down into the darkness at a steep angle, while the steps twisted around out of sight just two or three metres down.

Right. If there was a cave behind the beach at the foot of the cliff, then Dave had to assume this led down to it. And if Nicholas was nowhere else to be found, then Dave figured he must have come up to the stone circle to investigate – despite Bert's warnings, or maybe because of them – and ended up stumbling into whoever had brought that boat to the beach. And he must be down there now.

Dave took a breath. Had another look around him at the surrounding countryside – which still seemed deserted. And then took the first step down into the tunnel.

At irregular intervals the steps and the bits of pathway – such as they were – rejoined the rope in its more direct descent. Dave made his way down through the cliff as quickly as he dared, hanging onto the rope where he could and otherwise keeping at least one hand in contact with solid rock. At some stage, however, the rope running over his head began to move. He'd had hold of it at the time, and was startled enough to almost lose his balance, but steadied himself with both hands against the rough rock walls.

The fissure wound down through the cliff almost vertically. At two points so far, the makeshift stairs had been replaced by wooden ladders fastened to the rock in a ramshackle way.

Dave continued on, no longer using the rope which kept moving fairly steadily. Eventually a package hanging off the loose length of rope loomed into the circle of light cast by his torch. It was startling, but by then he'd half-expected it, so he simply crouched down where he was until the package trundled on past him. It seemed to be a canvas bag holding a clumsy collection of objects that rattled together. Whether that meant smuggling or not, Dave didn't care very much at this point.

What he cared about was Nicholas.

Eventually the fissure opened out into a larger cave, and Dave followed a foot-worn path further down until at last he could hear the waves surging onto the beach, and under it a murmur of voices. He switched off the torch, and carefully made his way nearer. He figured it was worth his while remaining hidden until he could work out what was going on, so Dave crept towards the cave mouth staying low behind a ridge of rocks.

At last he could look out past the far edge – and the first thing his gaze swooped upon was Nicholas. Dave's heart thudded in relief as he took in the sight of his husband, alive, in one piece and apparently unhurt. He was sitting on a rock next to Bert. They both seemed anxious, and concerned for each other, and Nicholas's posture seemed a little cowed. Dave suddenly felt swamped with hatred for whoever had bowed Nicholas's head and rounded his shoulders.

The apparent object of his hatred strode into view. It was Vincent, of course – looking rather spectacular, even Dave had to admit, with his wetsuit peeled off down to the waist and his chest still alluringly wet. The man was gesturing angrily and demanding, "Well, what d'you think we're gonna do now?!"

Bert gazed back at Vincent with pathetic sorrow, but Nicholas set his jaw. "You're going to let us part ways without any more threats," Nicholas said. "That's what's going to happen."

Vincent sneered. "What, so you can run off to the cops and spoil my game?"

"I don't even know what your game is." Nicholas turned to consider his companion again. "I get the impression that Bert wants out, but if you let him go – if you quit using him and there are no other victims, then I actually don't care very much about you carrying on smuggling or whatever."

"Don't try to con a con."

"I'm not." Nicholas's posture suddenly straightened and his tones and demeanour became more aristocratic than Dave had ever witnessed in him before. "I'm sure *my* class cares as little as *yours* does for legal restraints on self-interest."

Vincent's devilish eyes seemed to fire with fellow feeling. "You understand, then," he said, stepping forward to plead his case. "There's this old frigate down there. Not burdened with treasure, but enough to set a man up nicely. Finders keepers: that's fair, isn't it?"

"It seems fair to me," Nicholas said with convincing sincerity. "But the less you tell me, the less I know, if push ever comes to shove."

Vincent was too stirred up to quit, though. "It's three months in the clink and a five-grand fine just for not *telling* them about a treasure trove. Not to mention having to hand it over."

Nicholas dared to raise a sceptical brow. "They pay you for it, don't they?"

"Yeah, but as little as they can get away with. Anyway: finders keepers. Fair's fair."

"Agreed," Nicholas crisply replied. Then he turned to Bert, and said in a quietly encouraging voice, "Was there something you wanted to say to Vincent, Bert?"

A silence dragged while Bert gathered himself. He seemed oddly bashful for such a potentially dangerous situation. Eventually he said – to Nicholas – "I'm sorry. I'm sorry."

"Don't be. You must always ask your friends for help when you need it. Now, what did you want to say to Vincent … ?"

Bert finally brought himself to echo Nicholas's words in a small voice: "I want out, Vincent."

"Oh, *do* you?" Vincent retorted. "*Why?*"

"Don't wanna go to jail – nor pay such a fine!"

"Chances are we'll get away with this. No one knew until you got this fellow curious." Vincent gestured angrily at Nicholas.

"Feels as if everyone knows – and no one likes me for it – and it frets me – when all I want to worry about is fishing and taking a few people out on boat trips, and making them happy. I'm a simple man, Vincent. The simplest."

"Oh come on, Bert," Vincent said in increasing frustration. "It's almost winter, anyway. It's not like we'll have more than another one or two trips this season."

Bert sat there quite woebegone.

"See this season out with me, and then we take a break. We don't have to decide about next season – not for months yet."

Bert was upset, though he managed to repeat quite firmly, "I want out."

"And the cash?"

"Don't want it. Haven't used it." He gazed up at Vincent as if eager to please. "You can have it all back, Vincent, if you want. Well, almost all," he added with scrupulous honesty. "You know I had the *Teller*'s engine overhauled … You can have the rest!"

Vincent growled in annoyance, and turned away. "Where am I gonna find another boat? Who's gonna crew for me?"

Nicholas replied rather crisply, "I'm sure that's your own concern, and not Bert's. Not any more. Although," Nicholas added with a glint of humour, "if you try walking around town dressed like that I'm sure you'll find a man soon enough who's willing to do your bidding."

A finger stabbed through the air towards Nicholas. "Don't you *dare* count me in with your queer lot!"

"Well," Nicholas retorted, "quit taking advantage of a good man's affections, and I won't!"

A silence seemed to indicate that Vincent acknowledged the hits and was stuck for further arguments. Bert had apparently achieved his goal. Which would have felt better if it wasn't partly due to Vincent not wanting to be seen as Bert's partner in life as well as crime.

More importantly than that, though, Dave felt so bloody proud of Nicholas for having handled this with such firm tact. The only question that remained was how they could all withdraw from the current situation with good grace.

"Well," Nicholas eventually continued, apparently thinking along the same lines. "What usually happens now? Vincent follows his treasure up to the surface, and drives away in his suspiciously expensive car –"

Vincent swung back around to glare at him. Nicholas didn't even falter. Dave just loved him to the stars and back.

"– and Bert, you take the boat back to Cadgwith, do you?"

"I spend the night out on the boat, and go ashore at dawn."

"Oh ... because of the boat having to be hauled out of the sea? There isn't anyone to do that for you at this time of night?"

"That's right. It's not that there isn't, but it draws attention we don't want."

Nicholas nodded. "All right. So there's no reason why we three can't go our own separate ways, then, is there? You two just do as you usually do, and I'll climb up to the stones with Vincent and then head back to the cottage."

Bert gasped a little, and grasped Nicholas's closest hand. "No, you'd better come with me on the boat."

"If I don't show up until morning, David will be worried. He might already be wondering where I am. I can't do that to him – and you don't want him raising hell trying to find me."

Vincent complained in surly tones, "I'm not letting Bert go off, on his own or with you. Chances are you'd dock at Mullion, and turn me in."

"If I give you my word –" Nicholas began.

"I know how much that's worth, from my lot or from yours."

"Don't trust him," Bert said to Nicholas – in a mutter that carried perfectly well to Vincent and to Dave where he was still in hiding. "Don't go with him. Not on your own."

Vincent crossed his arms and stared at the other two forbiddingly. "There's no need to fear a 'convenient accident' happening to your friend,

Bert. If he fell down a ladder and died, you'd know just where to bring the cops, and who to blame. You'd be a witness, wouldn't you?"

"So you might hit me on the head, too," said Bert.

"Oh, for fuck's sake ... This is a sweet game, but not sweet enough to risk two killings for."

Bert, however, refused to be reassured; he clung to Nicholas's hand as if genuinely afraid for his life. Dave figured that it was time, finally, for him to make his presence known.

When Dave stepped forward into the light cast by the lanterns, Vincent was shocked rigid but too cool to want to show it, and Bert was confounded into doing little more than gaping and blinking at Dave – though he quickly pulled his hand away from Nicholas's as if badly caught out – while Nicholas burst into the brightest happiest grin. He instinctively started to stand up and come to Dave, but Vincent gestured menacingly to indicate that Nicholas should remain where he was, so Nicholas sank back down beside Bert. He still looked blissfully happy, though.

"What the hell – ?" said Vincent.

"Thought another witness might be useful," said Dave. "It takes murder right off the agenda."

"How long – ?"

"Long enough to know what's going on. I'm with Nicholas. If you let Bert out of your arrangement, we'll turn a blind eye to your treasure hunting. But people will know how to get in touch with us once we've left Cornwall, and we'd be happy to dob you in if you do the wrong thing by Bert. I think we're all in agreement on that, aren't we?"

There were nods all round – reluctant from Vincent, eager from Bert, and accompanied by a glowing grin from Nicholas.

"So now I think you let Nicholas accompany Bert on his boat. He can have the boat trip he wanted after all. And I'll climb back up through the cliff with you, Vincent, and see you on your way. We'll all be guarantors for the others, see? I'll drive down to Cadgwith, and wait for Bert and Nicholas to come in at dawn. If you're worried, Vincent, you'll have plenty of time to hide any evidence. Though what you'd do with the Maserati, I have no clue."

Silence.

"All right?" asked Dave.

Bert was beaming by now, and he shyly slipped his hand back into

Nicholas's. "Yes," he answered.

"Yes," Nicholas said, still watching Dave, though also squeezing Bert's hand in reassurance.

After a long moment, Vincent nodded again.

And so that's what they did.

Dave had few qualms about trusting Bert with Nicholas. The man seemed more besotted than ever, so surely would protect Nicholas with all but his life, and his shambolic helplessness seemed to fall away once he was dealing with his boat. Dave handed Nicholas into the dinghy, exchanging a significant look with his husband – and on a sudden flash of inspiration, he gave Nicholas his mobile phone, muttering, "Tell you why later; just take it." Nicholas did so with a nod, slipping it into his coat pocket. Then Dave helped Bert push the dinghy off into the sea. "See you in Cadgwith," Dave said for them all to hear, exuding nothing but confidence.

"See you, mate," Nicholas replied. His quiet use of the Aussie vernacular felt infinitely reassuring.

Bert nodded at Dave, solemnly conveying his sense of responsibility, before bending to take up the oars and adding a strong stroke to Dave's shove and the sea's flow.

It wasn't that Dave didn't have any misgivings over Nicholas's safety, but Dave knew that he himself was in more danger in Vincent's company, and he was content that it be so. In fact, he wouldn't have had it any other way.

Dave watched as Bert reached the *Fortune Teller*, fixed the dinghy, helped Nicholas aboard, and then weighed anchor. Nicholas waved cheerfully at Dave, before turning to talk with Bert. Soon the boat had quietly puttered away from land and then out of sight in a southerly direction.

"All right," Dave said brusquely to Vincent once he was sure that Nicholas was out of harm's way. "What do you need to do now?"

"Nothing," was the equally brusque reply. "Climb back up to the land above."

"Let's go, then."

With mocking politeness, Vincent swept his hand out to invite Dave to lead the way.

"No, thanks," Dave said, figuring that neither option was entirely safe, but keeping Vincent in his line of sight had to give Dave the advantage. "After you."

They both carried torches, and they were both fit, so the climb was a steady one, with Dave maintaining a careful couple of metres between himself and Vincent, and keeping a wary eye out for any 'accidentally' falling objects.

Soon they were making their way up the last few steps and clambering onto the level grass within the stone circle. They hadn't spoken since they'd left the beach. Dave watched Vincent unhook the bag of treasure from the top loop of rope – but then when Vincent bent to shift the huge altar stone back into place, the man said, "Turn around. I don't want you seeing the trick of this."

Dave backed away a few steps in order to keep his distance, and then obligingly turned. He stared out across the sea, and despite his intention to pay careful attention to Vincent, found himself searching ... After a moment Dave spotted a faint light and then a slight wake foaming pale behind a dark shape. Bert and Nicholas would be fine, Dave figured. No doubt Bert would regale Nicholas with seafaring tales for what remained of the night, while Nicholas waxed poetical about butterflies. Perhaps it was his imagination, but Dave could have sworn he heard a faint ring of laughter from over the water.

If he did, however, it was lost a moment later in a grinding noise and then a solid thump, which indicated that the stones had been returned to their rightful places. Dave turned back around. "Well. I doubt we'll be seeing each other again. But just in case," he continued, "you should know I recorded most of that on my mobile – and the phone is now out of harm's way with Nicholas. I'm really not interested in using that unless we hear you're taking advantage of Bert again, though."

It was a bluff, but Vincent fell for it. The man looked absolutely ropeable, and muttered a curse through gritted teeth.

"I'd wish you well –" Dave offered brightly.

"Save your breath," Vincent advised. And, slinging his bag of ill–gotten gains over one shoulder, he turned and strode off in the direction of the main road. No doubt the Maserati was tucked safely away somewhere nearby. Dave couldn't wish the Maserati itself ill, so instead of an accident in these narrow Cornish lanes Dave imagined a story involving Customs or the Tax

Office or whatever, and anonymous tips from concerned citizens … Surely Vincent wouldn't avoid justice for too much longer.

"And good riddance to you," Dave said under his breath. Once he was sure he was alone again, he turned and made his way down to the cottage.

Most of the night was already past, and there was only about two hours left until dawn by Dave's reckoning. He took a few moments to dress properly, and make up a thermos of strong coffee. And then he drove the Jaguar over to Cadgwith, and quietly parked down near the stony beach. After turning off the ignition, Dave got out and looked around, listening carefully. All was still and peaceful. He didn't seem to have disturbed anyone. No one came to ask difficult questions about his business there.

Dave sighed, and got back into the car, left his window cracked open for the sake of fresh air, and drank a cup of coffee. After half an hour or so he got out to wander back and forth on the asphalt in order to stretch his legs. There was no sign of Vincent having changed his mind and coming back to do away with witnesses. All in all, things seemed to be going their way.

Dave tried not to think too much, or let his imagination gear up into overdrive. He'd have brought the Kindle and read, but didn't want to attract attention with a light, nor end up too distracted to notice anything untoward. Instead Dave simply waited for the safe return of his husband. He let his mind dwell on memories of Nicholas, right from that first moment of clumsiness at the Brisbane airport when Nicholas had quite literally fallen at Dave's feet. Dave hadn't appreciated it at the time, but in retrospect he treasured Nicholas's bright smile as he lay there on the floor, already admiring what he saw. And Nicholas had been so confident in his pursuit of Dave – not due to arrogance, or having tickets on himself, Dave certainly knew that now if it had ever been in doubt. Instead Nicholas's happy confidence had been a gift from his family, so rich in unconditional love as they were.

After a while, Dave returned to the car and drank more coffee while standing there beside it. He considered the beautiful little cove in the moonlight, and lulled his anxieties with the sound of the waves crashing rhythmically in, one after the other and another one after that, endlessly.

Nicholas would be fine. No doubt he was enjoying himself out there on the sea on this magical night, with the dangers past and Bert adoring him. No doubt Bert was enjoying himself, too, and Dave had to hope that the man's crush on Nicholas would at least serve him better in the long run than his attraction to Vincent – though it was doomed to come to nothing. Nicholas Goring was a married man now, after all.

The time passed and Dave waited, sitting in the car again for a while, and then walking about. He drank more coffee, though he doubted he would have fallen asleep in any case. He took the time to examine the winch system and figure it out, thinking that he might have to be the one to use it once Bert's boat returned.

At last the horizon beyond the cove began lightening, and the world grew hushed with even the waves crashing calmly before running back down through the stones with a gentle sigh. The horizon glowed, and Dave's surroundings took on a cool grey clarity.

A light appeared in a cottage window behind him – he saw it in the rear view mirror – and then another. People were stirring.

And then just as the sun peeked up out of the sea and colour fled back into things, Dave heard a boat puttering near.

Someone had come down to the boats and seemed to be preparing to go out fishing for the day. "Morning," the man said to Dave, not questioning his presence.

"Morning," Dave replied.

The fisherman turned his head as the puttering drew closer. Dave thought he himself could recognise the boat by its engine noise, but he knew for sure when the man asked easily, "Old Bert been out for the night again?"

"Yes. He took my – my partner out for a trip."

"Oh, aye," the man agreed, apparently still finding nothing much to surprise him in all this.

Dave relaxed a little. And then the *Fortune Teller* appeared beyond the headland, and Dave could just make out Nicholas's tall slim figure beside Bert at the wheel – and Nicholas waved, which made Dave's heart thud in relief and gratitude for his safety – and Dave went to help the fisherman with the winch, silently singing a stirring song, for everything was working out just perfectly.

Bert slung a ladder over the side of the boat where it sat perched high, and then handed Nicholas over. Nicholas climbed down carefully, apparently still feeling his sea legs – and a moment later he was wound tight around Dave, deep in Dave's arms. They weren't too proud to cling to each other. "You're all right," Nicholas babbled. "David, you're all right."

"Of course I am," Dave stoutly replied. "You weren't fretting, were you?" Which was more for the benefit of the fisherman than anything else. The deal was that they wouldn't blow Vincent's cover, after all.

"Of course I was. And I bet you were fretting, too!"

"It's true, I was. But here you are, and you're all right."

They clung for a few moments longer, and then Bert was there beside them, watching Nicholas with a yearning undiminished. Nicholas played his part – detaching himself from Dave, shaking Bert's hand and saying, "Thank you, that was marvellous." He turned to Dave to add, "It was so great seeing the coast at night! So dramatic! And it was moonlit so we could see church spires and another standing stone and a ruined castle …"

Dave grinned at him. "I'm glad you enjoyed yourself." He shook Bert's hand, too, and thanked him, then said to his husband, "Shall we head home? I think there's some coffee left in the thermos, if you want it."

"I do," Nicholas replied with surprising intensity. "I *do* want it."

"Oh," managed Dave, hoping his blush didn't show up in the early morning light. And then he and Nicholas nodded farewell to Bert and the other fisherman – and headed for the Jaguar in a kind of controlled dash.

"It's their honeymoon," Bert could be heard indulgently explaining in their wake.

Nicholas rested his hand hot on Dave's thigh during the interminable few minutes it took to drive back to the cottage. They didn't speak.

As soon as they were inside, they were kissing mouthily damply while shedding clothes – their own and each other's – haphazardly stumbling their way through to the bedroom.

"Nicholas –" Dave managed as they tumbled into the room. Nicholas pushed at him so Dave fell back onto the dishevelled bed – then Nicholas was on hands and knees across him, reaching a long arm for the bedside drawer and the lube. "Nicholas –"

"Hush. It's all right," was the confident reply.

Dave helped Nicholas wriggle out of his boxer shorts – and then they were naked but for one of Dave's socks which he just couldn't be arsed about. Dave moaned a little in fear and anticipation as Nicholas squeezed out a generous dollop of the lube. It wasn't that this act had ever really hurt Dave, but then there was an edge to Nicholas's passion that morning that felt a little alarming. "Nicholas …" Dave groaned, his thighs already opening for the man.

But Nicholas hushed him again, straddled Dave's hips, knelt up tall – *and reached behind himself to apply the lube.*

"Oh God," Dave muttered. "Oh God."

And then Nicholas was positioning himself – lowering himself – and it was happening, it was happening, they were both gasping with the need, with the pain – for Nicholas was as tight as any virgin – but Dave knew Nicholas wanted it that way, he *wanted it* just exactly so, Dave could tell – so he clasped a hand to each of Nicholas's hips and tugged him down further – they both cried out in a joyous agony – Nicholas grasped at Dave's forearms to keep himself upright – and Nicholas let his weight sink further, he forced himself down even as Dave pushed himself up – and it was extraordinary, Dave had forgotten how extraordinary it was to thrust himself inside another human being – it was so hot, so hard, so glorious. Soon he was buried deep within Nicholas and Nicholas had given himself utterly over, his head slumping forward and his hands now loosening from where they'd marked Dave's skin, his arms now stretching wide as his head lifted and fell back – and Dave bucked up *hard*, brought his feet in close and took his weight on them – then as he lowered his hips again Nicholas carefully rose – and they crashed back together – and then they were *fucking* they were *fucking* – and it was raw and awesome and elemental, and Nicholas's deeply resounding groans meant that this was what he wanted, this was exactly what he'd wanted – and Dave took heart from that – he took courage and boldness from it – and after a few magnificent thrusts Dave grasped Nicholas's hips harder still, hauled him down and then pushed himself up so he was sitting with legs loosely crossed and Nicholas in his lap – Nicholas took Dave's head in both hands and devoured his mouth and cheeks with bites and licks and kisses – which was gorgeous but Dave couldn't thrust like that and he wanted to *thrust*, so Dave at last tumbled Nicholas over onto his back, those long legs aslant over Dave's back – and he thrust in hard, he thrust himself into Nicholas even while their right hands met on Nicholas's cock, and they tugged at him *hard* and *rough* until moments later he spilled with a guttural yell that reverberated all the way through Dave's cock and balls and they were both coming so damned forceful that sensation was a rush of dark ocean, and for a moment the stars blinked out.

"Oh God," said Dave.

"God, I *needed* that," said Nicholas. He seemed utterly happy, sprawled back in abandon – not in pain at all. Still, of course Dave had to check as best as he could that Nicholas was okay.

Dave hauled himself out of the bed and went to find a clean face washer, ran it under the hot water, and wrung it out. Returning to the bedroom, he knelt by Nicholas, grasped a hip and gently rolled him over. Nicholas went with a happy whoop, which on the whole indicated he was fine. Still, Dave took his responsibilities towards this man very seriously. He carefully wiped Nicholas clean, and looked for blood, but there was none, not even a speck.

"I'm fine," said Nicholas, still sounding blissfully happy.

"I'm glad," said Dave, rather inadequately though with a full heart. He tossed the face washer aside and collapsed to lie beside his love.

Nicholas rolled over again and they drew each other into a mutual hug. "I really needed that, David," Nicholas repeated, quietly this time. "Thank you."

"My pleasure," Dave replied quite honestly.

"Thank you for *not* being gentle with me," Nicholas persisted.

"Idiot," Dave grumbled. "Love you."

Nicholas sighed quite contentedly and wriggled in closer. "Love you, too." After a while they slept.

thirteen

"Your admirer is wanting to see you again," Dave announced. It was the following morning, and Dave had been taking the kitchen rubbish and recycling out to the bins when he'd seen Bert sitting on the altar stone up at the stone circle, waving eagerly, just as he'd done once before.

"Oh good," Nicholas brightly replied. Then he cast a half–apologetic look at Dave. "Well, you know … I wanted to be sure he's all right before we leave."

"Of course," Dave stoutly agreed, rather than making a pointed remark about the romance inherent in Nicholas and Bert's moonlit boat trip. "Look," he said, "are you really okay with letting Vincent go free? Can we live with that?"

"Can you?"

Dave shrugged. "Part of me wants to turn him in. But mostly, I guess I just want to be sure that Bert is all right."

"Me, too." Nicholas seemed to feel a mix of relief and guilt, but there didn't seem to be much they could do about that.

"Hopefully no one else gets hurt between now and whenever justice finally catches up with Vincent."

Which rather deflated poor Nicholas. "True."

Dave changed the subject. "Looks like there's more of those gold ribbons tied around the stones, too."

"Oh! So it was Bert, then? Even the flowers?"

Dave shrugged. "Guess so. Falling in love will make a man do unexpected things."

Nicholas just grinned at him so very happily.

By the time they got up to the stone circle, they found not only Bert up there but Maeve as well – and even old Joan, who apparently wasn't as sedentary as they'd assumed. The three locals appeared to be in a celebratory mood.

"All right, Bert?" asked Nicholas.

"All right, Nicholas," the old man replied with his cheeks pinker than ever and his shy smile almost as sweet as Nicholas's own.

"We wanted to thank you," said Maeve, with an expansive gesture that took in the nine gold ribbons each fluttering in the morning breeze. It was a cool day, but quite sunny, and rather delightfully fresh.

"Ah, then it was you the other day," Dave said. "And the flowers, too." He should have guessed already. Maeve had a white and gold frangipani bloom in her hair today – silk, of course, but beautiful nevertheless.

"Yes," she answered. Then as Maeve read their looks of relief, her face fell. "Oh ... That kind of creeped you out, didn't it?"

"We just didn't know who," Nicholas explained.

"Or what or why," Dave added.

"It was nice, though."

Maeve grimaced in remorse at Joan. "It was meant to be a handfasting ceremony ... without the actual hands. A gesture of support, yeah? We'd heard that some people have been a bit ... disapproving."

Nicholas was now gazing at Maeve with great interest. "A handfasting ceremony ... ?"

"Completely redundant, I know," she continued with a shrug. "You're already married."

"We had a civil partnership ceremony," Nicholas explained. "And we'll be registering our relationship in Queensland once we get there. But it's not marriage." Nicholas turned to Dave. "I figure that if we can ever get properly married – here or in Australia – we'll do that, too. Won't we?"

Dave had to laugh. "Is that *another* proposal?"

"Yes," Nicholas immediately replied, grinning like the most delightful of idiots.

"Then of course we will."

Nicholas soon turned a bit sheepish, however. "It's not that the civil partnership doesn't count. And I wouldn't put you through another whole big thing with everyone there, I promise. But the more anniversaries the merrier, right?"

Despite the fact there were other people there hanging on their every word, Dave took the time to think about that – and then leaned in close to quietly ask Nicholas, "It's not that you don't think I'm committed, right? I mean, you don't *need* an extra set of vows to be sure of me, do you?"

"Not in the slightest," Nicholas averred, lightly yet honestly. "I am *totally* sure of you."

"Okay, good. Is it about the visa thing, then? Proving our relationship to them?"

Nicholas paled, and metaphorically took a step back. "They'll think I'm trying too hard, won't they?"

Dave smiled, and lifted a hand, shaped it to that beautiful face. "They'll know you mean every single word." And when Nicholas seemed reassured, Dave straightened up again, then glanced at Maeve, wondering if this were even possible. He asked Nicholas – in his regular voice, so they'd all hear – "Nicholas Goring, you wanna get handfasted with me?"

"Yes," was the instant response, with the most gorgeous smile for Dave. "Yes, I do." Then Nicholas turned to Maeve. "If we can …"

Maeve turned to Joan. "Gran can do that for you. Can't you, Gran?"

The old woman nodded quite happily. Bert was beaming blissfully and yearning wistfully all at once. Nicholas looked like he was floating on air.

"Let's get that done, then," said Dave.

Which was how they found themselves later that afternoon, the five of them reconvened at the stone circle along with Margaret, who had closed the store for an hour so that she could attend as well. Joan was standing by the tallest stone nearest the sea, with Nicholas and Dave facing each other before her, and with Bert at Nicholas's shoulder and Maeve at Dave's as their witnesses. Nicholas had insisted it was Dave's turn to choose the clothes, so they were both in proper shirts, knitted sweaters and blue jeans. And Dave decided that the circle of standing stones was a pretty special place after all, and certainly more significant than the Disraeli Room, but mainly because he and Nicholas and their new friends were making it so.

Joan recited some words in Celtic or Cornish or whatever in a soothing cadence, and then Maeve read out parts of a poem by Thomas Hardy about him meeting his first wife Emma in Cornwall, which Maeve had adapted to fit the two men. Dave had never been much into poetry, but a few lines of it stayed with him: *'The man whom I did love so, and who loyally loved me.'* But, really, who cared about getting the genders right when the truth of the feelings transcended all?

'And shall he and I not go there once again now winter's nigh,
And the sweet things said that October say anew there by and by?'

Maeve finished there, and then Margaret gave them each a silk flower to hold – wattle for Dave and a rose for Nicholas. As they each clasped their flower to the other's wrist, Joan bound a gold ribbon around them, from one forearm to the other. Then she led them in their renewed vows.

"I David Taylor take thee Nicholas Goring to my wedded husband for a lifetime, till death us depart, and thereto I plight thee my troth."

Dave loved the quaint old words, so much more poetic than the formal vows for the civil partnership ceremony had been and definitely far more like a proper wedding.

Nicholas vowed the same, and not as tongue–stumblingly as Dave had done. Then they kissed with an intensity that even now felt new to them both. And it was done and done again, and no man nor woman would ever put them asunder. And if they even tried, Dave found himself fiercely thinking as he gazed into Nicholas's deep dark blue eyes – they'd have to deal with the stroppiest bloody Australian who'd ever lived.

corroboree

fourteen

Nicholas hated goodbyes so they were barely spending forty-eight hours in Buckinghamshire. They drove back from Cornwall in time for dinner on one day, and were flying out from Heathrow in the evening two days later. Nicholas had even asked that no one but the usual family members should be there – though of course he was inundated with phone calls, texts and emails from the others – so on that first night Dave and Nicholas sat down to eat with Richard, Robert and Penelope, Robin and Isabelle. Everyone was perfectly jovial, in an apparent effort to save Nicholas or themselves too much grief. Only Robin every now and then betrayed the tragedy of it all when the act cracked apart and his sorrow showed through. Young Robin's heart was breaking for the first time.

No matter how ready the general joviality, however, there could be no pretending that Nicholas wasn't leaving. Mrs Gilchrist was cooking every last one of Nicholas's favourite meals. Nicholas's room was strangely empty because Simon had organised the packing of the books, clothes and other belongings that they couldn't take with them on the plane; it was currently all on a container ship somewhere on its way to Australia.

Asked to fetch Nicholas for dinner on that first night, Dave had finally tracked him down in the garage, sitting curled up in the passenger seat of the MGB V8 roadster quietly talking with Frank Brambell who sat beside him with both hands on the wheel of the car he'd never drive again. Dave had crept away as best he could across the gravel driveway, and announced he'd failed in his hunt. Luckily for Mrs Gilchrist's peace of mind, however – not to mention Dave's – Nicholas showed up barely five minutes later.

On the full day Dave and Nicholas were in Buckinghamshire, the family held an afternoon tea to which were invited all the people associated with the estate and most of those living in the nearby village. The women – led by Frank's wife Agate – presented Nicholas and Dave with a handmade queen-sized wedding quilt which included their names and the date of their civil partnership ceremony in embroidery, and a colourful kaleidoscope of butterflies in patchwork. Dave was too astonished and Nicholas too moved to say very much in response, but Agate filled the silence with a humorous description of the women's quilting bees, such a creative shambles as they worked to a tight deadline, and then Richard thanked them very properly indeed on behalf of his beloved son and son–in–law.

Seeing their full names stitched into the quilt set Dave to thinking. He snuck away once the afternoon tea was done, and did some research on Nicholas's laptop. When a rather drained–looking Nicholas joined him in the half hour before dinner, Dave was all set. "I was thinking about our names," Dave announced.

"Yes?" Nicholas prompted, collapsing back onto his bed as if it were quite possible he would never move again.

"Our last names, I mean. We've each kept our own."

"Yes …" Nicholas agreed, somewhat warily.

"I figure you don't want to be Nicholas Taylor, and – no offence – I don't want to be Dave Goring."

Nicholas propped himself up on his elbows and considered Dave with narrowed eyes while he waited to hear where this was going.

"So I was thinking maybe we could do the double–barrel thing, and both be Goring Taylor."

Silence.

Dave suddenly lost his nerve. "If you think – I mean – Well, I don't want to presume –"

"You're perfectly entitled," Nicholas said, cutting him off.

"Really?"

"*Yes.*"

"We'd have to do it by Deed Poll, but –"

"No, that would be –"

"I figured you'd like it if we –"

"Awesome. That would be awesome."

"Cos we're a family now, yeah? Even if it's just the two of us."

Nicholas stared at him, *glowing* with intensity.

"If you think your family wouldn't mind, that is."

"David, they're your family, too, now." Nicholas got up, still looking drawn and pale but also charged with purpose. "He'll say yes, of course. He wouldn't even expect me to ask permission. But I want to talk to my father about it. All right?"

"Of course," Dave agreed, absolutely fine with that.

"I think he'll love it as much as I do," Nicholas continued, not moving from where he stood.

"Go on, then. If it's a good thing –"

"It's a good thing," Nicholas confirmed.

"Then go and make him happy. He deserves it."

Nicholas set off, but stopped by Dave to press a kiss to his temple. "Love you," he said.

"I know."

"I love you so very much – David Goring Taylor."

Dave grinned at him. "Exactly."

Nicholas hadn't returned by dinnertime, so Dave wandered downstairs on his own. Which was fine, of course.

Except that he happened to see Nicholas coming out of the study, and quietly closing the door behind him. And it was perfectly obvious that Nicholas was in tears.

Dave's first instinct was to see what he could do to make things better. But then he figured that actually he might just make it all worse. And anyway, Nicholas had his head down and was making for the downstairs bathroom. He wasn't looking for Dave, so maybe Dave should just let things be. He'd always known that this parting would break Nicholas's heart as well.

What with the Earl himself being absent as well, dinner was served fifteen minutes late. But when Richard appeared, he seemed fine, he seemed as robust as ever – and he shook Dave's hand very firmly, before announcing this latest news to the family with great pride.

Nicholas, still rather pale, held Dave's hand under the table and nevertheless had a good stab at eating the lamb shank casserole Mrs Gilchrist had prepared. And really, Dave had to assume that everything was going to be all right. They were all going to be all right. He just knew it.

Thanks to Richard, they flew first class to Australia, which of course was well-meant – but Dave found the unexpected surroundings a bit unnerving and Nicholas was subdued in any case. They did little more than hold hands and watch movies – manually synchronising them on both their screens – until at last an exhausted Nicholas fell asleep. Dave kept holding his hand, and just sat there, waiting through the hours of darkness. He hadn't travelled enough to have got the knack of sleeping on planes.

Dave didn't get much rest during the stopover at Singapore, either. Nicholas was still really out of it, so Dave just sat on the floor in the departure lounge with his back propped against a wall, and Nicholas lay himself out along the carpet with his head pillowed on Dave's thigh. He didn't fall asleep again, but Dave stroked his hair gently and Nicholas seemed to find that soothing.

Finally they touched down in Brisbane, a few minutes ahead of schedule. Denise came to meet them at the airport, and drove them home. She'd already stocked the fridge for them and made up the bed, so once she was sure they were sorted, she left them to it. The two of them still didn't talk much. After putting on a load of washing, Dave drove them into the city, and they wandered the botanic gardens for a while, just as they'd done when first they met.

It was a warm day, with an infinite blue sky. Nicholas seemed to draw strength from the sunlight as he tilted his face towards it, letting the sun find him under the brim of his Bluegrass Green Akubra. Dave watched him fondly, until at last Nicholas smiled at him – a little wobbly perhaps, but genuinely. They smiled at each other, and held hands – went home and made love, and slept. And on the next day they woke, and their new life together in Australia truly began.

Charlie came to visit them one day, bursting with a surprise. "You've been invited to a corroboree, mate."

Dave stared at him, flabbergasted. "You've been talking with the elders about the waterhole … ?"

"Yeah. And they're cautious. They're not giving much away. But they invited you – and Nicholas – to attend this corroboree. And more than that, Davey, they want *you* to actually take part in it."

"God!" Dave blurted. He hadn't really expected Charlie would get very far with his crazy notion that maybe this white fella should become the custodian of the old Dreamtime site Dave and Nicholas had rediscovered.

"Don't get too excited, mate, it's pretty much a show put on for the tourists. It's the real thing, but it's not the important stuff. There'll be no sacred boards, no secrets shared – you know?"

"Yeah, of course ... but that's really cool!"

Nicholas was watching all this with a glowing gaze. He'd always found it perfectly right and obvious that Dave could have a Dreamtime connection with the land, even if he was the wrong race, the wrong colour. But that was love for you. Nicholas would always see the best in him, even if Dave didn't quite believe it of himself.

"It's a small step, baby steps," Charlie continued. "You white fellas get impatient with us, I know, but at least they're showing an interest. At least they're doing you this courtesy."

"Not just a courtesy," Dave said, from the depths of his heart. "It's an honour. I feel really honoured."

Charlie grinned at him, and looked beautifully smug. "You'll be right, mate. You'll be just fine."

Before that could happen, however, Nicholas experienced his first Christmas in summer. He seemed rather bemused by it all. In the heat, Nicholas had taken to wearing a light t–shirt and long canvas shorts, staying in the shade as much as possible and wearing his Akubra when he couldn't, and of course drinking plenty of water with ice and lime juice. Dave was surprised to find that the Brisbane climate didn't seem to worry him too much. When Dave quizzed him about it, all Nicholas did was shrug and say, "I'm happy." Once he added, "I'm where I belong," and Dave didn't feel the need to ask so often after that.

On Christmas Day, Dave and Nicholas had Denise, Vittorio and Zoe over for lunch. They cooked steak, sausages and onions on the barbecue out on the veranda, while Zoe crawled around on the grass and wrestled happily with the colourful plush butterfly toys Nicholas had gifted her. Lunch was served with salads and damper, and then finished off with an Ice Cream Christmas Pudding from an old recipe that Dave's mum used to make.

Afterwards, Zoe napped while the adults stretched out on deck chairs and talked a little or maybe drifted off into a snooze. Eventually Denise announced that she and Vittorio were still trying to decide on a name for the baby they were expecting.

"Well, what have you got so far?" asked Dave.

"Nothing that both of us like."

"I like Zoe," he said musingly.

"Already taken."

They all laughed at her retort, before Dave explained, "I meant that was a good choice, so how did you settle on that?"

"Oh, long story," Denise brushed him off with.

"Really not relevant," Vittorio added.

Then Denise asked, "Nicholas, what are your favourite names?"

Nicholas blinked and returned her look for a long silent moment, obviously puzzled. "I've never really thought about it," he eventually answered. "I've always known I'm never going to have a child of my own to name."

"But if you did," Denise persisted, "what would it be?"

"Well …" He took his time with that, but the others let him. They each sipped at their beer or water–and–juice, and contemplated the backyard – which Dave felt was in pretty good shape despite having been abandoned for the entire spring season and more.

"Well," Nicholas eventually said, "I always thought Bethan is a nice name for a girl, and maybe … Aidan for a boy?"

"Cool," said Denise. "Dave, will those do?"

"Fine by me," he replied.

"There we go, then!" she said, exchanging a satisfied grin with Vittorio. "Problem solved."

"What?!" cried Nicholas.

"We figured that if you and Dave are the godparents – irreligious, mind you – then you might as well do the hard work for us."

Nicholas had been rendered speechless. Stranger things had happened, but not often. Dave went over to him, and knelt beside his chair, took him into a massive hug. They held onto each other tight. And Dave murmured into Nicholas's ear, "You're where you belong, husband. You're where you belong."

In the evening Dave and Nicholas drove down to the nearest beach on the

288 | Of Dreams and Ceremonies

Gold Coast, and wandered along the white sands in their Akubras as the sun westered. They drew a few odd looks for walking hand-in-hand, but no one bothered them.

After a long silence broken by nothing but the crash of the waves surging ashore, Nicholas said, half-surprised and half-contented, "I could get used to this."

"It's pretty good," Dave agreed.

Nicholas smiled at him with utter fondness. "It's idyllic." His hand was hot on Dave's thigh all the way back home to Brisbane.

The Greatest and Best Mystery in the World
To be honest, there are times when we're still trying to work each other out.

But my father says that even after we've been together for fifty years, David will still be able to surprise me. And not only is he probably right, I suspect that it's actually a good thing.

Because it seems to me ... the feeling that you already know all there is to know about another person, that you might even know them better than they know themselves – that's the death knell of a relationship, isn't it?

I can't imagine that ever happening for us.

David Goring Taylor, I want to spend the rest of my life trying to figure you out.

The corroboree was held in the new year on a *bora* ground long used for these public ceremonies, a clearing in the bush where there were large circles inscribed in the earth, with a pathway linking them together. The people started to gather together in the crisp morning air, both participants and audience, somehow mingling a sense of respect with a growing sense of excitement. Dave figured that was all right, though, as even Charlie was grinning with enthusiasm at the prospect of the rituals they'd enact that evening.

In fact, Charlie was again bursting with a surprise. "Nicholas my man, you've been invited to dance, too."

"Really?" Nicholas asked, gaping a little.

"With the women folk," Charlie added mischievously – though somehow they knew he was deadly serious. He looked from one to the other of their gobsmacked faces, and admitted, "They're taking the mick, of course. But the invitation's real enough. If you want to accept it."

A pause lengthened, and Dave scrambled for the right words to politely refuse on Nicholas's behalf.

Except that once Nicholas had found his voice, he said quite firmly, "Of course I will."

"You will ... ?!" Dave asked, flabbergasted yet again.

"Of course," said Nicholas. "Whatever you need, David. Whatever we need to do to make this work out for you."

"But I couldn't ask ..." He didn't think he could bear Nicholas being made fun of.

Nicholas drew himself up tall, and sniffed disdainfully. "I shall probably get to wear a better hat than you, so don't go thinking I'll be at all unhappy."

Dave barely had time to grasp his husband's hand in gratitude and exchange a look swelling with love before they were separated and each taken away to learn the songs and dances.

They were only taking part in the final song of the ceremony, but even so it took quite an effort to learn the unfamiliar words, and then the rhythm, and the melody, and finally the accompanying dance. There were three young Aboriginals who were learning along with Dave, however, and it didn't seem to come much more naturally to them than him. Charlie was participating, too, but he seemed to think it proper to leave Dave to his own devices. At least this song was the time at which all the disparate groups converged, so any mistakes Dave made would be hidden within the whole, just one person amidst about fifty others. But he was determined not to make any mistakes if he could possibly help it. He and Nicholas were the only white fellas participating in the corroboree, of course, and Dave felt all the force of the compliment again and again throughout the long day.

They each kept to their own group for a dinner which combined a Western barbecue with traditional bush tucker, and then it was time to dress. Dave was allowed to wear khaki shorts, though he felt that was cheating a little as the Aboriginal men wore a loincloth type of arrangement. He was barefoot, and adorned with all the same decorations, however, including strings of feathers hung around his neck and bound around his waist, and body paint. Not to mention an impressive conical head-dress also painted with significant designs.

At last it was time to begin. Even the audience had been taught a song, because the corroboree started with everyone joining in a general round of singing. Then the formal rituals began, with small groups of men and women each taking turns to enact a short Dreamtime story. Dave watched from the sidelines with the rest of the male participants, every now and then permitted to take part in providing percussion using the song sticks. He kept an eye out for Nicholas in the distant women's group, of course, but didn't manage to see him. Nicholas was probably trying to be discreet.

Finally they were ready for the big finale. A long pile of dry grass was set alight as the men moved into the *bora* ground, with the flames alternately illuminating and making silhouettes of the dancers' bodies. The audience were almost as enthralled by the drama of it as the dancers themselves were.

The men did their thing, with Dave at last discovering that maybe he had a feel for this after all. How awesome to be a part – no matter how temporarily – of this extraordinary community! The rhythm of the song keened through his blood and the melody grounded him as he stamped his feet and jumped, creating a pattern of tracks in the sandy ground.

Then the men pulled back again though they kept singing quietly with their thighs quivering – and at last there came the women, singing in counterpoint to the men, and approaching the *bora* ground in a united group with stamping feet and a sashaying dance step. And there was Nicholas, his beloved Nicholas, amongst them, singing right along with them, and dancing in his adorably clumsy way with every now and then a bit of show-tune pizzazz sneaking in there. Like Dave he was barefoot and wearing shorts, and like the women he had old dugs painted on his bare chest along with other patterns, and a broad swirling brim of feathers and leaves round his head like an earthly halo. He was all man, despite all or because of it. And Dave had never seen anything so beautiful, so wonderful before, and he faltered in his song, and just stood there for a moment, beaming at Nicholas – who glanced at him with delight kicking up the corner of his mouth – before Charlie nudged Dave, and he fell back into the rhythm and the joy of it with a full heart.

When the women retreated in their turn from the ground, then both groups renewed their songs and began approaching each other – Dave was one of the men approaching the women, dancing his way towards Nicholas, who was dancing towards him, too. And they met halfway, the men and the women, Nicholas and Dave – and it was probably horribly inappropriate but in that moment the love was everything, the love was all, so as the dance ended Dave took Nicholas's hands in his and he leaned in to press a kiss to his husband's mouth, and the whole camp erupted in laughter and a glorious cheer.

❖

Like Leaves
to a Tree

This wasn't at all how Dave Goring Taylor had intended to be spending the first Valentine's Day he'd shared with his husband. The plan was to fly up to Cairns, hire a 'prestige' car, stay at the Angsana Hotel & Resort in Palm Cove for a few nights, and take Nicholas to visit the Butterfly Sanctuary in Kuranda which apparently featured the largest aviary in Australia …

It was a great plan, even if Dave did say so himself. But of course on such a momentous occasion Sod's Law was working in overdrive, and so here they were stranded by the weather in the airport at Mackay.

"You can tell me you told me so, if you like," Nicholas offered with a half-smile that betrayed a hint of anxiety.

Dave guffawed. "If I learned one thing from Denise about relationships, it's to never say 'I told you so'."

"No doubt that's very wise."

They lapsed into silence again. The two of them were sitting on the cold hard floor of the arrivals lounge, with their backs propped against a wall, along with what must be a few hundred other travellers occupying whatever seats and space were available, in various states of disgruntlement. At least Dave and Nicholas had managed to maintain their cheerfulness despite the day's disappointments.

Nicholas glanced at his watch. "We'd have been landing by now."

"Landing or –" He couldn't say 'crashing'. It didn't even bear thinking about. "Or *not* landing …"

Nicholas actually let out a laugh. "Well, one way or another, we'd have made it to Cairns by now –"

"Maybe," Dave replied shortly. "But we might not have been in any fit state to go flitting about with your butterflies."

"I'm sorry." Nicholas turned a little towards him, and reached to discreetly brush his knuckles against the back of Dave's hand where it rested on his thigh. "I'll listen to you next time, I promise."

"Sure you will …"

"You were right –"

"The second thing I learned from Denise was to say 'You were right' as often as possible. So, full marks on that one."

Nicholas jostled him with an elbow, and pointedly continued, "We should have stayed at home, like you said. I just couldn't bear to give up on our plans! *Your* plans," he corrected himself, "which were absolutely perfect. I was sure it would all work out."

"I know. Don't worry about it." Dave sighed. Nicholas's optimism had been particularly contagious that morning – and, to be fair, while Dave had read up about the storms currently wreaking havoc in Cairns, the forecast had been for the worst of the conditions to remain out at sea, and to improve by the fifteenth. And after all, he reflected, even Qantas – infamous for their safety record – had thought it worthwhile for their plane to take off from Brisbane. But something unforeseen had happened with the clash of another weather system – Dave still wasn't sure he understood the full story of this damned imperfect storm, despite keeping an eye on the news channel playing on the TV monitors – and their pilot had decided to land in Mackay rather than risk proceeding any further. Unfortunately – or fortunately, rather – their pilot wasn't the only one, and by the time they were on the ground, it was announced that Cairns airport was in the process of closing to all but emergencies.

Group by group, the various airline staff were trying to make alternate arrangements for the stranded travellers, but who knew what options would be available by the time they made it to Dave and Nicholas …

"Okay," said Dave, "the first thing they're going to ask us – when it's finally our turn – is what our plans are. So what do we want to do? I'm guessing we'll have to stay here in Mackay overnight, but then what?"

"Are the storms still going to pass? I mean, they said it would all calm down again sometime tomorrow, didn't they?"

"Yes. And from what I can tell," Dave continued, nodding towards the TV monitors, "things will still improve. Maybe not as quickly as they'd thought, is all."

"Will everything up there be wrecked, though?"

Dave tilted his head to one side in a quibble. "We'd better wait and see. I don't think it's going to turn out to be a *huge* disaster – it's not like a cyclone or anything – so they'll probably make us welcome. It's better to go, and help the local economy, you know? Rather than avoid the place, thinking to save them the trouble."

Nicholas took a breath, and visibly tried to contain his eagerness. "Can we keep going, then? I know we'll have missed The Day Itself, but we can still have a nice few days together, can't we?"

"Sure. Absolutely." Dave nodded, and couldn't help but smile in response to Nicholas's grin.

"And there are the butterflies …" Nicholas couldn't help but add. "They were planning to release the *Papilio ulysses* into the aviary. It's not as beautiful as ours, but still …"

"Of course. We'll have to see about flights, though. We're halfway there, more or less, but it's still a long way, whichever direction we head. If there are flights to Cairns tomorrow, we'll go, yeah? But if there's only flights to Brisbane, then maybe we'd better go home."

Nicholas was caught between disappointment and hope. "We couldn't hire a car and drive?"

"Long way," Dave repeated, "especially if the weather's rough. Maybe not as far as driving from Lizard Point to John O'Groats, but nearly."

"Oh. All right." Nicholas settled beside him again, his brightness somewhat dimmed.

"Hey, we've still got Mackay," said Dave. "Nothing wrong with Mackay, is there, except it's not exactly where we wanted to be today."

And that earned him a loving look and a sweet smile – so really, Dave figured, things weren't so bad after all.

Two hours later, a minibus dropped them and another six people off at the A1 Park 'n' Rest Motel on the Bruce Highway on the outskirts of town. The two of them stood there in the car park for a moment as the others trudged over to Reception, taking in the sight of a relatively orderly building that appeared cheap if perhaps not overly cheerful. "Not exactly what I had in mind for tonight," Dave muttered.

"Hey," said Nicholas, "as long as there's a bed …" And he grinned cheekily and winked when Dave turned to consider him.

Dave chuckled almost despite himself, and they headed off after the other travellers, none of whom seemed to have retained their patience during what was admittedly a rather tiresome experience. They all crowded into Reception, where a rather large and lugubrious man waited with an old-fashioned bookings register open before him.

The first four travellers were dealt with slowly yet straightforwardly enough, before heading wearily off to their assigned rooms. Then the women ahead of Dave and Nicholas stepped forward, and were offered the last double – "If you don't mind sharing."

The two women looked at each other and shrugged as if resigned to a less than ideal situation. "No, fine, we can share," one of them said, stepping forward to take up the pen ready to sign.

"It's not like we haven't before," the other added with a sigh.

Dave glanced at Nicholas – though he hardly needed the encouragement – and stepped forward himself. "The *last* double?" he queried. "What does that leave us?"

The motel manager stared at him for a moment. "A twin."

"Well, look," said Dave. "It sounds like these ladies don't want to share – and frankly, we *do* –" A sudden silent tension vibrated through the room. "What with it being Valentine's Day and all," Dave finished feebly, trying like hell not to betray his embarrassment.

This being 'out' business was still a bit too new for Dave, and the manager's reaction both helped and hindered. The man sneered in distaste, which provoked Dave into blushing hard. On the other hand, it also steeled his resolve.

The two women were a *lot* more supportive. "Oh, they should definitely have the double," one said, while the other chipped in with, "That's so sweet!"

In a heavy silence the manager switched keys and wrote down a different room number for the women. They signed, and headed off with a cheery wish: "Have fun, you guys!"

"I'm sure we will!" Nicholas happily replied. "Thank you!"

Which left Dave to step up and sign where the manager pointed. Without a further word exchanged he was handed the keys, and that was that. He and Nicholas headed out – and Dave didn't look back, though he saw from the corner of his eye that Nicholas offered the manager a swish of his hips and a rather camp wave.

The room was clean and had everything they needed, and yet the whole enterprise had been spoiled for Dave. Nicholas put down his bag and sat on the bed, wriggling his hips with rather more serious intent before patting the bedcover beside him in invitation. But all Dave could think about was that someone at that very moment was imagining them exactly thus, and thinking of them with disdain. He knew it shouldn't matter. But it did.

"I can't," Dave rasped, pacing restlessly away and then back again.

"Oh, don't let that idiot spoil the mood …"

"I know I shouldn't –" Dave ground to a halt.

After a moment, Nicholas brightly offered, "Maybe I can help get you interested …" and he leant down to rummage in his bag for a moment, before sitting up again with a gift-wrapped box in his hands.

Which only made it all worse. "Oh fuuuck," Dave groaned. He turned to stare at his own bag, mentally reviewing its contents, but he already knew. Damn it. "Fuck, Nicholas – I left your present back home."

"Never mind," Nicholas immediately responded – though his tone betrayed the fact that he himself did mind, a little bit. "That just gives us something more to look forward to."

"I'm usually – you know. I'm usually so *organised* about trips and stuff."

"You are," Nicholas agreed. "And you would have been with this, if it had been a matter of life and death."

Which it wasn't, of course, but if Dave had learned a third thing from Denise, it was that sometimes the little things should be allowed to matter very much indeed. "Our first Valentine's Day. I wanted it to be *perfect*."

"It's *fine*, David. It'll be *fine*." Nicholas was beginning to sound a bit impatient with him. "Come here, and open your present, all right?"

"All right," he agreed. And with an unwelcome feeling of grudgingness he sat down beside Nicholas – not quite close enough to touch – and took the present he was offered onto his lap, and started drawing out the bow.

He took his time, and yet it was still too soon and he was still too unsettled when he finally lifted out the contents … which were all in a pale gold silk. Something sank heavily within him. There was a top, sort of like the slip he'd worn for Nicholas on their wedding night, with skinny shoulder straps. There was a feminine version of boxer shorts, with the legs kind of flaring out so they'd flounce or drape or whatever. And there were silken cords with tassels, that seemed originally intended for tying curtains rather than wrists. But, still. Dave got the idea. Especially when he lifted the shorts and saw that the crotch seam was split all the way from here to there, and he'd be able to wear them for the entire performance, no matter what Nicholas wanted to do with him.

Dave sighed. "I can't. I'm sorry, Nicholas. I just can't. Not now."

Nicholas echoed the sigh, and sat back to consider him for long horrible moments. "Is it because of that idiot at the desk?"

"Look, I know *I'm* the one being an idiot here –"

"No, you're not. David – I know this kind of thing …" Nicholas whispered a fingertip across the silk … "makes you feel vulnerable. So I'm never going to force you, all right?"

Dave was blushing ferociously by now. He managed to nod in acknowledgement. The problem wasn't that he didn't trust Nicholas.

"I guess I imagined us being safely tucked away in our suite at the Angsana tonight," Nicholas continued. "Nothing but luxury and comfort and beautiful things. I'm sure they'd have been a lot more welcoming, too!"

"They were," Dave managed in a strangled kind of voice. "When I called them – I explained – And anyway, now we've both changed our names – They were really cool about it."

"And so they should be," Nicholas tartly replied. He sighed again, and let a hand caress the silk that Dave still held in his hands. "Do you like the colour … ?" he asked wistfully. "I chose it because it's like your skin. You're darker where you're tanned, and paler where you're not, but you always looked as precious as gold to me …"

Nicholas leaned in a little closer, and Dave couldn't help but echo the move, so they met in the middle somewhere, temple resting against temple, and they communed there for a while.

"Well," Nicholas eventually concluded, sitting up again. "Let's put all that away, and save it for another time. I think I saw a spot of bushland further along the road. Shall we go for a walk?"

Dave nodded gratefully, and stood, and they began regathering themselves even as Nicholas continued nattering away.

"It's not quite how I imagined us working up an appetite before dinner, but I promise you I shall be perfectly happy …"

Dave defiantly held Nicholas's hand as they strolled across the motel's car park and headed along the broad strip of crabgrass that bordered the road. It was just as well they'd worn their coats, as the wind had picked up, there was a real chill to it now, and dark grey clouds were looming in the east. "Looks like we'll be catching the edge of the storm here," Dave remarked.

"Never mind," said Nicholas quite contentedly. "It's an adventure."

Dave clutched his hand tighter for a moment, and Nicholas returned the gesture, and then they walked on, at peace with each other.

Luckily the bushland wasn't fenced off, so they each crossed the drainage ditch with a long stride, and then wandered through between the trees. Despite a lack of undergrowth, within moments the human world quieted and receded – and a few paces later Dave was already feeling miles away from anything but the compacted brown dirt under their feet and the eucalyptus trees towering overhead with their sharp heady scent. The wind blustering in off the sea brought the tang of salt with it, and the soughing of the leaves far above them, but they were protected from the worst of the buffeting.

Soon they could have been anywhere at all; they could have been completely alone, surrounded by the bush which Dave knew could be deadly but in those moments felt like a cocoon. Maybe Nicholas sensed that, too, for after a while he stopped, and he turned to Dave, and then slowly – giving Dave plenty of time to pull away if that's what he wanted – slowly Nicholas drew Dave into his arms, and leant in close to kiss him, easily, gently, just a beautiful kiss, so loving …

Dave gave himself over to it, relaxed into the kiss, the embrace … and that heavy unhappy thing inside him at last just melted away as if it had never been. Nicholas had the power to do that, to make all things whole and well again, if only Dave would remember to let him … And yet it was Nicholas who broke the kiss to murmur with his lips still brushing against Dave's, "You make everything hale and healthy, David, I think you could mend the entire world if you put your mind to it." At which Dave huffed a laugh, and they pressed kisses to each other's mouths, cheeks, noses, chins, caressed skin against skin, rolled forehead against forehead, and held each other near, until –

splat

A large cold raindrop crashed onto the top of Dave's head, and when he startled back a little –

sploosh

Another fat raindrop landed on his cheekbone –

splot

He saw Nicholas startle and shiver, too, and then grimace …

Dave laughed, even as he heard the bulk of the rain approaching, rustling through the trees. "I thought kissing in the rain was meant to be romantic!"

Nicholas shook his head with a grin, and then had to lift his voice to be heard. "Any Englishman could tell you it's vastly overrated."

And then they turned as one, and were running back through the bush towards the road, still hand in hand, laughing as the rain pelted after them, leaping across the ditch already a small torrent of water. It didn't matter how fast they ran, of course, the rain caught up and swept over them – and they were drenched even before they reached the car park again. Dave was still laughing on the inside though, under his panting breath, and he was sure that Nicholas was, too.

At last they made it to their motel room, and Dave's cold fingers fumbled with the key – but then they burst through, and were inside, sheltered and protected. Nicholas seemed to have entirely forgotten his usual clumsiness as he turned to bolt the door, and then turned further to reach hands to the buttons of Dave's coat. "Have to get you out of those wet clothes," he murmured, his brow knotted with serious intent.

"Yes. You, too." And they were undressing each other, fingers stumbling, feet occasionally in the wrong place at the wrong time – but nothing could stop them, not now – and soon they were clambering together into the bed, hauling the covers up over themselves for the sake of warmth, and even though Nicholas's skin was a bit chilly, Dave could feel that he was brimming with heat on the inside, and he was moving over onto Dave with unshakeable purpose. They moved together then, they shifted together and against each other, knowing each other so well, the dry friction of it only inciting them to more, their arms and their mouths consuming, and their legs restlessly rubbing, as if Dave and Nicholas had to touch every possible bit of skin that they could, they had to touch and touch in as many places as they could, and it would never ever be quite enough.

It became clear to Dave then. It became so very clear to him that there they were, the two of them naked together in body and soul, and what more could they ever need? Fancy hotels and presents and silk playthings were all very nice, but this was what really mattered. When they were together like this then the love came easily, naturally, like leaves to a tree.

"Like leaves to a tree," Dave murmured, and Nicholas seemed to understand, for he replied, "Yes, my darling," and then they plunged into a pleasure so intense there were no more words wanted and none to be had.

"Best Valentine's Day *ever*," Nicholas concluded, a long while later as they lay curled together there in the warmth.

Dave kissed him for that.

❖

The Thousand Smiles of Nicholas Goring

*Life is not meant to be easy, my child,
but take courage: it can be delightful.*

George Bernard Shaw

one

"So," said Denise, "you're seven years married. Are you feeling the itch yet?"

Dave scowled over his mug of coffee. "No," was his honest response. But then he cast her a doubting look. "I always thought that was kind of a, uh – *gross* way to put it. I mean, if you're married, you shouldn't be out there catching the nasty kind of things that make you itch. Right?"

Denise laughed. "True. And if you're not feeling the urge to stray, Davey, then I guess all is well in Goring Taylor Land."

"Everything's fine with me and Nicholas, yeah." He considered her for a long moment, wondering what she was driving at. "But you know I'm the loyal sort. I wouldn't 'stray' even if things weren't fine."

"I know that, Davey," she offered reassuringly. She took a mouthful of her coffee, and they both stared contemplatively out beyond the backyard.

It was a warm winter's day in Brisbane, and the French windows were open to let in the fresh air. Denise and Vittorio's house was on a bit of a hill, so there was a view over the back fence of a wide stretch of rooftops and trees, and the cluster of taller buildings in the city centre, and then beyond that a blue haze which Dave could sometimes convince himself was the ocean. Dave squinted, adjusted his new glasses on his nose, and tried to judge how much further he could see now ... Well, the high-rises were certainly more sharply delineated, but he figured the ocean view was still more wishful thinking than not.

"How are you finding them?" Denise asked, lifting her chin to indicate the glasses. "Getting used to wearing them all day?"

"Yeah, they're fine." He added, "It's only the right eye that's short-sighted, you know. The left eye's spot on."

She snorted. "Oh, as long as you're only half defective, that's all right, then."

"Thanks!"

"Nah ..." Denise turned in her chair to consider him again. "You're

307

looking good, Davey. Those frames suit you. Very … I dunno. Somewhere between trendy and sophisticated."

"Thanks."

"Definitely sexy," she said –

– and his cheeks went pink, he just knew it. Dave stared studiously at his coffee mug on the table before him, and feebly offered his thanks yet again. It still mattered to him, just a little bit – even after all these years – that Denny might think him handsome. "Um …" He cleared his throat, and sought to change the subject. "Vittorio's at work, then?"

"Yes. And Nicholas is at uni?"

"Yes." He didn't dare look at her. They both knew where their husbands were. Somehow that hadn't changed the subject at all, but only intensified it.

Denise commented rather pointedly, "Zoe and Bethan are at school until three …"

A silence stretched.

"Um …" Then finally Dave dared to glance at her, and saw she was brimming over with mirth. He guffawed as she burst out laughing. "God!" he managed. "You had me thinking *you* were the one feeling an itch!"

"Nah … All's well in Agostini Land, too."

"Excellent."

They sat there for a while, drinking their coffee. Then Denise observed, "You *are* looking good, though, Dave. You always did, of course, but I have to say you're maturing very nicely indeed."

And he was blushing again. "God's sake, Denny," he grumbled. "What on Earth are you going on about?"

"I was just thinking … If you want to distract young Robin from Nicholas, that's certainly one way to go about it."

It was Dave's turn to snort. "I shouldn't think he'll ever get over Nicholas, not really … But after all this time … I mean, it'll have mellowed a bit, don't you reckon?"

"Ha! How old is he? Seventeen, eighteen?"

"Eighteen."

"Like *anything* feels mellow at that age – let alone love!"

Dave sighed, remembering his own devotion to Denise during his teens, thinking of Nicholas's steadfast passion for Frank Brambell, the Goring

308 | The Thousand Smiles of Nicholas Goring

family chauffeur. If Nicholas's nephew Robin was made of the same stuff, then there could be some shoal-filled waters to navigate during the next three months. "I'm sure it'll be fine," Dave said, not knowing whom he was trying to convince. "They've both been looking forward to this for, like, eighteen months or whatever. Since we went over there, two Christmases ago."

"He's flying in tomorrow, isn't he?"

"Yes, early start in the morning to go pick him up."

"Well, bring him over to dinner whenever suits – you know, once he's over the jet lag. I know you'll be wanting to head off to the waterhole, but it'd be good to see him again."

"Thanks, Denny." He smiled at her fondly, and they talked about matters less fundamental than love until it was finally time for Dave to mosey on home ... Before he quite left, though – before he'd opened the front screendoor – Dave turned and asked, "Things are really okay?"

"Course they are, Davey."

"No, uh – no nine-year itches for you?"

"Not even a twitch."

He leaned in to press an affectionate kiss to her cheek – and she took the opportunity to grab him in a rare shoulder-cracking hug. "I'm glad," he said, once she'd let him go again.

And she wrinkled her nose at him with a loving grin. "Me, too. See ya, mate."

"See ya, Denny." And he finally let himself out, and walked home.

When Nicholas got home from uni that evening, he announced that he didn't want much to eat for dinner. Dave examined him with an anxious gaze, looking for any signs of stress or pain. But Nicholas seemed no worse than a little tired, which was only to be expected at the end of a full working day – and a bright glance from under his brow soon convinced Dave that Nicholas was in fact feeling very well indeed. With a wink, Nicholas explained, "It'll be my last chance for a while to provoke you into making some noise ..."

Dave smiled, and returned his attention to the tomatoes he was chopping for the salad.

"I can't wait to see Robin again," Nicholas continued, coming over to press a kiss to Dave's nape and steal a slice of tomato from the chopping board, "but there's no denying a long-term house guest is going to prove damned inconvenient at times."

"You know you'll love having him here."

Nicholas murmured an agreement, before almost literally poking his nose into the salad bowl. "Your world-famous chicken and new potato salad ... ? Well, I was serious, you know. How about we have half now, and save the rest for after? I'm sure I can work us hard enough to earn a midnight snack."

"Always happy to rise to a challenge ..." Dave replied as smoothly as he could.

"Mmm ..." Nicholas's hand lowered again – but this time he boldly and unerringly cupped Dave's tackle through his jeans, and gave it an encouraging jostle. "Hold that thought! I'm just going to get changed."

Dave managed to touch a fleeting kiss to Nicholas's cheek even as he turned away, and then Dave had the chance to admire that fine tall figure walking out of the kitchen and into the hall. Nicholas always insisted on wearing a suit to work, though it wasn't at all necessary – but Dave couldn't deny the man looked absolutely gorgeous in suits. That day's effort was a dark blue, perfectly tailored to Nicholas's slim waist and strong shoulders.

Within a few minutes, Dave had finished preparing the salad, and dished out half of it into pasta bowls. He was covering the remaining salad with Glad Wrap prior to putting it in the fridge, when Nicholas reappeared – transformed into something more like a regular Aussie in a t-shirt and worn jeans, barefoot, and with his dark hair mussed. Nicholas grinned at him, and they exchanged a kiss full of promise before taking their dinner through to the lounge, and eating with Splayds while watching the ABC TV news.

Not that they paid much attention to the news; they sat there together in comfortable silence, or exchanged quiet comments and questions about their days. Nicholas had some kind of official affiliation with the university which enabled him to pursue his research; Dave wasn't sure exactly how it all worked, but Nicholas went in for at least one full day each week, and often more. Nicholas also did some teaching there, though right from the start he'd negotiated that being on a fairly casual basis, because he liked to be free to join Dave on his trips to the Outback. Not that Nicholas wanted to be included on every trip, whether it was with clients or even when Dave went to sing the Dreamtime songs with Charlie at the waterhole – but Nicholas liked it to be his own decision and, as he said, he could always justify any trip with research.

After they'd eaten the salad, Nicholas sat back – and Dave remembered to take his glasses off before being welcomed into the man's arms. Nicholas held him there warm and safe, pressing lazy kisses to his hair and stroking at his arms and chest and stomach, lulling him into a luxurious kind of comfort ... The TV burbled on until Nicholas reached for the remote and turned it off, and then the cosy silence was free to well between them. Eventually Nicholas tucked his head in beside Dave's, and murmured in his ear, "Anything in particular you feel like doing tonight ... ? Or anything you *don't* feel like doing?"

"Anything," Dave echoed – knowing very well that Nicholas would respect his wishes, but also trusting that whatever Nicholas wanted to do would be absolutely fine by him. "You're the creative one," he added, twisting a little to flash his lover a grin.

Nicholas laughed under his breath. "Well ... tonight I feel like ... going all out. Doing a bit of everything. Is that all right?"

"*Hell*, yes," Dave whispered fervently.

"And I want ... I want you to tell me how it feels."

Dave cast him a doubtful look.

"You know, just ... make a bit of noise. That's all."

"I can do that," said Dave, relaxing again. He'd long ago learned how a throaty guttural groan could add to the joy felt by his other senses, and he suspected he probably made plenty of other kinds of sounds, too, when in the heart of it.

"All right, then ..." After a moment, Nicholas carefully disengaged himself, and stood from the lounge – but when Dave went to get up, too, Nicholas said, "No, wait there."

Dave shivered in happy anticipation.

Nicholas returned in a few moments with a small bundle of things wrapped up in one of their silk slips, which he put down on the lounge out of Dave's reach before turning to stand in the middle of the room. "Come here," he gently asked Dave – and Dave happily went.

311

Nicholas leant in to brush a kiss across Dave's mouth, and then took Dave's face in both hands and kissed him hungrily, his tongue pushing out to lick across Dave's lips and then press inside. Dave sucked on him, rubbing his own tongue up against Nicholas's in a tender caress. Being so used to each other as they were, they hardly needed anything more than that to get in the mood.

More kisses pressed to his face, and Nicholas's hands running lightly across his shoulders, down to his waist – and then grasping the hem of his t-shirt and slowly lifting it up and off. Nicholas dropped to his knees, and grinned happily up at Dave while unbuttoning and unzipping Dave's jeans – and then his jeans and boxers were carefully eased down past his hip bones, past his cock already heavy with interest, and slid down his thighs and further until at last he could step out of them and stand there naked.

Nicholas stood, still dressed in jeans and t-shirt. "Your turn?" Dave asked, lifting his hands.

"Not yet," Nicholas replied with a smile that hinted at very thorough plans. He went over to the things he'd put on the lounge, and came back with the silk stockings. "All right?"

"I said anything," Dave replied – though he'd only worn these once before, and it had been on the strict understanding that Nicholas never asked Dave to shave his legs. 'As if,' Nicholas had scornfully retorted.

Nicholas knelt again, and gathered up one of the stockings, hands effortlessly rhythmic. Once he was ready, Dave lifted one foot, resting a hand on Nicholas's shoulder for balance, and watched as Nicholas carefully fitted the stocking over Dave's toes, settled it into place. Then he eased the sheer pale gold silk up Dave's leg, shaping it perfectly, until the top was snug around Dave's thigh. Nicholas reached for a ribbon, and tied it around the stocking to hold it in place with a golden bow. More kisses pressed to the bare skin above the silk, with an occasional 'accidental' nudge of nose or cheek against Dave's cock which hung thickly over his balls. Then the other leg received the same attentions, before Nicholas stood. A third ribbon was tied around Dave's left arm, about as high as it would go, and Nicholas caught up the long loose lengths in bow after bow.

Then, taking each of Dave's hands in his and holding them a little way out to each side as if to put Dave on display, Nicholas smiled at him with an appreciative twinkle in his eyes. "You really are the most gorgeous creature ..."

"Not better than butterflies," Dave protested, his voice already a bit rough.

"Better than butterflies," Nicholas confirmed with a nod.

To which Dave had no sensible response. But that was all right, because after a moment Nicholas pressed a kiss to his mouth, and then headed back to the lounge.

He returned with the butt plug and lube. "All right?" he asked again.

Dave simply nodded, and Nicholas walked around to kneel behind him, to kiss him *there* – and then, with the confidence of long familiarity, Nicholas broached him with two lubed fingers and then eased the plug inside. It sat snug within, filling him and promising there was more to come. Dave shivered a little – and Nicholas, who still knelt behind him, tapped his fingers against the plug's base, which turned the shiver into a shudder. Dave let out a sharp breath –

"No, come on," Nicholas murmured, pressing a kiss to Dave's rear. "Tonight I want to hear you."

Well, he'd feel foolish if he tried to manufacture a groan now, so Dave promised, "Next time."

"Good." Nicholas pressed another kiss to his skin – and then took a bite of flesh, not hard but startling.

"Ow!" cried Dave.

"Good," Nicholas repeated complacently. "That's more like it." Then he stood, and came around to smile with happy mischief at Dave, to take his hand. "Let's go to bed."

Dave happily followed him down the hall, walking only a little bit gingerly ...

Nicholas had Dave lie down in the middle of the bed, and then knelt beside him to use silk cords to tie each of Dave's wrists to the wooden slats of the bedhead directly above him. Dave tugged on the cords carefully as Nicholas drew away again, testing their firmness. They held – though as with the ribbons, they were only fastened with bows, and Dave could undo them himself at any time, if he needed to.

Nicholas pulled away again and stood, watching Dave with a bright heavy gaze as he took off his own clothes – and a moment later Nicholas was on all fours on the bed beside him, stealing a kiss from his mouth, then pushing down further to nuzzle at Dave's throat … Dave stretched tall in anticipation, luxuriating in the flex of his lower spine, feeling the weight and slight pressure of the plug within him – and he moaned a little encouragement as Nicholas unerringly found that particular place at the juncture of his neck and shoulder … moaned under his breath – until Nicholas took another bite at him, which provoked a grunt of protest, and then a muttered, "All right, all right!"

A rumbling kind of purr answered him, and then with slow deliberation Nicholas worked his way further down Dave's body, kissing and licking and nibbling at all the places he knew would drive Dave mad with wanting. It was enough incitement to have Dave making a needy little noise on each panting breath. By the time Nicholas was lapping at Dave's tackle, his cock was hot and hard and so damned *ready* … Nicholas was still taking his time, though, and would not be hurried along even though Dave wriggled impatiently, and rolled his hips, and pushed up against where Nicholas's hands were pinning him down.

At last Nicholas deigned to take Dave's cockhead into his mouth, and suckle it sweetly – but only for a few moments. Dave growled, and tugged at the restraints that meant he couldn't clutch at Nicholas or drag him closer.

"You've been doing very nicely," Nicholas commented, looking up at him from beyond Dave's proudly-standing cock. "Still a bit quiet, mind you – but I'm sure I'll have you shouting before long."

"Nnn," Dave said, in some disgruntlement.

"Words," Nicholas continued. "I think for now we need words."

Dave frowned at him suspiciously. "What words?"

"How about … you tell me what you want … and I'll do it."

A silence dragged – in which Nicholas did nothing but continue looking with confident hope up at Dave.

"And, you know …" Nicholas helpfully continued, "I won't do anything unless you tell me."

Dave shook his head. "Can't."

"No?"

"No! We won't end up doing *anything*!"

"Now, come on. You're not the shy inarticulate Aussie bloke you sometimes pretend to be. At least, not with *me*."

"I can't, Nicholas," Dave insisted. And to underscore his point, he glanced at his own cock, which had wilted a little. "I don't have the words. Not for this kind of thing."

"Well, then," Nicholas replied. "Never mind all that." And he obligingly bent his head to encourage Dave back into full-blooded life, with a hand slipping in below to roll and tug at his balls in a rhythm that had a fingertip regularly nudging at the base of the plug, sending a delicious vibration deep within him – and Dave played his part, at first embarrassed to be making an effort to translate sensations into sounds … but it felt surprisingly good, and the sounds transformed back into new sensations, quite apart from Nicholas rewarding him with exactly the right steady increase in intensity, and his free hand sliding up Dave's chest to pinch and rub at a nipple.

"Soon," Dave was eventually saying – though Nicholas seemed to only take this as a prompt to slow down. "Please," Dave was begging.

"*Mmm* …" Nicholas happily murmured around Dave's cock.

And still it went on and on, these thunderously awesome pleasures, until Dave began to fear that the final lightning strike would never quite happen. "*Please*, Nicholas …"

"*Mmm* … *!*"

And maybe Nicholas did want the words after all – "Please," Dave muttered – so then he gathered himself up tight and blurted, "Seize the fucking day, Nicholas – *right fucking now.*"

Which had exactly the opposite effect Dave had intended. Nicholas's mouth slid up off Dave's cock leaving it standing there damp with saliva and feeling the cold even on this warm day – and Nicholas sat up a little, while his hands kept working away at what they'd been doing, though gently now. "*Some* things," said Nicholas, with a smile that was probably a little shakier than Nicholas would have wanted, "are worth taking one's time over."

Dave really was out of words, so he just gazed up at Nicholas mutely, probably looking completely pitiful, for Nicholas kind of chuckled half-heartedly and then carefully withdrew his hands. At Dave's bereft protest, which sounded disconcertingly like a whimper, Nicholas nodded reassuringly – and he reached for the lube, and reached down between his own thighs to prepare himself.

"Soon," Nicholas whispered. "Soon, I promise."

And already he was straddling Dave's hips, and positioning himself – they didn't do this often, but it was often enough for it to all be quite instinctive – and then pushing down and further down onto Dave, taking him in and deeper in. Dave was all tensed up at this point, and virtually breathless with it, gazing up at his glorious contrary husband, and feeling the pressures of both having and being had … As soon as Nicholas was settled, he reached behind himself to play with Dave's balls, before at last beginning to rock his hips in a subtle move that threatened imminent devastation.

"Nicholas –" Dave said, his voice breaking with need and wonder.

"Ssh … it's all right."

Nicholas's cock bobbed stiffly as he moved, and Dave eyed it hungrily, wondering what Nicholas's plans were for his own pleasure. Perhaps he would toss himself off – but his right hand was currently toying with Dave's nipple again, and judging by the weight behind it, Dave thought Nicholas was pretty much propping himself upright at this point.

"Nicholas –" he tried again.

"Yes," Nicholas eventually said. After another moment or two, he managed to pause in his rhythm and lean forward far enough to pull at one of the cords, which fell free of the bedhead. Once Nicholas had resumed his chosen tasks, he nodded again at Dave, and said, "Make me come."

"My pleasure," Dave replied. And he reached down with the silk still binding his wrist, and bound his hand around Nicholas's gorgeous cock, and – after taking a moment to find the right timing – Dave began deliberately working away at a task that would be over all too soon.

Sure enough, Nicholas's head dropped back with a resounding groan, and his rhythms faltered – intensified for a moment – stilled – and then he was spurting his seed across Dave's belly, groaning again – and his tight arse was clutching at Dave's cock, Dave's own arse was clutching at the plug, Nicholas's hand was trembling on Dave's tender balls – and suddenly the end was upon him at last, and Dave drove up into Nicholas with a shout, and then another, all joy and relief and love …

They finally collapsed together – Nicholas barely summoning the energy to deal with the plug, but he did so while Dave released his other wrist – and Dave wrapped both arms around this awesome man, his husband, murmuring some nonsense about him being the best fuck in all the world, "the best lover ever", to which Nicholas murmured something that sounded pleased. And they settled there together in their bed, in their home, and after a while – forgetting all about that midnight snack – they slept.

The next morning saw Dave and Nicholas at the airport early to collect Robin. They joined the line-up leaning on the waist-high barriers, greeted with nods and friendly monosyllables from the drivers and tour operators and such, some of whom had known Dave since he was a kid. "Brought the missus with you, then?" one of them commented to Dave.

Nicholas snorted with quiet humour, but Dave answered seriously enough. "Yeah, his nephew's coming to visit for his summer holidays. Well, you know … it's winter here, summer up there."

"Got everything arse-about, them Poms."

"You just wait," Nicholas muttered darkly. "The magnetic poles will reverse, and then where will you be?"

"Still in God's own country, mate!"

"So you will," Nicholas happily responded. "And so will I!"

There was a general round of laughter, and then everyone fell back to their earlier silence or desultory talk. Nicholas nudged Dave with an elbow, and indicated the cold hard floor on the other side of the barriers. "That's where I was when I saw you for the very first time."

The guy on the other side of Dave asked, "Love at first sight, was it?"

"I get a lot of that," Dave remarked.

"What can you do?" was the sympathetic response.

"I fancied him so badly!" Nicholas declared. "It wasn't love, I don't suppose – not back then. But that's where it began. That's where our story began."

A resounding silence greeted this. *Far* too much information to be sharing with Aussie blokes of either gender. Dave was blushing, a little, but he couldn't deny that he was pleased. No doubt his own smile was as fond as one of Nicholas's, despite him trying to repress it. He hardly knew where to look.

But finally someone snorted, and someone else spluttered into laughter, and the embarrassment was lost in the general hubbub, or maybe just transformed into something else, something better. "Someone's overdone it with the coffee this morning," was one comment. – "That's why I never bring my missus along," another observed. – "Jeez, there's a decent hour and a private place for that kind of thing …"

Dave and Nicholas leant there on the barrier together, pressed shoulder to shoulder, letting the jibes wash over them. And eventually Dave dared to glance at his husband, and he saw Nicholas's lips curling in infinite amusement … and Dave could hardly even begin to measure his own happiness. He hadn't seen the edges of it for *years*.

"*Nicholas!*"

Finally Robin appeared, dressed in pale blue jeans, a pale pink polo shirt and a white jumper, pushing a trolley loaded with bags. A moment later Robin and Nicholas were dashing down either side of the barrier to at last meet in a massive hug, and Robin was babbling on at a million miles an hour, and only lifting his head from where it had been tucked against Nicholas's for the sake of gazing at his beloved uncle with tears in his eyes. He was as tall as Nicholas now, which was astonishing, though it seemed that his face hadn't kept pace with the rest of him, and Robin still looked rather younger than his years. It was kind of adorable to watch him drop a kiss on the tip of Nicholas's nose and then share a giggle.

"So," someone pondered, "are they *all* gay, then?" – "Couldn't be," someone else replied. "They'd have died out centuries ago."

Dave chuckled as he stood. "Just these two, in this family, I think."

"And yourself, mate."

"And myself," he agreed with a nod.

The first thing Robin did when they reached the car was to shuck off his jumper. "I thought it was meant to be winter here," he commented, lifting a quizzical hand to take in the warm bright sunny day.

"It *is* winter here," Dave confirmed.

Robin guffawed – and then he hardly quit talking the entire drive home, pausing only every now and then to allow Nicholas to get a response in or a question of his own. First the long flight and the stopover in Singapore were gone over in great detail. Nicholas interrupted at some point to ask, "Have you texted Simon to say you're here safely?"

"Oh, no. I'll do that now." And Robin proceeded to tap out a text on his smartphone while still talking away. He meandered his way into commentary on the family news, most of which Nicholas and Dave had already heard via one source or another.

Nicholas managed to restrain himself until they were turning in to their own road before asking, "And Frank? How's Frank doing?"

"Oh my God, he's a granddad now! Gemma had a baby girl."

"Yes, Simon emailed me. They're all well?"

"Absolutely. And Frank is like … *besotted*. I never got that before, about a parent or whatever falling in love with their child. Until I saw Frank, and it's like … his heart is no longer his own."

"I'm glad," Nicholas said, turning to look out the side window – but not before Dave glimpsed Nicholas's achingly poignant smile.

Robin quietened at last as Nicholas took him to the bedroom that would be his for the next three months – the one that used to be Dave's when he was growing up. Later on, while Dave's dad was still alive, Denise had moved in and shared the room with Dave, so it contained a double bed and wasn't filled with as much childish clutter as Robin might have expected.

Once Robin had shed his gear, Nicholas showed him around the rest of the house. "This is really nice!" was Robin's verdict as they joined Dave in the kitchen.

Dave handed him a cup of tea. "You sound surprised. Did you think I'd have Nicholas living in a corrugated iron shack?"

"No! No, of course not." Robin looked around him again, at the kitchen and family room, and the backyard full of greenery. "I've seen photos, of course, and everyone who's visited said it's great – but I didn't get to *feel* it until now. And it feels like home."

"It does, doesn't it?" Nicholas quietly agreed. "I felt that right away, too."

"Huh," said Dave, handing his husband a cup of coffee. "How I remember it is, the first time I brought you here, you promptly changed your plane tickets and went back to England six weeks early."

Nicholas took the coffee, put it down, and grabbed Dave's hand. "I *wanted* to stay – forever."

Dave coloured a little under Nicholas's earnest gaze – all too aware of

Robin's wistful yearning. "And now you can," Dave replied a little too brusquely. "Now you are." Then he cleared his throat and changed the subject. "Are you hungry, Robin? I thought I'd cook us a proper breakfast this morning. Eggs, bacon, sausages, toast ..."

Robin brightened immediately. "Marmalade and extra toast for after ... ?"

"And marmalade for after," Dave confirmed.

"See?" Nicholas commented to Robin. "He makes all our wishes come true."

The perils of having a house guest were soon made evident. Dave had done a load of washing on the morning of that first day, and had hung the bulk of it on the Hills Hoist in the backyard. A few items, however, the hand-washed silk items, he hung on the clothes airer and tucked it away out of sight in the main bedroom. He left the door open, as usual during the day, but assumed Robin would know better than to walk in uninvited ...

Dave discovered he'd been wrong about that when Robin wandered into the family room with the toe of one of the silk stockings pinched between thumb and forefinger and held at arm's length, his expression squeamish. Dave abruptly turned waratah red, and sat down on the nearest available chair.

"Unc-le Nich-o-laaas ..." Robin drawled.

Nicholas looked up from the newspaper he'd been reading, and promptly turned coldly unimpressed.

"You don't really *wear* these, do you?" Robin sounded more creeped out than disgusted, but still. It wasn't pleasant. "I never knew you were into *drag* ..."

"*Not* that it's any of your business," Nicholas tartly replied, turning a page of the newspaper, "but so what if I do?"

"Seriously? I always thought you were ... a man. A man who liked men."

"Things are generally a little more complicated than that," Nicholas replied in somewhat softer tones. He'd had the mercy to not even glance at Dave through all this. "I think you'll find ... there are infinite varieties of men and women and those in between."

"But *you're* not complicated," Robin insisted, letting his hand drop now.

"You've always been completely straightforward! Completely honest!"

"My darling, I'd rather be complicated than narrow-minded. Now, you go and put that back where you found it – *respectfully*, thank you – and then you can have a bit of a think about your reactions. I would have expected rather more acceptance, coming from *you*."

There was a brief struggling silence, and then at last Robin said in a humbled voice, "Yes, Uncle Nicholas. Sorry." And he turned and headed back down the hallway. A couple of moments later, the door to the guest bedroom could be heard to firmly close in what was, in context, a chagrined slam.

Nicholas continued reading the newspaper, letting Dave process all of that in whatever ways he needed to.

Eventually, after Nicholas turned another page, Dave asked quietly, "D'you mind him thinking that? I mean, that you're the one who wears them?"

Nicholas looked up at Dave, his gaze direct and relaxed, his smile gentle. "No, I don't mind. Don't worry about it."

Dave had to admire the man's insouciance. He shuddered in a belated reaction, and went to put the kettle on. And then he said, "You know, we still all have a lot to learn from you."

Nicholas shone a crinkly smile in his direction that did away with the last of Dave's anxieties.

two

Two days later Dave drove the Toyota Land Cruiser down the Warrego Highway, with Nicholas beside him in the passenger seat – and Robin in the back, paying far more attention to his smartphone than to the passing countryside. Nicholas caught Dave's glance, and twisted around for a moment to watch Robin sitting there with his head down ... Dave wondered if Nicholas was remembering, as Dave himself was, so very strongly, the first time he'd driven Nicholas down this road. *That* visiting Englishman had stared out the window, not wanting to miss a single detail of the scenery. *This* one seemed more concerned about not missing his friends' updated Facebook statuses.

Nicholas snorted. "Well – if you must – enjoy it while you can," he advised. "There's coverage in Charleville, but once we get near the waterhole, you won't get any signal at all."

Robin looked up at him with a woebegone face. "Not even a single bar?"

"No."

"Oh my God! *How* long are we staying there ... ?"

"Five or six days, I think." Nicholas glanced at Dave to confirm this.

"We're leaving a day earlier than I'd planned," said Dave, "so we can spend six at the waterhole – as long as Charlie's okay with that."

"*God* ..." Robin grumbled.

Nicholas turned around in his seat so he was facing the front again. "This is a privilege, you know. I hope you appreciate it! David hasn't taken anyone but me and Charlie to the waterhole in all these years."

"Oh." That had caught Robin's attention. "Why not?" he asked Dave.

Oddly enough, Dave found that he didn't have a ready answer. A beat of silence passed.

"It's a very special place," Nicholas supplied. "You've heard David and Charlie talk about the Dreaming ... ? The waterhole is a sacred site."

"So, like ... Aboriginal people go there?"

Another beat of silence.

"Well," said Nicholas. "It's quite difficult to find. Only David really knows the way."

"Not even you, Nicholas?"

"I don't drive, remember? Well, David taught me, but only for emergencies. And it's too far from anywhere to walk there. I've never even tried to get there on my own. I've never had to!"

"Oh." And Robin gazed out the side window rather pensively, his phone lying forgotten in his cupped hands.

If Dave had thought Robin looked afraid of being so far distant from civilisation, he would have offered reassurance. As it was, he let the peaceful silence grow. Nicholas quietly reached to rest a hand on Dave's thigh … and they drove on into the Outback.

They took their time with the journey, and reached Charleville on the second day. Once they'd checked in with Marge at the hotel, Robin started bouncing around insisting they go meet Charlie – "*Now*. Right now. Come *on*, guys."

Nicholas exchanged an indulgent smile-and-shrug with Dave, and obviously they had no objections to the plan, so they all headed down to the pub.

Charlie was sitting at their usual table, as if he'd known when they'd show up. He stood to greet them, and returned Robin's enthusiastic hug in kind. "Look at you!" he marvelled once they'd parted, looking over Robin from top to toe. "You're a man now."

Robin snorted. "I was, like, *eleven* last time we met!"

"So you were …" Charlie equably agreed.

"Charlie, I'll get us a beer," said Dave. "Nicholas?"

"Yes, please," said Nicholas, with a smile happily anticipating a treat. He didn't drink very often at all, but Dave knew well enough there was something about being in the Outback that called for a cool pour of amber.

"Robin? What d'you want to drink?"

"I'll have a beer, too, please. May I?"

Dave nodded, though he asked, "Have you got ID?"

"I have my driving licence. English, though."

"That's fine. Come to the bar with me, all right? Rosie will want to check it."

They drew a few stares, of course. Dave still attracted a bit of benign bemusement, and had done ever since he'd taken up with Nicholas; he'd long been used to letting that be. Robin, though, was a new face to ponder, and almost everything about him declared he was a visitor – not least the fact that he refused to wear his new Akubra indoors. This was despite Robin thinking he looked pretty cool in it, with which Dave had to agree. The young fella had insisted on the Graphite Grey, which Dave felt was too dark for practical purposes – but then Robin lived in England, so it wasn't as if he needed it all year round.

"You right, Dave?" asked Rosie when she reached them.

"Yeah, thanks. This is Robin." He nudged Robin with an elbow, prompting him to hand over his ID. "He's legal."

Rosie considered the card for a long moment, and then lifted her chin in acknowledgement as she handed it back. "What'll it be, Dave?"

"Four Cascades, thanks, mate."

The bloke sitting near them on a barstool had been gazing sideways at Dave this whole time. Dave offered him a brief nod, wondering if the guy was simply curious about the ocker who'd married the son of an English earl. Maybe that wasn't it, though, as eventually the guy asked, "New client, Mr Taylor?"

Dave's brow rose in surprise, as he was pretty sure they'd never met before – but he readily answered, "No, Robin's family. Not a business trip, this time."

Rosie came back with the beers, so Dave left it at that. He paid, exchanged polite nods all round, then he and Robin took the beers back to their table and settled in.

After they'd all taken their first appreciative mouthful, Charlie asked Robin, "You're here for the winter?"

"Yes, it's our summer holidays back home. The 'long vacation'. Dad said he'd pay for me to come here, if I got three A levels at grade A. And I did." Robin added with cheeky pride, "Actually, I got four!"

"Good for you," said Charlie, apparently understanding more about what that meant than Dave did.

"I had, like, a conditional offer from Oxford, so of course I was always gonna totally blitz it ... Dad didn't need to bribe me," he added with a beaming grin, "but I wasn't complaining!"

"It wasn't bribery," Nicholas said, correcting him. "It was a reward."

"Whatever. It meant I got to come see you – at *last* ..."

The two of them looked fondly at each other, and Nicholas said something soft that was meant for Robin alone.

Dave was feeling just as fond, but he took the opportunity to turn to Charlie and quietly ask, "That guy at the bar next to where I was standing … You know him?"

Charlie took another mouthful of beer, and discreetly lifted his gaze as he did so. "Yeah – know of him, anyway. Ted Walinski. Works as a surveyor."

"Huh," said Dave. "Never even heard of him."

"Why d'you ask?"

"He knows me! Well, my name, anyway, and what I do." Dave shrugged. "I don't suppose it matters, but if I meet someone through the business, I try to remember them, you know?"

"That's the smart thing to do," Charlie agreed, before they turned to more interesting concerns.

The next morning saw Dave driving down towards Cunnamulla, with Nicholas beside him and Charlie and Robin in the back. Nicholas's smile had a happy anticipatory kick to it, as it always did when they were heading for the waterhole. Charlie's usual cheerfulness was in full bubble, and even Robin had put his phone away to engage with the countryside and his companions.

"So, what's this place called?" Robin asked at some point about an hour into the journey.

Charlie replied, "It doesn't have a white-fella name."

"What's its black-fella name, then?" Robin persisted.

Dave glanced at Charlie via the rear-view mirror, but Charlie was the last person to take unnecessary offence when someone was genuinely interested and willing to learn. Nevertheless, Dave said, "We call the Indigenous people around here 'Murri', Robin, yeah?"

"Oh. Yeah, okay. What's its Murri name, Charlie?"

Charlie grinned at him. "Only your Uncle Davey and me know that."

"What, not even Nicholas?"

"Not even Nicholas," Charlie confirmed. He seemed to ponder this for a moment, and Dave himself was prompted to wonder whether or when that

325

should change. They'd kind of coasted along together on the current arrangements for a few years now – but who would he and Charlie pass the Dreamtime knowledge to, when it was time?

"What about –" Robin continued. "I mean, isn't there a tribe that belongs there?"

"Nah, there was but they're lost to us, mate. I had a friend, he was the last of 'em. He's the one who passed the songs to me. And I passed them on to Davey, because he was the one who found the place, when I never could."

"Wow," said Robin, gazing at Dave with a new level of respect.

Dave turned his head for a moment to acknowledge Robin with a rueful nod – and he caught Nicholas's proudly glowing grin in the corner of his eye on the way back. Dave had been staggered and humbled when Charlie first suggested all of this, and Dave remained so now. He caught up Nicholas's hand from where it rested on his thigh, and without taking his eyes from the road lifted it to his lips for a kiss. Nicholas returned the favour, bringing their joined hands over to his own mouth to press a kiss to the back of Dave's hand, before returning it to the wheel and his hand to Dave's thigh.

"Okay," Robin continued once they were done. "So we're gonna be holding our own ... like, mini corroboree or something?"

"Well," said Dave. "Charlie and I are."

"But I can watch, right?"

"I'm afraid not, Robin."

Charlie offered, "Some of it, he could, Davey."

Robin was unimpressed. "I bet you let Nicholas watch!"

"Huh," Dave huffed. "Yeah, but I shouldn't. Strictly speaking. So, don't tell Charlie, okay?"

Charlie just guffawed, as if he'd known it all along.

Nicholas diplomatically said, "You and I, Robin, we'll do the right thing and sit this one out."

Silence.

"It's *important*, Robin," Nicholas continued. "It's not just for fun."

"Yeah riiight ..." Robin drawled, turning away to stare out the window.

They just let him be after that. But from what Dave could see, Robin was doing more pondering than sulking. So maybe that was all right.

They stopped for lunch in Cunnamulla, indulging in cheesecake afterwards for no better reason than that they wouldn't be eating such things for a while. Then Dave filled up the Cruiser with petrol, and they headed west.

About half an hour out of town, Dave saw a sand-coloured Land Rover Discovery parked on the other side of the road, facing towards them. He slowed down a bit to see if anyone was in trouble. Nothing seemed wrong with the vehicle at least. However, the driver wasn't in sight.

"Call of nature?" Charlie surmised.

"Doesn't look like a flat tyre, anyway," Dave said.

"Careful ..." Charlie murmured when Dave slowed down further.

"Yeah," he replied shortly. "Nicholas. Can you see anything on your side? Scan, like, the full one-eighty. Robin, you have a look, too."

"All right." Nicholas sounded a bit puzzled, but he obligingly shifted in his seat, and the two Englishmen looked around. "I can't see anything but scrub and dirt. Robin?"

"Nothing, Uncle David."

"What are we looking for, exactly?"

But then just as they drew near the Land Rover, a figure stepped around from the far side of it, with a thermos and cup in his hands. It was the surveyor who'd spoken to Dave in the pub.

Dave let out a pent-up breath, and pulled to a stop, powering down his window to talk to the man. "You all right? Walinski, isn't it?"

"That's right, Mr Taylor." The man lifted one hand to push his hat back on his head, the better to hold a conversation. "Ted Walinski." He fixed the cup back on the thermos, and then reached to shake Dave's hand before offering a general nod to the others.

"You're all right out here? Not broken down, or anything?"

"No, she's right. Just felt like a cuppa, and didn't want to wait for Cunnamulla. Thanks for checking, though."

"No worries." Dave nodded, and after a beat of silence that wasn't filled, he said, "See ya round, then."

"Yeah. Thanks again!" Walinski stepped back, and lifted his hand in farewell.

Dave pulled away, and quickly eased up to his regular speed. He kept half an eye on the rear-view mirror, though, and noticed that Charlie had turned to watch as much as he could through his side window. Not that Walinski was doing anything more than pouring himself another cup of tea.

"All right?" Dave said to Charlie as the Land Rover receded to little more than a dot.

"Yeah," Charlie replied, resettling himself.

Nicholas was watching Dave with wary curiosity, but obviously knew better than to ask with Robin in hearing distance. And Dave wasn't even sure how much he wanted to tell Nicholas about ambushes and kidnappings and other nefarious things.

After another moment, Charlie turned to Robin. "D'you want me to teach you one of the songs your Uncle David's gonna be singing at the waterhole?"

"Hell, yes!" was the delighted reply.

Although some of the approach to the waterhole still felt counter-intuitive, Dave pretty much had the hang of it by now. There was a place where he always felt he had to turn right but knew he had to turn left, and another place where his instincts were to turn left which was actually correct. There was a worn old ridge of rocks like a skeletal spine poking out of the ground that he had to follow – it even had a kind of arrowhead formation at the far end – and he'd have to ask Charlie about all of that, because if he had the meaning right, the formation might actually feature in one of the songs. Then he had to pay careful attention to feel the gentle rise of the ground and drive at the correct angle up across it – and there would be nothing for a while, absolutely nothing. But then, finally, just as he was beginning to really give in to the doubt, the Land Cruiser would crest the edge of the wide flat valley that cradled their waterhole, and he would marvel at the fact that he'd managed the impossible yet again.

Nicholas and Charlie each let out a long sigh of relief as if they'd hardly even dared breathe for the past five minutes. Dave chuckled, and they did, too – and Robin was looking around him in vain for a miraculous change in the landscape, and asking, "What? What happened? Where are we?"

"We're almost at the waterhole," Dave said, shifting down a gear and then easing the Cruiser across onto the long shallow slope.

"It's right ahead of us," Nicholas added, pointing. "See the denser foliage there? That's the treetops breaking above ground level."

"No ..." Robin answered uncertainly, leaning forward as far as he could to align his sight down Nicholas's arm.

"Never mind. We'll be there in a few minutes. Just keep watching."

"What I reckon," Dave said conversationally – "not that I did anything more than high school geography. What I reckon is that a meteor hit, thousands or ten-thousands –" He looked doubtingly at Nicholas.

"Tens of thousands," Nicholas supplied.

"Yeah, that many years ago. And the meteor created this whole big crater – though it's been so long that it's fairly worn down now. And the meteor made the original hole there, too, and maybe it became a sinkhole, or opened up a cave system or something. And the depth of it means it's right near the underground water table, and *that's* what feeds the actual waterhole."

"Yeah ... ?" said Robin, apparently taking all of that in.

"Did you do geology?" Dave asked him.

"Yeah, a bit. I get what you're saying."

"Cos there's very little rain out here, hardly any run-off. But the actual waterhole itself is always full. It's always at the same level. So I reckon the water table somehow replenishes it."

"That's awesome," said Robin.

Dave laughed. "It is pretty awesome," he agreed. They were almost there now. He turned to the left once he could see the cliff edge, found the track that led down into the waterhole, but then pulled the Cruiser up and parked it nearby. He looked around at his companions. "It's Robin's first time here. What d'you say we walk down there, so he gets the full impact?"

"Absolutely," Nicholas said, his eyes as bright as his beautiful smile. He was already opening the door and swinging those long legs out and grabbing up his Akubra, all in one smooth move. The others followed suit, and a moment later the four of them were crossing over a slight ridge and then following the worn old layer of rock that served as a track down into the waterhole.

They walked in silence for a while, feeling the slightly cooler temperature as soon as they were below ground level and out of the direct sun. The cliff wall climbed steeply above them, a rich reddish-black, the edge of it sharp against the bright blue sky. Soon they reached the twist in the track that took them back around to the right.

Nicholas was grinning in anticipation, though even Dave knew it was the wrong season to be expecting to find anything more than the hibernating pupae of his butterflies. "Isn't this marvellous?" Nicholas asked Robin in hushed tones.

Charlie chuckled under his breath –

But Robin shivered. "It's kind of … well, not creepy, I guess."

"There's a magic here," Nicholas said.

"Okay, it's creepy," Robin concluded.

"It's not … familiar," Nicholas offered. "But you'll get used to it. Anyway. David belongs here, and so does Charlie, and they're happy that we're here, so the waterhole will be, too."

Robin was looking somewhat sceptical.

Charlie tilted his head as if considering or listening, and then announced, "Old man grunter, he's happy that you're here. This is his place, see?"

With more politeness than belief, Robin asked, "He's the Ancestor, right?"

"Right. He's sleeping down deep in the waterhole, he's a long time dreaming …"

Which, despite his obvious efforts to restrain himself, made Robin shiver all over again.

Dave tried another tack. "Well, how much d'you remember of your geology, Robin?"

"A bit."

"See the colours of the cliff walls and the rocks? What kind of stone d'you think that is?"

Robin scrunched up his face for a moment as he looked around. "Iron ore … ?"

"Exactly!"

"Which goes to make steel, doesn't it?"

"Yes! Well. I don't know for sure that it's iron ore, but that's my guess." They were walking through the trees and ground cover now, and then at last they were out in the open and approaching the jewel-bright pool of water itself. "I think the meteor – if that's what happened – drilled down into here."

Robin gasped. "You mean, it might still be down there, at the bottom of the pond? The meteor itself?"

"Maybe."

"Well, haven't you swum down there, to try to find it?"

330 | The Thousand Smiles of Nicholas Goring

The three adults were all completely taken aback by the notion.

"No," said Nicholas. "We don't disturb anything we don't have to."

"But –" said Robin.

"The Ancestor is dreaming down there," said Charlie. "It's not for us to wake him."

"But –"

"Anyway, the water's not safe," Dave concluded rather flatly. "Don't drink it, all right? We hardly even take a dip when we're here."

Robin sighed, and scuffed one sneakered foot through the dirt. "All right, all right," he mumbled.

A moment's silence fell heavily through them.

But then Nicholas said, with barely controlled excitement, "Shall I show you the butterflies? They're in their pupal stage at the moment."

Robin smiled at him indulgently, and peace returned. "Yes, please, Uncle Nicholas." And Dave watched as Robin slipped his hand into Nicholas's and the two of them headed further past the pool, past the old rockfall, and on towards the wattle.

When Dave announced he was going to head up and fetch the Cruiser, Robin got all panicky again. "You're not bringing it down here?!"

"Yeah, I am."

"But – how?"

"Down the same track we just walked."

Robin cast a wide-eyed stare at what little they could see of the old layer of rock through the foliage, and especially at where the track turned a corner near the bottom.

Dave scoffed a gentle laugh. "It's no worse than those narrow twisty lanes you call roads in England. In fact, it's better, cos at least you're not running along blindly between two great hedgerows."

"But – what if something goes wrong? Like another landslide," he added, gesturing behind him at the long-ago tumble of rocks. "How will we get out?"

"Robin," Dave said, "nothing's changed in here in the last seven years. Nothing but the trees slowly growing, and the butterflies emerging twice a year. I can't remember seeing even one fresh rock added to that fall over there."

"Yeah?"

"In fact, *that's* what used to not sit right with me. How everything stays the same. There aren't even any animals around to disturb things …" An edgy silence made Dave realise he'd better shut up sooner rather than later. "But that's good, right?" he tried. "What you see is what you get, no more and no less."

"Huh," said Robin.

"Well, anyway," Dave blundered on, given that neither Nicholas nor Charlie were gonna help him out, "if we're not back in Brisbane in a few days, Denise will call out the troops."

Robin squinted at him suspiciously. "I thought you were the only person who can find this place."

Dave assumed a lofty pose and told a white lie. "I left her detailed instructions, just in case."

At which Charlie snorted a chuckle, and Nicholas shook his head, ducking to hide a wry smile – so Robin was convinced. In fact, with what had to be youthful enthusiasm, he seemed to have a complete change of heart. "So, can I come with you, then? I wanna see how you get round that turn!"

Dave snorted, too. "Sure. Come on, then." And he escorted Robin back up the track, with the young fella chattering on as if he didn't have a care in the world.

They set up their campsite, Dave and Nicholas working with an efficiency based on years of shared habits, and Robin helping where he could. Nicholas helped Robin set up his own tent, which made Dave smile, remembering the first time Nicholas had helped Dave set up an earlier example of the same model. That was when Dave had first realised that Nicholas was stronger than he appeared; yet another small step on the long road to falling in love, had he but known it at the time.

Soon Nicholas and Robin had set up a second tent nearby. "So, this is for you two?" Robin asked.

"Well, no," Nicholas replied. "Dave and I like to sleep on a mattress on top of the Cruiser."

Robin's mouth twisted in distaste as he picked up on Nicholas's hint of self-consciousness. "What, out in the open? Where either of us could see you two ... getting it on?"

"Don't worry. I should think we can manage to restrain ourselves for a few days."

"You'd better!" Robin insisted. "I'm not hiding in my tent the whole time, and I didn't sign up for the full scenic tour!"

Nicholas manfully tried not to laugh, but then he glimpsed Dave's amusement and ended up spluttering in mirth. "I can assure you, Robin, that our tour guide comes highly recommended!"

"Uncle Nicholas ..." Robin said forebodingly.

"No, you're right. We'll promise to behave."

Robin shrugged his acquiescence. Then, after a moment, he indicated the second tent. "What's this for, then? In case it rains?"

"It probably won't rain. This is Charlie's tent."

Robin turned to find Charlie, where he was building a campfire for that evening. "You're sleeping *inside*?" He sounded scandalised.

"Yeah, and on that camp bed, too," Charlie replied, gesturing at where the bed waited to be unpacked and set up. "What, you think us black fellas all just lie down in the dirt to sleep?"

"Oh. No." Robin had gone red with shame. "Sorry."

"Ah, I'm messin' with ya," Charlie said with a chuckle, coming over to nudge warily at the bed with a toe. "Let's see if we can figure out how to put this together, eh? So my poor old bones can rest comfy tonight."

Robin offered him a tentative grin, which became a real one in response to Charlie's smile, and the two of them got to work.

On the day that Dave and Charlie would perform the Dreaming songs, Dave drove the Cruiser up out of the waterhole so that Nicholas and Robin could use it as their base. Robin slowly followed them on foot, exaggerating his reluctance for tragic effect.

Dave laughed under his breath, watching him, and turned to say quietly to Nicholas, "If he's going to be difficult, why don't you drive him out to where you can get a signal on his phone? That should cheer him up, to check in with his mates."

Nicholas looked a bit panicked. "*Me* drive him?"

"You know you can."

"You'd trust me with the Cruiser? What if I – ?"

"Of course I trust you with the Cruiser. You'll be fine. Remember what I said after our last driving lesson?"

"You'd trust me with your life."

"Exactly." That's what it had been about, after all. Dave liked to have backup plans for his backup plans, and he couldn't bear the thought of Nicholas stuck out there miles from anywhere if anything happened to Dave.

"But I've never – not without you in the passenger seat."

"You don't have to if you don't want to," Dave equably assured him. "It was just an idea. But I reckon you'd be fine. And won't Frank be proud to hear about it, from you or Robin?"

The corner of Nicholas's mouth betrayed him by twitching into a smile. "You know just where all my buttons are, don't you, David?"

"And exactly how to push them!" Dave grinned. "I figured that's why you married me."

They were alerted to Robin's presence by a groan. "Oh my God, don't you two ever give it a rest?"

"No, we don't," Nicholas tartly responded. "But don't worry. You can return the favour by being just as insufferable when you find your … special someone."

"Yeah right," Robin said with a scowl, before climbing into the back seat of the Cruiser with an enormous sigh.

Dave and Nicholas exchanged rueful looks, and Dave muttered, "We're not having any of our own, are we?"

Nicholas chuckled. "Don't worry. Only the sort we can give back."

"Have fun, then!" Dave said in brighter tones that would carry. "I'll come back up when we're done. We'll only be an hour or so."

"It's cool. We'll be fine. Enjoy yourself." And Nicholas kissed him, before heading over to the Cruiser.

When Dave turned for a last glimpse of him before descending into the waterhole, he was pleased to see Nicholas in the driver's seat, his hands and his gaze reacquainting themselves with the controls.

Dave knew the songs and dances by heart now. Within moments he had settled into a comfortable rhythm in tandem with Charlie, as they progressed down towards the pool, and then sang the story of the Ancestor that slept there.

Most of the Ancestors had emerged in human form during the Dreamtime, and the Barcoo grunter was no different. He had been woken to life when another Ancestor fell from the sky – Dave still wasn't too sure whether she was supposed to be a star or a bird or some other living creature, but obviously his pedantic white-fella mind linked her with the meteor which he thought had created the waterhole. The two Ancestors had loved each other and loved the land, wandering the area and singing the trees and shrubs into being. They bathed in the pool and mucked about together, splashing the water around so that the run-off formed the old creek beds that Dave could still trace today. Theirs was a barren love, until at last the fallen Ancestor had to return to her home in the sky. Old man grunter transformed into a fish, so that if he must be alone then he would sleep in the pool forever and remember the joy he'd felt there. But before he sank he cried a lament for his lost love, and his tears became the blue butterflies that still lived there even now.

That was Dave's favourite song: the lament and the beautiful things it created. It wrung his heart. Not that he ever told Charlie that, but no doubt Charlie could hear it in his voice.

There were another couple of songs that led them away from the waterhole again, and then they were done.

Dave had been conscious in the midst of the songs of a head cautiously peeking over the cliff edge high above and peering down at them. He thought it was Robin; a short while later he was proved correct when Nicholas appeared beside him. Nicholas indulged himself by watching for a moment or two – with infinite fondness and respect – but then he turned away and took Robin with him. Dave continued on, undisturbed, and if Charlie had noticed he pretended not to.

Dave always felt a sense of peace after performing the songs and dances. There was a sense of satisfaction, even a feeling of reverence. He couldn't explain it to himself, because he knew well enough that he didn't believe in the literal truth of the Dreaming. Imagining himself as a small part of the ongoing story told by Aboriginal culture, however, was a gift and a comfort.

Charlie was quiet for a while after they'd finished as well. Dave had developed a habit of leaving him and wandering off to kneel by a particular rock near the waterhole. When the first of the blue butterflies they'd discovered had died, Dave had buried it under this flat stone. He'd never confessed as much to Nicholas, let alone to Charlie, but he'd never forgotten either.

Once he'd paid his respects, Dave wandered back to sit cross-legged by Charlie, and then when he thought the time was right, Dave finally broke the silence. "The first few songs … they're about finding the waterhole, aren't they?"

"Yeah." Charlie pondered on this for a short while. "That's what you call the songlines … The paths from one sacred site to another."

"Yeah."

"Didn't help me, though. When I was looking for the place before you found it? Couldn't make head nor tail of it."

"I was thinking that – there's a ridge of rocks sticking out of the dirt that we drive beside, that pretty much points the way here. And there's the song about the lizard that goes to sleep and is buried, only there's a curve of its body still above ground. So, are those two things related? Like, are the rocks what remain of the lizard … ?"

Charlie was grinning at him fondly, proudly, which was answer enough, and then he muttered once more, "Old man grunter chose well when he chose you, Davey."

While he couldn't really believe that, Dave appreciated the thought more than he could say, so he nodded in acceptance. "I'll show you the place when we're driving out."

When he climbed up out of the waterhole, it was to discover that Nicholas had been brave enough to drive the Cruiser out to the edge of the shallow crater after all. Dave watched as they slowly returned, Nicholas carefully finding a way through the scrub and between the rocks; being far more careful with the Cruiser's paintwork than even Dave ever was. Soon Dave could make out the frown of concentration on Nicholas's face – which turned into a full-beam smile as Nicholas finally pulled up near Dave.

"Told you you're wonderful," Dave said, reaching through the open window to give Nicholas's shoulder a gentle shake.

"I suppose that every now and then I can … *rise* to the occasion."

Robin groaned from the back seat. "Oh my God, save me."

Dave ignored him, and asked Nicholas, "Are you gonna drive her down into the waterhole, then?"

"Oh hell no," Nicholas brightly replied. And he clambered over onto the passenger seat, while Dave laughed and climbed up inside.

They left the waterhole a few days later – and they saw the Land Rover Discovery again, soon after they found their way back onto a sealed road. It was parked as before, although this time Ted Walinski was sitting perched on the bull bar, again with his thermos. He lifted a hand in casual greeting as they neared.

Dave slowed to a stop and lowered the window. "You right, mate?"

"Yeah, sure. You always catch me on a tea break."

"All right, then." Dave nodded a farewell. "See ya round."

"Thanks for stopping." Walinski offered them all a smile as Dave pulled the Cruiser away. "See ya!"

"What's he doing?" Dave asked Charlie a few moments later, as Charlie had turned to keep an eye on him.

Charlie said, "Maybe he's looking for our dust trail ... He's not watching us, that's for sure."

Robin was all agog. "Could he, like, follow our tyre tracks back to the waterhole?"

"Maybe ..." Charlie said.

"If he can find where I turned onto the road, then good luck to him. It was too stony to have left an impression."

"I know fellas who could find it."

"Yeah, and I know *you* could," Dave fondly agreed.

"David," said Nicholas in worried tones, "do you really think he could find his way there?"

"Well, honestly, if he does then he's accomplished something a lot of people have failed at."

"David –"

"It's not like we own the place," Dave argued. "And I can pretty much guarantee your butterflies will be safe. Blokes out here, they respect what they find. Life can be a battle out here, and people respect that. You know?"

Charlie rumbled a thoughtful agreement. Nicholas subsided, though he looked unsettled. Robin was gaping at the potential for drama.

They remained silent almost right through to Charleville.

three

Back in Brisbane, they did the usual tourist things with Robin. They drove down to the Gold Coast beaches a few times, they wandered through the South Bank gardens, window-shopped in the city, browsed the markets, visited the Koala Sanctuary. Denise, Vittorio and the girls joined them for lunch on the paddle steamer that ran down the river, before heading into town to indulge in the most extravagant ice cream sundaes known to humanity.

Dave encouraged Robin to try abseiling at Kangaroo Point Cliffs, but he suspected he was on a losing wicket there, even after Nicholas gamely said he'd try it, too. "We owe it to David," Nicholas pointed out. "After all, we made him take us to the art gallery."

At which Robin just snorted.

"Don't tell your Uncle Nicholas," Dave stage-whispered, "but I actually kind of enjoyed that." Which was true, if only because Nicholas had made for an interesting and surprisingly knowledgeable guide, who knew more about the history of Australian art than Dave had even guessed at.

Dave had an Outback trip planned for late July with a family who wanted to fossick for opals, and another trip later on with a bunch of blokes who were more into pubs and off-roading, but Dave had delegated his other two business bookings to the retired couple who helped him out when needed. At least Robin was keen on the idea of him and Nicholas coming along on the fossicking trip, but otherwise he seemed content to simply hang out.

More to the point, Robin was perfectly happy to keep company with Nicholas. It was obvious Robin was still in love with Nicholas – and when Dave thought back to being eighteen and in love and on his summer holidays, he could perfectly understand Robin's lazy contentment.

One warm afternoon they were all three hanging out in the shade on the back veranda. Dave was stretched out on a recliner with his current Patrick O'Brian novel, while Robin was curled up on the swing chair beside his beloved Nicholas. Robin had been listening to his music, though he'd only had one earbud in, and Nicholas had been browsing through one of his glossier academic journals, but even such pleasing demands as these had been put aside. The backyard stretched before them, looking particularly green and lush, and when the leaves of the banana palms stirred in the occasional breeze they sounded as beautiful as the patter of gentle rain.

There was certainly a sense shared among the three men, Dave thought, of all being very right with the world. So it was no surprise or interruption when Robin softly announced, "I love it here. I really do."

Nicholas smiled broadly, and said, "I'm glad. I love it here, too."

"I can see why you had to come live here."

"It was David," Nicholas said. "David belongs here, and I belong with David." Nicholas exchanged a solemnly happy glance with Dave, before adding to Robin, "I didn't *want* to leave you all behind, you know."

"I know." Robin sighed, and the quiet returned for a while. Until Robin tentatively began again, "I was thinking …"

"Yes?" Nicholas prompted.

"I was thinking that … maybe I should defer my enrolment at Oxford, and spend some time here with you instead."

Nicholas's expression slipped from tranquil to troubled in a moment, though he seemed to be trying to remain calm on the surface. "Were you?" he asked in fairly neutral tones.

"Yes. Lots of people take a gap year before starting uni, you know?"

"They do," Nicholas allowed. "Usually there's some … purpose to it, though."

"Like there's any better purpose for me than being with *you*," Robin returned.

Dave tensed a little, and sensed that Nicholas did, too. That was about as blatant as Robin had ever been – in words anyway. For some reason it all seemed much safer if it remained unspoken, or at most a subject for teasing, no matter how well known.

Eventually Nicholas said, "Well, let's see how you're feeling in a couple of months –"

"Of *course* I'll still feel the same –"

"About the gap year, I mean. Your grandfather is coming over to collect you, remember? If you can convince *him* to leave you here rather than take you back to Oxford, then I won't get in your way. You can tell him you have a home here with us."

"Thank you!" Robin cried, sitting up to look at Nicholas with a bright smile as if it were all already agreed. "Oh, *thank you*, Nicholas!"

Dave snorted. Nicholas's father was a lovely guy, and particularly fond of Nicholas, but Dave had seen him in Formidable Mode. "If you're serious, Robin, you'd better come up with a better reason than just hanging out with us. I don't think Richard's going to be very impressed. *I* wouldn't want to have to argue your case for you."

Robin barely spared Dave a glance.

For some reason, Dave persisted, when really he knew he should be dissuading the young man. "What are you gonna be studying at uni? I know I should know already, but these things tend to go right over my head. Maybe you can do a year's study here that would be – well, relevant."

"I doubt it," said Robin. "I'm doing PPE."

"You're such a frightful snob!" Nicholas told Robin – before he took pity on Dave and explained, "PPE: Philosophy, Politics and Economics." He added wryly, "Robin's going to be prime minister one day."

"Not of Australia, I take it."

"No," and Nicholas intoned, "Prime Minister of the United Kingdom of Great Britain and Northern Ireland."

Robin didn't care about being teased. He was sitting sideways on the chair now with his leg folded under him, focussed entirely and intensely on his uncle. "Nicholas," Robin said.

"Yes?"

It seemed that Robin was determined to finally lay all his cards out on the table. "You know I'm in love with you, Nicholas. You've always known, haven't you?"

Nicholas took a long moment with that, and then looked up at Robin with a troubled grimace. Eventually he began, "Maybe you are in love, my dear –"

"*Don't* patronise me!"

"– but being in love passes."

"It *won't* pass."

"I'm just trying to say – don't go making any life-changing decisions, all right, Robin? Let's wait and see how you feel when Father –"

"Oh, *wait and see*," Robin grumbled. "You're not so old, are you, that you can't remember being fed up to the back teeth with being told to *wait and see*?"

That won a reluctant quirk of a smile from Nicholas, but he didn't give an inch. "In any case, Robin," he steadily continued, "I'm with David, and always will be, and that's all there is to say about that."

"But that doesn't matter," Robin earnestly continued, glancing again at Dave –

"I assure you it matters very much indeed!" Nicholas retorted.

"No, I mean – David, *you* don't mind, do you? Me being in love with Nicholas? It's not like anything's ever gonna happen."

Dave slowly swung around to put his feet on the ground and sat up to face the others more directly. He wasn't entirely confident about what to say for the best, but then he took another breath and gave it a shot. "It's not that I *mind*, but I think you'd be a lot happier if you loved someone who could love you back –"

"But he does."

"– in the same way." Dave sighed. "You know what I'm trying to say, Robin."

"But he does love me, and he lets me cuddle him, and he smiles at me, and I don't need anything more than that."

"Well," said Dave, "it's not that I don't understand about the smiles."

"So, you don't mind sharing, right?" Robin persisted. "Because, you know, he still loves you and cuddles you and smiles at you. It's not like I'm taking anything away from what you want."

Dave frowned, and looked to Nicholas for a way forward. "I'm stumped," he said.

Nicholas seemed more troubled than ever. "That's not all there is to love, Robin –"

"It's all I want."

"– and you'll forgive us for wanting you to have someone in your life who'll return your love in kind."

"I don't want to have sex with you!" Robin blurted. Into the silence, he continued in somewhat more reasonable tones, "I don't want to have sex with anyone."

Nicholas rubbed at his forehead in a way that caused Dave deep misgivings. "*What?*" Nicholas asked sharply.

"I'm – I'm –"

Oh God, thought Dave. *He's coming out. Just not the way we expected.*

"I'm asexual, you see." Robin looked from one to the other of them, pale and right on the edge. "I'm just not into all that."

"But," Nicholas gritted out, "you said you're in love with me."

"You can be into love and not into sex."

Nicholas scowled, and started massaging his own scalp, digging his fingers in as if desperate to relieve the tension.

"Nicholas –" Dave said.

"I'm all right," he replied, before turning back to Robin. "How do you know? Have you tried?"

Robin scowled right back. "Did you have to 'try' before you knew you were gay?"

"No, but you're – forgive me for saying so, but you're very *young*, Robin, and –"

"I'm eighteen! How old were you? You said you've always known. Well, I've always known, too. Even if I didn't have a word for it."

"No," said Nicholas. "Just – no."

Robin stared at him, somehow going paler still. The kid was terrified. "*Please*, Nicholas …"

"What?" Nicholas looked as if he were under siege. "What is it you want?"

"Just to *understand* –"

"You want me to understand? I don't even think *you* understand!"

"I do. I do. I know who I am, just like you did."

Nicholas groaned and shook his head, his gaze darting about as if desperate for inspiration. He looked at Dave, and looked away – and then realised. "You know what, Robin? David didn't know. When he was eighteen, he thought he was entirely straight. I just think you should allow for the fact that you might be … mistaken."

Robin turned to consider Dave with an anxious grimace, as if both needing and dreading to hear more.

Oh God. "Well …" Dave began, slowly and carefully. "Nicholas is right, as far as that goes. I was with Denise when I was your age. And I loved her, I really did. I thought I'd always be … with Denise. But looking back … When she admired other men, I always had an opinion. I thought it was like appreciating a beautiful sunset, you know? I thought I was just open-minded. I think we both … had a bit of a thing for Pete Murray. It was only later I realised that … straight guys don't think like that. Not even about Pete. Even when I met Nicholas, it took me ages to realise I'm actually

343

bisexual. I guess I was a bit …" What Aussie man would ever want to admit this? "I was a bit innocent, you know? Even a bit naïve, maybe."

"Innocent," Nicholas said with a nod, fastening onto this word. "You need to live more of your life, Robin, before you go deciding on labels like – Well. Deciding on fundamental things like that."

Robin had turned back to gape at Nicholas. "I thought *you* would understand, Nicholas. Even if no one else does, I thought you'd be the one who'd let me be who I am."

Nicholas scoffed a little. "Into love and not into sex? How does that even work?"

It had been a difficult enough situation as it was. Now Dave felt a cold stir of foreboding. "Nicholas –"

"I know *you're* into sex, Uncle Nicholas."

"Yes, I am," he returned in tones that Dave felt were a bit too defiant for such a sensitive conversation with young Robin.

"That doesn't mean everyone else has to be."

"Nicholas," said Dave. "Maybe you should give Robin the benefit of the doubt. At least for now. He's obviously put a lot of thought into this –"

Nicholas stared hard at Dave – and then dropped his head into his hands, and dug his fingers into his temples. He obviously had a headache. Dave's cold sense of foreboding deepened.

"Uncle Nicholas –" Robin began.

Dave was on his feet even before Nicholas was –

But in the event, Nicholas just walked past him, holding out a hand to indicate Dave needn't follow. "It's all right," he said. Dave had learned to trust him when he said that. "I'm all right." He was heading inside.

"Uncle Nicholas –"

"Sorry. I can't handle this right now." And Nicholas was through the French windows into the relative darkness of the house, sliding the screen-door closed behind him until it shut with a quiet *snick*.

Robin sat back down again.

So did Dave. They both stared at the wooden decking of the veranda, and then exchanged a cautious glance as if each checking the other was okay. Dave would rather be with Nicholas, taking care of him, but he couldn't abandon Robin. Not when Robin had just been rejected by the man he was in love with. "Are you all right?" Dave eventually asked.

Robin looked at him, pale yet steady. "All right enough. Is Nicholas – ?"

"He'll be fine. He'll drink his water-and-lime, and take a couple of pills for his headache. Maybe he'll read or have a nap. He'll be fine."

A solemn nod acknowledged all this. Then Robin sighed, settled back in the swing chair, and stared off into the abundant greenery of the yard. He snubbed a toe against the decking and pushed the chair back, and then let it swing in a gentle arc to and fro, to and fro.

Dave watched him. Robin had always seemed relatively young to him. It didn't help that whenever Nicholas was around, Robin turned as giddy as a bandicoot, but even so. Dave could have sworn he himself had been far more grown-up at eighteen, even if he had been an innocent in some ways. After all, at eighteen Dave had been working full-time with his dad, and Denise had moved into this house with them as Dave's partner. Dave had thought he'd known everything about how his life would be.

Well, Dave had been wrong about a lot of that – but looking at Robin now, Dave could see a maturity behind the youthful face, and a core of ... certainty. A calm confidence at the heart of him. An underlying self-possession. And *that* reminded Dave of Nicholas. If only the two of them could avoid falling out over this, perhaps Nicholas would come to see that, too.

"What are you thinking, Uncle David?"

"I was thinking that ... everything's going to be just fine."

"Good," said Robin. "That's good."

In the darkness that night, Dave surfaced from vague dreams as Nicholas's embrace tightened, as his hold on Dave became a grasp. "All right?" Dave muttered. "Nicholas?"

"Yes," Nicholas reassured him, though his breath was harsh in his throat as if he'd been running *hard*. His hands became demanding, and he grappled Dave under him, though he said, "Please –"

"Course," Dave said, already welcoming him with arms and thighs. It was so dark, Dave hardly even knew whether his eyes were open or not, but they definitely closed as Nicholas pressed his face into Dave's throat, as he bit at him and gnawed, and rumbled a growl that shuddered through Dave. Nicholas's cock hadn't caught up with the rest of him yet, but as he rubbed

345

himself against Dave's cock and balls, he soon hardened.

"David?" Nicholas asked.

"Not the whole hog, yeah?"

Nicholas grunted assent, and instead thrust up against him, hard and hot now and the friction just on the right side of bearable. Dave came almost without being aware of it, the dreams slipping through into reality and the pleasure pushing him back into a sweet daze. Nicholas had to work for his release, his cock sliding through the stickiness of Dave's spunk, his mouth alternating bites and kisses. Dave ran his hands down Nicholas's back, soothing him, maybe helping, maybe not. But then at last Nicholas came, and he collapsed into Dave's embrace, and Dave rocked him gently, voicing an incoherent murmur on every breath, until eventually Nicholas fell asleep.

Early the next morning, Charlie rang.

four

"Mate," Charlie said when Dave answered the phone.

Dave instinctively responded to the slight edge of worry to Charlie's tone. "What is it? What's wrong?"

There was a brief silence which Dave knew better than to interrupt. Then Charlie said, "I heard from people that Ted Walinski, that surveyor, has been asking questions in Cunnamulla."

Dave let a beat go by. "What kind of questions?"

"He has a lump of what he says is hematite, and he's showing it to the locals, asking if they know where it came from."

"Hematite being …"

"Iron ore."

Dave frowned over that, trying to ignore the sense of dread like lead in his stomach. "Are you sure?" He turned to find Robin sitting at the table in the family room, apparently playing some kind of game on his phone. "Robin, I've got an old geology textbook in the spare room. Would you fetch it for me?"

Robin didn't budge, but asked helpfully enough, "What do you want to know?"

"I want to check that hematite is the kind of iron ore that the mining companies are after."

A nod from Robin, as he swiped out of the game and started tapping away at the virtual keyboard.

Dave turned back to the phone. "Charlie." He took a breath. "Does that mean he's found the waterhole?"

"Walinski? Nah. But he's saying the rock came from west of town, out beyond the Aboriginal reserve."

Which caused more frowning. "But if he hasn't found the waterhole, then how does he know that's where the rock came from?"

"Guess he found it in the general area, and can't find his way further in, and you've made him curious." Charlie huffed a sigh, and Dave could perfectly visualise him round-faced with breath-filled cheeks. "It's not the actual Dreaming site he's interested in."

"No, but it's bad enough, isn't it?"

"It *is* bad," Robin chipped in.

Dave turned to face him, and held the phone in his direction, too, hoping that Charlie would hear. "Go on, then."

"Wikipedia says that iron ore containing hematite is what the mining companies like best, because it can go directly into the furnaces without any processing. They call it 'natural ore'. And it gets worse," Robin added.

By then Nicholas had come through from the lounge room, and was hovering anxiously. Charlie prompted, "Go on," in Dave's ear, which Dave passed on with an encouraging nod.

"It says that most reserves of natural ore have been used up already, or the ones that are accessible, anyway. So I guess that means," Robin said, looking at Dave with widened gaze, "they'll be really keen."

An edgy silence grew.

Nicholas sat down beside Robin, and tried to read the entry Robin had displayed on his phone, but really Nicholas couldn't tear his attention away from Dave.

Eventually Charlie said, "I'm heading down there, mate. To Cunnamulla. I'll see what's happening."

"I'll meet you there," said Dave.

Nicholas nodded, and stood up again. "I'll get us packed."

"Are you sure? We've got that fossicking trip coming up. Maybe you two should pace yourselves."

"No, we'll come," said Nicholas.

Dave lifted his chin at Robin. "It's a ten-hour drive, mate. You sure you're up for it?"

"We're coming, Uncle David," said Robin, also standing, like he meant business.

"We'll see you tonight, Charlie," said Dave.

"Take the Goondiwindi road," Charlie advised.

Dave didn't even bother asking why. "Will do. See ya, then."

"See ya."

"Shall we pack for a couple of nights?" Nicholas asked. "Or more, just in case?"

By the time they reached Cunnamulla that evening, there was already a buzz in the air. It was soon clear that the local community had been quick to extrapolate from a lump of reddish rock to a huge investment in the area from a well-funded mining company.

Dave, Nicholas and Robin found Charlie at the second of the pubs they tried. He was sitting back in a chair at a small table, with his arms crossed, looking as if his thoughts were miles away. Dave murmured a greeting, but when Charlie didn't respond, the three of them simply sat, and worked out what they would have for dinner. By the time Dave had been to the bar to order – including steak, potatoes and veg for Charlie – and returned with two beers and two lemonades, he'd overheard enough in any case.

"You know what happens to wages when the mining boys come to town?" one bloke asked his companion, purely rhetorically.

"They go through the roof, mate," was the complacent response.

"Mate, they'd go through the roof of a ten-storey building."

"So do prices, though," someone else chipped in.

"Reckon I can live with that."

"There's none ever come this far west, though," another guy fretfully observed.

"They'd come for 'shipping ore'. That's the quality stuff!"

"We've already got the railway," the first bloke reassured everyone in hearing distance, "and the airport, too."

Dave sat down again next to Nicholas with a sigh, and his husband gazed back at him worriedly.

"How long until dinner's ready?" asked Robin.

"Won't be long, mate. Ten, fifteen minutes."

"David," said Nicholas, leaning forward to speak quietly. "David, what about the butterflies?"

"They'll be all right. We'll do whatever it takes, Nicholas."

"David –"

"Maybe nothing will come of this anyway," Dave said, trying to remind himself of that fact. "And even if it did, it'll be obvious to everyone that we have to protect the butterflies. Quite apart from the – the rest."

He hadn't managed to quite say 'Dreamtime', because one of the younger blokes had come up to the table. "Did you hear?" he asked – not waiting for an answer before he continued. "They've found iron ore west of here."

"Yeah, we picked up on that," Dave replied in what he hoped were neutral

349

tones.

"Apparently it's somewhere near where you guys go camping, you know?"

They were all four of them silent, which probably wasn't the best response.

"Is that why you guys are here again? Gonna see if you can help find it?"

"Oh! No ... No ..." Dave tilted his head, trying to gather his thoughts. Lying didn't come easy, but he wasn't sure yet about where to draw the line between concealing and revealing the truth. "We're, uh – We've got a fossicking trip coming up, out Yowah way. Thought we'd scout the place. See if Charlie'll join us."

"Sure. Yowah nuts!" the young bloke responded enthusiastically.

Robin's eyebrows shot into his hairline. "Yowah nuts ... ? Sounds painful."

"They're opals," Dave explained to Robin. "You find them inside rocks," he indicated the size and rough shape with a cupped hand. "Reddish-brown rocks that look like large nuts – the sort you eat. Never mind that," he said as Nicholas's smirk grew. "Or maybe they look like gumnuts, I dunno. They're round or ellip- ... egg-shaped."

"How do you know the opals are in there, then?"

"You learn what to look for. You develop an eye for it."

"Cool!" Robin said, lighting up. "Oh, I'm going to find the most beautiful opal in all the world ..."

Charlie finally stirred out of his reverie. "Opals? Count me in."

The four of them ate their dinner in relative silence, each of them tired or downcast or both. Finally, once they were done and the table was cleared, Charlie leaned in and offered, "Like you said: maybe nothing will come of it."

But Dave shook his head. "We can't take the risk. Not on this." He pushed in closer, too, leaning his elbows on the table, trying to look casual. "Look. Can we head out to the reserve tomorrow, and maybe – finally – start a conversation with the Elders?"

Charlie pursed his lips. "It's all just been talk, hasn't it, and a few locals with dollar signs in their eyes."

"I know, but if something's gonna happen, then we want to stay one step ahead, right?"

A shrug from those eloquent shoulders, but then Charlie said, "Yeah, all right." A few minutes later he tipped a farewell nod to them, and headed out.

Dave sighed. "Come on, then," he said to the others. "Let's get checked in to the hotel."

Dave and Charlie had been here many times before. Once or twice a year, they came to the reserve, sat in a circle with the Elders and anyone else who happened to be there that day, and they spoke when they were spoken to but otherwise held their peace.

No one ever raised the matter of Charlie knowing the Dreaming songs for the waterhole when actually he shouldn't, nor about him having had the audacity to then pass them on to a white fella. Charlie had gone on his own to tell them that news, seven years ago now, and had reported that the circle of men and women had all talked and talked until everyone understood, and then they'd fallen quiet as they'd pondered the situation. There had been no conclusions reached, no judgement given.

Dave had gone to the reserve with Charlie a tactful month or so later, half-knowing that he should be forbidden from the sacred site, half-expecting to be quizzed or harassed about it all, but of course that wasn't the Murri way. Everyone still seemed to be taking it in and trying to work out what to think about the matter. Later he wondered if the Elders had decided on a 'wait and see' approach. None of the Murri spoke against him and Charlie keeping the songs alive, or at least not in Dave's hearing. Perhaps they, like Charlie, took the pragmatic view that the important thing was that the songs be sung, that the Earth's energies be renewed, that the relationship between land and people be maintained.

And so, in the 'eternal now' or 'everywhen' of Indigenous thinking, the Elders were pondering – and in Dave's white-fella view, time passed, and the whole thing became a fait accompli. Which was fine by Dave, and if it could have lasted through decades until it was finally time to find someone else to learn the songs, that would have been great. But it seemed that gubbah business – white-fella stuff – was going to intrude whether they were ready or not.

That day, Nicholas and Robin went to join the sociable mob which was gathered in front of the local store. They were soon sharing a drink and a jovial yarn with a range of people of all ages, all colours. After a few moments to make sure they were going to be okay, however, Dave and Charlie headed for the quieter group who were sitting in a loose circle under the shade of a huge red gum. There was a space that would fit the two of them and, as they approached, one of the Elders nodded – whether that was coincidental or not, Dave nodded a greeting, and he and Charlie settled cross-legged on the ground.

It was peacefully quiet in the circle, at just enough distance from the other mob that they couldn't make out specific words amidst the general talk – at least not until there was a scandalised "No way!" from Robin, which caused much merriment. Dave could make out Nicholas's laugh amidst the rest, which made him smile, and he exchanged a fond glance with Charlie.

Eventually, when there was a lull in the thoughts and meandering words of the group, Dave quietly asked, "May I talk to you, please? About the waterhole, about the Dreaming site where the Barcoo grunter sleeps." He didn't use the place's proper name, or the Ancestor's, even in this company. Neither did he have to explain further. It wasn't as if they didn't all know, even if they'd never spoken to him about it.

The lull became something more attentive, and a few of the others exchanged quiet words between themselves. After a while Dave sensed that he was welcome to continue, and Charlie murmured, "Yeah, go on."

"It's a very beautiful place," Dave surprised himself by saying. "It's precious. The water in the pool … it's like a jewel. The colours are so vivid … The layers of rock are red, and there's the green of the eucalypts, the gold of the wattle when it flowers. There are the butterflies, the most fantastic blue butterflies. My husband found them." He indicated Nicholas, though of course everyone there already knew about Dave and Nicholas. "The butterflies are unique, he thinks – but it's not only that. They're part of the Dreaming story about the waterhole, about the Ancestor who sleeps there and the Ancestor he loved who came down from the sky. It's a … a really incredible place."

He stumbled to a halt, having completely failed to reach the nub of the matter.

But then one of Elders nodded, and said, "We know you love the land."

Dave almost let out a gasp at that, and his eyes prickled embarrassingly. He hadn't expected to ever hear such a thing. Not ever. "Thank you," he said, not daring to even glance at Charlie for fear of the tears really welling up.

After a moment Dave considered what to say next. Even after such an acknowledgement, he wasn't going to ask permission to continue as custodian of the site, and risk a refusal. He had better pass on the news first, and then see where that left them.

"Look," Dave said, cutting right to the chase now, in his white-fella way. "The rock there – I think it's so red because it contains iron ore. And now a surveyor is trying to find it, and everyone in town is getting all excited, expecting a mining company to follow."

A silence fell after this great blurt. Dave looked around at faces that seemed even more enigmatic than usual. Charlie was looking pensive.

Eventually one of the men commented, "If they bring jobs and money, that's worth getting excited about."

"Well, yes," Dave agreed, his gut sinking. It was a fair point. "But I'm concerned that – that we make sure the Dreaming site isn't disturbed. And that the butterflies are safe."

"Yes," said one of the Elders, the one who'd nodded a welcome to Dave when he and Charlie first arrived. Dave didn't know his Indigenous name, but he went by the nickname 'Thursday'.

"Thank you, Thursday," Dave said. "I guess I just need to know that – if we have to make this official somehow – you'll support Charlie about him knowing the songs."

"No, mate," Charlie protested. "It's you that belongs there."

Dave turned to stare at him. *Are you kidding ... ?* "Mate, no one's gonna take that seriously!"

Charlie put on his most mulish expression, and insisted as he'd insisted before, "Old man grunter chose you." Then he kind of hunkered down inside himself as if withdrawing from all further discussion.

"I'll back you up, mate," Dave said, "but you've got to be the front man, if push comes to shove."

Silence.

Dave sighed, and fell into a ponder of his own. It wasn't that he had any firm plans yet, because he hardly knew what they'd be facing, but his initial sketches were already falling apart.

After a while, though, Thursday said, "You can speak for us, Dave. You can figure out what has to be done, and you can speak for us."

"I can?" he asked, somewhat flabbergasted.

"When it's time for us to speak, we will."

"Good. That's good. Wow." Dave hunkered down into himself, too, suddenly having a whole lot of rethinking to do. But he didn't neglect to say, "Thank you."

When he and Charlie finally got up to go, it wasn't only Thursday who nodded a farewell.

In town the next day, Dave ran into Ted Walinski as he, Nicholas and Robin were walking back from the shops. Part of Dave wondered if he should just push past the man on the grounds that sometimes discretion really is the better part of valour. Within the moment it took to reach him, though, Dave had decided that it was time to start taking a stand. "Morning," he said, pausing on the pavement in the shade of an awning.

"Morning, Mr Taylor," Walinski replied, stopping likewise, and nodding a genial greeting to them all.

"It's Goring Taylor now," Dave said.

"Right you are."

"Look," said Dave. "What are you up to?"

Walinski took a long cool look at him, and then glanced down at the pavement – almost as if miming a spit – before meeting his gaze again. "I'm doing some surveying for Mrs Wilson. Trying to establish her easterly boundaries."

"Henrietta Wilson?" She owned the larger of the two ranches on the far side of the waterhole.

"Yes. It's been dry, as you know. She wants to use more of her land to run her cattle, but it'll need fencing."

Dave considered the man. That was all fine, as far as it went, though the further east Henri Wilson pushed, the closer she'd get to the waterhole. Dave had to wonder if that was coincidence or not. He let that be, however, and tried another tack. "What about this rock you've been showing around? Getting everyone excited about mining rights."

Walinski started digging in his jeans pocket as soon as Dave said 'rock', and held it out to him. "Here, then."

Dave didn't take the thing, but peered at it, as did Nicholas and Robin. It did look very much like the rock in the cliffs that surrounded the waterhole. In fact, Dave had to suppress an instinctive *zing* running through him – though whether that was recognition or simple anxiety, he had no idea.

"Does it look familiar?" Walinski asked.

"Mate, it looks like a rock." Dave stood tall again, though he couldn't help crossing his arms. "Lot o' years gone by since my high school geology class."

Robin pitched in, perhaps hoping to confuse the issue. "It's not one of those Yowah nuts you were telling me about, Uncle David? You said they were a kind of reddish colour."

"No, mate, definitely not one of those." He asked Walinski, "So, what's your interest? You working for one of the mining companies now, or you gonna be selling to the highest bidder?"

Walinski shrugged, and quipped, "That's 'commercial in confidence', Mr Goring Taylor."

Dave let out a sigh. "So, this is really happening, isn't it?" He glanced at Nicholas, who nodded, with a tense expression on his face that Dave found nigh on unbearable. "Look, Mr Walinski," Dave said, turning to face the man square on. "There's a Dreamtime site out there, and there's a unique species of butterfly that Nicholas has written up in his … you know, academic journals and such. So, there's going to be some land that's off-limits."

A slow nod met this assertion, and after a long moment, Walinski said, "Thank you for telling me." He let a beat go by, and then lifted the rock between them again. "So, do you know where this is from?"

Dave took another breath, but then said, "I'll have to think about that."

"Fair enough."

"If I can help, I'll get back to you."

Walinski nodded, and held out his hand to shake. "Thank you, Mr Goring Taylor."

Dave shook the man's hand, more from a sense of fairness than an overwhelming sense of fellow feeling. And then they parted.

Dave, Nicholas and Robin continued back to the hotel in silence, though Dave sensed that Nicholas was barely restraining himself from speaking.

Finally, once they were in the privacy of the Land Cruiser heading back to Brisbane, Nicholas said, "The butterflies –"

"I know. I promise: we'll do whatever we have to, right?"

"Yes."

Dave glanced at his husband, really not liking to see anxiety so dark on Nicholas's brow. "You've done everything you can to document them, right? I mean, you've written articles, had them listed or – um, registered or whatever it is you do, yeah?"

"Yes." Nicholas returned his glance, a little rueful. "The only thing I couldn't do was really pinpoint the location. Though I described it as well as I was able."

"Of course, yeah."

A moment dragged by. Until finally Nicholas said, "Maybe we're the ones who need a surveyor."

Dave frowned over that, but he had to acknowledge, "Maybe you're right."

five

They arrived home late that night. Robin was hungry, so Dave began gathering the makings for an omelette, while Robin sat and shared his attention between watching Dave and checking his phone.

When Nicholas appeared, however, Robin put the phone down. Nicholas was looking a bit tired and careworn, but not unhappy. He diverted to press a grateful kiss to Dave's temple before going to sit opposite Robin – and then they were all quiet for a long moment.

Finally Robin said, "Uncle Nicholas –"

"Yes?" Nicholas prompted with the slightest of smiles, which seemed to be all he could muster.

"You know what we talked about … about me, I mean."

"Yes." Nicholas sat up, and leaned forward. Dropped his face into his hands and rubbed hard, as if trying to wake himself up. When he looked at Robin again, he said, "I'm sorry. Events kind of overtook us, didn't they?"

Robin took a breath. "I just want to know that we're … all right."

Nicholas put a bit more effort into his smile. "Of course we're all right, Robin. I love you no matter what. We both do. Always will."

"You don't understand, though, do you?"

"Does that matter?" Nicholas sat back again, turning a tad disgruntled despite himself. "Isn't unconditional love good enough any more?"

Robin's cheeks coloured in chagrin, and he picked up his phone again though he didn't look at it.

Dave had finished chopping the shallots and bacon, so he put them on to sauté – at a low heat, just in case the meal needed to be delayed.

Eventually Nicholas burst out, "I just think you're missing out on something – something marvellous. Maybe even –" He glanced at Dave, and seemed to grow in conviction. "Yes. One of the best bits of life."

"I'm perfectly happy being a virgin," Robin steadily replied, "and I probably always will be. It's not going to be, like … something I regret."

"But how do you *know* if you haven't tried?"

"How do you know you don't want to go to bed with a girl?"

"That's really *not* the same thing. I wish you'd stop trying to compare my situation to yours."

When Robin didn't reply, Dave put down the cheese he was grating, and tried, "Nicholas, perhaps you can just be happy that Robin is happy."

"How can he be happy at the *lack* of something?" Nicholas demanded.

"Well, I don't know. But it seems like he is. Doesn't it?"

Nicholas considered Dave. Considered Robin. Finally sighed, and gave in with a nod. "All right, yes. Fine. Robin, I'm happy if you're happy."

"I'm happy," Robin said, though in a very small voice.

"That's good, then," Nicholas concluded. "That's great." He got up and went to lean over Robin to give him a hug.

"Thank you, Uncle Nicholas."

"No worries," said Nicholas – which made Dave smile, as it was such an Aussie expression. But then Nicholas stood, and headed towards the hallway. "I'm going to bed," he announced, with an apologetic smile for Dave. "I'm sorry, that smells delicious, but I'm really not hungry."

"No worries," Dave said in turn, smiling fondly at his husband as he and Robin wished each other goodnight. "See you in a bit." Then Nicholas was gone, and Dave turned to Robin. "You're still hungry, I hope?"

"Too right, I am!"

"That's grand." And Dave poured the beaten eggs into the pan, where they sizzled in a most satisfying manner.

"I have an idea," Nicholas announced the next morning over breakfast.

Dave and Robin looked at him expectantly.

"It might not only be the butterflies that are unique. When I took a sample of the wattle to one of my colleagues in Flora, she couldn't identify it for certain. She said it was very close to two different species, but couldn't decide between them. So that's how I wrote it up, and I never really pursued it further. But maybe it's time."

Dave nodded, but asked, "Time for what?"

"Well ... maybe to bring back some proper samples for Lisa to analyse – if she has the resources. Though I'm sure she'd find a way to make it happen, wouldn't she? If it might be a new species of *Acacia*, I mean."

"She didn't pursue it before, though?"

Nicholas tilted his head in a quibble. "I may have over-emphasised the secret side of it being a sacred site. But it's been isolated for so long – the wattle, I mean – and in a symbiotic relationship of sorts with the butterflies. Whatever it used to be may well have evolved into something else by now."

"Symbiotic?" Dave said. "That makes it sound a bit – weird."

"Well, I just mean, given there don't seem to be any other insects around, and it's so sheltered there, it must be the butterflies that pollinate it. In return, it provides them with shelter and sustenance – and so on, and so on. It's this whole …"

"Great Circle of Life," Robin chipped in.

Nicholas laughed. "Yes, I was going to try for something more original, but that's it exactly."

Dave smiled at them both, and once the laughter had quietened, he said, "Would she come out on a trip, do you think, to see the wattle at the waterhole?"

"Oh," said Nicholas.

"Be better to see it in place, wouldn't it? In its natural habitat? And you don't want to take too much away as a sample. It's not like there's a lot of it, as it is."

"Oh, well. That would be great, and I'm sure she'd love to. But what about keeping the waterhole secret?"

"I've just been thinking, old man grunter won't mind me sharing it a bit wider. In fact, I'm thinking maybe it's time. And anyway, the place keeps its own secrets. We're still the only ones who've actually managed to find it, since Charlie's friend died."

"*You're* the one who finds it," Nicholas corrected him, "each and every time. All right, I'll talk to her today, and see what she thinks. Robin," he added, turning towards the young man. "Do you want to come to the university with me for the day? Shall we give David a break from all the Goring dramatics?"

"He's probably earned it," Robin agreed.

Dave just laughed.

Dave had business to pursue, in any case. He'd made an appointment for an initial interview with a lawyer at the Native Title Services organisation that covered the Cunnamulla region, and what with the fossicking trip coming up, he'd pushed to make it sooner rather than later.

So that afternoon Dave headed into the city, dressed in a proper shirt and trousers, and ended up sitting across a desk from a man of about Dave's own age or a bit younger, named Martin Bandjara. The place was obviously busy, with the phones in the main office ringing amidst ongoing chatter, and Martin's desk piled high with paperwork. He seemed genuinely interested in taking the time to engage with Dave, though, and when he asked, "How can I help you?" he seemed to really want to know.

"I'm interested," said Dave – "well, it's early days yet, but I'm interested in making a claim for Native Title."

"And you're acting on behalf of … ?"

"Myself, really. Or the Dreaming site, I guess. Basically, I'm looking to protect a Dreaming site."

Martin let a beat go by, and then he said, "Forgive me. But you look to be – white."

Dave huffed a breath that might almost have been a laugh. "I'm a white fella, yes. I realise this is probably a bit … unusual."

"You have an Indigenous predecessor, perhaps? A grandparent or great-grandparent?"

"Not that I know of. My dad's family were English; he emigrated, and I was born here. My mum's family were Irish and English originally, but they've been out here for generations."

"Ah, so there's a possibility one of them might have married an Indigenous person, or had a child with one, at least?"

Dave shook his head, beginning to realise that Martin's persistence didn't bode well for his case. "No, I really don't think so."

"The family might have … hidden the fact."

"I realise that times have changed, and for the better, but I don't think we've ever been the kind of people who would have felt ashamed of it."

Martin nodded. "Then – sorry – but what's your connection with this Dreaming site you mentioned?"

Dave told the story again, of how Charlie's friend had been the last of his tribe, and he'd passed the songs and stories to Charlie rather than let them be lost.

"And there's no chance that your mate Charlie has some kind of family connection with the tribe? Anything at all?"

"I wouldn't have thought so … No. I mean, that's the point, isn't it? His friend was already crossing the line in passing the songs to Charlie. And now Charlie seems to think I'm more entitled to them than he is."

Martin frowned in confusion. "Why exactly is that? I mean … if you don't mind me asking."

So Dave explained how Charlie hadn't been able to find the sacred site, but Dave had; and how Charlie had become convinced that Dave was the rightful custodian of the waterhole, especially once he'd discovered that Dave had been born in Cunnamulla, and conceived nearby as well. "So, you see," Dave concluded, "I've kind of inherited this in a … well, in a *spiritual* sense, yeah?" His face flamed. This was worse than talking about sex or love. "Not in the sense of bloodlines."

Martin considered him thoughtfully for long moments. Finally he said, "You seem sincere about this."

"Yeah, I am," he replied in easy tones despite the fact his face was still bright red.

"And you actually go there and perform the rituals every now and then?"

"Yes, of course. We haven't missed even one. Sometimes Charlie comes, too. Sometimes I go on my own. Well, with my – husband."

Martin didn't blink at that latest revelation. After a moment, he simply said, "Mr Goring Taylor –"

"Dave."

"Dave. I don't know what to tell you. It's remarkable that you've taken this responsibility so seriously. But – the Native Title Act is designed to recognise the traditional owners of the land, and their biological descendants."

"Ah."

"They are required to have continued to practise the traditional customs associated with that area, just as you have done, but –"

"No, I get it," said Dave, hardly able to bear hearing any more. "I've been naïve again, haven't I?"

"Not naïve," Martin protested. "In an ideal world –"

"Okay, so there's no chance," Dave concluded heavily.

"I'm afraid the right to claim, as the law currently stands, would have extinguished with the death of the last member of that tribe. If we tried to claim on the basis of a … a spiritual inheritance, then I doubt we'd get very far. To be honest, I'd love to try – to test the concept. But even if the Federal

Court took us seriously, they'd be wary of opening the floodgates. It would be setting a precedent for … well, for anyone to claim almost anything."

"I haven't invented this out of thin air," Dave argued. "I have a real concern for that waterhole. There's iron ore in the area, and a mining company has caught wind of it."

"You're …" Martin hesitated, and then asked almost apologetically, "You're interested in benefiting from the mining rights?"

"Not for myself, no, but if the Murri benefit from it, that's fine. I'm just wanting to protect that place."

Martin looked as if he were desperate to help. "Native Title isn't the answer," he concluded. "I only wish it were."

"Not even Charlie could claim Native Title?" Nicholas asked that evening.

"No biological connection," Dave confirmed. The three of them were sitting around the table in the family room, comparing notes about their days.

"So, what do we try next?"

Dave sighed. "The only real idea Martin and I came up with was to extend the reserve to include the area surrounding the waterhole. In which case, I can help, but it would have to be Thursday and his mob who make that happen."

"Well, that's all right, isn't it?"

"If it's made part of the reserve, then the people who live there will have a say in what happens, and they'll have the power to negotiate with a mining company. But there are plenty of locals who'll be happy for the work coming in – white fellas, Indigenous, or anyone else – and I can't say as I blame them. So I still feel like … well, like we need to do more to protect the waterhole itself, you know?"

"We might be able to help there. Do you want to tell him, Robin?"

Robin abruptly went pink, and stuttered a bit before saying, "Dr Munroe –"

"Lisa," Nicholas explained to Dave.

"– said she'd love to come out to the waterhole with us. She asked if she could bring her partner."

Nicholas grimaced. "I didn't mean *that* bit, Robin. I'm sorry, David.

I don't want to inundate the place with visitors."

"No, it's all right. I meant it about sharing."

"Go on, then, Robin," Nicholas said.

"W-w-well, Dr Munroe said she's very interested in the wattle, v-v-very interested indeed, and if it's rare then she can help protect it. And she asked if Nicholas had had the butterflies officially listed as 'Vulnerable'."

Nicholas was nodding along with this, sitting back in his seat and looking overly casual. "I've been a bit of an idiot not to have thought of this before. But the waterhole always seemed – so very secluded. Safe. And there's a sense there that nothing's changed for thousands of years, and probably won't for thousands yet."

"I know," Dave agreed. "Don't worry, I know what you mean. So, what's this vulnerable thing about?"

"We can nominate the *Ogyris davidi* species to be listed as 'Vulnerable' under the Nature Conservation Act. They're a textbook case, really." Nicholas counted off the points on his long fingers. "Their population is low; it's localised; it depends on a limited habitat; and that habitat might be at risk."

"Good," said Dave. "Okay. And once it's listed, what happens then?"

"Well, that opens up a number of possible activities, I suppose, but right now I'm thinking more about making it abundantly clear to any mining company that they can't just walk in and have everything their own way. If the waterhole is acknowledged as a Dreamtime site, in an Aboriginal reserve, with not one but two threatened species living there and nowhere else ..." Nicholas grimaced and shrugged, throwing his hands out in a plea. "That would be a solid first step, wouldn't it?"

"It's perfect," said Dave. He got up and went to lean over Nicholas, and wrapped him up in a big grateful hug – which provoked a happy rumbling growl from Nicholas. "You're awesome," Dave said. "Both of you," he added, glancing across the table at Robin.

Dave expected to find Robin grimacing in distaste or rolling his eyes, but instead the young fella was looking rather indulgent. The probable reason seemed fairly obvious to Dave. "So ..." he said, only loosening his hold on Nicholas enough so that they could all three converse. "Robin liked your mate Lisa, did he?"

Robin promptly blushed, but his smile was bright and uncomplicated.

363

"She was cool," he asserted. "She's like Uncle Nicholas, you know?"

Nicholas grinned. "I'm cool, am I? Wonders will never cease."

"You're pretty cool," Robin agreed. "But the thing I like is … you and Dr Munroe are both tall, dark and super intelligent."

Dave had to stand then, as his burst of laughter would have threatened Nicholas's eardrums.

"Oh my God …" Nicholas was drawling. "Robin has a type …"

Dave and Nicholas were curled up together under the doona that night. It was late and dark, and Robin was probably sound asleep, but nevertheless they whispered. "He's got a crush on Lisa … ?" Dave asked.

"Completely smitten," Nicholas confirmed, huffing a laugh under his breath.

"No change on the sexual side of things, though."

"I asked him afterwards, and he announced that he's asexual and bi-romantic." Nicholas shrugged. "I still don't understand, but he insists that romantic attraction and sexual attraction are two completely separate things."

"I think maybe he's right. I think maybe they are."

"Well," Nicholas responded – though how he could still sound tart while whispering, Dave had no idea. "Well, then you'd better explain it to me."

Dave let out a sigh. "I don't have the words to talk about that kind of thing, Nicholas."

"Try. You might surprise yourself."

"Anyway," Dave continued, letting his hands caress their way further down Nicholas's lithe body, "call me greedy, but I like having both mixed up together."

"Best thing in the world, having both," Nicholas agreed. He stretched out a little taller, pushed in a little closer.

Dave slipped a hand down to cup Nicholas's balls – and his cock, too, while it was still at rest – and he rolled the delicious handful in his palm. Nicholas groaned quietly and pushed closer still, wrapping his arms around Dave's shoulders. They bumped noses in the dark, but then they were kissing and mouthing hungrily. Soon Nicholas's cock was poking hard at Dave's wrist; he adjusted his hold slightly so he could rub the heel of his hand against it while still kneading his balls. A groan tore out of Nicholas, which Dave muffled with another kiss before gently shushing him.

"Quickly, then," Nicholas said, an insistent hand pushing down to wrap around Dave's cock. Nicholas shifted closer still, obviously wanting to wrap both their cocks up in one hand, as he'd liked to do ever since their first time together. Dave let go his own hold, but instead reached to bring Nicholas's leg up to hook around Dave's hip. By lifting up onto an elbow, Dave found he could reach down between Nicholas's thighs to tug at his balls from behind – which had Nicholas groaning again, and clinging on tight round his shoulders, round his cock. When Dave managed to grasp and rub at his own balls as well as Nicholas's, the orgasm hit them both like a lightning strike, and afterwards they lay welded together, panting and damp in each other's arms – and if they had after all made too much noise, in that moment Dave really didn't give a damn.

six

The clients for the fossicking trip were a well-off family who were quite happy to 'rough it' for a week, but wanted someone on hand who knew the ropes. It was hardly a challenging job, but Dave was perfectly happy to indulge them, especially as it meant he could give Nicholas and Robin a bit of a treat, working holiday though it was.

The three of them drove out to Cunnamulla again, and on the following morning went to meet the family who were flying in to Cunnamulla airport. Dave had talked to the father, Mike Baldry, on Skype a couple of times, so they recognised each other right away and shook hands heartily. Mike introduced his wife Suzanne, who seemed rather dauntingly elegant – until she grinned as broadly as her husband, and obliterated Dave's initial reservations. Their daughters Monica and Chloe were sixteen and fourteen years old respectively; the former was apparently going through the 'too cool for this' stage, but Robin and Chloe were soon nattering away excitedly.

Nicholas and Robin got the Baldrys' luggage neatly stowed in the back of the four-wheel drive Dave had rented for them, while Dave talked Mike through the controls, as he'd never driven anything beyond a regular sedan before. Not that they would be doing anything very challenging: it was sealed roads all the way to Yowah, and well-maintained graded roads after that.

The two vehicles proceeded in convoy into Cunnamulla, where they were going to have lunch before starting their journey. Apparently Monica thought that travelling with the gay couple was cooler than hanging out with her sister, so she sat in dignified silence in the Land Cruiser's back seat, while Robin joined Chloe in the back seat of the rental. Mike seemed to have no problems handling the vehicle during the short drive to town; in fact, it was all they could do to persuade him to take time out for lunch before starting the three-hour drive to Yowah.

Dave had chosen the town's restaurant as their lunch venue rather than one of the pubs, given the nature of the party, and that worked out well. The grub was simple in the best ways, and plentiful, and the conversation was promisingly cordial. Even Monica deigned to enjoy herself for a while.

"Can I hang with you guys?" she asked Dave and Nicholas afterwards.

Dave glanced at the other four who were still strolling down the pavement, chatting away. It seemed that Robin and Chloe were firm friends already; apparently they were bonding over a shared love of a series of films that Dave was only vaguely aware of. "If it's okay with your parents," he said to Monica, "it's okay with us."

"It's not, like, you have to talk to me or anything. I'll just listen to my music."

"That's fine," said Nicholas.

"And you don't have to watch what you say around me. I'm not a child."

"Understood. And if you did want to talk with us, that would be fine, too."

She went a bit pink, as if both pleased and embarrassed, so they let her turn away and slip her earbuds in.

Dave went over to the others, and rested a heavy hand on Robin's shoulder. "Can you put up with this one," he asked Mike and Suzanne, "if we stick with the current seating arrangements?"

Everyone was perfectly happy, so soon their small convoy was heading west along Adventure Way, with Dave in the lead. They stopped in Eulo for a cuppa and comfort break, and then continued on until they reached the intersection with the Opal By-Way which would take them to Yowah.

Once they'd made the turn, Dave pulled over to the side of the road, and switched off the Cruiser's ignition. Mike pulled in behind him neatly enough.

"Is something wrong?" Nicholas asked, though he didn't sound very worried.

"Nah," he replied, with a reassuring smile – though he flicked a glance in Monica's direction, trusting Nicholas to understand that meant Dave was being discreet. He climbed down from the cab, and went to say to the others, "Thought we could stretch our legs for a minute. How're ya goin', Mike? It's about another fifty clicks from here …"

Everyone was amenable to taking a short break. They all took a drink of water, and no one minded being reminded to wear their hats – not even Monica, thank heavens, who wore a straw hat with a wide circular rippling brim which Dave assumed she thought was cool.

That was all well and good – but his real reason for stopping was to check out the vehicle he was sure had been following them, more or less, since Cunnamulla. Soon it caught up to them, and passed without pausing, continuing along Adventure Way. It was a Land Rover Discovery, and Dave would have sworn the driver was Ted Walinski.

Dave had booked two of the cabins at the caravan park, one for each family. It had already been a long day, so they all concentrated on doggedly sorting out the luggage and settling in. A quick meal at the café brightened everyone up, though there were no disagreements about the notion of having an early night.

Soon after they'd all said goodnight, however, Dave heard a shriek and then further sounds of consternation from the neighbouring cabin. He headed over there at speed, with Nicholas and Robin at his heels. Dave wasn't overly surprised when he discovered the cause.

Monica was standing in the main room of the cabin with a green tree frog nestled trustingly in the palm of her hand. Her mother and sister, meanwhile – and even her father – were backed up just about as far away from her as they could get. "Are you kidding?" she was asking. "He's gorgeous! I mean, how *green* is that?" She lifted her hand, and Monica and the frog gazed intently into each other's eyes. "Aw … look at him … such a sweet little bloke."

Dave stood there just within the door, trying not to laugh, while Robin stayed by his side and peered at the frog from a safe distance.

Nicholas, of course, had no qualms about wildlife. "*Litoria caerulea*," he announced as he walked over to join Monica in her intent examination. "The Australian green tree frog. What a beautiful specimen! Where did you find him, Monica?"

"In the bathroom!" Suzanne announced with a horrified shudder. "Speaking of which … is it clear now?"

"Yes, Mum," replied the long-suffering Monica. "You're safe!"

"Oh, thank God," Suzanne muttered fervently – and made a dash for it round the edge of the room, keeping as far away from Monica as she could.

"How do you know it's a bloke?" Nicholas was asking meanwhile, leaning in close and gently prodding a finger at the frog as if wanting to turn it over and examine its chassis.

"Nicholas!" Dave protested.

Nicholas straightened up and looked at him. "Ah. Of course. I always forget that rule. Don't discuss the genitalia of frogs in front of the clients."

Monica snorted, Chloe giggled, and Mike did a little of both – while Robin dropped his face into his hands as if even he was occasionally befuddled by his beloved uncle.

"Come on, Monica," said Dave, thinking he'd better restore order. "I'll show you what's to be done with your new friend." He tilted his head towards the door, then led the way out.

She followed him trustingly enough, but protested, "You're not going to hurt him, are you?"

"Absolutely not."

Nicholas was walking with Monica, while the others hung back near the cabin, still keeping a safe distance. "A wise man once told me," Nicholas confided to Monica, "that people respect life out here."

The dark night hid Dave's smile.

"It's a beautiful country, but it can be harsh, so we all help each other out."

"Even the frogs?" Monica asked.

"Even the frogs," Nicholas affirmed.

A moment later Dave stopped by the large bucket kept near the amenities block. The sulphuric smell of the artesian bore water was stronger there, but Monica didn't seem to mind, and the frog certainly didn't. "Monica, if you pop him in here, he'll be taken out to the big dam in the morning, where he'll go on to live a long and happy life."

"Are you having me on?" she asked, hanging back.

"No." Dave shook his head solemnly, then indicated the bucket. "Look, he already has a mate to keep him company."

Monica edged close enough to peer in and see the other frog sitting there. "Won't they get bored? What are they going to do all night, sitting in a bucket?"

Nicholas's mouth quirked wickedly, and he was just about to answer – before Dave's look cut him off. "What?" Nicholas asked with a show of innocence. "I was only going to say they'll sing to each other, and maybe perform a duet or two."

"Sing?"

"Yes, that's their mates we can hear now," Nicholas whirled a finger through the night air.

Monica tilted her head to listen properly. "Oh! I thought that must be some kind of weird bird."

"It's the frogs. They'll be going all night, I'm afraid," said Nicholas. "But they sound happy, don't they?"

"Yeah ..." she reluctantly agreed.

"Your friend will be fine – and he'll be happier still once he's at the dam tomorrow. Anyway, even I'd rather sit in a bucket outside on a night like this, than be stuck in a bathroom."

"True," she said, stroking the frog's back with the tip of her finger. Finally she drew near, and gently placed the frog in the bucket beside his mate. "Goodnight," she wished him. "Sweet dreams – and sweeter songs."

Then they all trailed back towards the cabins.

"Uncle Nicholas ..." said Robin. "You'll check our bathroom, won't you? Very carefully."

"Of course," was the brisk reply. "Monica and I will be on regular Frog Patrol, I promise. Won't we, Monica?"

"Too right," she agreed with a laugh.

And finally they all started to settle, humans, frogs and all.

Dave loved the cool quiet peace of an Outback dawn. He woke early the next day and wandered down to the edge of the tiny town, to gaze across the fossicking fields and the wide flat land beyond. The enormous sky arched above in all its magnificent clarity. Everything was hushed for those last few minutes as the eastern sky shaded from blue to rose to gold. Then the sun lifted into view, and already the air felt a little warmer, and the frogs started singing along with the cicadas. Somewhere behind him, a screen-door swung smartly shut. Dave smiled, and headed back to the caravan park.

Robin was the next one to emerge from the cabins. He wandered towards Dave, who was taking care of the Cruiser. "Morning, Robin," Dave said. "Sleep all right?"

"Yes, thanks. How about you, Uncle David? Did you miss sleeping on top of the car?"

"Car?" he asked in horrified tones. "What car?"

Robin rolled his eyes. "The Land Cruiser. Did you miss her last night?"

Dave had to smile, but he said, "We only do that at the waterhole, you know."

"Uh huh, sure. Well, you know, what you do in the privacy of your own garage is none of my concern …"

A chortle burst out of him. Maybe Robin wasn't quite the innocent they'd assumed.

"We're all aware that Nicholas has to share your affections with … What have you named her?"

"Mate, it's just the Cruiser."

"Uh huh. Dave and the Cruiser, sitting in a tree, K I double S I N G."

He shook his head. He had no comeback for that. "I got nothin'," he admitted – though he was saved a moment later by Monica walking past in a set of black pyjamas, with another green tree frog in her cupped hands. "Morning, Monica."

"Hey," she greeted them, with a lift of her chin, and stayed her course towards the amenities block.

Dave trailed after her just in case, to make sure that nothing dire had accidentally happened to the other frogs – but there were three of them now in the bucket, and they all seemed perfectly content. Monica crouched down to place the fourth one in there, too. "They really will be okay, right?" she asked.

"Absolutely. The bloke and his wife who run this place, they'll come by soon – on Frog Patrol," he added, remembering Nicholas's term for it. "One of them will clear the bathrooms before people start using them, and they'll do the run out to the dam … Actually, if you want to get dressed, we could go with him. Or we could offer to do the run ourselves, and we'll be back in time for breakfast."

Her eyes lit up. "Cool!" She was already on her way back to their cabin. "I'll have a quick shower, all right? Don't let them go without us!"

Dave laughed, and returned to where Robin was propped against the Cruiser, contentedly checking his phone, then chuckling as he thumbed in a message or a Tweet. Well, at least Dave had one happy client, and it seemed he had a happy young family member as well.

After breakfast, the seven of them did the opal tour, which involved visiting an underground mine as well as a working open-cut mine. In both, they were shown the layers of sandstone and clay – and in between the two, the shallow layer in which the Yowah nuts might be found.

The guide was full of advice for their own fossicking ventures, so they were all keen to pick up the fossicking licences that Dave had already organised. Then he had to exert a bit of authority to insist everyone had a quick lunch before they drove down into the fossicking fields.

Mike, Robin and Chloe decided to find a couple of spots in which they could dig, while Suzanne, Monica and Nicholas wanted to 'noodle' or wander around looking for bits of 'colour'. Dave knew from past experience that it was surprising how much could be found on the ground, or in the mullock heaps. White fellas had been mining at Yowah since 1883, but until recently most people had only been interested in the precious opals to be found inside Yowah nuts. The 'matrix' stones, where specks and veins of opal graced the red-brown ironstone, had been discarded – but were now very popular. Dave found them just as beautiful as and even more intriguing than the proper opals, if he was honest.

There was no shade at the fossicking grounds, and the sunlight reflected back off the exposed clay and sandstone, occasionally creating a really harsh glare. Despite the fact that Nicholas was wearing his Akubra and sunnies, Dave wasn't surprised when Nicholas came over to quietly say he was going to head back to the cabin for a rest. "I just want to cool down," he explained apologetically.

"Not a problem. I'll drive you back."

"There's no need. It's not that far; I can walk."

"I'll drive you back." Dave jogged over to let the others know he'd be back in a few, and then walked with Nicholas over to the Cruiser. Five minutes later, even Dave was glad to be in the leafy shade of the caravan park, so he could imagine how relieved Nicholas was.

"Thank you, David. I'll be fine from here. Don't worry, all right?"

"Of course I worry," he said mildly. "That's my job." They exchanged a quick kiss before Nicholas climbed out of the Cruiser. "I put your lime juice in the fridge," Dave continued, "and there's plenty of bottled water in there, too."

Nicholas turned to smile at him with affection. "I love you," he said, before closing the passenger door.

"Love you, too," Dave replied, knowing Nicholas could lip-read at least that much perfectly well.

The affection warmed, and then Nicholas turned away to walk slowly yet steadily towards the cabin.

Dave turned the Cruiser and headed back to take care of his other charges.

The next day, though still warm, was a little cooler and a little cloudier, so Nicholas was comfortable enough to stay with the others through a long morning of fossicking. As it drew near lunchtime, however, he did take a sieve and a bucket of dirt and rock over to the slice of shade thrown by the Cruiser, and sat there on the ground to patiently sort through it all looking for colour.

Chloe and Mike each found a small Yowah nut that morning, which created a great deal of pent-up excitement, as of course they wouldn't know what was inside until the nuts were broken open. Nicholas observed in a learned manner, "For now, the opal inside both exists and *doesn't* exist ..."

Which made Suzanne and Robin crack up with laughter, while Monica hid an amused smile, and murmured, "Schrödinger's opal."

Dave, Mike and Chloe exchanged baffled looks.

Meanwhile, Suzanne had happily accumulated a small collection of chips of matrix opal found while noodling, to which Monica had been discreetly adding. "They're not worth anything, I know," Suzanne said, "but they'll look very pretty in a little bottle of water on my windowsill, and I'll shake them up so it looks different every day."

"Like a snow globe, only with opal!" Chloe agreed. "And they'll sparkle in the sunshine!"

In any case, Dave thought he could safely add Suzanne to the 'satisfied client' list.

After lunch at the café in the community centre, Dave took them all to his mate Ned's shop where – after the tension increased unbearably throughout his quiet examination – the two Yowah nuts were sliced neatly in half down their longest dimension. Of course, there was nothing of value to be found within. Chloe seemed the most disappointed, as her nut contained a core of solid powdery clay, which was the usual result.

"Chances are only one in a thousand that you'll find an opal inside," Ned told her, in commiserating tones.

"And how many have you cut lately?" Mike asked.

Ned's smile glinted in the shadow of his beard. "Reckon I'd be in the nine-hundreds."

"Well, then," Mike concluded, "we might get lucky later in the week."

Mike's was empty but at least in an interesting way: the hollow inside formed an almost perfect sphere. With a slice taken off the curve underneath, and a bit of surface buffing, each half could sit like a small bowl.

"What are you going to put in there, though?" Monica asked. "They're tiny! No use at all."

"I shall buy a pair of opal cufflinks," Mike replied, on his dignity, "and keep one in each half." And he headed off to browse the items that Ned had on display.

The others all followed him, and from there they descended into groans of yearning and adoration and despair. Dave was the only one to hang back, knowing how it went ... The items on display and for sale were beautiful – probably far beyond anything they'd imagined. But the most gorgeous specimens were also expensive, and rare, and therefore out of reach of most – though Dave saw that Mike began keeping an eye on what Suzanne was drawn to, so perhaps he could afford to really indulge her. For those without his deep pockets, the display both provoked their determination to do some serious fossicking, and also made them realise how unrealistic their hopes were of finding anything significant. All of which was why Dave tended to let people have a good fossick for a while before confronting them with the reality.

As the others wandered off to do some more browsing in other shops, Dave stayed behind to thank Ned, who hadn't charged them for cutting open the Yowah nuts. "No worries," was the reply. Then Ned lifted his chin in a westerly direction. "Beauty of a sunset this evening, I reckon."

"Thanks," said Dave, nodding an acknowledgement. At least sunsets were freely available to all who cared for them.

The sunsets at Yowah were generally known for their magnificence. Dave wasn't sure if there was a reason for that, or if it was just one of those things, but he made sure to never miss an opportunity to enjoy one.

That evening as the sun was westering, he and the Cruiser led Mike and the rental out to the Bluff, an abrupt cliff face a few clicks east of town. They were in plenty of time, so they drove to the further edge, where there was a view out across a seemingly infinite plain containing nothing but mulga. Around the lookout area were tall cairns made of piled stones, none of them fixed by anything other than judicious choices. They – except for Monica, who seemed to have reverted to being too cool – marvelled at these and at the view for a while, before heading back to the western edge of the Bluff, to look out over the town of Yowah to the far horizon.

For a while the sun hid behind a thick band of cloud – but then at the last possible moment, the light broke through, and the vista turned from gold to red to purple above them, lit by the sun and shaped by the clouds, as beautiful as any opal. They were all gobsmacked – even Monica.

It lasted for several minutes, in a hush that felt eternal, until eventually it began to fade, and then the sun slipped below the edge of the Earth, and the sky became a deepening purple.

They all remained quiet and still, except that Dave turned to Nicholas where he sat perched beside him on the Cruiser's roo bar. Dave turned to Nicholas, as gorgeous as any sunset, and took his face in both hands and kissed him, a real full-blooded kiss. When they broke apart, Nicholas grinned at him, lopsided with joy as if he hardly knew whether to laugh or weep – and then the two of them belatedly realised that everyone else was watching, but all of them fondly.

Nicholas announced, "Don't get me wrong, I love a good sunset, but David is by far the most beautiful thing in my life."

Dave found that he was a bit pink-cheeked at the compliment, but otherwise he was perfectly fine and bold and happy. It finally dawned on him that he hadn't felt embarrassed or self-conscious about loving another man for *ages* now. Which seemed like good cause to kiss Nicholas again, so he did, dragging him close with both arms wrapped around his waist – and the others cheered or laughed as was their wont.

They returned to the caravan park during the long dusk, and to everyone's surprise found Charlie sitting outside the cabins, tending a wood-burning barbecue with potatoes already baking in the embers.

"Charlie!" Dave was pleased enough to give the man a hug. While they were close he took the chance to quietly ask, "Anything wrong?"

"Nothing urgent." Charlie drew back to look him in the eye. "Nothing that can't wait."

Dave nodded, tried to wrestle his curiosity into submission, and turned to beckon the Baldry family forward from where they'd paused at a tactful distance. "Let me introduce you to a good mate of mine …"

Charlie announced that barbecuing was blokes' business, and delegated the work accordingly. Robin was sent to fetch folding chairs for the three women, and once they were settled comfortably he was to take care of their drinks and any other requirements. Dave and Nicholas were to chop vegetables and get them marinating in olive oil and lemon juice. Meanwhile Mike and Charlie took care of the sausages and steak – and then, in the last few minutes, they chargrilled the veg. Nicholas and Dave cut a cross into each potato, and pushed in a knob of butter and cracked pepper.

The results were plentiful, fresh and tasty. "I think I've died and gone to Heaven!" declared Suzanne as she finally sat back, replete.

"Awesome …" Chloe managed faintly.

"I'm taking you along on all my trips now," Dave said to Charlie.

"Like you could afford me," Charlie scoffed, which made everyone laugh while hanging onto their full bellies.

Charlie had put a large billy of water on to boil for bush tea, with a few gum leaves in it for flavour. Once that was ready, they all sat in comfortable silence for a while with the steam from their mugs of tea rising to the stars. The frogs sang to each other, while the cicadas provided a percussion track.

Eventually Robin said, "Charlie …"

"Yeah, mate?"

"Can you tell us a Dreamtime story about opals?"

Charlie rumbled in thought for a long moment before saying, "Reckon I can."

"Oh! Thank you."

Another long moment passed before Charlie began, but everyone was suitably patient and expectant. "There are different stories about opals in the different regions of Australia," Charlie said, "and I got to thinking that is probably right, because the opals are different, too.

"The story about opals in this country starts with an Ancestor in the form of a pelican. Old man pelican would travel and travel a long ways, from country to country and further. He'd carry his own food and drink in his dillybag: the pouch beneath his beak would always be full of water and fresh fish.

"One day, though, he died, on a hill north of here."

Robin asked in a hushed voice, "How did he die, Charlie?"

"Reckon I can't tell you that bit of the story."

"That's all right. I didn't know that Ancestors could die, though. I thought they just went back to sleep."

Charlie tilted his head in consideration. "Some do, some don't. You're right, though; most are sleeping." Then he continued, "When old man pelican died, the water in his pouch flowed out and made Cooper Creek – and the Barcoo River," Charlie added, with a nod to Dave – "and filled them full of fish. And it was his blood, seeping into the earth, that made the gold and the opal."

"Cool…"

"Some while after, the people living south of here, maybe in what we call New South Wales now, they wanted to know what was up here. So they sent another pelican to explore, and to tell them what he'd learned when he returned. He carried his water and his fish in his dillybag, because it was a long journey, and he'd been told not to stop.

"Pelican became tired, though, and he flew down to rest on top of a hill. This was the same hill where the Ancestor had died, and when Pelican looked about, he was filled with wonder at all the beautiful colours in the ground. No one had ever seen opal before, so he was very curious, and he started tapping at the stone with his beak. Soon he was chipping away at it, and sparks were flying, pretty in the sunlight. But the dry grasses nearby caught fire, and the flames rose high, and then they spread … The fire spread all the way back to Pelican's people where they were camped. That was the first time those people used fire for cooking their meat, just as we've done tonight. And that fire came from the opals, and the opals came from the blood of the pelican Ancestor."

"Oh!" cried Suzanne, who'd been absolutely spellbound – she burst into applause, before guiltily looking around to see if that was improper or not.

But of course it was fine, and everyone had already joined in, while Nicholas expressed thanks for them all.

There was a comfortable lull while people contemplated the story and what it might mean, and then began thinking about what might happen next. The evening wasn't quite over yet.

"Okay," said Monica, her tone indicating a determination to be brave. She stood up, then stilled again – when one of her hands started marking time, Dave realised she'd been listening for a rhythm from the frogs and cicadas. Monica looked at Chloe, nodding with the beat now, and Chloe picked it up with handclaps and a shift of her shoulders. They'd obviously done this many times before, though their parents were watching in startled wonder. "Y'all ready for this?" Monica asked – and she started rapping.

"We're off on a trip with a bloke named Dave
Still waters run deep, he's a bit of a rave.
Nick is his man till death do us part,
They got two bodies, one soul, they got one heart.

"Robin's their guy, but he is his own man,
He loves Tony and Pepper, he's a bit of a fan.
And God made Charlie from the rock and the clay,
Skin dark as night, and eyes bright as day.

"So we're off on a trip through this wide brown land,
And thanks due to Dave, we got it all to hand.
We got frogs, we got opals, we got purple skies,
And when we got baked potatoes, we don't need no fries.

"Yo," she concluded, and struck a pose.

The whole party – and half the occupants of the caravan park who'd gathered round – burst into delighted laughter and hearty applause. It was only now that Monica remembered to be embarrassed. She dropped her face into her hands with a groan. But Suzanne went to wrap her up in a great warm hug, and told her how magnificent she was – and the applause continued, while Robin declared, "That was wicked!" and Charlie agreed, "It was deadly, all right. The deadliest!"

"Nicholas," Monica said once things had quietened down a bit, "I'm sorry about 'Nick', but I'm not good enough to cope with three syllables."

"No need to apologise at all," he stoutly replied. "Nick is my rap name, don't you know."

It had been a really great evening, one of the best, but Dave was still relieved to finally get the chance to talk with Charlie. They sat at the kitchen table while Nicholas made a last round of tea, and Robin pottered about for a bit before saying goodnight and heading for his bedroom.

"So, did you have some news?" Dave eventually asked.

"Nothing urgent, mate, or I wouldn't have made you wait. Just talk about a mine meaning they'd put the railway through, and what that's gonna bring."

"People are still thinking about the jobs, then."

"Yeah. Can't really blame them."

"I know. But there are other things to think about, too."

Nicholas brought the tea over and sat down. "Cunnamulla is already on a railway line, isn't it?" he asked.

"It's the last stop on the line," Dave explained, "so they'd be extending it further west."

"Which means landowners along the way will be looking for recompense."

"And the two on the far side of the waterhole will be keen on a quicker way of getting their cattle to market." Dave sighed. "It'd mean massive infrastructure costs, though, even if they don't take it out as far as the floodplains."

"Mining's always high investment, isn't it?" Charlie observed with a shrug. "And if they reckon they're looking at natural ore, it's gonna pay its way."

"Yeah …"

Charlie left a long pause while they all gloomily contemplated the possibilities, tried to weigh the probabilities. Then he said, "You'll come with me to the reserve again, before you head home?"

"Yeah, I guess," said Dave, knowing he sounded reluctant.

Charlie cocked a curious brow at him, and Nicholas's expression was all sympathetic worry or maybe worried sympathy or whatever.

Dave confessed, "I'm just ... letting them down, you know?"

"What, cos you're not black?"

"Well, yeah, basically. The Native Title thing was just a daydream, wasn't it? I was such an idiot to even –" Dave cut himself off, and changed track. "Thursday and his mob might be able to get the reserve extended. Nicholas and Lisa might be able to protect the butterflies and the wattle. Where does that leave me? There's nothing I can do, and that place, that beautiful place –"

"You sing the songs, mate. You tell the stories."

Dave stared at Charlie for a long moment, but eventually he had to ask. "And that's enough, is it?"

"It's the only thing," said Charlie. "It's what really matters."

Nicholas nodded. "That's right at the heart of it."

"That place would have died already, without you."

"I'm not – I'm not –" He almost groaned with frustration. "I'm not doing more harm than good?"

"No, mate," said Charlie. "Old man grunter chose you for a reason."

Nicholas took Dave's hand in his, and said, "None of us could have even *found* the waterhole without you."

"You're a good man, Davey."

"Hear, hear," Nicholas agreed, squeezing Dave's hand and smiling at him, Nicholas's lips curled with such exquisite fondness and his eyes shining with such affection that Dave couldn't fail to be moved.

"We've got one heart," Nicholas murmured late that night in the darkness of their bedroom, his palm pressed just to the left of Dave's sternum.

"Mmm ..." Dave contentedly agreed. "I like that we've got two bodies, though." And he proceeded to demonstrate why.

On their last full day in Yowah, Dave and Nicholas got up just as the eastern sky was lightening, and walked down to the fossicking fields. They were already more than familiar with the area in which Robin and Chloe had been diligently working; it was straightforward enough to tuck a couple of uncut

Yowah nuts into the pile of dirt and rock they had yet to sort through, and a fragment of matrix opal as well. Then they headed towards the area where Suzanne had been noodling the previous day, amiably arguing as they did so about which direction she might head in next.

As they turned a corner round an outcrop of stone, they were startled to find that Monica had beaten them to it. She was crouched on the ground with her back to them, gently trailing a few fragments of matrix opal through the powdery dirt, before gathering them up again and scattering them in a long arc off to her right. When she stood and dusted off her hands, she looked around – and almost jumped out of her skin to see them looming behind her. "What are you two doing here?"

"Same as you, from the look of things," Nicholas replied with a grin. "That's good of you."

She shrugged. "You, too, then."

Dave said, "I guess we'd be overdoing it, if we left something here for your mum as well."

"You've taken care of the kids already?" Monica asked – and when they nodded, she pondered for a moment. "Well, we might be making it really obvious if everyone gets lucky this morning, but I'll show you where Dad was working, if you like. We'd better look out for him, as well!"

They were soon done, and then the three of them started back up the track towards town. In the still air they could hear the humans, pets and wildlife all starting to wake up. The day had already lost the dawn chill. "Going to be a warm one," Dave remarked. "You might want to take it easy today, Nicholas."

Dave received a small wry smile in reply, equal parts gratitude and stubbornness with a dash of sorrow.

"Well, before you put your feet up, Nicky GT," said Monica, "we're on Frog Patrol, remember? Otherwise half the tour group will be unfit for anything at all."

"Nicky GT … ?" Dave echoed.

"All I need now is some serious bling," Nicholas said in tones of complete satisfaction. "Oh, and a hit record, of course."

Monica snorted.

Suzanne soon started finding her seeded colour, and criss-crossed that area bent almost double in order to closely examine the ground.

Chloe was next – finding not one but both Yowah nuts. Her joy quickly faded, though, when she caught Robin looking indulgent, and realised she'd been fooled. Then suddenly she powered up again. "Robin! Did you put these here for me to find?"

He quickly shook his head. "Not me." Robin glanced at Mike, though, obviously thinking him the mastermind.

"It wasn't us, either," Mike said.

Chloe thought for a moment, and turned to Dave with a quizzical brow.

"My services don't extend that far," he announced with a straight face.

"Don't look at me," Nicholas added. "It's enough being on Frog Patrol every minute of the day."

Mike concluded, "You're becoming a very successful prospector, Chloe!"

"Yeah, you really are," Robin agreed, obviously believing in their denials.

Chloe's face as she basked in Robin's compliment was like a flower at last unfurling in the sun.

When she finally returned to her fossicking, Dave saw that Robin's expression fell into dismay.

The week drew to a close all too soon, and the two families prepared to part at Cunnamulla airport. Mike shook Dave's hand in a particularly emphatic way, and said a few un-blokey things about what a truly wonderful time they'd all had. "Thank you," he continued. "You made everything easy, and I don't doubt we did more in a day than we'd have managed in a week without you. It's been an absolute pleasure."

"No worries at all," Dave replied. "And I really appreciate you letting me bring Nicholas and Robin along. We've had a great time, too."

"It's been wonderful having them with us – and meeting Charlie, as well. We couldn't have asked for more."

Not everyone was as happy, of course. Chloe was in tears at being parted from Robin, and Robin was dealing with that with all the awkwardness of youth. The two of them were already following each other on Twitter, and had exchanged email addresses, but at Chloe's age every parting was tragic and forever. Meanwhile, Monica had withdrawn into her cool shell again, though she did make sure she caught Nicholas's and then Dave's eye, and nodded an acknowledgement. Dave knew she'd enjoyed the trip, perhaps almost despite herself – and it was Monica who finally put a comforting arm around Chloe's shoulders, and led her off towards the plane.

Mike and Suzanne both thanked Dave and Nicholas again, and farewelled Robin, and then they left, too. Dave and Nicholas watched for a while longer, to make sure everything was shipshape, and then they all three waved as the plane taxied off to the runway. Soon it lifted into the air, banked to the east, and was gone into the haze. The living quiet of the Outback returned.

Dave had his arm around Nicholas's shoulders, and Nicholas had an arm likewise around Dave's waist. Nicholas leaned in closer for a moment, tucking his head in against Dave's. "It's been the most perfect week," Nicholas said. "I've loved every minute of it."

"Me, too," said Dave, tightening his hold for a moment.

"Thank you, David," Nicholas said, standing tall again so they could talk eye to eye.

"No worries, mate. But what for?"

"For this." Nicholas gestured broadly. "For us, for our life here. For everything."

Dave looked at this man, his husband, and said, "I wouldn't have it any other way."

seven

Dave, Nicholas and Robin met Charlie at the Aboriginal reserve the next day. As before, Dave and Charlie went to sit with the gathered Elders while the other two went to hang out with the more sociable group in the shade thrown by the store and the neighbouring trees. Dave sat near a vacant spot, but a little removed from the circle, and Charlie settled beside him. Whatever certainty Dave had found last time he was here had gone again. He felt humbled. Thursday nodded a genial greeting at him, but Dave managed little more than a glum grimace, and then lowered his head.

After a while, Thursday prompted, "You think you bring bad news, Dave."

"Yeah. I should have known. Well, I did know, but I forgot for a while. It's hard to be taken seriously, when I'm obviously not Indigenous."

"You got no business with that place!" one of the others declared. "Charlie got no proper business, neither."

Dave had lifted his head at that, instinctively firing up, but he took a moment to consider his response. "The place itself, the waterhole, that's what's important. That's what comes first."

"You got no business performing the ceremonies."

"If there's someone more ... suitable to pass the songs to –" Dave felt a stab of pain even at the thought – "I'll pass them on."

"No," said Charlie in his stubbornest tones.

"If there's someone from your people who'll take it on," Dave insisted – but then he stalled.

"No," Charlie said again. "It was the Ancestors put these thoughts in my head. That old man grunter chose you for that place."

"And who'll come after me?" Dave asked, honestly wanting to know. "Who will I pass the songs to when it's time?"

Charlie shrugged that off. "It's not time yet."

"Well, anyway," Dave said, turning again to Thursday. "I don't think I can help much in using the white man's law to protect the site. Nicholas is doing what he can for the butterflies, and his friend for the wattle. We think they're unique, and they're going to have them officially listed as 'Vulnerable'. That might be enough in itself."

Thursday nodded thoughtfully.

"But," Dave continued, "I'm going to have to ask you to try to extend the reserve, to include the waterhole in your care. Will you do that, do you think?"

Another nod from Thursday, but the man who'd protested Dave's right to perform the ceremonies shifted ominously.

"I'm not asking for my own sake," Dave insisted, "but for the land's."

"We can apply to have it gazetted," one of the women said, "if you can tell us where exactly the waterhole is. None of us mob have been there."

"Fair point. I've been thinking about that. I've been thinking we probably need to hire a surveyor of our own. Even if that means we're opening it all up." Dave grimaced. "So, anyway, if you can … I think the sooner the better, right? Once people hear a mining company's involved, God only knows what interests come into play."

She nodded, and they all settled back into their thoughts, though some of them were happier than others.

After a while, when it felt as if it were about time to leave, Dave said a general "Thank you", and stood up.

"I'll stay here, mate," Charlie said, looking up at him.

"You sure? You want us to wait?"

"Nah, you go on. Young Robin'll be wanting his dinner. I'll get a lift into town later with one of this mob."

Dave went to round up his family, and take them back into Cunnamulla.

They'd decided on an early start the next day, so as to get back to Brisbane in reasonable time. Dave took their overnight bags out to the Cruiser while the morning was still cool and quiet and full of possibilities. Nicholas and Robin had gone to breakfast already, and promised to have a coffee ready for him when he met them there. All was well. Dave had slept soundly, and was recovering his usual sense of optimism. But a chill took him as he headed round to the back of the Cruiser and stowed the bags securely. Something was wrong.

Once he'd closed the rear door, he paced pensively along the length of her, carefully checking her out. The Cruiser was dusty, but that was only to be expected at this point. Her tyres seemed fully inflated. There weren't any scratches he didn't already know about.

It was only when Dave reached the bonnet and looked across that he realised. There was a bull's-eye break in the windscreen, with a starburst of cracks radiating out. He stood and stared at it for a long moment. It was serious; it would have to be fixed before they left Cunnamulla. But how the hell had it happened?

There was no way he wouldn't have noticed it the previous evening; it hadn't happened while he was driving from the reserve into town. Which meant that overnight, some kind of accident – or a deliberate drunken prank ... Not that there was a guilty rock sitting on the bonnet or on the road nearby ... Dave frowned, and pulled out his mobile.

First he took a few photos of the damage from different angles. Then he called the local garage, and asked if he could bring the Cruiser in for a replacement windscreen. They agreed, and said they could get it done pretty much right away.

By the time Dave had driven the Cruiser down there and walked back to the hotel, his coffee was cold.

"Did you report it to the police?" was Nicholas's first question once the coffee was replaced and Dave had explained where he'd been.

"No. Didn't seem much point."

"But –"

"It's fully covered by insurance. It's just annoying, really. We'll be leaving an hour later than we'd planned, but that's about all."

Nicholas let a beat go by, before saying, "Someone has deliberately damaged the Cruiser, and you're letting them get away with it?"

Dave shrugged, though of course it wasn't that he didn't care. "There's no proof it was anything but an accident. What could the police do? For that matter, there's no proof it didn't happen on the road yesterday."

Nicholas glanced from Dave to Robin and back again. "But it didn't, did it? We'd have known, wouldn't we?"

Dave brought out his phone, and showed Nicholas the photos.

"We'd have definitely known," Nicholas concluded. "So there's three witnesses, anyway."

"Three witnesses to say it didn't happen while I was driving – but that's all."

They pondered this. Dave drank his coffee.

Then Robin had a bright idea. "What about CCTV? There'll be footage of whoever did it. Or whatever happened."

Dave found himself reluctantly smiling. "Not out here, mate." He added with mock severity, "*Don't* run wild."

Nicholas was looking troubled, and absently rubbed a hand against his forehead in the way that always made Dave a bit anxious. That was the worst part about this: it pained Nicholas. Not that Nicholas was concerned for himself. "The poor Cruiser," he murmured, reaching to gently squeeze Dave's shoulder.

"Don't worry," said Robin. "Uncle David will kiss her better. She'll be *fine*."

"Eat your breakfast," Dave advised with a mock growl.

Of course, every time they drove through a town or some other location that had mobile reception, Robin's phone chimed to announce incoming messages. One, which arrived while they were passing through Dalby, seemed to put Robin in pensive frame of mind. Dave kept an eye on him in the rear-view mirror. Robin was doing nothing more than staring out the window at the unchanging scenery, so after about fifteen minutes of that Dave said, "You right, mate?"

Nicholas stirred and looked around, having fallen into his own reverie. "Robin ... ?"

"I'm all right." But Robin sighed, and after a moment he said, "Uncle Nicholas ..."

"Yes?"

"Has it been ... you know ... a real pain for you? Me being in love with you, I mean."

"No," Nicholas warmly replied. "No, of course not." He shifted around in his seat, so they could talk more directly. "Why do you ask?"

Robin grimaced, and didn't say anything.

Dave glanced at him in the mirror, and guessed, "Text message from Chloe?"

Another sigh, before Robin admitted, "Yeah." Then he asked Nicholas, "What am I supposed to do? I mean, it's not like ... it's not as if there's anything I *can* do! I'm *not* going to fall in love with her. She's just a kid, for a start!"

"Be kind to her," Nicholas promptly replied. "Be a friend. Be patient. That's a great deal to be getting on with. And it will pass. These things always do."

"Do they?" Robin asked in sceptical tones.

"Yes. You know – this is a secret, all right? But when I was her age … and when I was your age, too, for that matter! I was in love with someone who would never love me back. It could have been horrible, it could have broken my heart, but he was kind to me, and actually now I think it was the … second most perfect thing that ever happened to me."

Robin had his head down, but Dave sensed somehow that the mood had changed.

"If you can be her friend," Nicholas forged on, "Chloe might one day look back on this as something that made her happy."

Silence.

"Robin?" Nicholas prompted.

A muffled noise from Robin might have been a sob or a groan – but turned out to be a laugh. Robin was suddenly grinning at Nicholas and bubbling over with mirth. "I know you were in love with Frank Brambell, Nicholas!"

"Oh." Nicholas seemed rather affronted. "Do you?"

"And for that matter, you still are, a little bit. Sorry, Uncle David."

Dave laughed, too. "No worries," he assured Robin. "It was one of the first things I knew about your uncle. We'd hardly even said g'day and he told me he had a thing for chauffeurs."

"Were you driving at the time?"

"Yeah."

Robin thought that was hilarious. "Oh right, it's such a big secret he just blurts it out as soon as he sets foot in another country … Which is why I don't believe you, Nicholas, with all your 'This too shall pass'. As if it ever passed for you. And David still isn't totally over Denise either – are you?"

Dave cast him a wink via the mirror. "Yeah, maybe not."

Nicholas was still looking a bit pinched around the mouth. "How did you know?" he asked Robin when he could get a word in edgewise.

"Well … when I was young, I spent most of my life paying attention to you, didn't I? And there you were, spending most of your life paying attention to Frank."

"God! I tried so hard to be discreet. For his sake, you know? I never wanted to get him into trouble."

"It's all right," Robin said. "I don't think anyone else knew. Or didn't take it seriously, if they caught a hint. Except Simon, of course."

Nicholas shifted to sit back properly in his seat, as if he needed the support. "Simon knew?" He glanced at Dave –

And Dave confirmed this with a nod. "Simon knew."

"Oh God. Well. I suppose Simon always knew everything that was going on, didn't he?"

"Pretty much," Robin and Dave chorused – and then shared another laugh.

Poor Nicholas had just had his world rocked. But it didn't take him too long to rally. "All right, then. You have some good examples to follow, don't you, Robin? You treat Chloe as well as I treated you. As well as Denise treated David. Maybe not quite as well as Frank treated me," Nicholas added with a nostalgic kick to his smile. "You do that, and chances are she'll remember this last week as the happiest idyll of her life – at least until she meets the guy or girl who'll love her back." Nicholas's hand slipped over to rest warmly on Dave's thigh. "And then you'll have stood her in good stead, because her heart will still be whole, and her own to give."

Robin was gaping in wonder at all this. Eventually he blurted, "Nicholas? I do love you, you know."

Nicholas turned to smile at him with wistful whimsy. "I know, my dear. And I love you, too."

Despite which, Nicholas was soon back to bothering over Robin. "Did you hear him referring to Chloe as a kid?" he demanded of Dave once they were home, and closed bedroom doors separated them from Robin. "And Monica – who's two years younger than him – referred to him and Chloe as kids! I mean, that really was the most perfect week, don't get me wrong, but wouldn't you have expected him to befriend the older of the pair?"

"Aren't girls meant to grow up quicker than boys?" asked Dave. "At least, that's what I was always told. Maybe it was just cos Denise was always smarter than me, though."

Nicholas offered him a brief sympathetic smile, but was not diverted. "Monica was quite mature for her age, I suppose, and there's no denying Robin tends towards the opposite."

Dave emptied their bag of dirty clothes into the laundry hamper. "Maybe you could try taking him a little more seriously, Nicholas. Robin can seem like a different person when you're not around. When he's with you … it's almost like he reverts to the eleven-year-old boy you used to know back when you were living in England."

"Oh … I hadn't thought of that." Nicholas sat on the edge of the bed. "Oh yes, I see. I, uh … I know I get a bit giddy and drop at least a decade of intelligence when I'm with my father."

That made Dave laugh. "Giddy, yes. I reckon it's one of the reasons he adores you. But no one would ever call you unintelligent!"

Nicholas favoured Dave with a warm glowing smile – but then reverted to the topic of Robin with an irritable shrug. "Do you know, I'd almost started to think that the gap year was a good idea? I was beginning to think he wasn't ready yet – not for an intense course like PPE, anyway."

"Not that I know anything about the course, but I bet he's ready. He's clever, like you are – and I'm sure he knows his own mind, Nicholas."

But that led directly back to the question of Robin's sexuality, and it seemed Nicholas wasn't ready to talk sense about that yet.

There was a knock on the front door a couple of days later. Dave went to answer it, having no idea who it might be as they weren't expecting anyone. He opened the door to discover two men on the patio who didn't seem to be selling religion or a new energy plan. One of them was a white man with a sun-browned face, and the other Asian, perhaps Chinese – both of them middle-aged and wearing suits. "Can I help you?" Dave asked, having even less of an idea about what they wanted.

"Mr David Goring Taylor … ?" asked the white man.

"Yes."

"My name is Harvey. Fred Harvey. I represent the Reddy Eight mining company." He paused, and lifted a brow.

Dave's gut plummeted. "Oh. I see."

"Yes. I believe you've had some dealings already with a Mr Walinski, whose services have been retained by Reddy Eight." When he didn't receive a reply, Harvey indicated his companion, who stood a step beyond his right shoulder. "This is Mr Teng, who represents one of our major investors."

Teng respectfully inclined his head in greeting, so Dave did likewise – but he didn't make a move to open the screen-door, and he said in rather hard tones, "You come to my home … ?"

Harvey grimaced in what might pass as an apologetic expression. "If Taylor Outback Tours had a shopfront or office, I would have met you there. But it doesn't."

"And you couldn't have called first?"

"Would you have agreed to meet us?"

It was Dave's turn to grimace in acknowledgement. "Guess I might have put you off."

"But we need to talk," Harvey implacably continued. "Don't we?"

Dave weighed this up, but he concluded – as he supposed he must – that he should probably get this over with. "All right." He unlocked the screen-door, and swung it open. "Come in, then," he said ungraciously.

"Thank you," said Harvey. Teng offered another polite nod as he passed.

Dave didn't let them any further than the lounge room – which he and Nicholas used, though it was the most formal room of the house, such as it was. Of course Nicholas came through from the family room as soon as he realised they had guests, so Dave did the introductions. "This is my husband, Nicholas. Nicholas, this is Fred Harvey from the mining company, and Mr Teng from their investors."

"It's a pleasure to meet you," Nicholas smoothly replied, being the polite Englishman he still was – though Dave noted he didn't offer to shake hands with either man, nor did he offer their guests tea or coffee. "Would you care to sit down?"

Once they were all seated, each pair facing the other across the coffee table, Fred Harvey said, "I'll get right to the point, then."

"Please do," said Nicholas.

"I think we all know why Mr Teng and I are here. It seems, based on a very small sample, that there is a source of hematite out west of Cunnamulla. My company, Reddy Eight, naturally has an interest in that. But before this goes any further, we need to assess what's actually there." Harvey left a pause, but no one leapt in to either agree or disagree. "All right, then. It's not a difficult process to prove that enough volume of the stuff exists to make it worth our while to move in – or to prove that there *isn't* enough, if that's the case. I suspect it's in all our interests to at least establish that much."

Dave slowly took that in. Eventually he asked, "So, just to clarify, you don't even know for sure yet whether there's actually enough there to be worth mining?"

"That's correct, yes."

"And if there isn't … ?"

Harvey lifted his hands palm-out. "Your problem goes away."

Dave huffed a breath in surprise. "Okay, so what do you know about my 'problem', as you call it?"

Harvey took a moment with that, but then said, "We understand that there's some kind of … problem in accessing the site. That you're the only one who knows the way in." He shifted, betraying a moment's uncertainty. "To be honest, no one can explain to me exactly why that is."

Which drew another huff from Dave. "Not sure I can exactly explain that, either. But," he added, "that's not the whole story."

"No. There's a Dreamtime site out there, and songlines," Harvey said to Dave. Then he turned to Nicholas to add, "Not to mention vulnerable flora and fauna."

"Okay," said Dave. "So whether you understand or not, you've got to know I'll do anything I need to do to protect that place, and the things that live there."

"I respect that," said Harvey. "I do."

"Okay …" Dave repeated, knowing he sounded unconvinced.

"So why are you here?" Nicholas asked.

Harvey shifted forward a little, and said very directly to Dave, "We want to offer you a finder's fee, of sorts, if you'll lead Mr Walinski and a small team – geologists, surveyors – to the location of that hematite."

Dave stared back at him for a long moment, before glancing at Nicholas.

"Reddy Eight is in a position to be … generous. Very generous."

"I'm not the kind of bloke who can be bribed or bought," Dave said, though without much umbrage.

"I respect that as well," Harvey smoothly replied. "I'm discussing a service that you can provide us, and fair recompense for it."

"I've already got all I need," Dave said, with another glance at Nicholas.

392 | The Thousand Smiles of Nicholas Goring

"Though you probably already know that," he added with a bite to his tone. God only knew what kind of access a moneyed-up mining company had to individual financial records let alone more personal stuff.

"I understand, Mr Goring Taylor."

"And a lot of the locals are keen to have you out there. You don't need to deal with me to set that up."

"But it seems we need you to help find the place."

Dave ignored that for the moment. "And you'll need to be dealing with the Murri, because it's all going to end up as part of their reserve. If you're talking recompense, they're the ones who should have it."

"I admire your principles, Mr Goring Taylor. If you would prefer us to make a donation to the Aboriginal reserve rather than pay you a fee, that would be fine with us, and of course a certain percentage of jobs would be offered first to anyone in that community. Whatever you might think, Reddy Eight is not interested in destruction or desecration, but in cleanly extracting a resource that ultimately we all benefit from – and not only our friends in China," Harvey said with a nod to Teng. "Over half the weight of your Toyota Land Cruiser is due to the steel in it, you know."

Dave's reaction this time went beyond a huff; it was more like a bark of humourless laughter. "Now you're really getting personal!"

Harvey shrugged in something like an apology. "I only wanted to make a point, not cross any lines."

"All right." Dave took a long moment to consider, but he didn't figure anything had really changed. He looked at Nicholas again, but apparently Nicholas was trusting Dave to know what was right to say and do, just as Charlie was trusting Dave, and Thursday and his mob as well. Dave sighed. "Well," he finally said, "it's not that I'll never help, but I'm not ready to help yet. I need to make sure the Dreaming site will be safe. Once I'm sure of that, and I'm sure it's what most of the locals want, then I'll do whatever needs to be done. But not right now, and probably not real soon, either."

"Thank you, Mr Goring Taylor." Harvey stood, and offered his hand.

"Well, don't thank me yet," Dave said. But he also stood, and he shook the man's hand – and then Teng's as well.

"Thank you, sir," said Mr Teng, in an accent that mingled China and Australia.

"Right," said Dave. And he saw them to the door.

Once they were gone, Dave locked up again, and sank back against the door wondering what the hell would be thrown at him next. All he had to deal with immediately, however, was Nicholas stepping close, and lifting a gentle hand to cup Dave's face. "You were brilliant," Nicholas said.

"I wasn't. I'll try to be good enough, anyway."

"You're *bloody brilliant*," his husband insisted – and he pressed close for a full-on kiss as if that would prove it.

The next day that Nicholas went in to the uni, Dave drove Robin in to join Nicholas for lunch, and then the three of them went to talk with Lisa Munroe. Dave hadn't met her before, but could immediately see what had Robin interested. Anyone who had a taste for Nicholas could hardly fail to appreciate her tall lean figure and long face: the first impression of their likeness was almost uncanny. But she wore her dark hair in a thick plait, and her pointed chin was her prettiest feature while with Nicholas it was his plump pink lips. And Dave soon decided that while she had a lovely dimpled grin, it couldn't compete with Nicholas's range of smiles.

Robin was obviously still besotted – though, while he wasn't playing it cool, he seemed more thoughtful than starry-eyed now. Dave contemplated the situation while Lisa and Nicholas compared notes on their half-completed nomination forms for listing protected wildlife. Being bisexual himself made it easy enough for Dave to understand Robin being romantically inclined towards both genders. It was more difficult to get his head around the notion of not wanting to have sex with someone he was in love with – actually *not even wanting to* as opposed to not being able to for whatever reason. But Dave figured that if Robin was happy that way, there was no point in wanting him to be unhappy. What the odds were of Robin eventually meeting someone likewise inclined, and the two of them both falling in love … well, Dave didn't like to think. But surely it *was* possible. And in the meantime, there was … studying and working and eventually becoming prime minister, not to mention family and friends and all the other good things in life.

It must have seemed a bit weird for Lisa and Nicholas to finally look up from her computer and find both Robin and Dave in a reverie. Especially Dave, who was hardly known for being a thinker of any kind, let alone a deep one. Lisa laughed, and asked, "Solving the meaning of life, are we?"

Robin blushed – and Dave didn't have anything on his mind that he particularly wanted to share, so he glanced around in desperation, and as luck would have it the relevant paperwork was right there on Lisa's desk. "Just having a ponder on the Nature Conservation Act," he asserted, knowing that he probably wasn't fooling anyone.

There was more laughter in response, but then Lisa got right back to business. "I've been thinking about the waterhole itself," she said in serious tones. "Nicholas told me your theory, David, about the pool itself being fed directly from the water table."

"Um … yeah," Dave replied, wondering if he'd ever had a theory before. Obviously there was a first time for everything.

"If that's the case, then it raises the issue of any changes to the water table possibly affecting the level of water in the pool – and *that* might have a detrimental effect on the flora and fauna."

"Oh," said Dave, starting to scramble towards the full implications. Nicholas got there before him, and looked horrified. "You mean," Dave said, "even if the mining company kept their distance from the place itself, they might affect the water table, and that might …"

"Exactly."

"Oh God."

Nicholas stuttered a couple of times before managing to say, "The waterhole seems so timeless. Changeless. As if it hasn't been disturbed by anything for centuries."

"As if it's still dreaming," Dave found himself saying.

Nicholas stared at him, and then lifted a hand to his head as if he could hardly bear his own thoughts. "I've been thinking of it as almost … eternal. But nothing in nature is. Or only when you take the largest view of it all. The conservation of matter and energy means nothing is ever lost, but everything eventually changes. Everything has its season."

"A *natural* season," Robin protested. "Just because it will eventually be destroyed doesn't give us leave to destroy it now."

"Spoken like a true philosopher!" Nicholas replied, reaching a hand to ruffle Robin's hair. "And maybe you can tell me what there is in that field about a change in perception. I feel as if my perspective has just shifted one hundred and eighty degrees … One moment I'm thinking that the waterhole is changeless, and the next I'm thinking that the place exists in such a delicate balance, that actually it's ... unbearably fragile. And that scares the dickens out of me."

"All right," said Dave. "So that's one more thing to take into account."

"David, we really need to push this whole thing as hard as we can."

"I know," he replied, though he still felt as if all the important stuff was out of his hands. "You guys keep working on your nomination forms. We'll take Lisa out there as soon as we can – and if either of you have any ideas about a surveyor we can take, someone to help us pin down the location, that would be great. Otherwise I'll be looking up the Yellow Pages."

Nicholas came to sit by Dave, looking troubled and impatient. He didn't say anything, but then he hardly needed to.

After a thoughtful pause, Robin said, "Uncle David ... you know that man you talked to about Native Title? He'd know someone, wouldn't he? Or he'd know who to ask. I mean, they'd need to establish boundaries and such all the time."

Which earned Robin a broad happy grin from Lisa, and a particularly beautiful grin softened by affection from Nicholas – in the midst of which Dave's thanks went pretty much unheeded. Not that Dave minded one little bit.

The phone rang the next day, and Dave picked it up. "Hello, this is Dave."

"Hello, Mr Goring Taylor. This is Shirley Johns; I'm mayor of the shire council out at Cunnamulla."

"Ah," Dave responded rather intelligently, while reflecting that he probably should have been expecting this. "G'day, Shirley."

"G'day, David. Well, I won't beat about the bush, as you probably know why I'm calling."

"I can guess."

"Yes. I've had a couple of meetings with a Mr Fred Harvey of Reddy Eight. I believe you've met the man. He's interested in our natural resources, and we're interested in his investment. But we need your help."

"Yes, well, I'm interested in protecting something that's even more precious than iron ore."

"I'm sure I don't need to explain what a boon for the community it would be – and for the whole region – in terms of jobs and infrastructure. We'd be very grateful to you."

Dave sighed. "And I bet he passed on my answer. That hasn't changed."

"I confess I'm rather confused, David, about no one seeming to know where this place is. Can you at least tell me whose property it's on?"

"No, I can't – and that's not me being difficult. We've never been able to really pin it down."

"Mr Harvey mentioned that they've tried to locate it from the air as well. Apparently iron ore is quite obvious if you know what you're looking for. But they're left feeling as confused as I am."

"Well, I'm not surprised," Dave said – though he was, rather, by all of that. "The place isn't easy to find. I can't even explain why, really, unless you're prepared to believe that the Ancestors are protecting it, or something."

"I see," she said in sceptical tones.

"Shirley, once I'm sure the Dreaming site will be safe, I'll help. I've just got to be certain of that first. It's in *our* interests, now, to be able to locate it on a map, so I'm working out how to do that. But you'll understand I have my priorities."

After a moment she sighed, as if accepting at least a momentary defeat. "I understand – and for what it's worth, you were already well respected in town, David, just as your father always was. That's only increased in recent days."

He huffed a cynical laugh. "Flattery's not gonna do it for you, Shirley."

"It's not flattery if it's true. I'm sure I'm not speaking for myself alone when I say I very much appreciate the stand you're taking."

"Right. Okay, well, if that's the case, then if you can do anything to help Thursday's mob in extending the Aboriginal reserve to include the Dreaming site, I'd appreciate it. And I'll do what I can as soon as I can. That's as much as I'm able to promise right now."

"I understand," Shirley repeated, "and I'll do what I can as well, I promise you that. Thank you, David."

"Thank you, Shirley." And they each said goodbye, and hung up.

So there was someone else to add to the mix of interests precariously balanced around this issue. Dave's head hurt. But there was one thing he never lost sight of, and that was his sense of the true priorities. That had to count for something, surely.

There was another phone call late that night when the house was dark and they were all fast asleep. Nicholas kept a handset by his side of the bed, because of course a call in the middle of the night to him meant England. "Hello?" Nicholas answered blurrily, sounding as if he wasn't even half awake.

There was a long empty pause during which Dave stirred, and Nicholas turned on the bedside lamp.

"Hello?" Nicholas tried again, glancing at Dave with a frown. "Simon, is that you?"

Nothing.

"Father … ?"

Nothing. And then the line cut out. Dave could hear the dial tone kick in.

Nicholas turned off the handset and dropped it into his lap, before rubbing hard at his face for a moment. Then he picked up the phone again, and used speed dial to call the Goring family home in England. "Simon? It's Nicholas. Did you just try to phone us?"

"No, I didn't," Dave could hear Simon reply.

"We just had a call, that's all, but I missed answering it. I couldn't think who else it would be."

"If you can hold the line, Nicholas, I'll check with your father. Is everything all right with you?"

"Yes, everything's fine. I was calling to make sure everything's all right with you!"

"It must be very early in the morning there."

"Two-thirty," Nicholas replied, having checked his watch.

"No wonder you were worried." A few moments later, Richard had added his reassurances to Simon's that all was well.

"Never mind, then," Nicholas concluded. "Sorry to bother you. It must have been a wrong number."

"Goodnight, Nicholas," Richard said in farewell. "It was lovely to hear your voice. Sleep well now."

Nicholas put the handset back in its cradle, turned out the light, and lay back down in the bed. Dave shifted in close to snuggle up to him. "All right?"

asked Dave.

"Yes." Nicholas sounded wide awake. "There was someone on the line, you know. It wasn't just dead. I could hear them breathing."

Dave frowned, and finally suggested, "Some idiot dialled the wrong number, and then was too much of a wuss to admit it."

"I suppose," said Nicholas.

"Get some sleep," Dave urged. "Everyone's fine. It's okay to sleep now."

Nicholas sighed. "I suppose," he said again. But Dave suspected he'd be too fretful to really rest.

eight

Nicholas and Dave had decided that Dave would manage the next tour trip on his own. His clients this time were a bunch of blokes in their early twenties who basically wanted to camp out, go off-roading, do an extended crawl of Outback pubs, and generally behave like larrikins. Dave had figured it wouldn't be much fun for Nicholas and Robin to tag along, apart from which the clients might feel their style was being cramped.

Robin seemed to agree it would be a good idea to sit this one out; nevertheless he indulged in a bit of a sulk, perhaps because he'd enjoyed their Yowah trip so much. Nicholas likewise seemed torn in two about the decision, though in his more reasonable moments he agreed that he and Robin were better off at home. As for Dave, even after all these years he couldn't leave Nicholas behind without a serious pang.

This time he met up with his clients – six of them, almost indistinguishable from each other at first glance – in Toowoomba. From there a convoy of the Cruiser, a client's own Ford Territory, and a rental four-wheel drive headed through Dalby to Chinchilla, where they stopped for lunch at the RSL. Dave was intending a sober trip, for himself at least, to help ensure he could keep an eye on the others' safety, but he had to have a Cascade in honour of Chinchilla native Pete Murray – a ritual Dave and Denise used to observe religiously. He had a private chuckle, though, at the thought of telling this lot Pete's butterfly story, as he'd told Nicholas back in the days when they'd first met. It would take Pete telling it to provoke a suitable reaction in these blokes.

Dave received a call that evening from Denise, though it wasn't for the sake of sharing the Pete-love. She was instead passing on a message. "It's the Barton station," she said. "You were heading there on this trip, weren't you?"

"Yeah, for the off-roading."

"They've called to say they're restricting access to their land."

"Really?" he responded, feeling somewhat mystified. "I've never known them do that before. Did they say why?"

"No. It was Daryl who called, and he sounded a bit odd about it, like maybe he didn't agree himself. But what can he do? They're entitled."

"Of course they are. All right. I'll just reshuffle my plans a bit. These guys won't even notice."

"Having fun, are you?" Denise asked in wry tones.

"They make me feel old," Dave replied, "but mostly in a good way. Sometimes I even feel mature!"

"Crikey! Hang on to that, then."

"Will do."

It took a great deal of maturity for Dave not to swear loudly enough to wake the town early one morning in Charleville, when he came out of the hotel to find that not one but two of the Cruiser's tyres were flat. Luckily his clients were late risers, but by the time he'd swapped the wheels for the two spares, driven the Cruiser down to the garage and walked back, the blokes were straggling down for breakfast.

"We might have a slight delay in setting off," he announced. "I've had a couple of flat tyres."

"Oh," said Scott, the bloke who owned the Ford. "Is my Territory okay?"

"Didn't think to look." Dave accompanied Scott out to where the other two vehicles were parked, but they seemed all right, thank God or whichever Ancestor was watching over them.

"That's bad luck with the Cruiser," Scott observed as they stood there contemplating the Territory. "Both on the same side, I guess? You must have run over something that wouldn't say die."

"Bad luck, yeah," Dave agreed, provoked into further thought. He followed Scott back inside, and sat there frowning over a strong coffee. The thing was, Dave had never had more than one flat tyre at a time, and he certainly hadn't noticed anything wrong while driving the previous evening.

When he headed back to the garage, they announced they hadn't found any damage, though as requested they'd replaced the inner tubes anyway. "Better safe than stuffed," one of the mechanics opined. "Don't wanna get stuck out there."

"Ain't that the truth," Dave agreed. He contemplated the discarded inner tubes, which had been reinflated in an unsuccessful attempt to find the holes and patch them. "D'you think," he asked after long moments, "someone deliberately let them down? As a prank?"

The mechanic looked unimpressed. "Maybe. Can't think what else. Bit bloody-minded for a prank, but."

"Yeah …" Dave sighed, figuring he wasn't going to find an answer, or at least not that morning. "Look, would you keep them inflated for a while, and see if they do go down? It might be a really slow leak. Keep them, though. Sell them or use them, if they're okay. But I just want to know, one way or the other."

"No wuckers," the mechanic said, which of course was Australian for 'No fucking worries'. He lifted his chin in acknowledgement, and added, "Be seein' ya, then." The latter expressed a wish that it be so, and therefore that Dave stay safe out there.

"No wuckers," Dave replied.

Dave and his clients had planned to camp out that night. Of course Dave was an old hand at this by now, so he got the bulk of things set up efficiently despite the other blokes being more interested in teasing each other about who was going to share a tent with whom. Dave had his own tent, as usual, which was sacrosanct, and he managed to tactfully ignore the ribbing between his clients, who were obviously all concerned about being straight or at least being seen to be so. Some things were slow to change. Still, Dave reflected, they knew well enough that he had a husband at home, so they couldn't have been completely homophobic. "You all better sort it out," he eventually commented, "or one of you might end up sleeping in *my* tent."

There was a collective melodramatically indrawn breath, and then a solution was quickly found. Dave would be sleeping alone, which of course suited him perfectly.

It would be an understatement to say he was less happy with what he found once he'd further unpacked the Cruiser. A couple of items he took out were suspiciously wet – with water, thank God, rather than petrol or anything else – and when he finally got into the stuff stashed securely up against the back seat, he found that one of the containers of water was leaking. Maybe half of it was gone. Not that that mattered much in itself – Dave quickly checked the water they'd stored in each of the three vehicles, but the rest was all safe, and of course he always took as much water as he could reasonably carry on a trip. In this case, the seven of them could probably survive for a couple of weeks on what they still had, and they were actually planning to be back in town the next night.

However. Despite the fact that Dave always planned for accidents and emergencies – or maybe because of that fact – it was very rare that anything actually went wrong. And this loss of water followed hard on the heels of the flat tyres, and he'd had that broken windscreen not so long ago as well.

Dave upended the leaky container in order to save what he could, and they used the remaining water that evening. Nevertheless, once he'd had a ponder while cleaning out the Cruiser, Dave definitely felt he owed his clients an apology. "Flat tyres. Losing some of our water. I want you to know that I don't take these things lightly."

"No worries," said Scott. "It's clear you've got it covered."

Another one – named Matt – said, "Everyone told us how you haven't lost a client yet. Or not for years, anyway."

"Ha," said Dave, and reached to touch one of the larger branches which was waiting by the campfire.

"Anyone can have a run of bad luck," one of the others reassured him. Owen.

"Thanks. Well. I have a Plan B, C, D and E for just about everything, so I'm sure we'll be okay."

"Absolutely," they all agreed.

Dave sighed. Bad luck, Owen had called it. But Dave was honestly beginning to wonder …

The next morning, when they stopped just off the road for a tea break, Scott quietly approached Dave. Scott and his Ford Territory had been bringing up the rear in their convoy of three, and now he announced that he'd noticed something. "Maybe I'm just imagining things, but I think there's somebody following us."

"Why d'you think that?"

"Most of the time, there's just dust in the mirrors. But every now and then there's a tiny shape in the distance that looks like a four-wheel drive, and a dust cloud behind it."

"And that's just been this morning?"

Scott shrugged uncomfortably. "Dunno. Maybe yesterday, too."

Dave carefully didn't look around, but he asked Scott, "Can you see it now?"

"Nah … But you know … I don't have that good an imagination, yeah?"

"Understood." Dave thought about this while he drank about half a cup of tea. Then he said, "All right, if you don't mind helping, let's see if we can't sort out what's going on."

"Sure," said Scott.

So, next time there was cover enough to make it work, Dave pulled the Cruiser over and parked in the shelter of some trees and scrub. The other two vehicles carried steadily on as if nothing had happened, their dust clouds obscuring the fact that the convoy had lost a member.

Dave climbed out and watched the other vehicles for long moments, not really liking to let his clients head off on their own. Then he turned to peer through the foliage to see what, if anything, might be following them.

Soon enough, a pale-coloured four-wheel drive hove into view. Dave adjusted his glasses on his nose, and squinted hard. As the details came into view, Dave wasn't overly surprised to find that the vehicle was a sand-coloured Land Rover Discovery. Ted Walinski. And as far as Dave could make out, it seemed he was alone, or at least there was no one in the passenger seat, and no other vehicles following.

Dave took a breath – and just as the Land Rover pulled past the trees, Dave stepped into view with his hand out to flag the man down.

Walinski had obviously been fooled, but anyone driving out here needed quick reactions; he hit the brakes, but let the Land Rover continue on a little, stopping at an angle a wary distance away so he could keep an eye on Dave and the surrounds as he slowly climbed out and down to the ground. "Mr Goring Taylor," the man said, while pausing nearer his own vehicle than Dave's.

"What are you doing out here?" Dave asked in unimpressed tones.

Walinski shrugged. "Guess you know the answer to that."

"Following me."

Another shrug, which was neither confirmation nor denial.

"I'll save you the trouble. I'm not going anywhere near the waterhole, not this trip."

"Well, maybe you are, maybe you aren't."

Dave crossed his arms, and favoured the man with a hard gaze. "One of my water containers sprang a leak yesterday. Do I have you to thank for that?"

Walinski looked genuinely shocked. "No! Hell no."

"And two flat tyres, back in Charleville. Know anything about that?"

"No – and I wouldn't –"

Dave sighed, and lifted a hand to indicate it didn't need to be said. "No, all right, I know that." After all, Dave was talking about life-threatening stuff, and anyone who really belonged out here would never stoop so low.

Walinski gestured towards the Cruiser. "Everything all right?"

"Yeah," Dave replied with a sigh. "I was just wanting to ambush you."

"Looks like the cavalry are coming, anyway."

Dave shook his head in bemusement to see – and hear – the two vehicles containing his clients returning at speed. "I didn't ask them to do that. They were meant to stay right out of it." The young blokes were hollering as if they thought Dave might need rescuing. "Here," said Dave, holding his right hand out to Walinski. "So they don't get the wrong idea."

The two of them shook hands very deliberately, making a bit of a show of it, so Dave's clients were relatively calm again by the time they stepped out of the vehicles. "All right, Dave?" asked Scott.

"Yeah, mate, I'm fine."

Walinski backed away a little, but asked, "D'you need water? You said you'd lost some."

"No, we're fine. There's plenty left. Thanks, though."

"All right." Walinski lifted a hand in a general farewell, and headed back towards his Land Rover. "See ya, then."

The others called, "See ya!"

But Dave followed after Walinski, and said to him quietly, "Look, I told you and I told Fred Harvey: I'll help as soon as I can. I've just got to make sure that place is safe first. Then I'm not gonna stand in anyone's way."

"Understood," said Walinski. And they shook hands once more and then parted.

Denise called the next day with news of someone else who'd withdrawn off-road access to their property.

"For everyone," Dave asked, "or just for me?"

"Well, for everyone. I guess. I don't know … No, surely for everyone!"

"Right." Still. Dave had to wonder if he were being completely paranoid, thinking there was a message in there for Dave alone.

"Man, that was a bit of a rough trip," Dave announced, pretty much as soon as he was safely back home in Brisbane.

"Missed me, did you?" Nicholas asked cheekily.

"Yeah, o' course. But to be honest I was glad you and Robin didn't come." Dave groaned a little as he stretched out his shoulders and tried to roll the kinks out of them. "Have to admit I'm pretty knackered."

"Here, then," said Nicholas, "I have the solution." He came over to where Dave was propped against the breakfast bar, and pressed a mug of steaming hot tea into Dave's hands, pressed a kiss to his temple.

Dave grinned at him, still a total sucker for this guy, and happily so. "That'll do it, every time."

Nicholas gave him another kiss for that. "Was it worse than you've already told me?"

"Well, no ... But you know that I like things to go smoothly."

"Ah, but what's the point of having backup plans for your backup plans if you don't use them every now and then?"

Dave grimaced a quibble, though he had to acknowledge the point.

"And I'm sure your clients were more than satisfied. In fact, if I know you, they were downright happy about the whole trip!"

"Well, yeah, I did try to keep the drama off their radar."

"They probably didn't think it was anything more than business as usual, and I know very well you would have kept them safe."

Dave took a couple of mouthfuls of the tea, and then put down the mug so he could instead drag Nicholas close and wrap both arms around his waist. "Trying to talk me out of a good worry, are you?"

Nicholas rested his hands on Dave's shoulders and considered him for a long moment – and then he sighed and sagged a little, though he kept enough distance from Dave that they could talk to each other directly without squinting. "You haven't used the S word, but I know what you're thinking."

"I need to apologise for something ... ?"

That drew a muted laugh. "Not *sorry*, David. Sabotage."

Dave stared at Nicholas, his gut sinking. Stupidly, it made the problem all the more real to finally be voiced. And by Nicholas, too. So much for Dave protecting his husband from the nastier side of life.

"That's what you're thinking, isn't it? The windscreen, the tyres, the water. The landowners withdrawing permission for you to go off-road."

"Yes," Dave at last said a bit hoarsely. "That's what I'm thinking."

"But you don't think that ... Ted Walinski, for instance, is part of it."

"No, I don't think he is. Not that he's not trying in his own way ... Well, he doesn't worry me, not anymore. And maybe the rest isn't really a planned thing, but random. A few different people getting it into their heads to play pranks. Not like a planned campaign, you know?"

Nicholas's hands tightened on Dave's shoulders. "But it could become dangerous. What if you were out there in the middle of nowhere, and someone let all the Cruiser's tyres down?"

"I'd use the pump to refill them."

"And if you couldn't? I mean, what if the inner tubes were damaged?"

"I'd phone Charlie, and ask him to come get me."

"What if –"

"I'd grab the map, the compass, as much water as I could carry, and walk to the nearest station or town. And I'd leave messages every way I could, to let you all know where you could find me."

A silent moment passed, and then Nicholas reluctantly smiled. "I know you have all the answers."

Dave returned the smile, which prompted Nicholas's to become a more genuine thing. "So you don't need to worry about me, right?"

"Not so much about you, no. Although of course I do. As your husband, that's my privilege."

They shared a soppy grin, before Dave prompted, "What else are you worried about, then?"

Nicholas sighed, and pulled away from Dave's embrace. He paced off past the dining table, and then came back again. "What I'm worried about is the waterhole and the butterflies."

"I know," Dave said, making himself sound far more reassuring than he felt. "I know. I'm doing everything I can, Nicholas, I promise –"

"I know you are."

"The trouble is, I know I can't do anything much myself – but with you and Lisa, and Thursday and his lot, I figure we'll make it happen. We'll put it beyond any question of harm."

"But that's the problem," Nicholas replied in deadly calm tones. "It can never be put beyond any question, can it? It can never be entirely protected."

Dave stared at him, and his thoughts took on a desperate tinge. He tried to say something, but his throat was dry, and anyway Nicholas forged on.

"The waterhole exists in such a fragile balance. It wouldn't take much to destroy the habitat, or change it enough so that the butterflies can't adapt. If there are people out there willing to commit sabotage, then it has to occur to them that ... that they could simply make the environmental problems go away. If there's nothing left to protect –"

"But, then, what's the answer?" Dave blurted out. "If we just leave the place be, how long d'you think it will remain hidden?"

"I don't know."

"Sometimes I think someone's gonna spot it one day – from the air, maybe, or some random off-roader is gonna crest that ridge. Other times, I think ... that place is elsewhere ... it's elsewhen. And no one's ever gonna find it. Especially not if I don't risk leading anyone there or leaving a trail to follow."

Despite being a scientist, Nicholas was obviously intensely interested in this notion. "I don't pretend to understand – it's an entirely different way of thinking – but you're saying the waterhole is caught in its own Dreaming."

"Maybe. I just don't know. I wish I did. And anyway, what about the songs ... ?" Dave slumped a bit, and went to sit on the nearest dining chair. "I still need to – Well, no ... maybe I need to let that go. Let the whole thing go. It's not like many people agree with what Charlie did, passing the songs to me."

Nicholas dropped to his knees before Dave, and grabbed onto him hard. "No. No, you mustn't give up on that. It's important. Whoever's causing trouble, they can't make the cultural problems go away, can they?"

He grimaced again. "It's not like there's a whole lot of people who take me seriously."

"But it's still a Dreamtime site."

"But only if ... if the relationship between the land and the people is still alive. And I don't count."

"If the reserve is extended to include the waterhole, that makes it clear enough, and then the Murri will be better able to help protect it."

Dave sighed, and said in a small voice, "I'll just need to find someone – the right someone – to pass the songs to, and –"

"No, don't do that," Nicholas said, shaking him gently. "Not until you really have to. Old man grunter chose you, remember?" He laughed a little under his breath, but continued with quiet sincerity. "I realise you don't believe in the stories and songs in a *literal* way … but there's some part of you that … I don't know. That *feels* them as true. If that makes any kind of sense."

Dave stared at the man in mute wonder.

"Or, um … a part of you that *knows* the necessity. That's probably better. You can sense there's a reason for all this, a good reason – and seeing as it's about us humans being an intrinsic part of the environment, rather than something separate from it, then actually I think it's a bloody excellent reason!"

"Oh," said Dave.

"On top of which," Nicholas said, sailing remorselessly on, "it does you good. It makes you happy. After you've been singing the songs, you look so … utterly peaceful. It's lovely to see. I love being there with you afterwards. You're just so very … *you*."

"Oh," he managed.

"I don't want to give that up for *my* sake, let alone yours," Nicholas added with a laugh. He was about to sit back on his heels, having made his point, but Dave grabbed onto him in turn and leaned his head in close.

"It's the second best thing in my life," he admitted in a mumble that only Nicholas would understand.

Nicholas guffawed. "Second best after the Cruiser, I assume."

"Idiot," said Dave. And they shared a grin, and Nicholas's love and happiness shone bold from his bright eyes – and in that moment Dave felt as if he could take on the whole world and the horse it rode in on as well.

nine

What Dave found frustrating, though, was that there still seemed to be little he could do. He asked Charlie to come to Brisbane for a few days so Dave could talk through the idea of actually lodging a Native Title claim. "It probably wouldn't come to anything, but at least it makes the point."

"Nnn," Charlie replied rather noncommittally.

"That guy I talked to," Dave persisted, "Martin Bandjara. He said he wanted to test the idea, or he'd like to, anyway. And for that they need someone to give it a try, I guess."

"Mmm," said Charlie.

Dave lapsed into silence, having been round and round the matter a number of times, and feeling further than ever from a resolution.

The four of them were lazing about on the back patio while the banana palms rustled soothingly. Charlie had a beer, but the others were on water-and-lime. Robin was curled up on the swing chair with Nicholas, though he didn't look quite as blissful about it as he'd used to.

Nicholas was also fretting over something. Dave watched him patiently, until at last Nicholas stirred himself to ask, "Could I be part of the claim as well? Would that help or hinder, do you think?"

Which was rather unexpected. Charlie didn't react, even with an incoherent murmur. Dave scrunched up his face, and tentatively asked, "Because of the butterflies … ?"

"Well, yes. No. Sort of."

Dave glanced at Charlie again, but he seemed to have zoned out. Or was maybe mulling things over. "Sort of?" Dave prompted.

"I've just been thinking about the story. You know, the Dreamtime story about the waterhole. And I figured … I figured that it's *my* Ancestor who fell from the sky, right?"

No one responded, though Dave was listening hard.

"You know, I flew here, I came by plane … David, you came to meet me, I fell at your feet, and we … Well." Nicholas fell quiet, too.

Dave wondered what to say. But when he realised that Charlie was considering Nicholas thoughtfully, Dave decided to stay quiet at least for now.

After a long while, Charlie said, "You and Davey belong together, mate. You don't need no Dreaming story to tell you that."

"No, but ... it kind of works, doesn't it? He even ... I mean, if Dave's Ancestor is the Barcoo grunter, then he even made the butterflies that brought me back to him."

"It's a nice thought, mate," said Charlie.

"Are you saying ... I can't be part of it?"

"You *are* part of it," Dave insisted.

"I don't think Native Title can be the answer," Charlie finally concluded. "It won't work, whether it's me or Dave or the three of us making the claim. We'd be putting a whole lot of time, effort and money into something that was doomed."

"Oh," said Dave and Nicholas, both sounding rather dejected. "That's rather ... pragmatic of you," Nicholas added.

Charlie shrugged an agreement. A silence stretched.

After a while, Nicholas detached himself from Robin and came over to where Dave was stretched out on a recliner. Dave shifted up onto his side so that Nicholas could settle in behind him, spooning him closely in a comforting hug. Dave closed his eyes, and sank away for a while. This ... *this* was home and hearth and all good things.

"So, Robin ..." Charlie said. "I guess you'll be heading back to England soon."

"Three weeks and five days," Robin replied. "Granddad's coming here for the last ten days, and then we're flying back together."

"It'll be good to see him, that's for sure. Are you looking forward to being home again?"

"I suppose ..."

Dave opened his eyes, though he didn't shift from Nicholas's warm embrace. He asked with careful neutrality, "Are you still thinking about staying here, Robin?"

Charlie chortled appreciatively. "You looking to emigrate, too, mate?"

"I was thinking about ... maybe taking a gap year," Robin replied.

Nicholas had remained quiet and still through all this.

Dave suggested, "It only needs a slight adjustment in your ambitions. Prime Minister of Australia ain't such a bad thing to be."

Robin sniffed. "No ... once I've served my terms in Britain ... *three* terms,

I think ... I might consent to become Governor-General of Australia instead."

Dave and Charlie both had a hearty laugh over this, and Dave asked, "Don't you think we'll be a republic by then?"

"I don't know ..." Robin mused. "What do you think, Charlie?"

"I think we're a pretty independent mob," said Charlie.

"That's true," said Dave.

Nicholas shifted up onto an elbow, as if finally re-engaged by the conversation.

"But there's something to be said for the long-term view," Charlie continued. "I was reading the other day about how the British monarchy has been around for a thousand years. It's one of our longest surviving institutions. That has to mean something."

"Does it?" asked Dave, perhaps almost as astonished as the two Englishmen about where this was going.

"If they were doing such a bad job, they never would have survived this long."

"Right ..." Dave prompted.

"And the current lot, they're a good mob. So, I figured, what we should do, if we want to be a bit more independent, but not throw out all the good stuff ... What we should do is invite Prince Harry to be King of Australia."

Everyone stared at the man, absolutely stunned.

Eventually Nicholas said, "I like the way you think, Charlie. Very lateral!"

Dave let out a laugh, and said, "Yeah, Harry's enough of a larrikin!"

"What's a larrikin?" asked Robin.

"Oh, it means he'd fit right in." And by the time Dave had explained, Charlie had three firm converts to his rather unexpected cause.

Dave had a call from another of the landowners out west of Cunnamulla. By his reckoning he'd heard from all of them now. "Hello, Sandy," Dave said a bit guardedly once the guy had announced himself.

"Heh," said old Sandy under his breath, before launching right into the nub of the matter. "Now, I know some people have been a bit, uh ... uncooperative lately. Not letting you drive off-road and such."

"Well," said Dave. "It's their right. I respect that."

"I know you do. I know you do. So I figured I'd just come right out and say it. We could do with the railroad coming out our way, mate. You get that, I'm sure."

"I do get that," Dave agreed. "Cheap and easy transportation. I understand."

"So you'll understand we have an interest in Reddy Eight finding this iron ore, then."

Dave gusted a sigh. "Mate, I'm not against it myself. I just need to make sure this place is protected. This particular place. It's … unique."

"Yeah, your bloke found his butterflies there."

"Yeah." *The butterflies he named after me*, Dave couldn't quite add. "They're unique, too."

"Hasn't he, like … brought some out and raised them? Like in that aviary up at Kuranda, maybe?"

"He tried a couple of times, years ago now, but it never worked. They didn't survive. And he says it's too tropical up at Kuranda, for a start."

"I'm not saying we shouldn't protect them in the wild," Sandy said all too reasonably, "but don't you think he'd better try again?"

"Yeah. Probably." Dave frowned over that, and wondered why Nicholas hadn't persisted. If they had Charlie or Thursday take care of the butterflies somewhere out there near Cunnamulla, where the climate wasn't all that different …

"Just in case," said Sandy.

"But that's not all, anyway," Dave insisted. He sighed again, and thought twice, but then forced himself to say, "I don't believe in much, mate, but this place – it's sacred. I gotta put that first."

"Yeah, and I get that. I do. I figure …" Sandy paused for a moment, before rushing on. "There's kind of a 'no man's land' out there, isn't there? Somewhere east of Henri Wilson's place, south of the Abo reserve."

"Aboriginal," Dave corrected him.

"I mean it fondly, and I say it to their faces."

"Even so."

"Right, well. South of the Aboriginal reserve, east of Henri's. That kind of area. Am I right?"

Dave tilted his head in a quibble that of course the man wouldn't see. "Close enough."

"It's all right, I'm not gonna do anything about it. Just wanted to be sure I was on the right page."

"Yeah, you are."

"Not that 'page' is the right word. That's kinda vast."

"Look, Sandy, just give me some time, all right? I'm sure you'll get your railway in the end."

"Right, mate. Well, if you or your bloke need anything, let me or the missus know."

"Will do," said Dave. And they said goodbye and hung up.

A moment later – Dave had hardly even turned away from the phone – it rang again. "Yeah," said Dave as he picked it up. "D'you forget something, Sandy?"

There was no response.

But the line wasn't dead, either. There was an uncanny sense of presence. An echo of a breath.

"This is Dave Taylor. Who's that?"

Nothing.

"Right. Hanging up now." He waited a moment, but when there was no response Dave cut off the call and returned the handset. After a moment in which the phone didn't ring again, Dave wandered into the lounge room to find Nicholas tapping away on his laptop.

Nicholas glanced up at him, and then looked again, apparently picking up on Dave's pensive mood. "Are you all right, David?"

"Yeah. Just more pressure. God, it's honestly not that I don't empathise … And then another wrong number. Getting a few of them lately."

Nicholas sat back and crossed his arms over his chest and stared at him. "To be honest, I was trying not to think about this. But they're not wrong numbers, are they?"

It took a moment for Dave to click. "Seriously? You think it's harassment? Along with the … sabotage?"

"I didn't tell you, but when you were away for that week, I got a call almost every single night."

"What!" Dave was furious – at whoever the idiots were, but also a little bit at Nicholas. "You should have said."

"I was going to that first night you were back, but then they didn't call again – or not in the wee hours, anyway – and you already had enough on

414 | The Thousand Smiles of Nicholas Goring

your mind."

"Even so," Dave argued.

Nicholas frowned for a long moment, and then lifted a hand to rub at his forehead. "You know, I think my decision-making has gone a bit pear-shaped lately. Maybe I just haven't been getting enough sleep."

Dave swore under his breath that he could quite cheerfully kill whoever it was who'd been disturbing Nicholas. But at least this gave Dave one thing he could actually do something about. "Right. We're reporting it to Telstra. We can do that much, anyway!"

"No, you're right," said Nicholas, "and of course that's fine by me." His long fingers skittered across the keyboard as he closed whatever he was doing and opened a browser. "Come on, then. We can look up what to do on their website."

The three of them were eating dinner at the table in the family room that evening, with the ABC TV news on in the background providing its quiet litany of gloom, when a story came on about the Reddy Eight mining company. Dave reached for the remote to turn up the volume, and Nicholas glanced a plea to Robin to be quiet for a moment.

"Elvis Reddy, son of Noel Reddy and majority shareholder of new player Reddy Eight, had a surprise encounter today with business rival Leonard Harville," the newsreader said. The story cut to footage of a pair of men in business suits confronting each other with the puffed-up chests and sneering mouths Dave was more used to seeing outside pubs than courtrooms. Dave watched in disbelief as the scuffle became a swirl of colleagues, onlookers and reporters. The younger Reddy was soon yelling, and pointing hard accusations at the somewhat older and cooler Harville. "Just you beeping well wait," was the general tone of it. "I'm onto something beeping *big*." – Harville adjusted his cuffs. "Sure you are." – "Oh, you are going *down* …" The story cut back to the studio. "Stock prices for both companies have remained strong," the newsreader commented, absolutely deadpan, "though Reddy Eight has edged ahead slightly this afternoon."

Dave just gaped for a while as the next story played, until finally he blurted, "*That's* what this is all about?"

Nicholas shrugged a little, though he looked uncomfortable. "What can you expect, really?"

"Dunno," said Dave. "The Quiet Achiever, maybe?" He got up and went to look for Fred Harvey's business card.

"What are you doing?"

"Dunno," he repeated. "Being outraged, I guess." Dave dialled the man's mobile number.

The call was picked up right away. "Harvey here."

"Dave Goring Taylor," he announced.

"Mr Goring Taylor. What can I do for you?" There was an edge in Harvey's voice indicating that actually he could guess.

"*That's* who you work for?" Dave demanded. "*That* tosser?"

"Well. He certainly helps pay the bills."

"And that's all that matters to you, is it?"

"No," said Harvey, with no heat or resentment.

"Did his dad just *give* him the company to see what kind of mess junior would make?"

"No," Harvey repeated in exactly the same tones. "That's really not how any of the Reddy family do business."

Dave took a breath, and found himself lifting a hand to clutch at his forehead just as Nicholas would when trying to cope. "Look. I'm trying to protect this sacred place, these unique butterflies – and this guy you're working for, all it means to him is a chance to score a point in a dick-waving contest."

After a pause, Harvey suggested, "A healthy sense of business competition –"

"Right."

"They're business men, Mr Goring Taylor. They keep score with dollars. Not inches."

Dave sighed. "Well, I guess I knew it was all about money, didn't I?"

"Not just for Mr Reddy," Harvey argued. "It's still money and jobs and infrastructure for the people of Cunnamulla, the Murri, and that whole area."

"Yeah, I know. And it's steel for my next new Land Cruiser."

"Yes, sir." Harvey left a pause. "Does this really change anything, Mr Goring Taylor?"

"No," Dave had to admit. "No, I guess it doesn't." He was just about to

416 | The Thousand Smiles of Nicholas Goring

wind up the call, feeling entirely pathetic, when Harvey asked a question of his own.

"Mr Goring Taylor –"

"For heaven's sake, just call me Dave."

"Thank you. Dave. Have you seen the forecast for the coming rains? It's going to be one hell of a Wet season."

"Right …"

"Is the waterhole near the floodplains?"

Dave huffed a bit, and asked weakly, "Are you trying to trick me into revealing the location?"

"No, sir. I'm just passing on a concern."

"Well. I'll look into that, then."

"Right," they each concluded, before saying goodbye and hanging up.

Dave went back to the table and sat down by Nicholas. Robin had finished his dinner and wandered off somewhere, probably to his room, so Dave just launched right into the topic forever preying on his and Nicholas's minds. "Fred Harvey just said we should look at the forecast for this year's Wet. D'you know about that already?"

Nicholas was reaching for his laptop even as he replied with a frown, "No. Well, I'd heard it was going to be somewhat wetter than usual, but … are you saying he was trying to warn us about something?"

"Sounded like."

"God … All this time we've been fretting about anthropogenic threats, and it may all come down to a natural hazard instead."

Well, that was a new word for Dave, but he got the general gist. Within moments they were looking at a map of the Channel Country, the vast area through which the Georgina River, the Diamantina River and Cooper Creek drained into Lake Eyre. "Kati Thanda," Nicholas corrected Dave, giving the lake its proper Indigenous name.

"Kati Thanda," he agreed. "But the waterhole's hundreds of clicks away from all this, isn't it? A long way south-east of Channel Country."

"Yes …" Nicholas agreed slowly, his fingertips tracing out the waterhole's likely location. They'd at least managed to narrow down the area which contained it. "If it was going to be affected, we'd have weeks of notice. These things don't happen quickly."

"But what would we do in those weeks?"

Nicholas cast him an uneasy glance. "I'm not sure ..."

Dave persisted. "What about the water table, and the pool at the waterhole? Would a heavy Wet affect that?"

"Possibly. Though the water in the pool has remained level no matter what the season when we've visited, so I'm hoping that –"

"But if it floods," Dave persisted. "If it reaches high enough to affect the wattle and the butterflies."

Nicholas blanched, though his long fingers were as nimble as ever, darting about the keyboard and calling up information about the weather forecasts and likely effects. "If it floods, then it would have happened before at regular intervals. Perhaps every hundred years or so; that kind of timescale."

Dave was trying to understand so hard that his head was hurting. "Does that mean the butterflies have survived other floods, though? If there even have been any. Or does it mean the butterflies have only been there since the last flood? In which case they'd be threatened by another one."

Nicholas glanced at him, full of misgivings.

"But, no – they're in the songs, aren't they? So they date back as far as the songs do, which could be thousands of years ... Though I suppose the butterflies could have been added to the songs when they first appeared at the waterhole ... Oh God, I just don't know."

"I don't know, either."

"I've been thinking," Dave continued, "we really should try to create a backup, you know? Transplant some of the wattle, and try to establish the butterflies elsewhere. Maybe there's a sheltered waterhole somewhere on the Aboriginal reserve that they'd let us use."

Nicholas had sat back now, and was watching Dave carefully, with his hands resting cupped in his lap.

"We could fence it off, and there'd be someone there who'd help us take care of them. I know you haven't had much luck in bringing the butterfly eggs and such back here, but the climate wouldn't be so different out there, would it?"

There was a small but very genuine smile on Nicholas's face by now, and his eyes were glowing with affection. Once Dave had finally wound his way to a halt, Nicholas paused for a beat, and then leaned in and quietly teased, "You and your backup plans."

"Is it a good idea, though?"

"Yes. Yes, of course. And if we succeed with one colony, then we should try for more as well. I wonder if I could find someone out there who actually has an aviary …"

"I'll ask Charlie to ask around."

Nicholas's smile had widened, but also turned poignant. "You know … I'm so used to thinking of the waterhole as … well, as *ours*. And the butterflies, too. I almost … I almost didn't want to bring any of the butterflies back here. But we're going to have to share them, aren't we?"

"Yes," Dave solemnly replied, "I think we are. But we've had them to ourselves for years and years, haven't we?"

"So many good memories there … The first time we made love. The first time we kissed properly."

Dave felt his cheeks heating, and other parts of him, too. "I know." He added with a wry grin, "It's not like we have to share *that*."

But Nicholas wasn't ready to laugh about it. "Lazing about, getting to know each other … All those long conversations we had, all those words and thoughts meandering along the riverbeds, diverting into billabongs, flowing out into lakes …"

Dave snorted a chuckle. "That must have been you. My conversational skills are more like a dry old creek bed."

"They are not! And anyway, we found other ways to communicate … other things to learn about each other."

"Oh, is that what we're calling it now?" Dave retorted, his chuckle becoming a laugh.

Nicholas sighed. "I wish we could go out there again, just you and me alone for one last time."

"I know. But we really need to get a surveyor out there, and Lisa said she's gonna come, too, didn't she? And her partner."

"I suppose …"

"And I don't know that I want to give Ted Walinski yet another chance to track us there. We should try to keep control over when and how this happens. Shouldn't we?"

"Yes – but can't we skive off 'real life' for a few days? Don't we deserve that? We could just drop everything and go tomorrow."

Dave frowned, not sure exactly how seriously to take Nicholas. This might be just a verbal whimsy of his, after all. "What about Robin? You're not suggesting we, uh … I dunno, leave him behind with Denise and Vittorio or whatever?"

While it was fairly obvious from Nicholas's defeated expression that he agreed they couldn't abandon Robin even to the care of their best friends, unfortunately Nicholas didn't voice a denial.

"Uncle Nicholas … ?" Robin was standing in the doorway, frozen in the act of bringing a used mug back to the kitchen.

"Oh God," Nicholas groaned – though he sounded more annoyed than apologetic. "I'm sorry, Robin, of course we won't go without you."

"It's all right," Robin replied, stiffly on his dignity. "I know where your priorities lie."

"Well, it's not as if we're going, anyway, so don't worry about it."

"Nicholas …" Dave murmured, wondering at this unusual ungraciousness.

"I'd understand," Robin said. "You can dump me at Denise's, if you want."

Nicholas shifted around on his chair to confront Robin a little more directly. "How can you possibly understand? You're asexual, remember?"

Robin flushed, and came further into the room, clutching at the mug. "I know about *love*, remember? I'm just not into sex."

That dragged a growl out of Nicholas. He sounded almost *agonisingly* frustrated. "I might agree that you know about love, if you didn't always fall for the inaccessible. Me. Lisa. That's not love, it's infatuation."

"Oh right," Robin scoffed. "So it was infatuation you felt for Frank, was it?"

Nicholas sniffed. "Ah, but Frank wasn't so inaccessible as all that."

"Nicholas!" Dave protested, knowing that if Nicholas were thinking clearly he'd be a lot more discreet.

A guilty look glanced off Dave, and then Nicholas continued a little more reasonably, "One day, Robin, someone you care for will be ready, willing and able to return the compliment … and you should at least *try*."

"Sure! And one day, Nicholas, you should *try* with a woman."

The two of them glared daggers at each other.

Dave sighed, and sat back in his chair. "That's enough from both of you," he said.

And maybe they even agreed, for the silence resounded. But Nicholas did nothing more than cross his arms, and Robin just lifted his nose and looked haughty.

"Look," Dave continued. "I have no idea what either of you can say to make this better, so I reckon you're just gonna have to agree to disagree. All right?"

Nothing.

"Isn't that what unconditional love is all about? Not, uh … imposing conditions on each other," Dave finished rather weakly.

Robin stared hard at Nicholas, as if expecting him to make the first move. But Nicholas, despite allegedly being the more mature one of the pair, pressed his mouth into a flat line and looked elsewhere. After another long moment, Robin put the mug down on the kitchen counter rather heavily, and returned to his room.

And Nicholas wouldn't unwind again even for Dave's sake.

ten

It finally happened the very next morning. Dave's world collapsed.

Dave and Vittorio had planned a trip out to the camping store at Enoggera, and Dave figured he'd better take Nicholas and Robin as well, rather than leave them to stew in each other's company. The four of them made a rather subdued group wandering the aisles while Dave advised Vittorio on the Agostini family's camping needs. Each of them were wheeling trolleys, as Dave took the opportunity to collect a few necessaries for himself as he went.

It didn't take long before Robin and his smartphone hung back long enough to lose them, and then at least Nicholas relaxed a little.

"What's happened between you two?" Vittorio asked in his blunt Italian-Australian way.

Nicholas shrugged in reply with a weak wry smile. "Dave will tell you it's the same old same old. We can't agree to disagree."

"You'll be all right," Vittorio concluded.

"Both too stubborn for our own good," Nicholas said.

"You'll work it out."

"I don't know …"

They'd reached the aisle of day packs and hiking packs, which lit Vittorio up like it was Christmas. "So here we have," said Dave, "your basic backpack porn …"

That at least earned him a guffaw from Nicholas and a chuckle from Vittorio. And after Vittorio had found himself the perfect backpack, the three of them wound on through the store, and finally met a marginally more sociable Robin at the registers. A short while later they were in the car park, shifting their purchases into their vehicles. Once that was done, a brief silence stretched.

Vittorio, meaning well, offered, "Robin, do you want to come home with me and help me organise all this? I'm sure Denise would be happy for the company. The girls have been nothing but mischief lately, but they always behave for you."

Robin scowled, though he answered politely enough, "No, thank you, Uncle Vittorio, but please say hello to Denise for me."

"All right, no worries."

Dave shook Vittorio's hand, and conveyed his thanks for the thought with a feeling expression.

He was aware of Nicholas standing a little way behind him, his stance a bit off-kilter. "I wish my father were here," Nicholas commented rather vaguely.

"Not long now," Dave reassured him, checking that the Cruiser's rear door was firmly fastened, and mentally trying to do the maths. Was Richard due to arrive in ten days now, or nine?

"David –" Nicholas was reaching towards him, helplessly too far away.

Dave was already turning towards him, was already starting to fear – when Nicholas seemed to just fold down into a wrecked heap on the ground. For a millisecond, for an eternity, Dave stared in horror.

Then – *"Nicholas!"* – he was crouching at Nicholas's side, hands trying to secure him, gaze desperately trying to find the things he needed to know, the things he needed to do.

Nicholas's hands were at his head, and he let out a wail that seemed all the more stricken for being strangled.

Robin echoed the wail, louder and stronger, and then cried out his name – *"Nicholas!"*

Dave kept one hand on Nicholas – he couldn't not be hanging on – but his other hand was fumbling for his phone.

Vittorio was a step ahead of him. Even in the middle of that moment, Dave didn't forgive himself for that. Vittorio had already found his mobile, dialled 000, was saying, "Ambulance, please. *Immediately.*"

Robin looked like he was about to fall over himself, or fall onto Nicholas – and Vittorio was one step ahead of Dave there, too – Vittorio suddenly slid an arm around Robin's waist to secure him and spun around with his momentum to keep him clear. All the while, Vittorio was calmly explaining the situation, giving Nicholas's name, and even that of his neurologist.

Dave's attention returned to the only place it belonged.

Nicholas moaned miserably, clutching at his head, and then one eye peered up at Dave through his fingers, blearily, warily.

"Help's on the way," Dave reassured him. "Hang on, all right? Help is on the way."

Nicholas tried to say something, maybe only Dave's name, maybe something important, and Dave tried desperately to read it in his eyes instead. When he couldn't, Dave resorted to the only words he knew to say.

"Hang in there, Nicholas. Stay with me, all right? Help will be here very soon, I promise."

There was the sound of running feet as others gathered, urgent questions, Robin's distraught sobs and pleas, and above all the sound of Vittorio's calm commanding voice. Thank God for Vittorio. It turned out that Dave wasn't much use after all, so thank God for Vittorio.

Nicholas's eyelids drooped a little, and maybe he wanted to escape the pain, but Dave was determined to keep him awake and aware. "Stay with me, Nicholas, don't leave me, all right?"

Dave eased Nicholas into a more comfortable position, cradling him gently, supporting his poor head, making sure he could breathe.

"I know it hurts. I know it hurts, but I love you," Dave said. "I love you so much, I know you know that, I know you love me, oh God I know it hurts but God please don't leave me …"

Nicholas was looking up at him rather piteously – and then, horribly, his expression slid away and he became blank. Not even peaceful; just blank.

"Please don't leave me, *please* – I'll do *anything* –"

There were sirens.

"Help's coming. D'you hear that? Help's coming. Hang on, Nicholas. Hang onto me, hang on for me. *Please*."

Then Dave himself had to let go. Firm hands pried Nicholas away from him, and he had to let go. He could be brave enough to do that much, at least. "Aneurysm," he blurted, and was about to say more –

"We've been briefed, sir." The medics were careful but brisk. They established Nicholas was alive. They needed to get him to hospital. That was all. Dave crouched there, watching, but within moments Nicholas was bundled neatly onto a gurney, oxygen mask over his face, eyes closed peacefully as if there were no pain any more and there never had been … Dave's heart wrenched in his chest.

"Sir?" one of the medics asked as they gently hefted Nicholas into the ambulance.

"I'm his husband," Dave said clearly and strongly.

"Come with us, then."

He climbed aboard and sat where they showed him. He rested a hand on

Nicholas's shoulder.

At the last moment he thought to look back out through the doors – before they closed he saw Robin sagging in Vittorio's arms, crying his eyes out – and above that was – oddly – Vittorio's smile shining confidently, almost proudly, as if knowing all would be well.

"All will be well," Dave murmured to Nicholas, who surely couldn't hear him. "All will be well," he repeated, knowing that it mattered anyway. "Nicholas – husband – all will be well. I promise."

The ambulance ride was relatively quiet, oddly insulated as they were from the sirens. One of the medics drove with a reassuring economy of effort, while the other sat in the back, monitoring Nicholas, and relaying information to the hospital, occasionally asking Dave questions, all of which he knew the answer to, thank God. He soon discovered that Dr Williams, Nicholas's consulting neurologist, was on a shift at the hospital, and he'd be making ready to receive him. If emergency surgery was required, then it would be someone else undertaking it – but informed by the man Nicholas had chosen and talked with at length.

"Tell him thank you, if you can," Dave asked, as at least one knot of the thousand in his gut relaxed a little.

"Will do," was the medic's reply.

"We're almost there," the driver added.

"Thank you," Dave said again. If this was going to happen, then – short of Nicholas actually having been in the hospital at the time he collapsed – it was happening in almost the best way it could, with the best chances of them all pulling him through. Dave didn't like the fact that Nicholas was unconscious, but at least that meant he wasn't suffering. Dave gently firmed his hold on Nicholas's shoulder, then bent over to press a kiss to that pale forehead, looking bare now with most of the thick dark hair swept off to one side. This was probably the quietest moment they'd have together for some while now. "Nicholas," he whispered – and then he ran out of words, no longer in that urgent place he'd been only moments before, where he'd blurted out any reassuring nonsense or urgent plea that crossed his mind. Dave sighed. "Nicholas …"

Minutes later, an eternity later, they were at the hospital, and Nicholas was being slid out of the ambulance on his gurney – and chaos erupted, though it probably only seemed like chaos because Dave wasn't initiated into the whys and wherefores of what was happening. There was a lot of clipped talk back and forth, cold clinical talk about the man he loved, and at some point in some corridor Dave was held back from following any further. He watched yearningly, drinking in every moment in which he could see his husband, until at last too soon Nicholas was gone, and the nurse who'd held Dave's arm finally released him with a pat, and said, "He's in good hands, Mr Taylor, the very best – and for you, for you there are forms to complete, so very many forms."

Dave dragged his gaze away from the empty corridor, the closed door, and found that he could, after all, summon a weak kind of smile. "Oh good," he responded a bit hollowly.

And the nurse chuckled appreciatively under his breath and led Dave away.

He'd hardly even worked his way through the first two bits of paperwork before Denise, Vittorio and Robin were there. Dave stood, letting everything fall away, and he walked forward into an intense group hug. They all just held each other for a long hard moment, heads tucked in together – but then of course the others wanted news, they needed to know, so they each stepped back a little, just a little, except Robin who clung like a limpet to Dave's side. Dave kept him there with a comforting arm around his shoulders.

"What's happening?" asked Denise. "Is he – ?"

"He's being diagnosed," Dave said, saving her from saying any other kind of D word. "He's in Intensive Care. Dr Williams is with him. There's no visitors allowed, of course."

She looked gobsmacked. "Diagnosed? Don't they *know*? Isn't it *obvious*?"

"Well, no. They have to be sure. No point in doing brain surgery if it turns out to be a migraine."

Denise turned to Vittorio. "But you said –"

Dave didn't want to hear that either. "I know. We all saw it. Looked like a – like a stroke." He swallowed hard over that bitter word. "But when a CT scan confirms that, and confirms the location – then it'll be surgery of one sort or another."

The four of them fell silent contemplating this enormity.

Finally Denise said briskly, "Well, we're here for as long as it takes, all right? Whatever you or Nicholas need, we're here for you."

"Thanks, that's great. That's really great. But it's gonna take a while, and there won't be much to do other than wait."

"That's all right." She left a beat. "They were ... hopeful, right?"

"I dunno. No one's said much yet." Dave looked around at the others, and realised he was probably going to end up reassuring them more than being reassured. "Look, I don't like that he was unconscious even in the ambulance, but we got him here quickly – thanks to Vittorio – and nothing worse happened. As far as I know, there's been no complications. So let's go with 'cautiously optimistic', yeah? That's how his doctor always put it. If we got him here in time – which we did – we could be cautiously optimistic."

Robin sagged heavily against Dave and muttered, "It's my fault, though, isn't it, it's all my fault."

"No," they soothed. "No, of course not." And Dave asked, "Why would you even think that?"

"Because, you know, I was always arguing with him about – well, you know what. I was always – making him mad."

"It is *not* your fault, Robin. You don't even need to think about going there. We always knew that if this was gonna happen, it was gonna happen, no matter where we were or what was going on."

"I guess," Robin whispered doubtingly.

"I'm just thanking God we weren't out at the waterhole or somewhere, a hundred clicks from help."

Robin nodded, though he lacked conviction.

"What about his family?" asked Vittorio. "When are you going to call them?"

"It's the middle of the night in England. At first I thought I'd give it a couple of hours, cos maybe we'll have some news by then. But then I figured Richard might want to catch the first flight out in the morning, and we should give them as much notice as possible." Dave tightened his hold on Robin for a moment. "What d'you reckon? Do you think your grandfather will want to drop everything and come over right away?"

"Yes." Robin was still wide-eyed and tear-stained, but seemed marginally more comforted.

"Good. Nicholas will like that, too. So we'll do what we can to make that happen." Dave took a breath. What hadn't he thought of yet? There were probably a thousand things, and he wanted to get things sorted as much as he could so that once Nicholas was back in the wards, Dave would be free to just be with him. "Oh. Where are Zoe and Bethan?" he asked.

"At my mother's," Vittorio replied in easy tones. "She loves having them all to herself, so don't worry about them, Dave. You don't have to worry about anything other than you and Nicholas, all right?"

Dave looked at him feelingly. Gratefully. "All right. And please say thanks to Maria for me."

Denise took Robin off to the cafeteria to fetch them all drinks, and Dave took the opportunity to call Simon. It was midday in Australia, which meant it would be three in the morning in England. Simon's habit was to always be up by six, but early starts wouldn't make a three a.m. phone call any easier to deal with. Still, Dave figured they'd expect him to call, under the circumstances.

Dave felt he had himself pretty much together, and he tried to make the phone call as brief, calm and informative as it needed to be. He still must have sounded shaken, though, because Simon ended up reassuring him. "You've done everything we could have wanted for Nicholas, and more besides. Thank you, David."

"Well, there's no call to be thanking me yet. If there ever will be!"

Simon took a breath, as if about to say something before changing his mind. After a moment he said, "I'll go and tell Richard myself now, David, then I'll call you or text you with the details. I'm sure you're right: he'll want to be there with Nicholas just as soon as he can."

"No worries. One of us will come pick him up at the airport. If I'm needed here, it'll be Denise or Vittorio, all right? Just let us know when."

"Oh," said Simon, "and what about Robin? Is Robin all right?"

"Yeah, as much as can be expected. Um … he and Nicholas had been disagreeing about something – I mean, not when it happened, but over the past few days – so Robin's a bit upset about that. Otherwise, he's coping."

"Good. Please give him our love – give everyone our love – and reassure Robin and Nicholas that Richard will be there just as soon as he can."

"No worries," said Dave. And with that they said their farewells and hung up.

Dave took a long breath and tucked the phone away in his pocket. Then he sat back down to do some more paperwork – though he suspected most of it was just a ploy to distract him and keep him out of the way. Although that was proved to be the cynical view when the nurse came to fetch the first completed form, quickly reading through it and verbally double-checking that Nicholas hadn't eaten anything since an early breakfast.

Dave was through the third form and on to the fourth before he thought to ask. "Vittorio."

"Mmm?"

"Why were you smiling? I mean, when we were in the ambulance about to leave. I looked out and you were smiling."

"It's not that I wasn't unhappy about Nicholas," Vittorio began.

"No, I know that." Dave looked at him. "I didn't take it the wrong way. It just made me wonder."

"Well," said Vittorio, settling down into his seat and even now faintly echoing the smile. "I was just remembering how you used to go bright red, like a tomato, every time you called Nicholas your husband or said you were his. So much has changed since then, Dave. So much has changed, and for the better."

Dave nodded, and bent his head over the paperwork again. But he couldn't quite focus on the words or the lines. He frowned over them some more, and tried it without his glasses, but it was hopeless. He put it aside for now.

After a while, in a very small voice, he admitted, "I'd give anything to go back to this morning, and keep things exactly the way they were."

Vittorio nodded, too, and reached for a moment to grasp his hand. "I know, Dave. We all would."

Dr Williams appeared soon after Denise and Robin returned with polystyrene cups of coffee and tea, and bottles of water. Dave stood to meet the neurologist and shake his hand. "Is he all right?" Dave blurted, not bothering with the social niceties.

The slightest pause – which could signify anything – before Dr Williams replied, "There's been no change, no worsening of his condition. May I speak freely?" he asked, with a tactful glance at the others.

"They're family," Dave said. Though he was glad enough when Denise went to put an arm around Robin's shoulders.

"We've done a CT scan, and there has been quite a bleed, I'm afraid, but it's exactly where we'd expect it based on his history. It's as accessible as these things can be, and we've already relieved some of the pressure. But Nicholas is still unconscious, David." And Williams waited for a response.

Dave nodded curtly to indicate his understanding. He knew that Nicholas's chances would have been far better if he'd remained conscious.

"We have one of the best neurosurgeons available – and I mean one of the best in the country, not just in Brisbane. She and I have consulted at length, and with other specialists, and we've decided that early surgery is called for under the circumstances. If he were conscious, we'd wait for twenty-four hours to allow for the swelling to subside. But, in fact, Nicholas is being prepared for surgery now."

Dave nodded again, unable to trust his voice. Though he wanted to know –

"We've decided on clipping," Dr Williams continued, as if he knew exactly what Dave was thinking.

That meant a craniotomy. Brain surgery. Dave swayed a little, but Vittorio was there at his elbow.

"As you know, it's a more invasive method than coiling, but there are also lower rates of recurrence and re-bleeding."

Dave managed to say, "I know." What the doctor was tactfully not spelling out was that there were higher risks from the operation itself with clipping, though the long-term effects were better than with coiling. If Nicholas came through this, then he'd be best placed for a good recovery and less danger of any future ruptures. "I understand," Dave offered.

"Of course Nicholas talked through the options with me at some length, so he knew what he'd be facing. I feel confident he'd understand our decision."

"No, that's fine," Dave said, though his throat felt like it was jammed up badly. "Shouldn't you be with him?"

"Yes, I'll be there throughout. But do you have any questions?"

"How long?"

"The operation might take up to six hours, David. If there's anything to report I'll let you know, but I'm afraid you'll have rather a wait."

"That's all right," he said roughly. "I have to be here."

"Nicholas will be glad of it," Dr Williams reassured him. And then, with a kind nod and a half-smile for them all, he turned and left.

Dave sat down.

The others sat down, too, and were silent – though Dave suspected that was because they knew a hell of a lot less than Dave did about exactly what was happening and what the ramifications were. Even if Nicholas survived the operation and the next couple of days, there was a good chance he'd suffer some loss of function, whether physical or mental. There was a good chance he'd change in some ways. Though of course he'd still be Dave's husband, and Dave his, so the fundamental things would remain regardless.

And Nicholas hadn't been scared in those last moments. He'd known what was happening, and Dave had hated the way Nicholas had gone kind of blank, but he wasn't scared. He'd peered up at Dave quite calmly, all things considered.

"He wasn't scared," Dave said, conscious for once of thinking out loud.

"Of course not," said Denise. "And you know what? It'll be all right."

"Will it?" he asked, wondering how she could possibly know that.

"Whatever happens, it'll be all right, Davey. You've both been so wise. No unfinished business, that's the secret. Nicholas was always about seizing the day – and what with you being you, Dave, you both lived your lives to the full."

"Me being me?" he queried.

"You being such an obliging bloke," she said with a cheerful wink. "No unfinished business. Either way, that works for you."

"Either way," he echoed, unwanted images flickering through his head of what might well be his bittersweet future. Bitter with loss, sweet with memories. "Well," Dave said, conscious not only of himself but of Robin sitting beside him. "Let's not go there just yet. There's every reason to think Nicholas will be fine. Cautiously optimistic, remember?"

"Oh, absolutely," Denise and Vittorio agreed. "Cautiously optimistic, it is!"

Dave called Simon back – and then spoke to Richard about the surgery. They both agreed it was a good decision, and reassured each other it would all work out well. Then Simon came back on the line with details of when Richard's flight would arrive, early the following evening, Australian time.

Afterwards, Dave called Charlie and broke the news. Charlie was silent for long moments, and Dave kept him company throughout. And then Charlie announced, "I'll be there tomorrow, mate."

"Of course," Dave replied. "I'm guessing I'll be here at the hospital, but if you go to the house first, you've still got the keys, right?"

"Right." Charlie seemed preoccupied with something, which was hardly surprising, so after Charlie asked Dave to call back with any significant news and Dave agreed, they ended the call.

And then all Dave had to do was sit back down and wait. Doing nothing could be the hardest thing of all.

Robin soon distracted himself with his phone, putting his earbuds in to listen to his music while browsing the net and tweeting to his friends. He seemed to have friends globally, because no matter what time it was he always had someone to exchange messages with.

Whether deliberately or not, Vittorio also took the opportunity to slip down more comfortably on the low couch and doze off with his head back, peacefully snoring. Denise and Dave shared a wry look.

"What should we do with them?" Dave quietly asked. "I mean, if it's gonna be six hours. If I'm remembering right, it'll be at least four. Should we send Vittorio and Robin off to Maria's as well? No point in everyone hanging around if they don't need to."

"Let's play that by ear. See how they go. I'm sure they'd rather be here if they can, and we can always get them to run errands if they look like going stir-crazy."

"Errands?" Dave asked, feeling absolutely blank.

Denise huffed a laugh. "Fetching phone chargers for you and Robin, for a start!"

"Good thinking."

"And we will have to eat at some point. I know you'll tell me you don't feel like it," she added, overriding his protest, "but you have to keep your strength up for later, for when Nicholas needs you."

Dave shifted forward on his seat so as to talk to her more confidentially, and Denise shifted likewise. "Look, I have to tell you how great Vittorio was. I know you know that already, but …"

She gave him a soft grin. "Always good to hear it again."

"And it turns out I was useless," Dave continued even as he rolled his eyes in impatience at his own self-pity. "If it wasn't for Vittorio phoning for the ambulance –"

"You'd have done it if you had to, of course you would. But you didn't have to. You took care of Nicholas instead."

Even so. Dave had expected more of himself. Richard and Simon and the rest of Nicholas's family had expected more from him, too.

"You've done your bit," Denise added in bolstering tones, "and chances are good you'll have more of that to do."

"What's my bit, then?"

"Making him happy. Nicholas has been living the dream these past seven years, that's been perfectly obvious. That's what counts. Not who was first to dial triple zero."

Dave sighed, and dropped his head, and thought for a long moment. But then, he'd never hidden anything from his oldest friend. "Denny. Chances are I'll lose him. You know that, right? I'm hoping for the best. But I faced this a long time ago. Chances are he won't come back from this."

Denise leant forward and wrapped her arms around his shoulders, tucked her head in close to his. "I know, Davey. I know, my darling. I've done my homework, too. But whatever happens, we'll deal with it, all right? You won't be alone, no matter what."

"I know," he whispered, scarily close to tears.

"And you'll always know you did everything you possibly could. You loved him as thoroughly as he ever wished for. No one in the world can ask more from you than that."

"Denny …"

She heard or maybe felt the tremor, and withdrew a little to look at him directly. "But we need to be brave for now, all right, Davey love? For Robin's sake, if nothing else. We need to go with 'cautiously optimistic'."

"I know." He nodded, and let a shudder run through him, and then he was fine again. Or fine enough. Like Denise said, he'd deal with it. He'd been preparing to do that for seven years now.

eleven

After an eternity – Vittorio told Dave later that it had been just under five hours – Dr Williams finally appeared and walked towards them with a pleasantly neutral expression. Dave stood, cold with dread, hot with hope. The others stood beside him, Robin clinging to one arm and Denise holding his other hand, with Vittorio bracing them both up. Dave nodded wordlessly at the doctor in a greeting, a query, an affirmation. *It's okay, I'm ready. Whatever it is, I'm ready.*

Dr Williams looked at them all with a friendly glance, and then at last said, "Nicholas has come through the operation very well."

They all sighed and sagged in relief.

"*But,*" Dr Williams added, "we're not out of the woods yet."

Dave nodded again, indicating that he should continue.

"The clipping was successful, and we were able to remove all the excess fluid. There was no sign of any other irregularity. Nicholas is breathing well on his own; in fact, all his vitals are quite acceptable. He's stronger than he looks," Williams added with a slight smile.

"Yes," Dave managed to say. He remembered his own satisfaction with that discovery, so many years ago.

"The next twenty-four hours will be crucial. To be honest, the next three or four weeks will bring plenty of challenges. But for now, let's concentrate on this one day at a time."

"Yes."

"We're going to maintain an induced coma overnight, to enable him to rest, to assist in reducing the swelling. In the morning, if Nicholas seems in as good a state as he is now – and certainly if there's been any improvement – then we'll slowly bring him around."

They all looked at each other, on a sudden surge of hope.

"I must warn you, though," Williams continued in heavy tones, "not to expect too much. We won't be able to assess for a while if there's been any long-term damage and, even if there hasn't, Nicholas will probably seem quite dazed and slow to respond. He will probably be confused at where he finds himself, even though he's anticipated this for years. Don't be too disheartened. And I know I can rely on you all to respond kindly and calmly."

Dave's heart thudded urgently. "Does that mean we can see him?"

"David, I want you to come through to the ICU and sit with him overnight. Will you do that?"

He frowned, wondering why there was even a question. "Yes, of course."

"I'm afraid I can only have one of you through there, but I think it's important. I can't cite any empirical evidence, but to have you sitting with him, holding his hand, talking to him – in my view, it can only aid his recovery."

Dave blanched. "*Talk* to him?"

Denise tightened her grip on his hand. "You'll know what to say, mate."

"No, I, uh … Words were never my strong suit, you know?"

"You're underestimating yourself," Denise advised.

"Even your presence will be beneficial, David," Dr Williams said, "but your voice as well would be even more so."

Robin pushed close to murmur, "You can tell him something from me, Uncle David. You can tell him how much I love him, and you can tell him I'm sorry for arguing with him all the time."

Dave looked at Robin directly. "Yeah, I'll tell him that. And you know he'd want me to tell you it's okay, and he loves you, and he's sorry, too, right?"

"Yeah, I know …"

"Good," the doctor replied, rather more briskly. "Have you eaten at all, David?"

"Not really."

"Well, let your family take you up to the cafeteria for a sandwich and a juice to see you through, and then come to the ICU. I'll meet you there."

Denise insisted that she'd stay in the waiting area overnight, just in case Dave needed her for anything – "Anything at all." After some verbal rambling among them all, it was agreed that Vittorio would take Robin and go to his mother's to join her and the girls. Robin veered wildly between relief at escaping the hospital for a while and guilt at leaving Nicholas, but the others pointed out to him at length that he wouldn't be able to see Nicholas until later the next morning even in the best case scenario, and he finally allowed himself to be persuaded.

Eventually Vittorio and Robin left, after hugging Dave warmly, and then

Denise accompanied him up to the ICU. Dave introduced himself to the nurse at the station, with Denise hanging onto his hand as if unwilling to let him go.

The nurse welcomed Dave with a smile. "I can take you to Mr Goring Taylor now. Dr Williams is already with him." Though she cast a doubting glance at Denise.

"I promise I won't cross the threshold if you'll let me take a peek," Denise said. "I just want to see for myself he's still with us, yeah?"

Dave backed this up with a hopeful expression, suddenly realising that he would actually appreciate having Denise there. God only knew whether Denise had this in mind as well, but it occurred to Dave that he might find the initial sight of a post-op Nicholas rather shocking. Denise could shore him up through that, and from then on he reckoned he'd be fine. He thought he could cope with anything, just so long as he could get his bearings first.

The nurse only took a moment to agree, and then beckoned them down the ward. It seemed that each patient was in their own separate room, though the walls along the main corridor were all glass, presumably so the nursing staff could easily keep an eye on everyone. Part of Dave relaxed at the thought that whatever kind of one-sided conversation he had with Nicholas that night wouldn't be overheard – and it was probably only fair on the other patients that they didn't need to suffer through his illiterate ramblings on top of everything else.

And then they were there. The nurse indicated a particular doorway, and Denise came to a halt just outside – and Dave did, too, clinging as hard to her hand as ever she'd clung to him.

Nicholas lay in a wide hospital bed, on his back and neatly arranged – far more neatly than he slept normally – with the bed propping his head and torso up at an angle. An oxygen mask covered much of his face, and tubes ran into or out of his left hand. A drip was, presumably, providing nutrition, which was surely a good sign. Dave braced himself to look further – and saw a pristine bandage wrapped around Nicholas's head, with a tumble of dark hair poking out the top. The area around Nicholas's eyes seemed a little puffy, a little bruised. But that was it. All right, Dave probably didn't need to fear witnessing anything truly horrific, and anyway he would bear even that if he had to. It wasn't that Dave didn't know something about anatomy and biology.

There were monitors and other machines to either side of the bed, and Dr Williams was carefully considering one and taking notes on a clipboard. He finally looked up and said, "Come in, David. And Denise, isn't it? You can come in for a moment, too, if you wish. I hope you'll find Nicholas's condition reassuring."

"Yes," she said.

"He's pale," Dave blurted. And it was true. Under Nicholas's usual softly-burnished tan, he seemed utterly white. "Has he – Did he – lose a lot of blood or something?"

"Not so much that we had to give him a transfusion. The fluid –" Williams tapped his pen against the drip bag – "will not only keep him hydrated and nourished but also help him replenish his own stocks, as it were."

"He looks fine, all things considered," was Denise's verdict.

Dave was more hesitant. "Dunno. He looks … tired." Perhaps it took a husband's scrutiny to see that while Nicholas appeared to be resting peacefully, he still looked drawn as if having been through an ordeal. Which he had, after all.

"Are you going to be all right?" Denise asked Dave, obviously concerned.

"Of course I am. Hanging out with Nicholas … What else should I be doing?"

She grinned at him, and pressed a rare kiss to his cheek. "You're such a good bloke, Dave." Then she let him go. "Well. You know where I'll be if you need me. For anything, all right?"

"Anything at all," he agreed. And he managed to press a kiss to her cheek, too, before they parted.

Soon enough, Dave was sitting at Nicholas's bedside, and he was carefully shaping his own hand around Nicholas's, trying not to jar him or startle him. Dr Williams had beat a tactful retreat, and while the door to the room was open, Dave was pretty much alone with Nicholas. Still, it took him forever to find his voice.

"Hey, Nicholas," he finally murmured roughly, softly. "Hey, it's me. Dave – David. I guess – I guess if you can hear me, then you just heard Dr Williams telling me all over again to talk to you. Which is probably, like, the last thing you want, really. You probably just want to sleep quietly, don't you? So I'm not gonna keep this up all night, but I'll be here regardless, all right? I'll be here with you."

Dave sighed. "I've missed you. I've missed working things out with you. Isn't that crazy? I kept thinking, oh, if only I could talk to Nicholas about Nicholas being – well, being in surgery, for instance. Nicholas would have the right ideas about what to do. You know, about you. Being in surgery … Oh never mind, I don't even know what I was thinking, really."

A pause stretched into a silence. Surely he wasn't done already? Nah, he could manage more than that. He could at least get the easy stuff out of the way. "Um, so Robin wanted me to tell you how much he loves you, and he's sorry. I told him you loved him, and you were sorry, too. I know you wouldn't have wanted this happening while you and he were disagreeing, but I also know you've already forgiven each other and all that, so let's consider that sorted, yeah? And then I'll just need to convince Robin it's okay. I'm sure he'll see that once he's over the shock.

"Oh, and your father is on his way. He'll be on a plane already. I called Simon, and they were going to make sure Richard would be on the first possible flight. So you'll have your wish. D'you remember saying you wanted to see him? Right before all this happened. I guess maybe you felt it coming, did you? Anyway, he'll be here tomorrow evening. They're going to wake you up tomorrow morning, and you'll be able to see me and Robin, and then Richard will be here. I know that'll make you happy.

"I don't know if they'll let Denise and Vittorio in, not while you're still in the ICU, but they've been here all day with me. Denise is still here. She's going to sleep on the couch in the waiting room so she'll be here if we need her. I know you know they love you. They love you like family. You have to –"

Dave looked at his husband, the dark eyelashes casting a long shadow down those pale cheekbones. He'd have loved to reach up and brush fingertips across those plump pink lips, but didn't trust himself to be gentle enough. Perhaps it was only in his imagination – he should have checked with Dr Williams – but Dave thought any touch might reverberate through Nicholas and hurt him. When his very brain was tender, it seemed that any sensation at all would be too much.

Well, instead he could cradle Nicholas's hand, and keep talking, he supposed. Not that he could remember what he'd been going on about. "What else is there to talk about? God, it seems like forever ago, but it was only this morning when we were talking for real, and you were answering back. And I've missed you since then, I've missed you so much.

"But that's all right. I don't want you feeling bad about that. I guess you'll be in here for a few weeks, and of course I'll come visit you every day, but the nights are going to be so long without you, that bed of ours will feel so empty."

Dave made himself stop and regroup. "I should be talking about happier things. I should be giving you reasons to come back to me. If you need reasons."

And then he frowned over that for a while. Nicholas slept quietly, and the monitors hummed along. Dave did some hard thinking.

"Nicholas," he eventually said. "You once told me ... It's a long time ago now, but it really struck me. Back when we were first together, it must have been, out at the waterhole. You once said that ... that under some circumstances ... you'd prefer to die."

Dave sighed, and let that sit between them.

"And, you know ... it's not like I don't understand. I really do, actually. If it were me, in some situations I'd be hoping that you – or Denise – would be brave enough to pull the plug. So, anyway, if that's what I'm meant to be talking to you about ... Is it? I don't know. Maybe Dr Williams even ... maybe he means for this to be me saying a proper goodbye to you. D'you think?"

Dave traced a careful fingertip along the back of Nicholas's hand, from each of the four knuckles to his wrist and back again. "Can you tell? From the inside, I mean. Can you tell how things are going to be? What you've lost and what you've kept." He took a breath, staring down at that beloved hand. "If you can tell already, and if you're sure it'll be unbearable for you ... then I can be brave enough to let you go. I can. It'll be the hardest thing ever, but I'll do it. All right?"

Dave risked a glance up at that beautiful face, and wondered if he was imagining that Nicholas looked as if he were listening. Dave cleared his throat, and tried to continue – but couldn't until he'd dropped his gaze to Nicholas's hand again. "If you want to slip away ... or if you want to stay asleep so long they give up on you ... then I'll understand. I promise. I want what's best for you."

He let that sit between them, too. He wanted Nicholas to know – if indeed he was hearing any of this – that Dave was serious.

But then he took a deep breath and said, "If you want to stay, though, under any conditions at all, then God I'd give anything for that. *Anything*. I don't care, d'you hear? If you're not entirely the same man you used to be – I don't care. You'll always be Nicholas. You'll always be my husband. And I'll always want you in my life. I *promise*. No matter what."

Dave took off his glasses and put his head down then; he rested his forehead lightly against their joined hands, and perhaps he got a little more than damp-eyed for a while.

Finally, though, Dave found the wherewithal to lift his head and look lovingly at Nicholas, and even crack a wavering kind of smile. "Anyway, don't you remember? We have opals to find, and butterflies, too, and sunsets to watch. We've got family and friends to love, and people to share the Outback with, and our godchildren to have fun with and learn from – and then hand back at the end of the day. We've got each other to take care of, and love – I love you so much, you know – and oh God, there's plenty of sex to have, too. Or hey, there's plenty of kissing and cuddling to be done, even if … even if we can't –" He didn't follow that thought to its logical conclusion, for fear of Nicholas discovering another reason to slip away.

"And there's songs to be sung, and stories to be told, and there always will be. There's so much life we've yet to live, Nicholas. I mean, don't come back to me unless you really want to, but … d'you remember Monica Baldry made up that rap song about us?" And Dave softly sang, "*Nick is his man till death do us part; They got two bodies, one soul, they got one heart.* Wasn't that cool? That was just about the most perfect trip … And there'll be more like that, I reckon. I'd love to share them with you."

Dave soon found himself spinning a yarn about another awesome trip they might take, and all the adventures they might have, the wonders they might see. And then there was another one, and another, each more brilliant than the last, and there were beautiful butterflies to be found and there was sex to be had under the myriad stars, and the marvels of salt lakes and billabongs and cave paintings to visit. Dave talked himself into a stupor, until at last he couldn't help but lay his head down beside his hand joined to Nicholas's … and in his dreams they were holding hands, and they took flight together into a sky as beautiful as an opal, and they soared.

Dave woke confused and bleary with a crick in his neck and something buzzing that shouldn't be. A moment later he realised the latter was his phone, which he'd switched to silent and vibrate, before stuffing it into his jeans pocket.

He carefully lifted his head, and turned a hopeful gaze on Nicholas. There seemed little change, though maybe Nicholas wasn't quite as pale as Dave had expected, maybe he was a little less puffy. A harder look made him think he might be imagining it, but his first impression had been a surprise. Nicholas was still asleep, was still looking untroubled. At least, Dave figured, he wasn't in pain, and that wasn't such a bad bottom line.

His phone started buzzing again, so he hauled it out – glancing towards the corridor a tad guiltily, though there were no witnesses, or none that were conscious, and anyway he'd wanted to be available if Denise or Simon needed him. Dave answered the call – "H'lo" – without checking the display.

"Davey, it's Charlie."

"H'lo, Charlie." Dave looked around at the window, and judged from the paling darkness that it was almost dawn. "Always the early bird, you," he said fondly.

"How is he, mate?"

Dave looked his husband again. "Still asleep. I was, too. Um, he looks kinda the same as last night. At first I thought there's a bit more colour to him, but maybe that's wishful thinking."

"Okay, good. So he's hanging in there."

"Yeah. I guess they'd – they'd have woken me, wouldn't they? If there was anything to tell me. I must have been out of it for two or three hours."

"I've got a song for him, all right, mate? A healing song."

The light outside warmed a little.

"Davey?"

"Yeah, I'm here. Yeah, okay. That's good."

"It's as close as I can tell to his Dreaming. Robin?" Charlie asked. "What do I do with this now?"

"What?" Dave asked, still struggling to wake up properly. "You're at Maria's, Charlie?"

441

"Nah, I've just got Robin on the other line. It's a convention call, or something. Hang on a sec."

"*Conference* call, Charlie," came Robin's voice. "Morning, Uncle David. Did you tell Nicholas for me?"

"Yeah, I told him, mate," Dave gently replied.

"Good." Then Robin went through a few instructions for Charlie about swiping and tapping and such, all of which was Greek to Dave who still had the old-fashioned kind of keyboard phone.

Not too long after, an Aboriginal chant began in Dave's ear, accompanied by the percussive beat of clapsticks. It was a mesmerising sound, and while it felt changeless it was also strangely hopeful. The same long refrain repeated again and then again – or maybe Charlie just had it on a loop – and in any case it felt oddly familiar to Dave. Before he'd even heard it through once he was already humming along, and after a while he held the phone at a slight distance so perhaps Nicholas could hear something of it, too. Dave began quietly chanting. He didn't understand the words, but he recognised the sort of sounds they made, the vowels and the consonants, and he could copy that well enough.

After a time, Robin said, "Uncle David? If I talk Charlie through sending you the sound file, can you play it to Nicholas, do you think?"

"I guess," Dave replied. "But he's hearing it now, and I'm singing it to him."

"That's enough," said Charlie. "That's everything he needs."

It was fully light outside when Dr Williams appeared not long after, walking in to find Dave chanting softly to Nicholas, trying to sound both soothing and encouraging – though he stopped abruptly as soon as he realised they had company.

The doctor smiled, and said, "That sounded nice."

"It's a healing song, apparently. Something to do with Nicholas's Dreaming. I think he has Butterfly Dreaming."

"Excellent." The doctor checked the various machines and charts, and studied Nicholas himself in between times. Then he made some notes on his clipboard.

Dave wasn't feeling very patient, however. "Is he doing all right?"

442 | The Thousand Smiles of Nicholas Goring

Dr Williams smiled at him. "What do you think?"

"Well," said Dave, considering Nicholas again. "He seems pretty much the same to me. Maybe not quite as pale?"

"I thought so, too." Williams studied Nicholas some more – then announced, "We'll try letting him wake up later this morning. Why don't you go tell Denise the good news, and the two of you can have some breakfast. Take your time, there's no rush."

Dave nodded, though he asked, "Then I can come back, right?"

"Of course, David. Then you can come back."

By the time Dave returned, though, something was very different. Dave's heart thudded hard when he realised.

Nicholas was scowling. Rather blearily, it was true, but Dr Williams was sitting by the bed talking quietly, and Nicholas was scowling, looking oddly restless for someone who was barely even moving his face.

"D'you see that, Denny?" Dave whispered.

"Oh that's marvellous!" she whispered back. She stopped at the threshold, and tried to let go of Dave's hand. "Go on, then! Go say hello."

Williams looked around, and beckoned Dave forward. He went with trepidation, more scared now than he'd been since all this began. Eventually he reached the chair he'd been sitting on all night, on the opposite side of the bed than Williams. And he sank to sit down, moving carefully. Not wanting to startle or confuse Nicholas with any unexpected movement. He didn't quite dare reach to take his husband's hand. Instead, into the rustling beeping quivering silence, he said, "Nicholas?"

At which Nicholas scowled some more, and then his gaze wandered haphazardly across to finally settle on Dave. A long moment while Nicholas tried to focus on him, finally squinting a bit, as if he didn't quite dare believe it really was Dave. But then at last he seemed to comprehend or maybe simply accept, and the frown lifted as if by magic and the scowl smoothed away – and one corner of that gorgeous mouth quirked into a smile.

"Nicholas ..." Dave murmured happily, reaching now to gently cradle Nicholas's hand in his own, just as he'd been holding it all night. "Oh Nicholas ... you little beauty. Oh thank God. Thank the Ancestors! Everything's going to be all right."

Nicholas's hand clutched briefly at his, though it seemed to require quite an effort, and then he could be seen to be forming a word. Dave and Dr Williams just waited, letting him take his time. Eventually Nicholas stuttered out, "S-s-song," though the G was more implied than spoken.

Dave burst into a grin. "You heard that? Charlie found it for me. It was a healing song."

Nicholas, however, seemed to want to roll his eyes impatiently. He got about halfway through that and gave up, then tried saying another word. "L-lines ..."

"Lines?" Dave only took a moment. "Songlines? Is that what you're saying?"

Nicholas nodded a little, and seemed content enough with that for now.

"Cool," said Dave. "I'm gonna ask you to tell me more about that later, all right? But songlines, yeah? It's so cool you said that."

Nicholas's eyes started slipping closed, though he fought it for a moment, still trying to look at Dave.

"Yes, I think it's time for a nap, Nicholas," Dr Williams said. "You're doing very well, but let's not tire you out on the first day."

"I'll see ya later, Nicholas," Dave added as reassuringly as he knew how. He bent his head to press a kiss to the back of Nicholas's hand, hoping Nicholas would take that sensation with him into sleep. "I'll see you later, husband."

Once he was settled again, no longer lying quite so neatly in the bed, Dr Williams led Dave back out of the room. "Why don't you let Denise take you home for the rest of the morning, David? Have a few hours of sleep."

"But –"

"You'll be more use to him then."

Well, Dave couldn't really argue with that. "Can I come back this afternoon? And his father. His dad's flying over from England; he'll be here this evening. He can come visit, right?"

"Come back at three, David, and his father can join you for a little while this evening. But then I want you to take the night off, all right? Nicholas is in excellent hands here, I promise you."

"I know," Dave agreed with a smile. Denise appeared beside him again, and took his hand ready to take him away. "Thank you, Doctor."

"And thank *you*, David."

444 | The Thousand Smiles of Nicholas Goring

After which graciousness, Dave decided to save any further protests for later. With one last look at his beloved husband, Dave turned for home.

Nicholas slept most of the afternoon – a natural sleep, not induced, and apparently occasionally troubled by dreams – but Dave was content to simply sit beside him and hold his hand. Dave figured Nicholas needed most of all to rest, but when he was awake he spent half the time scowling, and even when he looked at Dave his instinctive smile sometimes seemed reluctant. Maybe Nicholas was simply feeling impatient already with where he found himself.

Denise had taken Robin to meet Richard off the plane from England, and brought him directly to the hospital. The reunion of father and son had tears springing even to Dave's eyes.

"Oh my boy," Richard murmured, walking towards the bed as if it were the last stage of a long pilgrimage. Dave brought him around to Nicholas's right side, so Richard could grasp Nicholas's hand without fear of disturbing any of the tubes and such. Richard collapsed to sit on the chair, and murmured again, "Oh my dear boy." The two of them gazed at each other fiercely. Nicholas hadn't said anything since he'd first woken that morning, but his look now spoke eloquently enough. Dave left them to it, and went to regather himself by the nurses' station.

About half an hour later, Richard was gently ushered out by one of the nurses. "He's asleep," Richard said to Dave, his tone full of wonder. "He's truly resting. I've been told to go do likewise. I couldn't sleep on the plane, that's true, but I think I will be able to sleep tonight, now that I've seen him."

"He's doing all right," Dave said, as reassuringly as he could.

"So much better than I'd expected. Better than I dared to hope." Richard looked at him feelingly. "*Thank* you, David. I'm sure we have you to thank for taking such great care of him."

"Well," he responded with an uncomfortable shrug. "I wish I'd done more."

"Nonsense, my boy," said Richard, drawing him into a hug. "You've been everything that we ever hoped for, and more besides."

Neither of them was too proud to cling for a while, but then they took a moment to regroup. Dave cleared his throat. "Why don't we go throw ourselves on Denise's mercy, and see if Vittorio will cook us dinner? I could do with a great big bowl of pasta. Sheer comfort food, you know?"

"I can't imagine anything better," Richard agreed.

twelve

In an astonishingly short period of time – a matter of a few days – Nicholas was well on the way to recovery. He was moved into a room in one of the regular wards, and soon the nurses had him out of bed and sitting up in a chair for a couple of hours each day. He still hardly spoke at all, but it was obvious from his awareness and his reactions that he was as bright and engaged as ever. Dr Williams counselled Dave and Richard to talk to Nicholas, and include him in conversations, just as they normally would when talking with him, and let Nicholas take his own time in choosing to reply. There would be plenty of chances to push a little later, whether gently or firmly, once he was further past the trauma.

"D'you think he's worried that he's lost his abilities, or something?" Dave asked. "Cos I don't reckon he has. I mean, he's still as sharp as a tack. He always knows exactly what's going on."

"Well, like you, I suspect it would be more about the worry than the actuality," Williams agreed. "But let's not push him just yet."

Richard huffed a little under his breath and fondly observed, "He's more than able to convey his meaning, in any case. He's still vain enough to be fretting about the hair you needed to shave off!"

They all had a quiet guilty chuckle about that. Dave regathered himself first. "I'll have to talk to his barber. Later, of course, once the wound's properly healed. Maybe he can visit the house, and come up with some sort of style that makes it look deliberate."

Richard looked at Dave very fondly. "You think of everything."

"Actually, what I'm more worried about," Dave blurted, forever unwilling to forgive himself for his inadequacies, "is the scowling. I mean, what's that about?"

"He never scowls at you, David," Richard pointed out.

"And not at you, either. But pretty much everyone else – even the doc here, and Nicholas has been seeing you for seven years now, hasn't he? I reckon he thinks of you as a friend."

Williams inclined his head. "Thank you. But again, let's wait and see. It might not be anything to worry about in the long-term. It might be a temporary disorientation, or a period of adjustment, or simply impatience."

Richard didn't huff, but actually laughed a little this time. "My dear boy has always tended towards impatience, I'm afraid."

"He's not bad-tempered, though," Dave argued, "and he's not the sort who doesn't like people."

After a moment, the doctor said, "We've talked about the possibility of some changes in behaviour or personality. I suspect from what we've seen that, if there are any, they'll be relatively minor. But it is possible you're seeing a shift in his nature."

Richard turned a worried glance on Dave – who replied before he could think twice about it, "It's not like I mind. Have you really looked at him when he scowls? He's like this great big beautiful thunderstorm."

The other two men laughed heartily.

"He's totally awesome. I'll just keep an eye out for lightning bolts, is all."

Dave experienced a bit of a lightning bolt himself the next morning. He was sitting with Nicholas – and Dave had him to himself for once, as Vittorio had taken Richard and Robin out for the day – and he was reading out loud from one of his own Patrick O'Brian books. There was a passage that had the officers and crew each bonding through the singing of songs, and when Dave came to a chapter break, he put his Kindle aside.

He pondered for a moment, and then met Nicholas's quizzical look. "D'you remember the first thing you said to me when you woke up after the operation?" Dave asked. He left a pause, in which Nicholas lifted his chin slightly in an equivocal answer. "You said 'songlines'. I've been so curious about why. I hope you'll tell me about it one day." Dave left a rather longer pause, though not as if it were an unexpected thing to do. Then he continued, "I was thinking about that song Charlie gave me, too – you know, the one he had me sing to you. Did that have something to do with the songlines?"

Nicholas ducked his head briefly to one side. No.

"No worries," Dave said. "It's not as if I don't like a bit of mystery …"

Then Nicholas said, very clearly, "I followed the songs back to you."

Dave stared at him, rather startled to say the least.

"I would have found my way back, with or without Charlie."

"Would you?" Dave asked, trying to understand, while also trying not to betray his joyous sense of relief that obviously Nicholas was perfectly able to speak even if he didn't choose to.

"I followed the path of the songlines."

Dave's jaw dropped. "Oh ..." Two and two finally started adding up to make seven. "Oh, mate! I think I'm having ... Well, never mind that. That's awesome! Now we know you'll always be able to find your way back to me, and probably I will, too, in that case – I mean, find my way to you."

Nicholas nodded a little impatiently, obviously knowing something else was going on.

Dave scrambled for words, for sense. "I think I'm having one of those epi- epif- epicentre things."

Nicholas grinned a bit lopsidedly. "Epiphany."

"Exactly. Oh my God," said Dave. "I've finally figured it out. About the waterhole. I know what I have to do."

Nicholas's grin turned fuller, and he didn't speak again, but his eyes were just *glowing* with love and pride.

"You're brilliant, you know that?" Dave asked. "But what if I have to go do this? *Now*, I mean. Will you be all right if I leave you here for a couple of days, while Richard and Robin are still around to look after you?"

Nicholas favoured him with a half-scowl. But then he ducked his chin in a nod.

"God, I love you *so* much ... And it's not like Richard doesn't deserve some proper time with you, yeah?" Dave was already standing, and reaching into his pocket for his phone. "I love you so much, but I've got to call Charlie, all right?"

Of course it was all right. Nicholas smiled at him with an arch kind of sweetness, and his long fingers plucked at the Kindle and lifted it – apparently to give himself something to frown at while Dave made his phone call.

Early in the morning two days later, Dave was standing on a low flat hill in the mulga scrub west of Cunnamulla. Charlie and another Indigenous man named Kalti stood with him.

Waiting below them on the plain was a gathering of friends and strangers. Denise was there with the Cruiser, with Bethan and Zoe in the back. Robin had, surprisingly, decided to abandon Nicholas and come as well. His presence might or might not be explained by the fact that Lisa Munroe was there, though he didn't seem to mind that Lisa had brought her partner Debbie. Ted Walinski was there with his Land Rover, and he'd brought Fred Harvey and Mr Teng with him. Mayor Shirley Johns was there, too, accompanied by Henri Wilson, who owned the big station out to the west of the waterhole. The Native Title guy Martin Bandjara had driven from Brisbane overnight to be part of it. And there was a hearteningly large group of Murri from the reserve and elsewhere, too – including Thursday, magnificently attired in native accessories, a headdress, and swirls of paint but otherwise as good as naked.

Dave took a breath. It was vital that he had witnesses, but oh what a disaster this would be if he messed up.

"You right, mate?" Charlie asked.

"Sure." Dave nodded. "Let's do this, yeah?"

"Yeah. Absolutely."

Dave turned to Kalti, and nodded respectfully. "Okay, so if I'm right, your songline brings you here. And mine starts here. So, would you mind singing the song about this place? If you can share it?"

Kalti nodded, took a couple of paces away, and with no further ado launched into a chant which resounded clearly in the cool morning air.

Within moments Dave was grinning, knowing already that they were off to a perfect start. His own song for this place, the very first of the sequence of songs he'd learned, consisted of exactly the same words, and though the tune was slightly different, the two songs belonged together. As soon as he realised that, Dave started singing, too. Kalti's gaze fixed on him – perhaps he had doubted, as surely most of them did – but now he knew. Charlie had withdrawn a little, and remained silent as if making the point that he wasn't driving this, though he was paying close attention. In fact, everyone was watching and listening in varying degrees of surprise and satisfaction – and of course not everyone would get on board even if Dave succeeded in this, but thank the Ancestors he was off to a good start.

"That song," he said when they were done, "the words: they're something about a small plain on a large plain, right? I never realised what that was about, until now, but it's this hill."

"That's good, mate," said Kalti. "That's right. You done good."

"Will you come with us, then? Come to the waterhole with us."

Kalti glanced at Charlie, but not like he was seeking permission. "Yeah, mate," he said to Dave. "I'll come."

While they were still on the hill, Dave began murmuring the next song, scanning the land towards the west, looking for the next location on the songline. It had to be somewhere visible, towards which he could navigate. He couldn't immediately think how the song helped him, though, so he quit singing and said to Charlie, "This is about a snake Ancestor gliding over the ground, isn't it?" It wasn't just the words that told him that, but the undulating rhythm.

Charlie considered for long moments, and then suggested, "*Through* the ground, I think."

"*Through* the ground," Dave muttered, wondering how the hell that worked. But when he looked again, he glimpsed something on the horizon that might help. When he adjusted his glasses on his nose and looked again, he saw a slight but sharp dip in the line of the horizon. He pointed this out to Charlie and Kalti. "Like that? See that kind of … valley? It only looks like a notch from here, but could the snake have gone through there?"

"You beauty!" Charlie cried. "That's it, of course!"

"Cool," said Dave. And singing the song under his breath, he strode down to the level ground, and then struck out across the plain. He was aware of Charlie and Kalti following just behind, and then beyond them a convoy of four vehicles lurched slowly into gear and trailed along, accompanied by a goodly number of people on foot.

They covered just under twenty-three kilometres in this way, making for quite a long day. Dave would interpret the songs in terms of what he could see in the landscape, sometimes with help from Charlie, Kalti and Thursday but mostly on his own. There was only one song that completely stumped them all – and when they decided to have faith and strike out in the same general direction, they soon came to a rocky outcrop that had apparently broken apart or collapsed some decades before, but which had probably once been visible from some distance.

The very last song in the sequence was about a frilled-neck lizard Ancestor who had gone to sleep so long ago that now you could only see his back poking out of the ground. Dave had already figured this related to the worn old ridge of rocks that he'd long followed on his way to the waterhole, as the formation did look just like a spine curving up out of the ground and back down again. The pattern of rocks that he used to think of as an arrowhead at one end could instead be interpreted as a frill at half-mast.

"We're almost there," he said to his companions, unable to suppress his excitement. The ridge of rocks pointed them in exactly the right direction to take them up across the rise that would eventually reveal ... the wide valley that contained the waterhole.

Dave paused on the crest of the rise in the warm glow of late afternoon sunshine, and let the others catch up with him. Those people in the vehicles climbed out and joined the group, which somehow felt larger than it should be, almost as if it were thick with spirits.

"That's it there," Dave announced, pointing towards where the trees and scrub were thickest. "That's the waterhole." Not that any of them other than Charlie would realise quite what they were looking at, not yet. "Come on!" Dave cried, and he strode down the long slope into the valley.

They all followed after him, and any tiredness was lost in a hubbub of excitement. Soon Dave was standing at the entrance to the waterhole. The vehicles were left parked at a respectful distance, and the people gathered around Dave. He looked at them all, sharing the moment with the people he loved, and the people he respected. The excitement became more of a fully charged hush ... and when the timing was perfectly right, Dave turned and led the way down into this beautiful sacred place.

It was more than time to share the beauty with the world. Even the butterflies seemed to agree. Dave hadn't expected them to have emerged from the chrysalis yet, but a kaleidoscope of blue scraps of sky rose to meet them. His companions gasped in wonder, and Robin cried, "Oh, Nicholas!" He added more quietly, "Oh, I wish he were here ..."

Soon the odd assortment of people were scattered across the sandy ground by the pool itself, marvelling at the gorgeous colours, revelling in the lush sense of peace which even this large gathering of humans couldn't dispel.

Without the slightest sense of self-consciousness Dave took up the long-familiar stance, and began chanting the first of the songs about the waterhole itself, sharing the story about the Barcoo grunter Ancestor, and his love who fell from the sky. Charlie fell into step beside him, and they worked through the sequence of songs and dances – agreeing with little more than a glance which must be kept secret – while the others settled to sit in a large circle around them.

Once they were done, they were met with hearty cheers and applause, as everyone celebrated with them. Charlie put his arm around Dave's shoulders to squeeze him tight, giving Dave all the kudos, though Dave knew well enough they shared it between them. "There's another few songs that lead away from here," Dave explained, "that take the songline further out to the west. But I reckon we'll save them for next time. Let's just hang out here for what's left of the day, right?"

"Right," everyone agreed with a happy laugh.

Dave sat beside Charlie and watched as Thursday and Kalti set a small fire going and then lay green eucalyptus leaves on it. The leaves created smoke, which Dave knew was intended to cleanse both the area and the people in it, and symbolise a new beginning. The sharp scent of the leaves was itself stimulating; everyone touched by it smiled.

Thursday beckoned Dave into the place where the smoke was thickest, and gestured through it as if covering Dave with smoke from head to toe. Charlie advised, "Slough off what you don't need, mate. Let the smoke take it." Dave felt immeasurably lighter. He closed his eyes, listening to Thursday and Kalti chant a song of renewal.

Eventually the smoke dwindled, and people began stirring, about to get up and start exploring, when instead they fell quiet.

Thursday was stepping through the circle to Dave with a dillybag in his hand. When he reached Dave's side, he lifted a wooden board from the bag, and silently handed it over.

Dave took it carefully, and considered the painting on the one flat surface. As with most traditional Aboriginal images, it showed the landscape from above, from a bird's-eye view as it were. There was something about the shapes this depicted that felt very familiar – and it only took a moment for Dave to twig. "Oh! Oh, that's the waterhole!" He traced the concentric shapes, not quite daring to touch them. God only knew how old this was. "This is the valley, the crater," Dave said, indicating the largest, almost perfectly round circle. "This is the sinkhole, which we're in," he added, gesturing at the ellipse in the centre of the circle. "And this is the pool." It was an irregular shape towards one end of the sinkhole, pretty much exactly matching the pool itself. There were two people sitting by the water, one male and one female. "Are these the Ancestors, then?" he asked Thursday.

The old man nodded. He was looking happy, and very satisfied. When Dave tried to hand back the board, Thursday shook his head and stepped away.

"But –" said Dave.

Thursday drew near again, but only to give him the dillybag. "It's yours now, Dave. You belong in this place."

And Dave could feel himself beaming with joy. He had hoped to prove a point that day. He hadn't even considered that he might receive such recognition. "Thank you," he said, slipping the board safely back into the bag, and cradling it in both arms against his chest. "Thank you."

The gathering settled after that into the happiest picnic there had ever been, with everyone mingling and chatting happily, or wandering around gazing in quiet awe at the natural beauties of the waterhole. The butterflies continued their happy dance in the day's warmth, occasionally deigning to settle on someone's outstretched hand. Robin was taking plenty of photos with his smartphone so that Nicholas could eventually share in it as well.

Charlie was marvelling. "You do belong in this place, Davey. The Ancestor called you to him, before you even knew the songs."

"I guess so," said Dave. It was a mystery he didn't have an answer for, so Charlie's interpretation made as much sense as anything else.

"I knew all the songs," Charlie continued, giving Dave yet another one-armed hug. "I knew all the same songs, and I couldn't find this place. I couldn't do what you just did. I couldn't follow the songlines."

"Oh well. I guess the Ancestor just decided it was time."

"You're a good man, Davey Taylor."

He grinned at Charlie but bashfully shrugged off the compliment – and instead went to talk to Ted Walinski, who was puzzling over some kind of satnav device. "Not picking up a signal?"

"No, not even a weak one." Walinski looked at him a bit sheepishly. "I'm starting to understand now. I thought you were just being …"

"Difficult?"

"Something like that." He gestured at the red and black cliffs that surrounded them. "Maybe the depth of the sinkhole is interfering with the signal. We'd need a satellite to be almost directly overhead."

"Maybe," said Dave. "But I never got a signal from up at ground level, either. This whole area has been kind of … hidden."

Walinski was sceptical, of course. "Are you saying you believe in – ?"

"I guess we'd all explain it in different ways," said Dave.

"We flew over this area, I'm sure we did. The scrub and the trees would have hidden the sinkhole, I guess, but I don't understand why we didn't spot the crater."

Dave shrugged. "I don't have any answers for you that don't involve the Dreaming, and I know how hard that is for a white fella to accept."

Walinski turned to something he felt surer of. "I wasn't wrong about the hematite, though. That's magnificent!"

"It *is* magnificent," Fred Harvey agreed, wandering up to them with a complacent expression on his face. "Well, you've made your point, Mr Goring Taylor, and I think we can promise you that Reddy Eight will be taking great care not to cause this place any harm."

"But you'll still be looking to start mining in the region," Dave confirmed.

"Yes, but with the smallest possible footprint, I can assure you of that."

Dave sighed, though not unhappily. "I'd like to hear that from Elvis Reddy himself, but I don't mind hearing it from you in the meantime."

"I can do you one better." Harvey nodded his head towards where Mr Teng was sitting serenely meditating by the pool. Teng was still in his expensive shirt and trousers, but his shoes and socks were off, and on top of them were neatly piled his suit jacket and tie. "You can hear it directly from the man with the money, just as soon as you'd like to ask him."

"Oh!" Dave wondered why he hadn't guessed that already. "Mr Teng is actually the major investor?"

"Indeed." Harvey grinned at him. "Like I said, Dave, you've made your point. Well played."

And when Harvey offered his hand, Dave shook it with perfect equanimity.

Once Harvey and Walinski had wandered off, Dave looked around to see

455

that Robin had taken Lisa and Debbie over to the wattle, and the young man was standing there watching with Bethan and Zoe while Lisa examined the plant just as thoroughly and excitedly as ever Nicholas had examined the butterflies.

Denise came over to Dave, and rubbed an affectionate hand up his arm. "This place is *beautiful*. No wonder you and Nicholas love it so."

"Yeah," said Dave, "but it was time to share. The butterflies don't seem to mind, anyway."

"They're astonishing!" she said. "I had no idea … I mean, to see them alive …"

"So, we're trying to get this place included in the Aboriginal reserve; the Department has agreed in principle. But we're also going to try to establish the wattle and some of the butterflies near another waterhole on the reserve. If we set that up properly for visitors, then that helps protect this, if you see what I mean. Nicholas and Lisa are paranoid about how fragile the environment is here."

Denise nodded. "Look, I admire you sharing the waterhole with us, Davey, but I think most people would understand you not opening it up as a tourist site, you know?"

He shrugged, feeling a bit reluctant himself. "I guess we'll have to consult the Ancestor about that!" he offered, more than half seriously.

Charlie, who'd been pondering the pool, heard them and came closer. "The Ancestor is dreaming happy," he declared. "You're right. It was time for him to welcome more of us in."

"It wasn't that we ever wanted to be selfish about it," Dave said. "We never thought we were more … well, more entitled to enjoy it than anyone else."

"Of course not," Charlie bracingly replied. "But you wanted to bring it back to life, and that takes time. You weren't in a rush, Davey, and neither should you be. You know, even Nicholas isn't always about seizing the day."

Denise snorted with laughter, in which Dave joined, and the happy sounds of mirth and quiet wonder and Mr Teng chanting a song of his own – all these lovely sounds mingled and rose and danced in the bright air with the butterflies. Everything seemed vivid and alive, and there was a sense somehow that it was all stirring. Sap was flowing through veins, water was welling through rock, and light was sparkling warmth in all it touched. The timeless feel of the waterhole had shifted, as if somehow it had become part of the world again, part of today, part of a story that wasn't yet fully told.

Dave wandered over to Ted Walinski, and said, "Try your GPS again, would you?"

Walinski did so – and after a long moment he received a signal loud and clear. He looked up at Dave in surprise.

Dave nodded, and headed over to Robin. "Do me a favour, mate? Choose your best photo of the butterflies, and try sending it to Nicholas."

Robin looked doubtful, but he didn't argue. He swiped through the images, and then quickly tapped out a text and sent it. His brow shot up once he realised the message had actually gone. A few moments later the phone rang, and Robin answered it. "Hello, Uncle Nicholas! ... No, I know they are, they're just *gorgeous*. ... Yes, he did it. ... No, we're still here, we're at the waterhole. ... I know! It's awesome!"

Dave grinned and wandered away, and found a rock to sit down upon. For long moments he watched the others revelling in this place and each other. Charlie and the Mayor were sharing a yarn that made them both laugh; Lisa was showing Teng the wattle; Denise and the girls were teaching Robin a song. Dave hardly dared even think it, but he suspected that somehow he'd just accomplished something that was utterly impossible. It was the most humbling, the most wonderful thing he'd experienced in his *life*.

Well, next to Nicholas's love, of course. Nothing could be more humbling or wonderful than that. But this came pretty darned close.

epilogue

Despite some last minute bravado from Robin about taking a gap year, in response to which the earl carefully did not panic, the two Englishmen headed home as planned in time for Robin to start the new academic year at Oxford. However, there was much talk about the Goring family observing Christmas in Australia that year, or as many of them as could make it, so Nicholas and Dave would be seeing them again soon.

In the meantime, Dave spent every available moment at the hospital, while making sure that everything was clean and ready and comfortable at home for when Nicholas was finally discharged. He figured it couldn't be much longer now, as Nicholas was pretty much mobile – if currently rather slower than he had been, and almost indiscernibly weaker on the left side. Nicholas was using the time as thoroughly as he could, to pursue as much physical rehab as Dr Williams would let him.

Otherwise, the scowls persisted, and Nicholas still didn't speak any more than he had to. Dr Williams never came up with a definitive explanation for this, or at least not in the physical sense, so Dave tried to simply accept it as one of the inexplicable changes he'd been warned about. He knew how lucky he was to have Nicholas with him at all, so it seemed ridiculously ungrateful to wish everything would return to 'normal'. Crucially, when it was just Nicholas and Dave together, then Nicholas relaxed and was happy, and Dave thought it was perfectly clear that Nicholas was just as sharp and clever and *engaged* as he'd ever been. Not to mention just as outrageous.

One afternoon they were hanging out in Nicholas's room quite innocently, and every now and then talking together about nothing much. Dave was slouched back in the chair, and Nicholas was lying in the bed. At some point after a lull in conversation, Nicholas stretched out tall and rolled back his shoulders, first one and then the other, so that Dave's spine lengthened and popped in sympathy.

And then out of the blue Nicholas asked, as if knowing the answer, "Have you been tossing off without me?"

"What?!" spluttered Dave.

"You heard me." Nicholas rolled onto his side and curled up so he could look directly at Dave. "Have you been taking care of yourself ... seeing as

I'm not there to take care of you?"

"Well," said Dave, knowing that his cheeks were burning red, "yes, I suppose." He added in a dismissive tone, "A couple of times, that's all."

Nicholas interpreted that to mean "Not so great?"

"Not without you, no," Dave replied quite evenly. What he didn't say was that it had only been about solace, really. Not pleasure. Just a way of feeling less alone in their enormous bed. The joys of being with Nicholas had spoiled him even for wanking. Dave sighed.

"Well," said Nicholas, "I think you should hop up here on the bed, and let me have a try."

Dave just stared at him for a long moment. And then glanced at the door, which was of course held wide open by one of those magnetic mechanisms. People bustled along the corridor, or ambled along, taking the opportunity to stare in at them as they went. At least the walls were solid here in the wards, and not made of glass as they were in the ICU. But still. It was mid-afternoon in a public building, and anyone might walk in on them.

"Come on," said Nicholas, shifting back on the bed so that Dave would have room to lie beside him.

Perhaps spooning would be the easiest way, and wouldn't it be glorious to have Nicholas pressed up close against his back, tucked up tight against him from top to toe, reaching around to wrap his clever loving hand around Dave's cock ... Not that Dave was actually thinking about doing this.

"Come on," Nicholas repeated, reaching that very hand out towards him. "I've missed you ..."

"Oh my God, you're serious."

"Of course I am. Haven't you missed me?"

"You know I have." Dave frowned at him, and darted a pointed glance at Nicholas's nether regions. "I'd gotten the impression that ... you weren't quite fully recovered yet."

"I'm not," came the tart response. "But that doesn't mean I'm incapable of helping you out. And anyway ... there's more to miss than orgasms, isn't there?"

"Kissing and cuddling," Dave agreed.

Nicholas patted the bed beside him. "Come on, then, husband."

Dave groaned in frustration and annoyance. "There's no lock on the door!"

"What, and you don't have a backup plan for that … ?"

Oh God! Dave stared at the man, appalled and aroused in equal measure. Then after a long long moment he pushed himself up from the chair, and headed out to the nurses' station.

Luckily one of the nurses they were most friendly with was on duty. Dave paused for a moment, and then when she looked up enquiringly, he leaned in closer to speak confidentially. "Um … is there such a thing as … as a 'Do Not Disturb' sign we can place on the door?"

She gazed back at him for a moment without blinking an eye. "You're not taking advantage of my patient, are you, Mr Taylor?"

"Actually, it's more like I'm the one being taken advantage of." He held up a hand palm-out. "No, that wasn't funny. Or true. To be honest … I doubt we'll be doing more than cuddling, anyway."

"No worries," she said. "Just had to be sure." She reached into a drawer, and came out with something that looked very much like a hotel's 'Do Not Disturb' sign but read 'Private Consultation'. "Here you are. Put this on the door handle. And draw the curtain round the bed, too, at least down the side facing the door. I'll keep an eye out, but I can't promise no one will blunder in."

"That's all right," he said. "I'll take my chances."

"Have fun," she offered with a wink.

He blushed even harder, and retreated in as good an order as he could manage.

Nicholas didn't speak when Dave returned, but just lay there on his back watching as Dave sorted out the sign and quietly closed the door, then drew the curtain down one side and along the foot of the bed. Neither of them liked to feel too enclosed, so he was happy enough to leave the other side open and, while that was opposite the window, they were on too high a floor to be overlooked by anything but the sky.

As Dave took off his glasses and then heeled off his shoes, Nicholas turned onto his side to face the window and shifted back again to make room. Dave went to clamber on, but paused when Nicholas voiced an inarticulate protest.

"I am *not* getting naked for you," Dave insisted, interpreting this correctly. "Not here."

"You could just take off your jeans …"

"No, mate. I'm sorry, but no."

After a moment, Nicholas tipped up his chin in agreement, and Dave climbed up onto the bed, which was unnervingly higher off the floor than a regular one. He settled quite naturally with his back to Nicholas so they were spooning, with Nicholas encompassing him warm and strong just as Dave had imagined.

Nicholas shifted up on an elbow to look at Dave, and push closer still for a kiss. "There … That's sweet …" He chuckled in quiet happiness. "Remember how we used to while away whole afternoons like this, back at the waterhole, on the bonnet of the Cruiser … ?"

Dave snuffled a laugh. With the top half of the bed propped up at an angle, it was almost exactly like lying up against the Cruiser's windscreen. "Yeah, I remember …"

Nicholas didn't say anything more, but pressed a kiss to Dave's hair, to the sensitive spot by his ear, to his cheek, to his forehead – and then to his mouth. Another. And then they settled into a proper kiss, lush and gorgeous. Dave slipped his hand back to mould to Nicholas's hip, and Nicholas spread his palm and fingers and thumb against Dave's chest just over his heart, rubbed at him reassuringly and then slowly caressed his way down further and further still until he could slip his hand in under the hem of Dave's t-shirt and flatten warm against Dave's belly.

A peaceful warm hush had fallen, and they might have been anywhere. They might have been safe alone together at the waterhole – and in any case, Dave had sprung to full happy life, so that when Nicholas asked at last, "Let me?" Dave replied in roughened tones, "O' course." And then that hand slid under the waistband of his jeans and into his boxers, and there was just room enough for the palm and the inside of Nicholas's wrist to rub at Dave's eager cock while those fingers pushed tantalisingly at his balls – and it had been so long, too long. Within moments Dave's spunk was gushing forth and he voiced a quiet "Oh!" of wonder, and as the pleasure slowly started ebbing away he opened his eyes to see Nicholas gazing down at him with infinite affection.

They stayed there holding each other's gaze for a long while, with Nicholas's hand gently cradling Dave's tackle as if he loved it soft and tender as much as he did hard and rampant. Eventually Dave remarked, "Well, okay, I guess you're starting to get the hang of this."

Nicholas's mouth quirked in delight. "Excellent. Give me another seven years to practise, and who knows what I might achieve!"

"Mate, and I'd give you another seventy after that, if I could."

"Deal," said Nicholas. And he looked down at Dave with the most gorgeous smile: half besotted, half wry, full of hope, and wholly Dave's.

One thousand and three, Dave happily noted – and he pressed a smile of his own to those plump pink lips, and let his eyes convey the entire marvellous heart of the matter. *Nicholas Goring Taylor, I love you true.*

❖

About Julie Bozza

Ordinary people are extraordinary. We can all aspire to decency, generosity, respect, honesty – and the power of love (all kinds of love!) can help us grow into our best selves.

I write stories about 'ordinary' people finding their answers in themselves and each other. I write about friends and lovers, and the families we create for ourselves. I explore the depth and the meaning, the fun and the possibilities, in 'everyday' experiences and relationships. I believe that embodying these things is how we can live our lives more fully.

Creative works help us each find our own clarity and our own joy. Readers bring their hearts and souls to reading, just as authors bring their hearts and souls to writing – and together we make a whole.

I read books, lots of books, and watch films. I admire art, and love theatre and music. I try to be an awesome partner, sister, daughter, friend. I live an engaged and examined life. And I strive to write as honestly as I can.

I have lived in two countries – England and Australia – which has helped widen my perspective, and I have travelled as well. I love learning, and have completed courses in all kinds of things. My careers have been in Human Resources, and in eLearning and training, so there has always been a focus on my fellow human beings and on understanding, conveying, sharing information.

Knitting gives me some down time and the chance to craft something with my hands. Coffee gives me stimulation and a certain street cred. My favourite colour has segued from pure blue to dark purple, and seems to be segueing again to marine blues.

I think John Keats is the best person who has ever lived.

And that's me! Julie Bozza. Quirky. Queer. Sincere.

If you want to know more, please do come find me at juliebozza.com and libra-tiger.com.

Titles by Julie Bozza

The Butterfly Hunter Trilogy:
    Butterfly Hunter
    Of Dreams and Ceremonies
    Like Leaves to a Tree
    The Thousand Smiles of Nicholas Goring

Albert J. Sterne:
    The Definitive Albert J. Sterne
    Albert J. Sterne: Future Bright, Past Imperfect

Novels and Novellas:
    The Apothecary's Garden
    The Fine Point of His Soul
    Homosapien … a fantasy about pro wrestling
    Mitch Rebecki Gets a Life
    A Night with the Knight of the Burning Pestle
    A Threefold Cord
    The 'True Love' Solution
    The Valley of the Shadow of Death

Stories and Anthologies:
    Call to Arms
    A Certain Persuasion
    An English Heaven
    No Holds Bard
    A Pride of Poppies

Made in the USA
Columbia, SC
17 December 2024